ALIBIS IN ARKANSAS

THREE ROMANCE MYSTERIES

CHRISTINE LYNXWILER
JAN REYNOLDS
SANDY GASKIN

BARBOUR
PUBLISHING

Published by Barbour Publishing, Inc., P.O. Box 719, Uhrichsville, OH 44683, www.barbourbooks.com

Our mission is to publish and distribute inspirational products offering exceptional value and biblical encouragement to the masses.

 Member of the
Evangelical Christian
Publishers Association

Printed in the United States of America.

ALIBIS IN ARKANSAS

DEATH ON A DEADLINE

1

LAKE VIEW MONITOR

Help Wanted

Early morning paper route available. Good pay. Must have dependable vehicle. Apply in person at the Lake View Monitor *office, 243 Main St.*

Hey! Dog! Stop digging up the yard!" I waved my arms wildly.
Mama had predicted more than once that curiosity would be my downfall. The instant I let that dog's incessant barking propel me out of bed, my fate was as sealed as the proverbial curious cat's. Especially once I peeked through the living room blinds and ran out on the porch, long Mickey Mouse gown flapping in the September breeze.

The startled golden retriever scooped up a brownish object in his mouth and galumphed down the sidewalk toward downtown. I squinted into the rainy mist. Was that my missing Dooney & Bourke wallet clutched in his teeth? I was off the porch and halfway down my driveway before I even realized my bare feet were splashing cold water against my legs.

The dog turned back for a split second as if to confirm I was behind him, then picked up the pace to a quick trot. We'd almost reached the city park—mercifully without seeing another human—and I was gaining on the dog when he looked back again. My brain finally kicked into gear. I was playing right into his hands. . .um, paws. I halted in my tracks.

He skidded to a stop. I dropped to my knees in a shallow puddle of water, but I managed to hold out a friendly-looking hand. *See? No threat here, buddy,* I thought with clenched teeth. "Here, doggy, doggy." Okay, so I have a cat, but how much different can it be? Apparently not much, because the golden retriever did that head-tilt thing and then sidled back to me, still clutching the brown object in his teeth.

"Give it to me, buddy."

To my shock, he dropped the slobbery wallet into my outstretched hand. *Ugh.* It wasn't a Dooney & Bourke. It wasn't even a Dooney & Bourke knock-off. This billfold was plain brown wet leather. I held it between my finger and thumb and flicked it open. A familiar face stared up at me from the Arkansas driver's license inside the flap. Hank Templeton, hard-hitting editor of the *Lake View Monitor*. Hank the Crank, people not as nice as me called him behind his back. Even I had to admit he could easily be a founding member of the Grumpy Old Men Society, if there were such a thing.

His wife, Marge, was probably wringing her hands and trying to convince him she hadn't misplaced his wallet. I felt sorry for her. But not enough to show up at her door dressed like this. I'd do my good deed and take it by their house on my way to work.

I wrapped my arms around myself and bent my head against the wind. As I trudged through the rain, the retriever matched me step for step. "Shoo. Go home."

The collarless dog ignored my words. So I returned the favor and ignored his presence as I hurried home. My house came into view—slightly run-down, barely above low rent, but the light in the window beckoned like a flag at the finish line. And a hot shower would be my trophy.

Almost to the driveway. The hum of a motor behind me interrupted my mental victory dance. I quickened my pace. Maybe if I didn't look at the driver, he wouldn't notice me.

After all, why would he notice inconspicuous me? Barefoot in my night-gown? Oh, and how could I forget? The dog. Stuck to my side like a stray sock to a pair of rayon running shorts fresh from the dryer. The car slowed. *Please, please, please be a total stranger needing directions to the diner.*

The horn blew directly behind my right ear, and I turned instinctively. Great. Brendan Stiles. My date for tomorrow night.

He rolled down his window. "Hey, Jenna. Out for a stroll?" Dark hair and eyes, nice smile, even those cute little wire-rim glasses that made him look geeky but handsome. The local pharmacist and I had dated three times in the last month or so. The last two Sundays, he'd even shown up at church. Seemed ideal on the surface. Especially once I'd gotten used to covering his stingy tips for the waitress and overlooking the fact that he monopolized the conversation most of the time. But so far—big shock—no chemistry, at least on my part. And after seeing me today with no makeup and my hair frizzed out, probably no chemistry on his part, either. A fact over which I couldn't work up a great deal of distress.

I held up my soggy prize. "Had to see a dog about a wallet."

At his quizzical look, I spilled the whole story.

He laughed. In a nice way. "Want me to drop it off at Hank's office?"

"That's okay. I'll take it by the house." This was the most helpful I'd ever seen him. Maybe there was still hope.

"You sure? I'm going right by there. Why don't you let me take it?"

Okay, I'm cranky before I get my coffee, but he had just crossed over the line from helpful into obnoxiously persistent. *Never doubt your first instincts.*

"Thanks anyway."

"Have it your way. See you tomorrow night." He sped away.

I jogged up the driveway and slipped into the house, closing the door firmly against the dog's nose. A girl has to draw the line somewhere. I'd already been adopted by a neurotic cat that had to go to work with me every day because she couldn't stand to be alone.

On the way to work, I stopped at Hank and Marge's but got no answer in spite of my relentless doorbell ringing. I jumped back in the car, determined to make up my lost time. Hard to do, since my boss's long-ago run-in with the zoning committee had forced him to build outside the city limits. As I negotiated the crooks and turns of the hilly road, I thought about Brendan's easy acceptance of my wild appearance and felt a pang of guilt that I'd been less than impressed with him. Again.

I pulled into the Lake View Athletic Club parking lot, not as early as usual but with minutes to spare. Two women jogged in place outside the door in matching hot pink T-shirts and tight black leggings. Against the cream-colored siding of the building, they looked like oversized flamingos.

They were obviously newbies—their eagerness gave them away, as well as the T-shirts, still new-looking, straight from the club's sports shop, my name in big letters on the back. With my strawberry blond hair, I wouldn't be caught dead in hot pink, but thankfully, Bob doesn't make me wear the shirts. Just sell them.

No matter how much my boss insists we have to capitalize on my name, I'll never get used to seeing GET IN THE SWIM WITH JENNA STAFFORD emblazoned across the backs of perfect strangers or, worse still, people I know. Talk about cheesy. I *am* Jenna Stafford, and I don't even have a T-shirt with my name on it. But they sell like hotcakes, and I get a percentage of the profits in addition to my meager salary.

From the pink ladies' disgruntled looks, they'd counted on my habit of opening early. They should have been glad it was my day to open and not Gail's. The college student was always late. But they weren't looking for reasons to be glad.

Nothing starts a morning off better than dealing with a couple of irritated flamingos. Unless it's chasing a dog through the rain in your nightgown. Surely the day could only go up from here.

I clutched the cat carrier in one hand and unlocked the door, flipping on light switches as I went.

As the ladies followed me down the hallway past the U-shaped receptionist station and deserted smoothie bar, I stared straight ahead, praying they wouldn't mention the pictures that adorned the walls—a much younger me at various swim meets. Bob's insistence, again.

For about two months, at the tender age of sixteen, I'd been America's

Olympic darling. Even though I left Lake View for college two years later and didn't move back for nearly a decade, the local residents still remember my summer of fame. Or shame, depending on how much stock you put into winning. Hence the booming T-shirt sales. Which proves that under Bob Pryor's good-ole-boy exterior beats the heart of a shrewd businessman.

I wouldn't call him a vulture, but when I gave up teaching and moved back to Lake View three years ago, he showed up with a job offer before my suitcases were unpacked. The position didn't pay much more than flipping burgers, but being able to swim every day in any weather was incentive enough. And his promise to retire in a couple of years and sell me the health club at a reasonable price had sealed the deal. Plus it saved me the humiliation of pounding the pavement in my old hometown. And of admitting my failures.

Those "couple of years" were up, though, and lately I suspected my boss had been avoiding my offers to buy the business. Even his current Caribbean cruise with Wilma smacked more of a need to elude me than of a need to re-spark the romance in his forty-year marriage. But with him gone, at least I would have the office to myself. Which worked for my Greta Garbo mood.

Unfortunately, the office stayed deserted as the day flew by in a blur of small problems and needy members. I didn't even get to darken the office door until four, when I finally nabbed a bottle of water from my little fridge and sank into my chair. Neuro jumped up on my walnut desk, rubbing her bumpy yellow fur against my arm, purring loudly. "Come here, you." I cradled her in my arms and relaxed.

Hayley, my ten-year-old niece, burst into the room. As she slammed down in the chair across from my desk, arms crossed, Neuro skittered off my lap and disappeared behind the file cabinet.

"Having a good day, I see."

"Mom's out there in the hallway." Hayley spat out the words. "Signing *us* up for gymnastics."

"You and Rachel don't want to take gymnastics anymore?"

She gave me the are-you-a-total-moron? look ten-year-olds do best. "*Rachel* wants to."

"Oh." Poor Carly. The twins had been identical, not only in looks, but in likes, for so long that we all tended to think of them as one entity.

A tap on the door interrupted our meaningful aunt-niece communication. "Hayley, sugar, there you are. I figured I'd find you in here." Carly gave me a distracted grin. "Hey, Jenna."

My sister brought her focus back to the still-scowling Hayley. "Can you do me a favor and go tell Rachel I'm in Aunt Jenna's office? She's down by the sign-up sheets."

Hayley rolled her eyes and mumbled something I couldn't quite make out.

"Don't give me that attitude, young lady," Carly said, drawing herself up to her full five feet two inches.

Hayley left with no more mumbling, and Neuro immediately scampered out of her hiding place. That cat can sense a mood better than most people I know.

"Help." Carly plopped into the chair her daughter had vacated. "Mama's words keep comin' out of my mouth."

I nodded. "When you said 'young lady,' I cringed and ducked."

"You notice Hayley didn't. I try to be tough, but I'll never have my bluff in on them like Mama did us." My sister is a wonderful mother with enough insecurity to keep a therapist busy for life. She's always been a little unsure of herself, but as a single mom raising three kids, she often falls prey to self-doubt.

"Are you going to make Hayley take gymnastics this year?" I kept my voice neutral. I'd seen so many miserable kids whose parents signed them up for classes they didn't want to take, but I couldn't make Carly's decisions for her.

"Who knows? I didn't end up puttin' her name on the list." She sighed. "I remember when I was eleven, Mama and Daddy let me quit swimming. I felt like *I'd* won the Olympics."

That was the year I'd turned seven. I'd already taken top prize in several competitions by then. A recurring thought surfaced for the gazillionth time. *Was I the cause of my big sister's lack of confidence in her abilities?*

"I swear those girls of mine are gonna be the death of me. I could've kissed Mama's feet when she offered to babysit tonight."

In spite of my tiredness, I grinned. How did my sister end up with such a soft Southern drawl? We were both born and raised in Lake View, Arkansas, and everyone around here says "y'all." But Carly takes it a step further. She lived in Atlanta for several years, and now she drops her *g*'s and softens her *r*'s like she's a native Georgian. Must be the *Gone with the Wind* effect. Turns every woman within a hundred-mile radius into Scarlett O'Hara.

"I'll get off work in about an hour. Why don't you come by the house after you take the kids home and we'll go get a bite to eat?"

"I thought you'd never ask." Carly ran her fingers through her short dark curls—a nervous habit that gives her a perpetually tousled look, reminiscent of a fifties starlet. But I knew that underneath that Betty Boop exterior beat a Betty Crocker heart. "Can you guarantee there won't be any ten-year-olds there?"

"C'mon, Car. This fighting won't last forever. By the time Hayley and Rachel are in high school, they'll be best friends again."

"Ya think?" She relaxed in her chair. Neuro took Carly's chilled-out posture as an invitation and leaped into her lap.

Carly pushed the cat off, but Neuro bounced back up like a Super Ball.

She pushed again; Neuro bounced up again. "I give up, Baldy," she muttered.

"Hey. . ." I snatched Neurosis off her lap. "Cut the name-calling. She has a problem. But we're working on it."

"She's a cat," Carly drawled, making *cat* two syllables. "A cat that pulls her hair out. How do you work on that? Kitty therapy?"

Covering Neuro's ears with my hands, I dropped my voice to a whisper. "She only does it when she's alone. So I'm trying not to leave her alone much." The cat wiggled her head out from under my hands.

"Oh!" Carly sat straight up in her chair. "The weirdest thing happened earlier."

"What?"

"After I picked the girls up at school, they begged to go to Dairy King. I'm tellin' you, Jen, there's a secret ingredient in school lunches, programmed to fizzle out at exactly three o'clock. Remember how Mama used to have milk and cookies ready when we'd get off the bus? Anyway, I caved."

So far, so normal. My sister could never tell anything straight out. You had to drag it out of her in bits and pieces. Today was no exception. "And?"

"When we turned onto Main Street, I had to stomp on the brakes. The place was crawling with police cars."

"A wreck?"

She shook her head. "No. The whole Main Street Park was roped off with yellow tape, but for the life of me, I can't imagine why. When I slowed down and asked the police officer directing traffic what was going on, he said"—Carly tucked her chin and mimicked the deep voice—" 'Official police business, ma'am. Keep moving, please.' So I kept moving. The kids were dyin' for hot fudge sundaes anyway."

"That's weird. Wonder if somebody stole the mayor's car again? Remember a couple of years ago when those three kids took it for a joyride?"

Carly laughed and fished a rubber band out of the little jar on my desk. "Byron was fit to be tied, wasn't he? I saw a clip of an interview with him and Amelia on Channel 8's Web site. The esteemed first lady of Lake View kept saying, 'We've been violated.' But the mayor was literally hopping mad." She twisted the rubber band around her finger.

"His temper is as big as his ego." I stopped short of saying what we both knew. *And both are considerably larger than his brain.*

"Speaking of ego, you know what? Maybe John's dog got off its leash in the park and he used his power as police chief to commandeer the whole department to help him find it."

We've known John since the sandbox, so we never miss an opportunity to give him a hard time about his "powerful" position as police chief of our little town. But Carly's tongue-in-cheek scenario made me think of my early morning chase. "That reminds me. . ."

When I finished the story, she laughed. "I can see you now—holding up that billfold, trying to act normal in front of Brendan."

Ack. "I just remembered I didn't get an answer when I rang the bell at the Templetons' this morning. I meant to call later, but it's been wild here today."

"So you still have his wallet?"

"Sure do. I feel awful. Then again, if he hadn't lost it, I wouldn't have had to run in the rain this morning."

"Well, like I always say, when in doubt, blame a man." She shot me with the rubber band.

"Ouch." I rubbed my arm and tucked the rubber band in my pocket. "Seriously, though—I wish we knew what happened. I may swing by the park on my way home. After that I can drop Hank's wallet off at the *Monitor* and kill two birds with one stone."

"Going by the park won't do you any good. You know you'll get into it with John if he catches you snooping around. Might as well watch the news and save yourself the grief."

Carly had the curiosity of a dishrag sometimes.

"So are the kids adjusting to their new school?"

"They haven't said much." Carly narrowed her eyes. "Why? Have you heard something?"

Now she was curious. Guess it depended on the subject. "No. As far as I know, there haven't been any problems. The girls seem to love it here."

I picked up our family picture from my desk and worried the dust off the oak frame with my finger. Sixteen-year-old Zac towered over his mom and even stood a good four inches above my five-six. How had he grown up so quickly? Suddenly I felt old. "I know Zac didn't want to move, but he seems to be settling in. Is he still enjoying his paper route?"

Carly shrugged. "Who knows? Sugar, I do good to get three words out of him." A rueful grin flitted across her face. "Usually the three are *Mom, I'm hungry.*"

"What did I tell you?" I smiled. "Normal teenage boy who happened to get in with the wrong crowd. You worry too much."

"Maybe so. I hate that he has to leave the house while it's still dark. 'Try the school golf team,' I said. But no, he had to have *private* lessons from a pro." Carly held up her hand. "You don't have to remind me. I know I'm the one who told him he'd have to come up with the money on his own. But for goodness' sake, I never dreamed he'd want lessons bad enough to get a job. Especially not one that starts before daylight."

"He loves golf."

"Just like his daddy," Carly said. "Only Zac's got talent. Travis didn't play

13

very well, but he always had to watch those tournaments on TV." She sighed. "I kind of wish Zac didn't remember that."

"You think subconsciously he hopes that if he's good at golf, his dad will see him in some tournament on television and love him enough to come back home?"

Carly arched an eyebrow. "In other words, is he living in a dream world? Don't think I haven't thought about that. The therapist said every time Zac hits a milestone in his life, the rejection issues might start up again. I guess sixteen *is* a milestone."

My stomach clenched the way it always did when I thought about Travis. Running off to California with Miss Stick Figure ten years ago had been more important to the loser than sticking around to help Carly raise their six-year-old son and unborn twins. Okay, so her name wasn't Miss Stick Figure, but that's how I always thought of the anorexic model he'd latched onto—as a caricature, rather than a real person.

"Whatever the reason, golf means a lot to Zac. I probably should have just given him the money for the lessons." Carly's words jarred me back to the present.

"No, he'll appreciate it more in the long run this way. And a job will keep him busy and out of trouble. Remember what Mama always says about idle hands."

Speaking of idle hands, I pulled a rag from my bottom drawer and gave my desktop pictures a hasty dusting. Guilt never loses its power, even when served as leftovers from childhood.

Carly grinned and nodded toward the cloth. "Afraid the devil might be lookin' for a new workshop?"

If only I'd known how busy the devil already was in our sleepy little town, I definitely wouldn't have laughed.

2

LAKE VIEW MONITOR

Advertisement

STAFFORD CABINS

1500 Stafford Lane
(870) 555-3993
Affordable Lakeside Resort
Ten Spacious, Clean Cabins
Reasonable Rates
Family Owned and Operated
RV Parking Available
Call for Reservations

Y'all come back now, ya hear?

I should have listened to Carly and skipped the park. The six o'clock news would have given me more information than I'd gotten from John when I tried to climb over the yellow tape. And without the childish name-calling.

"Jen, you're the last person that needs to be here." John gave me his chief-of-police stone-faced glare. "Go home."

Lucky for him, I had it on good authority—his wife, Denise—that he was a softy inside. "You going to arrest me if I don't?" I picked up a gum wrapper near my feet and put it in my pocket. *See what a model citizen I am? I hate litter.*

"This is a serious police matter."

Obviously, somebody's been watching too many cop shows. He's starting to learn the vernacular.

He spun away from me in a classic dismissal technique then must have decided I might not take the hint. He turned back and hiked up the waist of his uniform pants with an air of authority. "You need to go home."

In a minute, he'd be tucking his thumbs in his waistband and patting his spare tire with his fingers. My friend was morphing into the sheriff from

Smokey and the Bandit before my very eyes. What was with the go-home mantra? "Just tell me what's going on." I nodded to the bright yellow tape stretched around the Bradford pear trees behind him. "Did someone get her purse snatched? Or did you find a dead body in the bushes?"

He ran his hand over his face. "Do you have to be so nosy?"

I didn't answer, and he turned to walk away.

"Fine!" I called to his back. "I've got to return Hank's wallet over at the *Monitor*! Maybe he'll have some answers!"

"What?" John's head snapped around. For the first time, he didn't seem in any hurry for me to leave. "Why do you have Hank's wallet?"

I allowed myself a grin. Maybe my funny story would loosen up our esteemed chief. Though it's a well-guarded police secret, he does have a sense of humor. For the third time that day, I recounted the early morning dog chase, leaving out Brendan's appearance. John didn't need to know everything. Or so I thought. Twenty minutes later—after I'd answered a hundred questions ranging from "What time was it when you first saw the dog?" to "Did you see anyone else while you were out?"—I'd changed my mind. And, of course, in answer to the last question, I had to tell John about running into Brendan.

"Why are you asking me so many questions?" I'd patiently answered his. Surely he could answer mine. "Was Hank's billfold stolen?"

John snapped his lips together so definitely that I wouldn't have been surprised if he'd made a locking motion with his fingers by his mouth and pretended to throw away the key. Instead, he frowned. "I can't say right now."

"How convenient."

"You've got the wallet with you?"

I pulled the billfold out of my pocket, and John latched onto it.

"What do you want with it?" I refused to let it go.

"I thought I'd save you some trouble and get it back to its rightful owner." He tugged.

Yeah, right. "You don't want me to talk to Hank." I tugged back.

"Look, Jenna, didn't anybody ever tell you curiosity killed the cat?" He tugged again, but his eyes weren't angry anymore. Instead, something that looked suspiciously like concern clouded his gaze.

That proverb kept cropping up in my life. Maybe it *was* time to go home. I let go of the wallet and left John regaining his balance as I crunched across the leaf-covered parking area to my car. Even the Quik-Mart across the road was overrun with cops. But it was hard to tell if that was because of the store's proximity to the park or the appeal of the best doughnuts in town.

I reached in the driver's window and unlocked the door. Leaving the windows down about four inches probably wasn't very smart at a crime scene, but my cat had to have air.

"You don't think I'm nosy, do you, Neuro?"

She blinked at me from her travel carrier. But she didn't make a sound. Okay, I admit I waited for a response. Maybe I needed to get out more.

❖

When I pulled into my driveway, I saw Carly relaxing on my porch swing, her feet up on the railing and her red-painted toenails peeking out of her brown leather sandals. The golden retriever lay on the porch next to her, looking way too at home. I tromped up the steps, clutching Neuro's carrier in my hand.

"You went by the park anyway, didn't you?" Carly called.

"Yep."

"And had a fuss with John." It wasn't a question. My sister obviously had no confidence in my diplomatic skills.

I set the carrier down to get my key out of my purse, ignoring Carly's knowing look. "Actually, he was nice enough to take Hank's wallet off my hands and save me the trouble of returning it." The dog trotted over and looked into the carrier, his tail wagging against the wooden porch. Neuro hissed and spat. "But yes, we had words. And I'm pretty sure he had an ulterior motive for taking the billfold, since he interrogated me about how I got it." I slid the key into the lock and maneuvered Neuro inside. "Want to say, 'I told you so'?"

"I would, but I'm too hungry." Carly followed me in, and for the second time that day, I shut the door in the dog's face. Inside the house, I released the carrier latch, and Neuro jumped up on the bay window to continue taunting the canine from a safer distance.

"Me, too. What do you want to eat?"

"Do you feel like getting a pizza?" Carly grimaced. "Not that I can afford the points."

"Pizza sounds good." I can't believe she worries about dieting with her curves. Every male in the vicinity stops and stares when she walks by. With my boyish figure, if a man whistles when I'm around, I assume he's calling his dog. But that's life. We always want what we don't have. "Let me get a quick shower and we'll go."

As I twisted my hair up on top of my head and secured it with a bear-claw clip, I had an epiphany. Since I'd come back to Lake View after my meltdown, I'd actually been pretty happy with my life—a family who loved me, a low-pressure job I enjoyed, an undemanding social schedule.

But then came my twenty-eighth birthday. I'm not sure why this insignificant milestone hit me so hard. Maybe I was still dealing with Colton's death. Although I think the counseling had helped me come to grips with that. Or it could have been that, even though Carly had been divorced forever, at least she had three wonderful kids, and they were her world. I was on a waxed slide to thirty with no hint of romance in sight.

ALIBIS IN ARKANSAS

To celebrate that particular birthday, Carly and the kids had come up from Atlanta for the weekend. Mama babysat while Carly and I stayed up half the night at my place watching an Elvis movie marathon. As the *Love Me Tender* credits rolled, I confessed I was afraid I'd grow old alone. Then she blew me away with a confession of her own. She thought Travis's defection had given me a deep-seated lack of trust in the male race. Yep. She accused me to my face of sabotaging my own relationships because of my reluctance to commit.

I'm not sure how it happened, but by the time the sun came up, I had committed to a deadline. Find Mr. Right or, as I told Carly, Mr. As Good as It Gets by my thirtieth birthday. Or at least make a serious effort.

And even though I'm the first to admit I have commitment issues, I've tried. I honestly have. As the hot water showered down on me, I ran through the list of possible candidates one more time.

One man I went out with made a pass at the waitress before we even ordered. And I'll never forget the cop who leaned over to me in the middle of the movie and said, "So I guess if we start dating, I can work out at the club for free?" Then there was a guy from our singles' group at church who brought over an *X-Files* DVD for us to watch. I actually enjoyed the episode, but after it was over, he showed me passages in the Bible that he claimed proved Jesus died for aliens, too.

The list could go on. Unfortunately. Which led me to Brendan Stiles. Maybe my date with him tomorrow night would be better than I expected. A girl could hope. It had been almost two years since that night I set the deadline with Carly as my witness. My big 3-0 was less than four months away.

After my shower, I found Carly sitting in the living room, flipping through the channels. Neuro amused herself by scratching at the pile of clean blankets. I picked up a quilt and tossed one end to Carly. "Make yourself useful."

"Thanks. I never get to fold laundry." She stood and took the proffered corners and joined me in a ritual we'd performed together since elementary school. Mama had taught us simple steps to accompany the chore of folding towels and sheets, as well as quilts and blankets. Between our own house and the ten cabins we rented out, there'd been plenty of work to keep us busy.

"Remember how Mama always made work a game?" Carly seemed to read my mind.

"Yes." I'd helped with the cabins, but my swim training had come first. The bulk of the work had fallen to Carly.

"She doesn't understand why I can't do the same thing with the twins and Zac." Carly slammed a folded quilt onto the pile. "Maybe now since we're living with her, she'll see it's not as easy to teach kids things these days."

For Carly, that constituted a tirade. I didn't know what to say.

She flopped back onto the couch. "I guess that sounded ungrateful, didn't it? I'm thankful Mama and Daddy let us move in with them. And goodness knows, I need the job helping out with the cabins. But Zac is like a stranger these days, and for the life of me, I can't figure out what's happened to my precious little twins. . . ."

"I know." The twins had gone from being as close as two pieces of gum in the same wrapper to elevating sibling rivalry to an art form. And as for Zac, well, teenagers are hard to figure out. I'd learned that firsthand when I taught PE and coached. Anything could happen. I shuddered. Anything at all.

My phone on the end table rang. With the instinct of a mother whose children are not with her, Carly glanced at the caller ID.

She groaned. "Oh no. I bet the twins are at it again."

I nodded for her to answer the phone.

"Hi, Mama. The girls drivin' you nuts?" Carly held the handset between her ear and her shoulder and picked up a quilt to fold.

All the color left her face. She slammed the phone down and shot to her feet, dropping the quilt as if it burned her hands.

I grabbed her arm. "What's wrong? What did Mama say?"

"The police." She jerked away from me and snatched her keys from the table.

"What about the police?" Carly's legs are shorter, but I found myself running to keep up with her as she darted down the hallway to the door.

"Zac."

Was I going to have to shake the facts out of her? "Carly, talk to me here. What do the police have to do with Zac? Is he in trouble?"

"I don't know. Oh my goodness." Tears streamed down her face.

As we reached the car, I gently pried the keys from her fingers. "I'll drive."

She nodded. "It's Hank Templeton. They found his body in the park."

I clapped my hand to my mouth. "His wallet."

Carly sobbed. "He's been murdered. They want to question Zac."

My mind raced as we flew down the road to our parents' house. My sixteen-year-old nephew couldn't hurt someone if his life depended on it. But surely no one in Lake View was capable of murder. Some vagrant must have stumbled into our safe little town, decided to lift Hank's wallet, and had gotten carried away. We all knew the editor and owner of the *Lake View Monitor* walked home from the newspaper office every night through the park. Maybe he'd surprised some bum on a bench. Knowing Hank, he probably shook him awake and demanded he stop loitering. But still my heart ached that the grouchy old man was dead.

Had the dog gotten the wallet from the murderer? Or from Hank's body in the park? The park. The mystery of the park's yellow tape was solved, but why question Zac? A paperboy. "Wait a minute, Carly. If Hank's been murdered, it's only natural they'd want to talk to his employees, right?"

She looked at me as if I had two heads. "You think that's it? That they're talking to all the people who work at the newspaper?"

"I'm sure of it."

She sank back against the seat and covered her face with her hands. "I was afraid that they'd found out about Atlanta."

I eased the car into the Stafford Cabins entryway and gasped. A black-and-white patrol car sat in the driveway. Flashing blue lights imprinted the surreal scene in my mind as two police officers started toward us. Ed and Seth, just a couple of locals with badges. Seth I knew especially well because he was the cop who'd gone out with me, hoping to get a free membership to the health club. Still, we hadn't ended on bad terms. Surely they didn't need blue lights to ask Zac some questions.

Daddy stood with his arm around Mama, and the twins huddled against them.

I squeezed Carly's arm. "Don't think the worst. Let's just pray."

Carly peeked between her fingers. "Oh Lord, please help us. Hasn't Zac been through enough? Haven't we all?"

I breathed a prayer of my own as Zac pulled in right behind us.

The policemen marched past us to Zac's jeep. Carly and I erupted out of her car in time to hear Ed ask Zac to step out of the vehicle.

"We need to ask you some questions about your relationship with Hank Templeton."

"Like what?" Zac's voice shook, but he stepped out onto the gravel. My heart thudded against my rib cage as we followed the officers up to the porch.

"Hank's been murdered," Carly blurted, then gasped as Ed gave her a hard glare.

"Son, where were you this morning around four thirty?" he asked.

"He was at work." Carly's voice cracked.

Ed glared at her again, and an ashen-faced Zac looked at the ground. Flash back to an adorable four-year-old ducking his head when his mom asked if he'd put crayons in the VCR. This was so not good. I knew Zac didn't kill Hank, but he looked so guilty.

"Is that true?" Ed kept his gaze on Zac.

Zac slowly shook his head. "I was just drivin' around town."

Carly dug her fingernails into my arm. "Zac?" She sounded like she'd been sucking helium. "What about your paper route?"

"Hank fired me three days ago, Mom. I'm sorry." My nephew, who hadn't even cried when he broke his collarbone, swiped tears from his cheeks.

Carly put her hand over her mouth, but her eyes screamed.

Ed frowned. "So let me get this straight. You didn't have a job anymore, but you still left home before daylight?"

As if we were all attached at the neck by a wire, our heads swiveled toward Zac. *Please let him have a good explanation.*

"I figured Mr. Templeton might get over it in a few days and let me come back to work; then I wouldn't hafta tell my mom."

As dumb as that sounded, I'm sure it made perfect sense to a sixteen-year-old. He'd probably thought Carly would make him quit his golf lessons.

"Witnesses say you had a loud argument with Mr. Templeton when he fired you. Is that true?" Seth shot me an apologetic glance. In spite of our one disastrous date, he practically lived at the club. And paid his own way. Zac nodded.

"I'm afraid you're going to have to go downtown with us to answer some more questions." Officer Ed Arnett looked like he'd rather be in the dentist chair than on Mama and Daddy's front porch. He turned to Carly. "You'll have to come, too, since he's a minor."

Carly staggered as if an invisible force had slammed into her. I reached out to steady her, trying to ignore my own trembling legs. Mama put her arms protectively around her granddaughters. "Girls, let's go in the house."

As Hayley and Rachel reluctantly obeyed, I drew strength from the normalcy in Mama's voice, even though I knew it was forced. If only Carly and I, and especially Zac, were young enough to "go in the house" with Mama instead of facing the harsh reality on the porch.

Even at sixty, Daddy stood tall and straight beside Zac and Carly. As a boy, he'd been a swimmer—an Olympic hopeful until he'd torn his rotator cuff in a sandlot baseball game. When we were growing up, he was a deputy sheriff, and though those days were long gone, he still carried himself with the air of a humble president—in control but not arrogant. "Now, Ed, listen here. Zac's not going anywhere without me. I'll take him and his mom to the station, and you boys can follow us."

Ed, the grizzled-before-his-time veteran cop, didn't seem to mind a bit that his old Little League coach had just referred to him as a "boy." Instead, he nodded and glanced at his young partner. "Seth? What do you think?"

"Sure, that'd be okay."

As ridiculous as this was, if I kept telling myself that the police officers were only doing their job, maybe I could keep from slugging them.

Daddy turned to me and pushed an errant strand of hair behind my ear. "Stay with your mama and the girls, honey. We'll talk to John and get this worked out and call you when we know anything."

Unlike Carly, who had butted heads with our parents on a regular basis right up until she ran off with Travis on the night of her high school graduation,

I'd rarely ever disagreed with Mama or Daddy. But this was the exception. I belonged with Carly and Zac. "I'll help Mama get the girls settled and then meet y'all at the station."

His eyes widened, and I lifted my chin.

Without a word, he nodded then shepherded Carly and Zac into his crew cab truck.

3

Lake View Monitor

Monitor Mourns Editor

The body of Lake View Monitor *editor and owner, Hank Templeton, was discovered early Friday morning in Main Street Park, the victim of an apparent homicide. The local police department is withholding details pending an investigation. . . .*

Twenty minutes later, I rushed into the Lake View police station. Before I could ask the uniformed desk clerk for information, I spotted Carly slumped on a bench.

The haunted look in her eyes took me back to the days right after Travis left. Ten years of healing down the tubes.

"Daddy wouldn't allow them to question Zac without a lawyer, but they'd only let one of us stay with him until the attorney gets here." She shrugged. "I told him to do it. He's a rock." She nodded down at the twisted tissue in her hands. "I'm a basket case."

I sank onto the wooden bench and put my arm around her shoulders. "Why don't I call Denise?" Sometimes John's wife was the only one who could get the hard-line chief of police to see reason.

Carly shook her head. "Daddy talked to John when we first got here. John said he wished there was something he could do, but there's not. He can't afford to do us any special favors. Especially in a high-profile case like this."

Hank Templeton. Married into one of the wealthiest families in Lake View. And although they despised each other, he and Mayor Byron Stanton, who had married into the same family, had been brothers-in-law.

John and his department would be under tremendous pressure to solve this case. But surely they wouldn't railroad an innocent sixteen-year-old. "So you called a lawyer?"

Carly nodded. "Daddy thought we should get Alex Campbell since he's back in town." She looked up at me. "Are you okay with that?"

I could almost hear the rusty hinges on the corner of my heart where I'd stashed all my unresolved feelings for Alex Campbell. I gave the door a mental shove and was gratified to hear it clink shut once more. "Sure. I'm fine with it."

Alex's dad had been my swim coach from the time I was eight. Alex was two years older, but he let me tag along after him. Until I turned fourteen and he started tagging after me.

Alex and swimming. My two youthful obsessions. Both lost the summer before I turned seventeen. When I slunk home from the Olympics in need of a friend, Alex left for college, and since his parents moved away shortly after, he'd never returned.

Until now.

A door across the hall opened. John stepped out and, studiously ignoring me, motioned to Carly. Maybe I'd gone too far at the park today. But so had he! Tricking me into giving him Hank's wallet. "Carly, I think you need to come on in here with your dad and Zac, after all."

I stood with Carly and gave her a hug. "I'll be out here praying for y'all," I whispered.

"Thanks." Carly hurried into the room.

"John, can I talk to you for a minute?"

He turned around and glared at me. "Don't you think we've talked enough today, Jen?"

"Aw, c'mon, John. You know I don't think you're power hungry. And among other things, you called me a busybody!" My anger flared. "Plus, you basically lied to me about Hank's wallet! But you don't see me pouting. This is my nephew we're talking about." John and I had bickered all through school. Even though he's married now and the well-respected chief of police, we still argued like five-year-olds. But this was serious.

"Look, Jenna, it's been a long day for all of us. I'm worried about Zac, too. But the best thing you can do for him now is let the police handle it." He hurried down the hall before I could protest.

Alone on the bench, I murmured a prayer then flipped open my cell phone and called Mama. I couldn't imagine being at home with no way of knowing what was going on.

"Mama?"

"Jen!" She lowered her voice. "What's happened?"

"Carly and Daddy are in a room with Zac. They're waiting for Alex Campbell. Daddy called him."

"Oh, good." I could hear the relief in Mama's tone. Alex still inspired confidence in people, even after all these years.

Daddy had been drinking coffee at the Lake View Diner with the same bunch of men every weekday morning for the last twenty years. It usually took a year or two for a newcomer to break into the group, but when Alex had come back to town recently to hang out his shingle, he'd been accepted immediately into their early morning circle.

"Yes, Alex will no doubt save the day." I regretted the sarcasm as soon as it left my lips. But not nearly as much as I did when I heard a masculine cough beside me.

"Thanks for the vote of confidence."

As I looked up into his gorgeous blue eyes, I barely remembered saying good-bye to Mama.

After hearing about it for a month, I was seeing it for myself. Alex Campbell had, indeed, come home.

◆

Early Saturday morning, I popped open a tube of crescent rolls as Carly stumbled, bleary-eyed, into the kitchen. I felt a little guilty thinking about food at a time like this, but we didn't ever get that pizza, and my sandwich from lunch yesterday was long gone.

"Hey. Did you get any sleep?"

"A little bit. Mama insisted I take something." Carly grimaced. "I'm sorry you couldn't."

Right after my granddad's death several years ago, Mama had given us each a sleeping pill. Carly had slept like a log, but I'd bounced off the walls all night, finally falling asleep in the middle of the funeral. Then it took forever for them to wake me up. No matter what the disaster now, no one in my family would ever offer me another sleeping pill.

Carly shrugged. "Actually, not sleeping was probably a blessing. At least you didn't have any bad dreams." She pulled a mug off the shelf and padded over to the coffeepot. "I appreciate your staying here all night and helping get the kids to bed. After Alex got there and they started questioning Zac, I figured Mama needed you more than we did."

"Yep. Holding down that wooden bench didn't seem all that important." No need to mention that once Alex arrived, I'd practically run out of the station. "Speaking of Zac. . ." I pushed the creamer toward her then put the rolls in the oven and set the timer. "How's he taking all this?"

"Like anybody would, I guess. He feels guilty for not telling me about getting fired, but he can't believe the police would think he might be a murderer. Ah, Jen, he's terrified." Carly perched on a bar stool. "And I'll tell you, so am I." She put her head in her hands.

My heart wrenched. "I know. I am, too."

Carly looked up, tears sliding down her cheeks. "But regardless of Zac's *record*, you know he wouldn't hurt a flea."

"Of course I do. But we know him." We'd known he actually *was* holding a package for a friend when the police found drugs in his locker in Atlanta.

Carly had started making plans to move back to Lake View shortly after the incident.

Carly grimaced. "And the police don't."

I handed her a tissue. "I didn't get a chance to ask you last night, with everyone so wiped out. Why'd Hank fire Zac?"

"Tuesday morning that old wreck Zac calls a car wouldn't start, and he had to give it a boost off my battery. He never even woke me up. My baby's growin' up so fast." She sniffed and wiped her eyes. "Anyway, when he finally got to work, Hank lit into him for being late. Zac told him about the car, but Hank still didn't let up."

I felt a surge of irritation at Hank, but then I remembered he was dead and immediately felt guilty. "Hank always could be hard to take. Remember how he used to yell at us if Beauty ever went to the bathroom in the edge of his yard when we were walking her?"

"Yeah, well, unfortunately, with half of the newspaper staff there, Hank fired him, and Zac yelled that he'd be sorry."

"Oh no." I sank onto the stool beside her. "No wonder the police are questioning him. Did you ask him what he meant?"

Carly nodded. "He said he was thinking about how many of the other delivery people were slackers and how he had been trying so hard to do it right." As she spoke, tears spilled down her cheeks again. "So he meant that Hank was losing someone who cared about doing a good job. He thought Hank would be sorry when he realized it."

"I can see that."

"I can see it, too, but it sounds bad, doesn't it?"

"Yeah." I knew Carly didn't want false words of reassurance. Maybe it was time to change the subject. "So did Alex handle things okay?" Heat rushed to my cheeks as I remembered his overhearing me talking to Mama last night. The perfect ending to the perfect day. Not.

"Yes." She wiped her eyes and glanced at me. "Are you sure you don't have a problem with Alex being Zac's lawyer?"

"I'm sure. Why should I?"

"Why should you? Sugar, this is me you're talking to. Remember? That torch you carried for him made the Olympic torch look like a little birthday candle. And it broke my heart, too, when he left town that summer without sayin' good-bye to you."

Actually, he had called, but I'd refused to talk to him. The agony of my defeat was still too fresh. I was seventeen. Who knew he'd never call again?

"Anyway, he said it was good to see you and asked what you were doing these days."

"Really?" I grimaced at my high-pitched tone. I took a sip of my coffee and tried to sound casual. "Strange we haven't seen him at church."

"He's been closing out his old office on the weekends. Had to go again today, actually. But he'll be at church tomorrow."

"That's nice. So what did you tell him?" I picked an imaginary fleck from my Eeyore pajama bottoms. "About me, I mean."

"Oh, not much. I'm pretty sure Daddy had already bragged up your job at the health club and made you sound like a partner." She frowned. "Which you should be. At the very least. So I told him you were seeing Brendan."

I flinched.

"Was I wrong?" Carly raised an eyebrow.

I shrugged. "Not really. I canceled for tonight, though." The oven timer went off, and I pulled the rolls out. "Can you grab the butter and jelly?"

"Sure." Carly retrieved them from the refrigerator and put them next to the basket of hot rolls. "Anyway, for the life of me, I don't know what we would have done without Alex. He believed Zac about last year's trouble."

"Sounds like he has good judgment." Although, surely, if he'd had very good judgment, he'd never have stayed away from Lake View for so long. I pushed a buttered roll toward Carly. Enough about Alex.

"Thanks." She cradled the hot bread in both hands. "I'm not counting points today."

"I noticed you set out the real butter." That detail, more than anything, made me realize the extreme level of her stress.

"Sometimes you have to have the real thing." She squeezed a big glob of strawberry jelly onto the roll and took a bite.

"Zac still asleep?"

"Probably. Bless his heart, he was worn out. I guess Mama and Daddy went out to breakfast this morning?" She looked around the kitchen as if expecting our parents to pop out of the cabinets. "I told them last night, the more normal we can keep things, the better."

Our parents rarely splurged, but their Saturday breakfasts out were a time for them to talk over the week. They sure had a lot to talk about this morning. "Do you think the police will question Zac again?"

"I don't know." Carly finished off her coffee. "They told him not to leave town." She wiped her hands on her napkin. "For the life of me, I can't imagine why they took Zac in. A lot of people had run-ins with Hank. You know what? On the way home, Zac told us that even his golf teacher had a fight with Hank recently."

"Do the police know that?" I felt a little guilty, hoping to incriminate someone else, but *someone* murdered Hank, and it wasn't Zac.

"Don't you dare tell them!" We spun around to see Zac standing in the doorway, his eyes red-rimmed. "Elliott didn't kill Hank!"

"I'm sure he didn't." Carly's quiet tone couldn't hide her frustration. "But neither did you."

"Mom, Elliott got mad at Hank over something you might understand. His fiancée left him."

"What did that have to do with Hank?" I asked casually, my heart in my throat. Had Hank been cheating on Marge and been killed by a jealous boyfriend?

"Not Hank, the paper. It had something to do with the paper. I don't know what." Zac stomped over to the refrigerator and snagged a single-serving bottle of orange juice. He glared at his mom as he popped the top. "I'm sorry I even told you. He was only trying to make me feel better about getting fired."

"I understand, son, but—" Carly cast me a pleading glance.

"Want a crescent roll?" When in doubt, distract.

Sure enough, Zac nodded and took one. Another dangerous situation defused with food. "I'm going out to the course."

"Today?" Carly looked dumbfounded.

Zac grunted. "I'm a suspect, not a prisoner." He snatched one more roll and blew out like a spring tornado.

We sat in silence for a few seconds; then Carly swiveled her bar stool back and forth. "You know, I can't help but wonder. . ."

"What?"

"Well, we know Zac didn't kill Hank. And Zac's positive Elliott didn't. So who did?"

"Good question. I've been thinking the same thing." I picked up Carly's dishes. "They always say it's most likely a family member. But somehow I can't imagine Marge killing anyone." Like an eccentric old aunt, Marge had been around as long as I could remember, giving us gum after church when we were little and buying chocolate bars and Girl Scout cookies from us as we grew older. Her sister, Amelia, relished her high-profile role as the mayor's wife, but Marge had seemed content in her middle-class life with cantankerous old Hank.

"Oh, I don't know." An impish grin flitted across Carly's tired face. "Maybe she finally managed to nag him to death," she drawled.

"Carly Elizabeth Reece! You are so bad."

"I was kidding." Her smile disappeared. "But I shouldn't have said it. It's hard enough to get along with a normal man. Marge deserves a badge of honor for putting up with Hank's bad temper and know-it-all attitude for so many years."

"Well, we've known her forever. I can't believe she killed him, so who does that leave?" I wrung out the dishcloth and wiped off the counter.

"You're the one who's always got your nose in those murder mysteries. You tell me."

I rolled my eyes. "Oh yes, that makes me an expert." I tossed the cloth into the sink. "Seriously, though—if we could find out who did it, that would clear Zac."

"We? You got a frog in your pocket?" Carly's voice squeaked, and she shook her head. "I get scared readin' those books. I'm not about to live one."

"Not even for Zac?" Yes, that was below the belt, but if I was going to get to the bottom of this, I had to have help.

Carly shook her head again. "The best thing we can do for Zac is pray and let the police do their job. They'll find the killer, and that'll prove Zac's innocence."

Where had I heard that before? Was Carly the mouthpiece for the chief of police now? "I know. You're right, and we *will* pray. But they say God helps those who help themselves, so—"

"Oh, Jen, that's not even in the Bible. Besides, this is too important for us to play detective. We don't want to make things worse for Zac." Carly hesitated. "Sugar, your track record's not that great. Remember in school how mixed up things would get every time you decided to 'help' figure things out?"

I bristled. "I've helped plenty of people."

Carly's smile was gentle. "Like Susan?"

"How was I supposed to know that girl with Barry was his cousin? They were picking out jewelry together."

"Yeah, gifts for the groomsmen."

"Once I cleared up the misunderstanding, they got back together." They'd even been able to get the same date and time for the ceremony. All I'd really done was inject a little excitement into their post-engagement/pre-wedding lull.

"And marked you off the invitation list."

Some people. One little mistake and they never let you live it down. I shrugged. "This is different. What can it hurt if we do a little innocent snooping?"

"What can it *hurt*?" Carly's animated face was such a contrast to her earlier tears that it was almost worth the disagreement. "Are you kidding? This isn't a game or some high school prank. You're talkin' about goin' after a cold-blooded killer."

4

LAKE VIEW MONITOR

Obituary

Respected editor and owner of the Lake View Monitor, *Henry (Hank)
Theodore Templeton, died Friday morning. (See front-page story for details.)*

*Templeton is survived by his beloved wife, Margaret Smith
Templeton; one son, Henry Theodore Templeton Jr., currently in Europe;
two sisters, Elisen Bradenburg of Arizona and Lilly Jordan of Missouri;
and numerous nieces and nephews.*

*Templeton was a member of the local VFW, the Lake View Zoning
Committee, and the Lake View Chamber of Commerce. Funeral
arrangements are pending.*

Green bean casserole and marshmallow salad. Haute cuisine for dummies. Normally this would have been the perfect opportunity for Carly to display her culinary skills. Cooking actually helped her to relieve stress, but she was exhausted, so Mama and I opted for quick and easy.

Poor Marge. How would she react to Zac's being a suspect in her husband's murder? I was in no hurry to find out. If Mama hadn't played the Christian-duty card, I wouldn't be standing here this fine Saturday afternoon ringing the Templetons' doorbell.

Marge's best friend, Lois, opened the door. "Thanks for coming by." Her hushed tone matched her somber face. I suppose with her being the town librarian, *whisper* is her native language.

"How's Marge?" Mama asked.

Lois shook her head. "I think she's still in shock."

We nodded and followed her through the standing-room-only crowd. Everyone from church and the neighborhood had turned out to pay their respects to Hank's widow. In the South we show our sympathy with food offerings, and judging by the number of steaming dishes filling the table, everyone in Lake View felt sorry for Marge.

We squeezed our own offerings into the sea of casseroles. Lois would have her hands full after the funeral, helping Marge discreetly dispose of the leftovers.

"You ladies come in and have a seat." Lois gestured toward the living room. When we stepped in, it was as if someone had hit the MUTE button. We nodded politely into the silence.

The news of Zac's trip downtown had definitely made its way around the local grapevine. Mama always said, "Good news travels fast, but bad news travels faster," and she was right again.

A low-hum chorus of greetings floated in our direction; then mercifully, the guests went back to their quiet conversations. Lois motioned toward the chintz couch, and the gray-haired Llewellen sisters scooted closer together to make room for us. After we settled in, Lois perched on the arm of Marge's overstuffed chair and patted her on the back. "Is there anything I can get for you?" She reminded me of an anxious lady-in-waiting.

"No, thanks. I'm fine." Marge smiled at us. "Elizabeth. Jenna. It's good to see you. Theo's on his way, Jenna. I know he'll want to see you." Marge's eyes were red and swollen, but her abnormally high-pitched voice and pseudo-perky attitude suggested that the doctor had probably given her some pills to lessen the shock.

"Marge, we're so sorry to hear about Hank's death. Lake View won't be the same without him."

That was true. Mama always knew the right thing to say. If it had been left up to me, I probably wouldn't have mentioned Hank. And if I had—well, let's just say it's a good thing I let Mama do the talking.

Marge beamed. "Hank loved Lake View. The newspaper was his life." Her smile froze then melted into a frown. "Amelia used to say he should have married the *Monitor* instead of me."

Now there's a thought. Since the wife is the most likely suspect, maybe the Monitor *killed him.*

Valium was probably responsible for this emotional roller coaster, but the wistful tone in her voice clutched at my heart. Hank had been a pain, but he'd been *her* pain.

"Amelia. *Humph*," Lois muttered, looking as if she'd taken a drink of curdled milk.

Mama leaned forward and patted Marge's hand. "Hank was lucky to have you, Marge. He loved you very much."

Suddenly, Marge plopped back against the chair. "He had a funny way of showing it sometimes." Tears spilled onto her cheeks.

A million questions flooded my mind, and I barely stopped them before they tumbled out of my mouth. Had Hank been abusive? Something beyond your garden-variety crankiness? I settled for a hopefully leading, "Oh?"

Mama glared at me, and I could see she knew I was trying to launch a little investigation of my own. How do mothers do that?

"Hank did love you, Marge," Lois said soothingly.

"Yes, I'm sure he did, but you know as well as I do, by the time the bridge club meets Monday, they'll be wondering if I murdered him." Marge squeaked on the last word.

The Llewellen sisters gasped, and even Mama looked a little nonplussed. This visit had suddenly gone from obligatory to interesting.

"No, they won't!" Mama and Lois chorused.

I opened my mouth to gently ask why they would think that, but before I could speak, Marge burst out, "Oh yes, they will." Her gaze darted from side to side, and she lowered her voice to a conspiratorial whisper. "You know how people talk." She nodded to Mama. "Look at how the news spread about Zac being arrested."

"He wasn't actually arrest—," Mama started.

"Can you believe they took that poor child down to the police station? Isn't that the most ridiculous thing you've ever heard? Why, they even came around here asking *me* all kinds of questions. Why didn't I call and report Hank missing?" She shook her head, and her tight curls sprang back and forth. "Why would I call? I never know what time Hank's going to get home. Everybody knows how late he works when he's got his mind on a story. Besides, Lois had one of those twenty-four-hour bugs. I couldn't leave her alone, so I stayed with her. I never dreamed he didn't come home. Isn't that right, Lois?"

Lois nodded, but for a second, I thought I saw a warning expression in her eyes.

Marge looked back to us. "You tell that sweet boy not to worry. I know he didn't kill Hank."

"It's kind of you to be concerned about Zac, Marge," Mama said. "He had a rough night last night, and so did his mother. We'd better get home and check on them." Mama stood, and I quickly did the same. My mother could always be counted on to extricate us gracefully from an awkward social situation. And situations didn't get much more awkward than this.

Marge pushed to her feet and hugged me. The familiar smells of spearmint gum and perm solution transported me back to childhood. Marge was odd, but she deserved to know who killed her husband. And if I had my way, she would.

The doorbell rang. Marge gave Mama a hug and excused herself to answer it.

Mama squeezed Lois's hand. "I'm glad you're here with her."

"Thank you. She'd do the same for me." Her solemn gaze flickered to include me.

I nodded. "Have they made any arrangements yet?"

"Poor Marge." Lois dabbed her eyes with a tissue. "The. . ." She cleared her throat and glanced toward the foyer, where a weeping Marge was enfolded in the rather large embrace of the church secretary. "The authorities say the body won't be released for at least two weeks. Marge doesn't think it's fair to Hank's memory to wait."

"Bless her heart." Mama's voice was soft with sympathy.

"Yes," Lois said. "She's scheduled a memorial service for him at the church Monday afternoon. They'll put a special notice in Sunday's paper."

We hugged Lois and patted Marge's heaving back one more time on the way out the door. When the latch clicked behind us, I glanced at my mother. "You did good, Mama. I felt sorry for Marge, but the air in there was too thick with weirdness."

She frowned. "Marge has always been a little. . .hmm. . .unusual, especially the last year or so, but today was strange, even for her. Poor thing. Even if she was under his thumb all those years, Hank's death has to be hard on her."

"I know. I wish there were more we could do."

"We can visit her whether we enjoy her company right now or not."

If I'd said that, I'd have sounded like Pollyanna, but Mama just sounded gracious.

I reached in my pocket for the keys. "Yeah, but there might be something else we could do, too." Maybe if I led up to this slowly, I could slide under the Mama-meter.

"What do you mean?"

"I don't know. We know a lot of people. Don't you think if we tried, we might figure out what happened to Hank?"

Mama groaned as she walked around to the passenger side. "Jenna, honey. . ."

"Don't worry. Carly's already given me that speech about minding my own business. You don't have to." That is one disadvantage to having a big sister. I hear every for-your-own-good talk twice.

"Why do I get the feeling you didn't listen to her, either?"

I slid into the driver's seat and chose not to answer. As I turned the key, a black car rounded the corner. "Talk about the consummate politician. I never dreamed he would show up here." I nodded toward the Mercedes that was the trademark of Lake View mayor Byron Stanton.

I should have known, though. The mayor was bound to be happy that Hank's scathing editorials were a thing of the past, but he'd squeeze out a few tears for the public's benefit, his classically handsome face twisted into a mournful expression.

Mama nodded. "Looks like he even coaxed Amelia into coming with him. She and Marge haven't spoken in years," she said. "I wonder if they will today."

I braked. "Want to go back and watch?" I nearly laughed aloud at the look of distaste on her face. "Mama, I'm kidding!"

"I know you are. It's just always bothered me that two sisters who were as close as Marge and Amelia used to be could let their husbands pull them apart. Marge needs her sister's support at a time like this. Maybe they can mend fences."

"Maybe so." I thought of the last few editorials Hank had written. "But you know how when somebody dies, there's a tendency to canonize them. Marge may take up the torch and continue the 'Lord Byron' editorials."

"Let's hope not. I agree Byron *is* egotistical, but Hank ran that into the ground. I'm sure our mayor was sick to death of it."

I glanced quickly at Mama. "Sick to death, huh? Interesting choice of words."

❖

The solemn music drifted into the foyer as Carly and I entered the church building. Carly kept her gaze fixed on the faded gold and maroon carpet and stepped back for me to take the lead. She'd tried to beg off, claiming that people would think it was in poor taste for her to attend the memorial service on account of her son's being a suspect, but I wasn't about to come by myself. And I wasn't about to miss it.

"Why did I let you talk me into this?" Carly muttered into my shoulder blades.

I knew the answer to that one but kept my mouth shut. She owed me big-time after the Pampered Chef party I'd endured for her a couple of weeks ago.

I signed our names in the guest book, and we walked to the back row, where three aisle seats were empty.

Carly slid into the inside seat with a low growl. "Honestly, I think I should just go home."

"Relax, it'll be fine."

"Sure it will be. But staying at home with a good book would have been *much* finer," Carly snapped.

I lowered my voice to a soft whisper. "You know, they say the best place to find a murderer is at the victim's funeral."

"But we're not interested in finding a murderer." Her voice rose on the last word.

"Shh. Yes, we are." I turned back toward the front. "Look."

"What?" She followed my gaze and spotted Brendan offering his condolences to Marge. "Brendan? What's he doing here?"

"I have no idea." He hugged Marge then leaned down to embrace Lois, who was sitting next to her bereaved friend.

"Maybe he's a friend of the family."

"Are you ever going to go out with him again?"

"Someday," I said without looking up from the program the funeral director had handed me as we entered, "when there's not so much going on."

"Yeah." Carly sighed. "Surely Zac will be cleared soon. The idea of him murdering someone is ridiculous. And the idea of us attending the victim's funeral is even more ridiculous."

I stuck the program into Carly's black satchel. "If we find the killer, Zac'll be cleared."

"Jenna, we are not—"

"I know we're not officially investigating, but if we pick up a little clue here or there that would exonerate Zac, what can it hurt?"

"That's it. I'm leaving." Carly started to rise, but I put my hand on her arm. "Wait. Look."

A short, trim man in a dark suit and a red and yellow floral tie walked past us. The well-preserved blond on his arm was decked out in designer black down to her stiletto heels.

"Yeah. Byron and Amelia. So what?" Carly pulled her arm away from me. "They *are* Hank's sister-in-law and brother-in-law. It seems natural to me they would be here."

"Does his million-dollar smile look strained to you? A little stiff? Hers, too, for that matter?"

"Why, yes. Now that you mention it, I wouldn't give you but a hundred thousand for it today," Carly drawled.

"I'm serious," I said.

"Me, too. Have you ever read that Nancy Drew mystery where Nancy suspects everyone and ends up looking like an idiot?"

"No." I turned my attention back to the mayor. He was greeting people as if this were a parade and he and his wife the only float.

"Me, either, but I'm sure there is one."

I rolled my eyes. "If you'd help me look around instead of wasting time wishing you weren't here, we might learn something."

Carly sighed and stared straight ahead.

Shoulder to shoulder, people filled the pews, and the last few aisles, including the one we sat in, consisted of mostly occupied white folding chairs.

I methodically scanned each row, spotting Don Samuels, the butcher from Piggly Wiggly. Two rows down, Angelo Petronelli from Petronelli Bakery sat with his family. *The butcher, the baker—all we need now is the candlestick maker.* Immediately Chrysalis Summer, owner of that little bead and candle shop on Main Street, passed in front of my view. Now everyone was accounted for at the funeral of one of Lake View's most prominent citizens.

The newspaper employees were all seated in one section, along with their families. Something about the slumped figure with a blond buzz cut caught my eye.

"Car!" I hissed.

She glanced at me. "What?"

"Does the back of that head look familiar to you?" I pointed discreetly, covering my finger with my hand. "Right there, on the other side, four rows up," I whispered.

Carly clutched my hand. "It's Zac."

I winced and pried her death grip loose. I nodded, but my mind was spinning. Why would Zac be here? Why hadn't he told us he was coming? He was supposed to be in school. "Who's that sitting by him?"

"It looks like Elliott, his golf instructor." The hurt fled from Carly's face, replaced by determination. "I'm going to go talk to Zac."

"Wait a minute," I said. Making a scene at the funeral wouldn't be a good thing for Zac, and Carly's taut face had *scene* written all over it. "Let's think about this. If he didn't mention he was coming, he probably didn't want you to know. Did you tell him you were going to be here?"

She shook her head.

"Don't you think home would be a better place to discuss it with him? Or at least wait until after the service?"

She nodded and sat back, biting her lip.

"Excuse me, ladies."

I jerked around to meet Alex Campbell's intent gaze. He seemed to be making a habit of sneaking up on me.

"May I sit here?" he whispered.

I nodded dumbly. Carly slid into the vacant seat farther into the row, and I automatically followed suit.

Alex leaned over toward me. "Hey, water girl. How's life in the deep end?" His standard greeting to me as long as I can remember.

"I'm not so crazy about being in over my head anymore," I whispered, my pulse pounding as loud as my words.

Thankfully, before I had to tread any more dangerous water, Brother Johnson stood and approached the podium. The music and muted conversation stopped.

5

LAKE VIEW MONITOR

Advertisement

LAKE VIEW DINER GOLFER'S SPECIAL

Bring in a golf tee for $1 off a "club" sandwich.

I admired the preacher who could make heavy-handed Hank sound like a candidate for sainthood. But I was glad for Marge's sake that he could come up with comforting words. Theo, Hank's son, had barely made it home in time for the funeral, but he seemed to be holding up very well. Since there was no casket, after the closing prayer, we stood respectfully while Hank's family filed out. What a shame Amelia wasn't close enough to her sister to comfort her at a time like this.

Once we were all outside, I hugged Marge, then Theo.

"Jenna, it's so good to see you."

"You, too, Theo. I'm just sorry about the circumstances." We hugged again, and he took his mom to speak to someone else.

I turned around to find Carly and Alex standing behind me.

"Would you ladies like to get a bite to eat?" Alex lowered his voice. "Or is it bad manners to talk about food right after a funeral?"

I glanced around the parking lot at the huddled groups of people engrossed in conversation. There were fewer tearful faces than I'd ever seen after a death in the community. Even Marge, flanked by Theo and Lois, looked exhausted but calm.

Alex cleared his throat, and I pulled my attention back to him.

He raised one eyebrow. "Why do I get the feeling you're not considering my etiquette question?"

I loved how he could arch his eyebrow. Why couldn't I do that? "I think once you're outside the building, anything goes. Especially since there's not a graveside service."

"In that case, how about lunch?" Alex's smile included both Carly and me.

But Carly's stare focused on something in the distance. I followed her gaze. Zac. Getting into a car with his golf teacher.

"Thanks, Alex," Carly murmured, keeping her eye on the car. "Actually, I need to run an *errand* right now." She motioned toward me. "Why don't you two go eat?"

"Another time," I said, trying my best to mimic Mama's natural grace for getting out of a sticky situation. "I'll just go with you, Car. In case you need help with your *errand*."

Alex frowned. "Why do I feel like there's a whole conversation going on that I'm not hearing?"

So I'd failed miserably in my attempt at a graceful exit. "Carly's got a lot on her mind."

Carly shook her head. "This is something I need to deal with on my own. Alex, will you drop Jenna off at home when y'all finish eating?"

"I'd be happy to."

Carly's heels click-clacked across the asphalt lot before I could frame a reply. From now on I was taking my own vehicle everywhere I went. Who'd known when my sister had offered to drive that she'd pawn me off—like a bag of old clothes for Goodwill—before the day was over? Still, short of chasing her down, I had little choice now. I was stuck going to eat with Alex.

Poor me. I could think of worse situations to be stuck in. Maybe giving in with grace would be more my thing. I smiled. "The diner?" It had been our hangout for so many years, it was hard to imagine eating anywhere else with him.

"I was going to suggest it if you didn't." He guided me toward his vehicle a few yards away.

I stopped. Even though he'd been driving a hand-me-down car from his dad when he'd left town, all these years I'd pictured him with a four-wheel-drive truck. Not the kind with oversized wheels that loomed over everything else on the highway. Alex had never been showy like that. Just a rough-and-ready truck.

Exactly like the one sitting in front of me right now.

"You don't like it?" He held the passenger door open for me.

The last thing I wanted was for him to know that he'd even crossed my mind over the years, much less that I'd imagined what kind of vehicle he drove. "It's fine."

When he slid in and buckled his seat belt, I checked mine. Alex had always been famous for going from zero to sixty in seconds. "Do you still drive like you're in NASCAR?"

"I've mellowed some over the years." He gave me a slow grin.

Great. The only thing I could imagine more dangerous to my emotional equilibrium than Alex Campbell was a mellow Alex Campbell.

When Alex and I walked into the Lake View Diner together, we automatically headed toward the booth nearest the jukebox. I slid in across from him, and for a second it was as if the hands on the big-faced clock over the counter were flying around backward, taking us back to a time when swimming practice and competitions had kept me busy. But every bit of free time I'd had, I'd spent with Alex, often in this very place. I had moved on, and so had Alex, but some memories you never outgrow.

We should have gone to McDonald's.

I scrambled for a safe topic, one not obviously stilted, yet several degrees this side of nostalgic. "How did Coach's gallbladder surgery go? In the last card I got from them, your mom mentioned he was scheduled to have it done."

"It went fine. You keep in touch with Mom and Dad?" Alex sounded surprised.

"Why not?" I loved Alex's parents. After the Olympics, Coach must have been disappointed, especially when I decided to quit, but he hadn't made me feel bad.

"I thought—well, I wasn't sure how you felt about them after Dad practically deserted you when you didn't win." Alex picked up a menu and studied the selections with more concentration than they deserved, considering we'd had the diner's entire menu memorized fifteen years ago and it hadn't changed a whole lot since then.

I put my hand on the slightly greasy laminated card he held in front of him like a shield and pulled it down so I could see his eyes. "What exactly do you mean, deserted me? I lost, it was over, and I chose to stop. If anyone should have been disappointed, it was your dad. I failed him, not the other way around." I sounded abrupt, but I didn't want pity. Truthfully, Alex's desertion was the one that had shaken the foundation of my world. Not that I'd ever admit that to him. Hard enough to admit it to myself.

"And anyway, your parents needed to move close to your granddad—remember how sick he was? I'm sure they would have stayed here if I was still competing, but I think it may have been a relief when they were able to leave."

Alex laid the menu on the table. "I guess they didn't have much of a choice, but I never quit thinking of Lake View as home. Most of all I missed—"

"Can I get y'all something to drink?" Debbie pushed back her frosted hair with one hand and offered Alex a dazzling smile.

We agreed to try the new peach tea, and she sashayed back to the kitchen with enough twist in her step to draw almost every male eye in the place. But the man across the table kept his gaze on me. That was a good sign. Now how to nudge him back to where he was before Debbie showed up? What had he missed? The small-town atmosphere? The diner's homemade pecan pie?

"So, water girl. What's been happening in your life? Besides the obvious?"

Unfortunate fact number one: Once a conversation has been interrupted, there's no going back.

"Not much. I guess you probably know I gave up teaching a few years ago and came back home. I've been working at the health club ever since."

"I heard Bob was supposed to have sold you the place by now."

I rolled my eyes. "Of course you did. No such thing as personal business in this town, is there?" I wondered what he'd heard about why I quit teaching.

"Not last time I checked. Must make John's job easier, though. He shouldn't have any trouble finding someone willing to tell him who killed Hank and why."

Just as Alex spoke, Debbie waltzed up and plunked two tall glasses of iced peach tea down on the table. "That man sure knew how to rile people up."

I looked up at her with interest. "Hank?"

"Mm-hmm. Half of his lunch meetings ended with yelling." She lowered her voice. "Seeing as how the newspaper is right around the corner, he was a regular."

Alex nodded. "I'm sorry for your loss."

Startled, I choked on my tea. He shrugged and gave an imperceptible shake of his head, like *What was I supposed to say?*

"Who did he shout with mostly?" I asked when I'd gotten my breath back. Alex might not recognize that Debbie wanted to tell what she knew, but I sure did.

"Now that you mention it, the last person I remember him being in here with was Brendan Stiles." She leaned toward us. "You know, that new pharmacist over at Lake View Drugstore."

Apparently the fact that I'd dated said pharmacist hadn't been newsworthy enough to merit a swing on the gossip grapevine. "Yes, I know who you mean." Was it my imagination, or was Alex narrowing his eyes at me? I turned back toward Debbie. "What were they talking about?"

"I don't know." She shot a glance toward the counter, where someone's ham and cheese sitting under the heat lamp was growing staler by the minute. "Maybe Marge."

"What about Marge?" The gentle tap on my leg wasn't my imagination. Alex kicked me under the table.

"Well, I heard Hank say, 'My wife,' and then something about 'a bag.' I thought maybe Brendan was insulting Marge. But that's all I heard."

"You must hear a lot, Debbie," I said and sipped my tea.

"More than you'd believe."

"I think I'll have the turkey and dressing," Alex said.

I returned his kick.

Debbie frowned then slapped her forehead. "Of course. What was I thinking, standing here gabbing when you need to order?" She flipped her pad open and jotted down our choices, then bustled to the kitchen.

"Aren't you Chatty Cathy?" He raised an eyebrow. "Or is it Nancy Drew?"

Boy, what was it with him and Carly and the Nancy Drew thing? I ignored that part of his question and laughed. "You always said I talked too much, remember?"

"That was when I was twelve and trying to catch a fish, and you wanted to discuss the most effective swim strokes." He reached toward my hand, I think, but ended up bumping my tea glass instead.

I grabbed it to keep it from tipping over.

"You don't want to get involved in a murder investigation, Jenna."

"I don't want my nephew to go to jail for something he didn't do, Alex," I said, mocking his slightly patronizing tone.

He flicked at a speck on the plastic tablecloth. "It's my job to keep him out of jail. Don't you trust me?"

I stared at his chiseled jaw. The slight five o'clock shadow would have made most men appear unkempt and messy. Instead, it gave Alex the rugged air of a hardworking hero, too busy saving the world to shave. "I trust you." *As long as it's not my heart at risk.* From the corner of my eye, I saw Debbie enter the three-stall restroom to the right of the kitchen.

"I'm glad to hear that." This time he connected with my hand and clasped it loosely. "I don't want you to get in over your head."

In spite of the tingle down my arm at his touch, or maybe because of it, I slipped my hand from his and pushed to my feet. "I've spent half my life in the deep end, remember? Excuse me." I wove my way through the tables to the restroom.

Debbie stood at the vanity, reapplying her lipstick.

"Hey."

In the mirror, she met my eyes. "You dating Alex?"

"No."

She smacked her red lips. "I was hoping you'd say that."

I suddenly remembered hearing at the beauty shop that Debbie's husband ran off with a woman from River Falls. Sympathy warred with my desire to tell her to stay away from Alex Campbell until I decided how I felt about him.

"About Hank. If you remember more details about his conversation with Brendan, or anybody else for that matter, will you give me a holler?"

She turned the faucet on and stared at me. "I heard about your nephew. That's too bad." She squirted soap on her hands and rubbed them together under the stream. "You sure you're not dating Alex?"

"I think I'd know."

"In that case, I'll call you if I think of anything."

"Thanks." I scribbled my cell number on the back of a blank ticket for her and hurried back to my seat.

In a few minutes, Debbie brought our order. She never referred to our bathroom conversation but turned the full force of her charm on Alex. As far as I could tell, he was unaffected. I was surprised by how happy that made me.

As we were driving home, Alex glanced over at me. "You're not going to let this drop, are you?"

"Whatever do you mean?" I borrowed Carly's thickest Southern accent, the words dripping innocence.

"If I remember one thing about you, it's that once you get a bone between your teeth, you never let go."

"Are you calling me a dog?" When had I stopped engaging my brain before my mouth?

"Hardly." That one word spoke volumes.

I blushed and stared out the window.

"Promise me something," Alex said.

"What's that?" I murmured, not daring to tear my gaze away from the houses we were passing.

"At least keep me in the loop on your questions and the answers you get. As Zac's lawyer, I'd like to know anything that might affect his case."

"Oh, so this is purely professional?" The words popped out of their own accord, I promise.

"No. Not purely." He flipped on the blinker and glanced at me. "As your friend, I want to know if you're doing anything that might endanger you, too."

I nodded. Friends to the end. "Don't worry, Alex. I'm not planning on getting myself killed."

"Yeah, but here's the kicker." Alex smoothly navigated the truck into my driveway. "I'm pretty sure Hank wasn't, either."

"Point taken. I'll be discreet." I unfastened my seat belt. "Thanks for lunch."

"Let's do it again sometime."

"Sounds fun." Suddenly it felt as if I were waiting for a good-bye kiss. The thought propelled me out of the truck, and I practically ran up the sidewalk, almost tripping over the golden dog who had taken up a permanent position on my porch. Once there was a safe distance between Alex and me, I turned to wave. He was looking at me with an inscrutable expression. Probably thinking I was still crazy after all these years.

❖

I confess I closed my eyes when I let go of the ball. But when I opened them, there wasn't a white pin standing. Again. As the electronic scoreboard excitedly flashed a big *X*, I turned to face Brendan Stiles. My date for the evening stared at the scorekeeper's monitor, his lips pinched together like someone had laced his cola with pure lemon juice.

"*Whoo-hoo!* Another strike! Sweetie, don't you want to ditch your date and join our team?" Francee Moore called to me from the next lane. "We sure could use you tonight, what with Millie Jo out sick!" She cocked an eyebrow at Brendan. "We'll let him watch!"

"You know the rules, Francee." Joyce Simms from the Shear Joy team balanced her monogrammed bowling ball on her hip and glared at Francee. "Only employees are allowed on the team."

Francee rolled her eyes at the woman in purple and yellow polyester and muttered to me, "Shear Joy should lose for sheer bad taste." She slapped one hand against the delicately intertwining *C-N-C* embroidered on her light blue and navy blouse, roughly in the direction of her heart, and ran the fingers of her other hand through her short, spiked red hair. "Jenna, I promise to pay you six bucks an hour to wash hair one day a year. You choose the day. How about it?"

I could feel Brendan's gaze boring into my back. My cheeks burned. "Thanks, Francee. Looks like Cut 'n' Curl is doing fine without me, though. We're just here for fun."

And some fun it had been so far. Brendan and I were finally getting around to our date that had been postponed because of Hank's untimely demise. I'd suggested bowling, thinking a little physical activity would be better than sitting across a table making awkward conversation. My mistake. Even tepid dinner conversation would have been an improvement over the competitive tension that had been in the air ever since we walked into the musty-smelling building. The only thing stronger than Brendan's determination to win was the magnetic pull of the gutter on his ball. He couldn't roll it straight to save his life.

"Fine. Have it your way." Francee laughed. "Joyce Sims is liable to throw that bowling ball at me if we win anyway. Sports can be dangerous."

"They sure can," a small blond beside her piped up. "One of my perms today said the police found a golf club they think someone used to kill Hank Templeton."

"Really?" I glanced at Brendan, who had abandoned his pout and was listening intently. "Whose club was it?"

"They don't know. But I reckon they're going to try to find out."

As she finished speaking, a Shear Joy team member made a strike, and pandemonium broke out.

"So a golf club was the murder weapon," I said to Brendan, then suddenly remembered what Debbie at the diner had said about Hank's heated conversation with the local pharmacist. "Did Hank play golf?" I was pretty sure he had, considering his and Marge's house backed up to the golf course, but I wanted to hear from Brendan how well he knew Hank, without asking outright.

"How should I know? I barely knew the man."

"Didn't you say you were on a zoning committee with him?"

He rolled his eyes at me. "Well, yeah. And I'm sure I saw him from a distance when I went into the news office to take out an ad for a cashier, too, but that hardly constitutes knowing him."

Neither of us mentioned the fact that Brendan played golf. It didn't seem possible that I might be on a date with a murderer, but it was time I faced facts. Someone in our town had probably killed Hank. "You never had lunch with him or anything?" I asked, fully aware that if Alex were here, he'd be kicking me under the figurative table.

Brendan looked at me as if I'd sprouted green antennae and grown an extra head. "Me have lunch with Hank? Why would I?"

I didn't spend three years teaching school without learning to recognize an evasive answer. I also knew that sometimes you're better off to let things drop for the time being. "It's your turn to bowl."

Brendan threw two quick gutter balls then collapsed back in his seat. I picked up my ball from the rack, but his next question stopped me short.

"Maybe you should be thinking a little closer to home. Didn't you say your nephew was taking golf lessons?"

"So?"

Brendan tapped the table with the pencil. "It's perfectly understandable."

I huffed. "What's understandable?"

"You're in denial."

"Denial? About Zac?" I tried to suck air into my lungs, but it felt as though they were trapped on a one-dimensional planet and refused to expand. "Zac didn't do it," I said through gritted teeth.

"Okay, whatever you say."

We'd abandoned all pretext of bowling, but I still clutched the neon green ball. I ran my hand over the slick, cool surface and fought the urge to lift it to my hot cheeks. Or better yet, slam it into Brendan's smug face. The muscles in my jaw ached. My daily Bible study was from James, and I was trying desperately to control my tongue, but biting it until it bled might be a little extreme. "I think it's time for us to call it a night." I put the ball back on the rack beside us.

Brendan pushed to his feet, the look on his face reeking of false concern. "Jenna, honey, I didn't mean to hurt your feelings, but it's true the family is often the last to know."

"I guess I'm the last to know a lot of things." I ground out the words as I changed shoes. When I'd finished, I stood and leaned toward Brendan, speaking softly for his ears only. "Like the fact that I'd rather spend every Friday night for the rest of my life at home, painting my cat's toenails, than go out with you again."

I didn't mind the walk home. The night air had never felt so cool and fresh. Some places were stale with bad company.

6

LAKE VIEW MONITOR

Help Wanted

Part-time position available. Qualified applicant must have common sense and grammar skills. Send résumé to P.O. Box 34213, Lake View, AR 72001. Salary commensurate with experience.

O *omph!"* Carly grunted. "That ball has it in for me." Her racket clattered to the hardwood floor. She laughed and sank down beside it. "Forget it, Jen. Racquetball isn't my game."

"You don't know that! You haven't even given it a chance." I leaned against the wall and crossed my arms, giving my sister a measured glance. "Besides, it beats staying home and moping."

Carly rubbed an angry-looking red spot on her leg. "At least staying home wasn't giving me bruises. Besides, have you ever tried to mope around ten-year-old twins? Let's call Mama and ask her how much moping she's getting done tonight."

"Nice try. Come on. Give it a few more minutes. If you still don't like it, we'll change and head to the sauna."

Carly got to her feet and waved her racket around over her head with a grin. "Boomerang ball? Crazy sister? Sauna at the end? Bring it on." She resumed the stance I'd shown her—knees slightly bent.

For the next ten minutes, she gave it her all. But when she collapsed to the floor again, gasping for air between her giggles, even I had to admit defeat.

Celebrating the end of the game, Carly did a victory dance into the locker room then collapsed onto the wooden bench across from the silver metal lockers. "Why couldn't we have played something a little less strenuous?"

"Like what? Golf?" Since finding out about the discovery of the murderous club last Friday night, Carly and I had made a list of every golfer we knew. After Carly's meeting with Elliott on the day of Hank's funeral, we weren't sure where to put him on the list. On one hand, Carly said he was charming and attractive, but on the other, there was no rule saying a killer couldn't be good-looking, was there?

But Carly's mother-tiger claws had come out when she heard what Brendan said about Zac, so the pharmacist's name was at the top of the list, circled in red. Zac, Alex, and I were at the bottom. The in-between included the golf pro, Byron, Amelia, and a good portion of Lake View's population.

"Even a deadly sport like golf is better than racquetball," Carly huffed.

I couldn't have asked for a better opening. "I'm glad you think so, because I have a plan."

She rolled her eyes. "Mercy, Jenna, how do you do it? You have more plans than Blue Cross."

"So you don't want to hear it?"

"You know I'll bite. What did you have in mind?"

"We're going to play golf this Saturday at the country club."

"We? You and me?"

I blushed. This part of my plan could be misconstrued as my having an ulterior motive. "You, me, and Alex." I pulled my swimsuit from my locker and clicked the metal door shut. "Of course, we'll need a fourth. So I've called the club and reserved their resident golf pro to play with us. That would be Elliott."

"Nancy Drew's on the case again. I can see the wheels turning. You want to get to the bottom of Elliott's fight with Hank and find out if he's missing a golf club."

"That's the plan in a nutshell."

"Works for me." Carly picked up her towel. "Somehow I can't see him as a killer, but I think we do need to get to know him a little better."

"Exactly." I was relieved that she wasn't putting up a fight. But a little surprised.

"Have you mentioned this to Alex?"

"No, but he'll go along with it." I fiddled with my swimsuit strap.

"Oh my. One post-funeral lunch date and you're pretty confident of your charms, aren't you?" She gave me a wide grin.

"Not really, but he did say to keep him up-to-date on my investigation."

Carly popped me with her towel. "Get outta here. He was okay with you playing Jenna Stafford, Girl Detective?"

"Once he realized he couldn't stop me, I guess he figured better to be in the loop than out of it."

"Smart man. When is tee time?"

"Elliott's supposed to meet us there at 7:00 a.m."

"Just thinking about getting out on the greens that early makes me look forward to a lazy sauna session right now," Carly drawled.

After we stretched out on benches in the empty sauna room, Carly covered her eyes with her extra towel. I did the same and allowed the quiet humidity to penetrate the sore places of my soul.

"I needed this."

I raised a corner of my towel and saw Carly peering at me across the dimly lit room. "Thanks for dragging me out of the house," she murmured and let her towel back down over her eyes.

"I'm glad you came."

For several minutes, the only sound in the room was our breathing.

Then Carly broke the silence. "You know, I haven't been attracted to any man since Travis left." Long pause. "Until now."

Shock kept me quiet.

"But there's something different about Elliott. And he acted like he felt the same about me."

Sweat trickled between my shoulder blades, and I rubbed my back against the nubby towel.

"Wow." I didn't know what else to say.

"I know. It's weird." I heard her shift on the boards. "And why would someone like him be interested in me? He probably makes every woman feel that way."

"Carly, don't be ridiculous. Of course he'd be interested in you. Any man in his right mind would be."

"Let's just drop it, okay?" Even in the dark I could tell Carly was embarrassed by her confession.

"Okay."

Silence reigned.

When I'd enjoyed all the soul soothing I could stand, I pushed to a sitting position. "Did you see the ad in the paper?"

"Uh-uh," Carly answered without opening her mouth or moving her towel.

From the sound of her voice, I could tell she was in no hurry to join me in the land of the sitting, but I can only take so much inactivity. "You didn't? For the job at the paper?"

"Oh. Yeah, I saw that. So?" Carly tucked the towel tighter around her eyes.

"So?" I lifted her towel, and one brown eye glared at me. "So I thought one of us should apply."

Carly sat up. She wiped the sweat from her face and neck and looked at me as if I were out of my mind. "Why?"

I rolled my eyes. "So we could be at the newspaper office. . .undercover."

Carly shook her head. "From Nancy Drew to Charlie's Angel in one fell swoop. I'm not doing it."

"Fine. I will."

"You're going to send a résumé?"

"No, actually, I thought I'd stop by tomorrow and talk to Marge." As the last few words came out of my mouth, the sauna room door opened.

Amelia Stanton breezed into the dimly lit room, her neon-orange bikini reminding me of fog lights. Carly sat up and shot me a look. Had Amelia heard us?

We didn't have to wonder long.

"Hi, dears." Amelia arranged an extra-thick towel on the bench and sank down, covering her eyes with another one. "I wish *I* could visit Marge. But unfortunately, she doesn't want to see me."

I gave a mental groan. What could we say to that? "Really? I'm sorry to hear that." I tried a trick I'd learned from John and made the end of the sentence sound like a question, hoping to trigger an explanation.

"Yes," Amelia said, her voice more languid. "She blames me for Hank's death, or at least Byron, and me by extension."

"Why?" Enough tricks. My direct question hung in the damp hot air.

"Nancy Drew," Carly mouthed at me and narrowed her eyes.

"Who knows?" Amelia rearranged her towel. "When we were younger, Marge and I were as close as you two. But then we drifted apart. We might have patched it up, but after we married. . ." She folded her hands across her taut stomach. "Well, I never blamed her. A woman has to stand by her husband. Even if he's wrong."

I raised an eyebrow at Carly. "Hank came between you?"

"Oh my. That's an understatement."

I wondered if the reclining position combined with my clinical-questioning technique reminded Amelia of talking with her psychiatrist, because the words kept pouring out.

"He hated Byron." Even though we were the only ones in the room, she lowered her voice to a conspiratorial whisper. "Almost from the day we married."

"So I guess it's a relief to you in a way that he's gone?"

Carly put her hand to her mouth and bit back a choking cough. I ignored her.

Amelia was quiet for a few seconds, and I was afraid she was going to tell me to mind my own business, but when she spoke, her voice was soft. "It was like winning the lottery. Or at least it would be, if Marge would allow me back into her life."

Carly made a cutting motion across her neck, but I averted my gaze from her and took the big plunge. "Do you have any idea who might have killed him?"

"My stars, honey. How would I know? Hank had more enemies than a

Saks Fifth Avenue has dressing rooms."

Carly stood and motioned frantically to me that we needed to go.

I ignored her. "Byron must have hated Hank, as well."

Amelia pulled the towel back from her eyes, and Carly froze in mid-motion. "Hank put Byron through hell. But Byron didn't kill him." Every ounce of ditzy blond was gone as Amelia leveled a steely gaze on me. "And believe me, Jenna Stafford, if you try to pin it on him, you'll be sorry."

Carly latched onto my arm. "Amelia, it's been nice talking to you. I hope you and Marge work things out. Mama's got the twins, and we have to go." She tossed an artificial laugh over her shoulder as she shoved me out of the room. "Can't be late for our curfew."

As soon as we were back in the locker room, I swung around to glare at Carly. "Why did you do that? She was spilling her guts."

"Oh yeah. I could see that." Carly met my glare and added a touch of sarcasm to her own. "In between threatening to spill *your* guts if you don't butt out."

"She didn't say that." I snatched up a towel and headed for the showers.

"Jenna, maybe you need to rethink the whole 'common sense' requirement of that newspaper ad. What part of 'You'll be sorry' do you not understand?"

I spun to face her. "Car, I just want to clear Zac."

Carly's shoulders slumped. "So do I. But you scare me. You have to be more careful."

"If you would help me, then you could keep me out of trouble."

Carly laughed. "Nice try, sis. It would take an army to keep you out of trouble once you set your head to playing detective."

"But you'll help me?"

"Was there ever any doubt?" Carly brushed past me and headed for the showers.

❖

Déjà vu. Standing outside Marge's door with food. Again. I nervously clutched the pot of Carly's cheesy Mexican broccoli soup. Too bad Mama wasn't with me to make sure I said the right thing. Maybe the food would speak louder than words. Carly and I figured the funeral fare had been either eaten or ruined by now. With only herself to feed, Marge could heat this up one bowlful at a time.

Footsteps sounded on the hardwood floor, and the ornate door creaked open. "Jenna, honey, come in." Her kiss on my cheek enveloped me in the sweet scent of spearmint. I returned her embrace, shocked by how fragile she felt. As if a hug would crush her.

"How are you?"

"Okay, I guess. Hasn't sunk in yet, I don't think." This was a much more subdued, less manic Marge than when we'd brought food before the funeral.

Dark circles underlined her bloodshot eyes, and when she brushed her hair back from her face with a trembling hand, a stray tear splashed down her face. "Why would someone do such a thing to Hank?"

Motive wasn't a problem. I could think of five reasons right off the top of my head why someone would kill Hank, but those aren't the things you share with grieving widows. So I shrugged. "It's a strange world out there." I patted her arm awkwardly. *Carly is so much better at this than I am. I should have let her skip the funeral and come here with me instead.* How did I miss out on the sympathetic, knowing-just-what-to-say gene?

Life's not fair.

And that sad fact was even more evident when Marge and I sat down in the darkened living room. The quiet of the house covered us like a blanket. No football playing on the TV or local news blasting from the radio. No Hank calling for a glass of tea. No wonder Marge was going bananas.

"Are you sleeping well?"

She twisted a tissue in her hands. "Not really."

"Can't you get Doc Brown to give you something?" I remembered how much perkier she'd been when we'd come over with food before the funeral. I'd thought she'd acted weird then, and maybe under the influence, but now—in my humble, nonmedical opinion—a little more of whatever she'd been taking that day seemed to be in order.

She shredded the tissue into strips as if she were about to embark on a papier-mâché adventure, then peered up at me, looking much older than her sixty-something years. "I'd rather feel the pain than lose who I am."

"I understand, but—"

Her trembling hand closed on mine. "You're a sweet girl, Jenna. I appreciate you."

"Thanks, Marge." I cleared my throat. What I was about to do bordered on taking advantage—and I had to admit that clearing Zac's name was my biggest motivator. Still, if I could find the murderer and, by doing that, give Marge peace, my conscience could stand the hammering. "I noticed you had an ad in the paper for a part-time position." I smiled gently. "I have good grammar skills and at least a little common sense."

"Why didn't I think of that?" Marge murmured, almost as if she were talking to herself. "I know you were a coach, but didn't you teach, too?"

"Yes, ma'am." Physical education and swimming, but did she really need to know that?

"You'd be perfect."

"Really?" All of my persuasive arguments, along with the crisp résumé in my purse—useless. Was there such a thing as too easy? "What does the position entail?"

"Before I tell you, you have to give me your word that you won't share this secret with anyone."

"Does that include Carly? If I can guarantee she won't repeat it?" I knew myself. I was going to tell Carly whatever it was. And I had enough guilt for taking advantage of Marge's grief. I wasn't about to start out our professional relationship by lying to her.

Marge seemed to think it over, then sighed. "No one should be expected to keep a secret from her sister. Especially not when they're close. You can tell Carly. But no one else. Agreed?" In the dim light, the firm set of her jaw reminded me of Hank. Maybe she wasn't as fragile as she seemed.

I agreed, and for the next ten minutes, Marge allowed me into the magical, mysterious world of the local advice columnist, Dear Prudence, also known as Dear Pru. Dear Pru was required to sign a legally binding confidentiality contract promising to keep his or her identity secret or face legal consequences. Hank had to let the last Dear Pru go due to irresponsible answers. He'd been handling the letters himself for the last few weeks.

Marge was anxious to fill the position, and before I left her house, I had a key to the newspaper office and a part-time job moonlighting at the paper. Literally. Eventually I would do most of my work from home, but in the beginning I'd be using the letters already received and sorted in a file at the office. While there, I could look through the past questions and answers to familiarize myself with the job. I agreed to work during that rare time no one was at the office—Tuesday nights after five. Marge officially hired me for a night-shift typist position I could use as a cover in the unlikely event someone ran into me then.

My mind reeled with the possibilities by the time I got to my car. In order to go undercover to investigate the newspaper office, I'd just taken an undercover job working for the newspaper. Did that make me a double agent? Or a crazy woman with more curiosity than brains?

7

Dear Prudence,
 My fiancé's job requires him to be outside on his feet all day. We hardly ever go out or do the fun things we used to do. Even though he says he still loves me, he wants to rent a movie and order takeout every night. He claims this is an investment in our future—that he's working extra hard to build his reputation and that his schedule will smooth out later. But my life is boring and empty. What should I do?

 Lonely in Lake View

Dear Lonely,
 Don't waste time waiting for a man to make you happy. Get a life. Take charge of your own destiny and lose the loser.

 Prudence

When Carly and I arrived at the country club early Saturday morning, Alex and Elliott were standing beside two golf carts at the edge of the course, chatting like old friends. Alex waved and motioned us over then went back to talking. Elliott, strikingly handsome in a broad-shouldered Pierce Brosnan way, seemed genuinely interested in Alex's conversation. I never would have guessed he was getting paid for his time if I wasn't the one paying him.

"They look as though they stepped off the pages of *Golf Digest*," I muttered to Carly as we walked through the breezeway toward the men. "And here I am, straight from the clearance section in Uniforms 'R' Us."

"Oh, sweetie, you'd look good in anything." Carly looked down at herself. "I don't know why I wore this. I'm a walking flag. One of those extra-large ones."

"You silly goose, you could double for a finalist in the Miss Fourth of July pageant." For some unknown reason, Carly had decided to go patriotic today. Red, white, and blue from her stars-and-stripes sun visor down to her little flag-adorned red toenails peeking out of her walking sandals. I teased her, but

I had to admit the ensemble looked good on her.

My closet hadn't yielded anything nearly as coordinated or snazzy. Last time Francee cut my hair, she mentioned that royal blue makes my eyes "pop," so I threw on a royal blue polo shirt with my favorite pair of khakis. Unfortunately, her fashion advice backfired when I walked into the club this morning and realized I was dressed exactly like the greens maintenance crew, sans the monogram above the shirt pocket.

"Are we supposed to get some clubs at the desk?"

"No—I reserved them, but Alex said he'd pick them up."

Carly nudged me. "So is this your second date?"

I snorted. "It better not be, considering I'm the one who asked him to come, and I'm paying the greens fee and club rental. Besides, the first one wasn't a date, either. He asked both of us, but you—"

"Methinks thou dost protest too much," Carly interrupted in that smarmy way of big sisters everywhere. She looped her arm in mine and whispered in my ear, "You're babbling."

I had no chance to deny it, because we'd reached the men. I hadn't allowed myself to think of the personal implications when I'd called Alex and asked him to play golf with us. But faced with being close to him, in a situation of my own engineering, my knees trembled. His heart-stopping smile didn't help.

He introduced me to Elliott, and I shook the man's hand while trying to take his measure as a person. Not an easy thing with a quick handshake. Did he look like a killer? No. But I'd come to the sad conclusion that Hank's murderer may very well not be sporting an ear-to-lip scar and an evil grin.

When Elliott shook Carly's hand, he didn't let go immediately. "It's great to see you again. Zac talks about you so much, I feel like I already know you."

Like Carly was going to be taken in by that line. Zac loved his mom, but at sixteen, he wasn't going to be talking about her to his golf instructor. And we both knew it.

Carly snatched her hand away, and her face turned as red as a flag stripe. She stammered, "Thanks. Good to see you again, too."

Unlike me, my sister is unrattleable when it comes to the opposite sex. Going through trial by fire with Travis seemed to sear her what-will-a-man-think? nerve. Or so I'd always thought—until today. But she was obviously more than a little shaken by her attraction to the smooth golf pro.

My hackles rose. Did this man, who very well may have killed Hank and charmed my nephew into allowing himself to be blamed for it, now conspire to seduce my sister so that she wouldn't recognize him for what he was? "Elliott, I'm so glad you were available to work today," I said, stepping neatly between my sister and the murder-minded Don Juan.

"Thanks. Wouldn't have missed it." Instead of being angry at my rudeness,

Elliott sounded like he meant it.

Alex put his hand on my arm. "Shall we get started?"

We played the first hole quickly. It was a long par three, but that didn't stop Elliott from getting a birdie. "Show off," I muttered under my breath while Carly cheered. Hadn't she ever heard that in golf you were supposed to clap quietly and say, "Ahh," when someone did well?

Thrilled with her beginner's-luck bogey, Carly allowed Elliott to guide her to the front golf cart, where he solicitously helped her get settled into the passenger seat then went around and hopped in behind the wheel. As Alex and I were loading into our cart, he shot me a sideways glance. "What's the deal? I've never seen you be so rude."

"A golf club killed Hank Templeton," I hissed. "Zac told us Elliott had a huge fight with Hank before the murder. Do you want to see Carly taken in by a killer?"

"No," Alex whispered as he guided us along the cart path, "but I find it hard to believe he's the killer."

"And you're basing that on what? A five-minute conversation with him this morning?"

"Actually, he eats breakfast with us at the diner."

"And the fact that he tolerates Alice's cooking exonerates him?"

He ran a hand through his short blond hair and sighed. "Jenna, if you're going to play detective—not that I'm advocating that—but if you are, you're going to have to learn to keep your cool." We slowly puttered toward the second hole, where Elliott and Carly were already picking out their clubs. "If he is the murderer, you've tipped him off to your suspicion immediately. Is that what you want?"

At the clear sound of worry in his voice, my anger fizzled out like a bottle-rocket dud, and my face burned. "Obviously not. I just can't stand to think of someone taking advantage of Carly after it's taken her so long to rebuild her life."

"Come to think of it, he asked me about her before Hank's murder, so maybe he really likes her." He pulled our cart up beside Carly and Elliott's, effectively ending the discussion.

After playing three holes of the nine-hole course, Carly grabbed a paper cone from the cooler and filled it with water. "Break time," she announced and plopped down into one of the side-by-side golf carts. I grabbed my own water and took the open spot beside her before Elliott could. I'd tolerated his and Carly's banter, but I still didn't trust him completely. Alex sent me an I-know-what-you're-up-to look as he and Elliott sat in the cart beside us.

"Did y'all hear that the police think Hank was killed with a golf club?" I asked the air in general.

Carly squirmed a little beside me. She'd been gung ho when I'd planned this, but clearly her interest in Elliott was coloring her willingness to play detective.

"I heard that." Alex said Carly's rehearsed line, even though he hadn't been in on our planning. I could have kissed him. I pulled myself from fantasyland and jumped back into the script.

"Wonder whose club it was?" I watched Elliott's face closely, not expecting an answer but wanting to see his reaction.

He stood abruptly, crushed his empty water cone in his fist, and tossed it in the trash barrel. I got out of his cart and climbed into mine by Alex. When we reached the next hole, Elliott stomped up to the tee box, his expression dark. "This is actually none of your business, and I'm only telling you because I know you're worried about Zac, but the police came here this week asking questions." He glanced at Carly. "They think the murder weapon was one of our rentals."

I waved my own driver. "Like this?"

"Yes."

"So it should be easy enough to check the records and see who didn't turn their club back in, shouldn't it?" Alex asked. His tone was casual, but he stepped slightly between Elliott and me. My hero.

"Not necessarily. Think about it. If you were a clerk making six dollars an hour, would you worry about making sure missing clubs are accounted for?" He waved a hand toward the wide expanse of rolling hills. "We find them out on the greens all the time." Either he deserved an Emmy or he was an innocent man. Right now, in my book, it was a toss-up.

"So it's the perfect murder weapon," I said.

"Ew," Carly interjected. "No such thing." She placed her ball in the tee box, stepped back, and took a practice swing.

"No, Jenna's right," Alex mused. "Untraceable, not belonging to any one person. It's not like they can investigate the country club as a murder suspect." He walked over to slide an iron from his bag.

No, but they could take the country club's golf pro in for questioning. "Did the police talk to you personally?"

Elliott looked at me, then at Carly, who had stopped midswing. "Yes, they did. I had an argument with Hank a few weeks before his murder."

"What about?" I fiddled with my wristband and pretended the question was normal.

Elliott's tanned face reddened. "I felt that his newspaper mishandled a personal matter."

"Did he agree?"

"Actually, he did promise to take care of the person responsible." Elliott clutched his iron with white knuckles. "Are we here today for you to question me? Or is there any chance you want to play golf?" He sounded more resigned than angry, and I felt bad. He'd been more forthcoming than I would have been if faced with such interrogation.

Carly took her position at the tee box, refusing to look at me. "Y'all, if they'd put a windmill down there by the cup, I just know I could get a hole in one."

Elliott's face relaxed, and Alex grinned. Carly had effectively defused the situation, and I had no doubt my who?-li'l-ole-me? sister had done it on purpose.

"Or maybe a little doghouse with a door to hit the ball through?" I joined in.

"Just use your imagination," Elliott coached.

Carly promptly hit her ball out of bounds.

"I don't think he meant for you to close your eyes, Car," I teased.

Elliott eyed Alex and me. "I'd say that calls for a mulligan, wouldn't y'all?"

"Sure," Alex answered quickly.

"What's a mulligan?" I asked, convinced that Alex didn't know what it was, either, but in the tradition of men everywhere refused to admit his ignorance.

"Yeah, because if it's a sandwich, especially a breakfast one, that sounds good." Carly glared in the direction of her missing ball.

Elliott laughed, and so did Alex, so maybe he did know what it was.

"A mulligan is a do-over. When you're playing with friends, you can get a chance to do it over if everyone agrees." Elliott grinned at Carly.

"A sandwich would be better. But she can definitely do it over." I smiled. Elliott was being a remarkably good sport. The least I could do was try to be one, too. I could always move him up on the suspect list later if I needed to.

Carly's inexperience balanced Elliott's professional status; plus, after his initial burst of irritation, he was holding back a little, so by the eighth hole, we were about even.

"What's the par on this one?" I asked, adjusting my royal blue cap and scoping out the shot.

"Three." Alex smiled.

"Sounds like the perfect place for me to make a birdie."

"You dream big, don't you?"

"Nothing wrong with that, is there?" I swung with all my might, and the ball flew for a good distance then dropped to the ground, just short of the green.

"Oh no!" Carly stamped her foot.

"Who's your partner, me or her?" Elliott asked her, laughing. Then he turned to me. "Don't worry about it—you're still doing great."

"Easy for you to say." I grinned, hoping he would accept it as an apology for earlier. "But thanks."

"No problem."

A few minutes later, on the way to the next hole, Alex slowed to a stop and looked over at me. Carly and Elliott's cart disappeared over the hill, and no one else was in sight.

I'd been thinking about who killed Hank, but Alex's intense gaze sent the mystery fleeing from my mind. "What?"

"You still pouting about missing that birdie?"

"Nah. It wasn't even close." I shivered. Not nearly as close as his face to mine.

"People don't always get it right on the first try, water girl." Alex leaned a little closer, and I was pretty sure we weren't talking about golf anymore. "Sometimes things worth having are worth a second shot, don't you agree?" he whispered.

My heart pounded in my throat, and I nodded.

He sat back in his seat. "Good." He pushed the pedal and buzzed along merrily to the last hole, keeping his attention on the path.

Forget murder. My heart may not survive another shot with Alex Campbell.

8

Murder Investigation

Local police are investigating the recent murder of Hank Templeton, but no arrests have been made. "We are following every lead," says Police Chief John Conner. He declined to comment on the cause of death, although sources report that a murder weapon was found. "Mr. Templeton's body was sent to the Arkansas State Crime Lab at Little Rock for an autopsy," the chief added.

Y ou know, the first few weeks Alex was back in town, I didn't see him at all, but now, everywhere I go, there he is." The alley seemed to grow darker and more menacing as I fumbled with the key to the back door of the newspaper office.

Carly followed my gaze to the right. "Church on Sunday and the diner last night. That's not really everywhere you go. You didn't see him at work today. . . ." Her voice, already distracted, drifted off.

I froze with the key in the lock. "Is that something moving?"

Carly clutched my arm, and we peered into the narrow alley alongside the red-brick building. A long line of tall evergreen shrubs shielded the dark thoroughfare from the park. I looked behind us at the guard light shining down on my car in the paved lot adjoining Main Street Park, mentally measuring the distance. *Maybe we should make a break for it.*

A calico cat darted out of the alley, followed closely by a gray tabby. They disappeared into the park. I let out my breath, and Carly released my arm with a nervous giggle.

"Whew. We have to get a grip," Carly whispered as I turned the key in the lock and pushed open the door.

"Yeah, I'd planned on not turning on many lights, but I think we need a new plan." I flipped on the light switches and lit up the back half of the building. From the road, a passerby wouldn't be able to see these lights, but it was enough illumination to shove away the last of the creepy feeling we'd had.

Five minutes later, we found the Dear Pru file exactly where Marge told me it would be, in Hank's office. We sat down, one on each side of the desk, and I spread the letters out in front of us.

I picked up one out of last month's archives and began to read aloud. "'Dear Pru, I get no respect around here. What do you think I should do?' Signed, 'Trampled.'"

"Is there an answer?" Carly asked.

I nodded. "'Dear Trampled, respect can't be asked for; it has to be demanded. You're only trampled if you let yourself be. So stand up and be counted.'"

"Hmm. Blunt, but I guess that makes sense. This is going to be kind of hard, isn't it?" Carly held up a current letter. "'Dear Prudence, I'm fourteen and my parents won't give me any privacy. I'm a good kid, but they think because I'm a teenager I'm automatically bad. What should I do?' Signed, 'Need Some Space.'"

"Oh, that's a good one. Put it over to the side for me to answer later." I was hoping to start on some fairly easy ones. And garner some wisdom from the previous Dear Prudences.

Carly jerked. "What's that noise?" The popping sound followed by creaking noises echoed in the quiet, empty building.

"I think it's the heater coming on. Let's don't get all jumpy again." I was nervous, too, but I wouldn't mention that to Carly. "We have a right to be here, remember?" And if anyone saw us here, well, I was an employee.

"*You* have a right to be here, not me." Technically, Carly was right, but even though I was acting bravely, I was really glad she was here with me.

"Don't be silly. You're my assistant."

"Without pay, right?"

"Yes, but with a lot of honor. So, honored assistant, how many unopened letters are there?"

She shuffled through them. "About ten."

"Marge said there would be between five and fifteen every week. They're all local, so at least it's not like a deluge of letters." I'd envisioned huge mailbags before Marge had told me that little tidbit. Apparently the citizens of Lake View didn't need advice all that much. Or if they did, they didn't realize it.

"That doesn't give you much to choose from if you answer three each week." She ripped another one open. "'Dear Prudence, my husband thinks if we exchange all our lightbulbs for long-lasting ones, we'll save loads of money. I think it's wasteful to throw away a bulb that hasn't burned out yet. What do you think?' Signed, 'In the Dark.'"

I rolled my eyes. "Trash," we said together, and Carly tossed it in the round metal can by the desk.

For the next several minutes, we pored over the letters and replies, reading bits aloud. After I'd gathered the current ones to take home and try to answer and a few of the archives for reference, I lowered my voice. "We'd better start looking if we're going to find any clues to Hank's murder."

I flipped on the computer.

"What are you doing?" Carly walked over to stand behind me.

"I just want to check his history. I'm sure the police already did, but maybe we'll see something they missed."

"Won't you need a password?"

I pointed at the screen. "Thankfully, Hank saved it." I logged on and pulled up his history for the last twenty days. There were the usual Web sites—weather, sports, news. No pornography or online gambling sites had been visited within the last twenty days.

"Look at this flyer I found stuck in the Dear Pru archives." Carly held up a bright yellow brochure. "'Makeover for Couples! Two-for-One Special at the Luxury Spa in Memphis, Thursday, September 5, through Sunday, September 8. Surprise your Special Someone with a spa weekend featuring Botox and collagen injections in the privacy of your Luxury suite with your own personal attendant. Tanning beds, permanent makeup, and elimination of spider veins and unsightly age spots included. No need to grow old together gracefully when you can stay young for each other forever.'"

I looked up from the computer. "Weird. Marge said Hank was handling Dear Pru when he died. I guess he stuck that in there. Maybe he was going to surprise Marge."

She shuddered. "Eww. Can you see Hank and Marge getting makeovers?"

Before I could answer, my cursor moved to the more recent sites in the computer's history and I gasped. "Look at this. Oh my goodness. Why would he have all these? There are at least a hundred sites about prescription drugs."

"Must be for a story."

"I'm sure. But about what?"

"Drugs?" Carly chuckled. "Just a guess, Nancy Drew."

The rest of the history showed nothing important, so I shut down the computer.

"I'll look through the file cabinet, and you check his desk."

I slid open the first metal drawer and stared at the file tabs. Most of them didn't seem pertinent. Then my gaze fell on a tab marked CURRENT EDITORIALS. I plucked it from the drawer.

"Listen to this. This was the editorial that was supposed to go out the week after Hank died. It's not completely done, but listen." I waved the paper in Carly's face. "'Our esteemed mayor is up to his eyebrows in more than the citizens of Lake View can ever imagine.' What do you think Hank meant by that?"

"No idea. Oh, you should read this letter. I'm sixteen and my parents are so out of touch. I feel like I can't talk to them about anything.' Isn't that just so sad?" Carly hadn't moved from her chair, still enthralled with the Dear Pru letters.

"Carly, stop reading those letters and help me look."

She reluctantly left the letters, and we opened every drawer of Hank's massive, battle-scarred oak desk. If there were any clues there, we weren't smart enough to find them.

"Let's take a break and have a cup of coffee. Newspaper offices are known for having coffee, right?" In the break room, Carly put some fresh coffee in the Brewmaster and I poked around in the cabinets.

"Ever wonder what newspaper employees keep in their refrigerator?" Carly opened the door and peered inside. "Ketchup, mustard, and French vanilla creamer. That's it."

"Glad you cleared up that little mystery for me." I took two cups off the shelf and filled them with hot coffee. "Check out the freezer—maybe there's some Häagen-Dazs or Ben & Jerry's."

"Nope. Just some ice and a brown paper bag." Carly shut the freezer door and sipped her coffee.

"What's in the bag?"

"Are you serious?" Carly asked.

"Sure. Maybe it's cold cash."

Carly opened the door, retrieved the bag, and shook the frost off it. "Looks like medicine of some kind." She pulled out several prescription bottles and set them on the table. "Oxycontin. Isn't that a prescription painkiller?"

I shook one. Empty. I shook another one. Empty, too. Every bottle was empty. "The label says ANNE MANSFIELD. Who's that?"

"No idea. This one's for Josephine Winston," Carly said, showing me the one she held. "Never heard of her, either. You?"

"Nope."

We sorted them out by names and ended up with three for Josephine, four for Anne. "Who would be sick enough to gather up different women's empty pill bottles?"

"Maybe there was some kind of plastic drive and we just didn't hear about it? A recycle-your-old-pill-bottles thing? And these accidentally got put in the freezer instead of with the others?"

"But they're all painkillers," I mused.

Carly nodded and ran her finger over the bottle label. "Why would anyone have these?"

"I don't know. Unless it was for a story Hank was doing. The one he did the Web research for. They're all from Lake View Pharmacy and all dated within the last few months."

"Oh well, it was more interesting than ice cream but not near as tasty." Carly shoved the bottles back into the sack and started to put them back in the freezer.

"Wait. Maybe I should take them to Marge and ask her if she knows what they're for."

"If you think these have anything to do with Hank's murder, you need to take them straight to John." Carly sounded like the bossy older sister she was.

"If they did, don't you think John would have confiscated them when the police searched this place?" I scribbled the names from the labels on the outside of my folder and stuffed the bag back into the freezer.

The heat kicked off with a loud *pop,* and Carly jumped. "C'mon, girl. Let's clean up this mess and get out of here. I've enjoyed about all of this place I can stand."

She might be a tad on the bossy side, but in this case, I completely agreed with her.

Two hours later, I pulled my old threadbare terry robe around me and sat down on the love seat with the Dear Prudence file. I sketched out some rough-draft answers to a couple of letters then pulled one out of the archive. The previous Dear Prudence had been much more forceful with her advice than I was. Was that good or bad? I scanned the letter and then read it again more carefully. Could it be? I scooped up the cordless and punched in Carly's cell number. She answered on the fourth ring. "Tell me this is important."

"Already in bed?"

"Hmm. It's ten thirty. I have to get up at six. Yes, as lazy at it seems to you, I'm in bed." She cleared her throat and laughed. "But I'm awake now. So what's up?"

"I need you to listen to this Dear Prudence letter."

"I thought I was the one addicted to them—"

I didn't let her finish. " 'Dear Prudence, my fiancé's job requires him to be outside on his feet all day. We hardly ever go out or do the fun things we used to do. Even though he says he still loves me, he just wants to rent a movie and order takeout every night. He claims this is an investment in our future— that he's working extra hard to build his reputation and that his schedule will smooth out later. But my life is boring and empty. What should I do?' It's signed 'Lonely in Lake View'!"

"Fascinatin'," Carly drawled. "Sounds like she's got some serious growing up to do. And this is worth waking me up for because. . . ?"

"It has to be written by Elliott's fiancée." I'd not been surer of anything since we'd started trying to solve this mystery.

"How do you figure that?"

"Listen to the answer. 'Don't waste time waiting for a man to make you happy. Get a life. Take charge of your own destiny and lose the loser.'"

"Ouch."

"Remember what Zac said about Elliott's girlfriend leaving over something to do with the newspaper? If an anonymous columnist gave your fiancée that kind of advice and she left you, wouldn't you confront the editor?"

"Probably. But I wouldn't kill him." Carly was definitely wide-awake now and apparently remembering the chemistry between her and the handsome golf pro.

"You would if you were obsessed with the woman. And a little bit psycho."

Silence.

"Carly, I'm sorry. I know he seems nice, but we have to consider all the possibilities."

"Yeah, you may be right. Move him to the top of the list for now."

I hung up feeling lower than a snake's belly. My sister deserved whatever happiness she could find, and for all I knew, Elliott was a fine Christian man. But she was right. For now, he belonged at the top of our suspect list.

LAKE VIEW MONITOR

Lost and Found

Found: Male golden retriever, Fri., Sept. 6, near Main Street Park. If you have information about this dog, call (870) 555-3232 and leave a message.

I could sleep through a lot of noises. Dripping faucet, worn-out refrigerator motor, Neuro snoring. But even I couldn't sleep soundly enough to ignore a dog howling outside the front door at four in the morning.

I threw back the comforter and slipped on the Tweety Bird slippers Carly had bought me as some kind of sick prank on Neuro. I don't think they bothered the cat, but Carly got a kick out of them. Neuro raised her head and blinked sleepily at me from her position at the foot of the bed. I stumbled down the hall to the front door. The cat, wide-awake now, was hot on my heels.

I stopped, hand on the knob. What if someone was torturing that poor dog so I'd unlock my door in the middle of the night? The howls were blood-curdling. With a murderer on the loose in Lake View, a girl couldn't be too careful. I peeked out the window. The golden retriever was so pressed against my front door, he was barely visible, but I knew he was there by the endless off-key song. Persistence. I admired that in people, but it was downright annoying in a dog.

I'd put cat food out for him the last couple of days, praying he wouldn't get sick. Other than his ceaseless attempts to get into the house, he seemed happy enough. He didn't even bark at Neuro anymore, and I'm almost positive I caught them rubbing noses through the window last night.

So why howl now? I couldn't help but suspect he'd calculated his odds of catching me in that particular sleep-deprived state that will make a person do almost anything to go back to la-la land. And as bad as I hated to admit it, he'd chosen his time wisely.

I picked Neuro up and opened the front door. For a brief second, he hesitated, then bounded into the house. Neuro stiffened and snuggled closer to me. I reached out one hand to pat the dog on the head. "Will the laundry room do, Mr. Persistence?"

He chuffed in what I hoped was agreement.

"I'll have to shut the door." I resisted the urge to talk anymore. If I got too awake, I'd take him back outside where he belonged. A couple of dirty towels made a soft bed, and I filled an empty Cool Whip dish with water. He drank a little then chased his tail around in a circle and collapsed on the towels, smiling. "Good night, Mr. Persi," I said softly and closed the door.

When it was time to get up and start the day, I was stunned to find no mess in the laundry room. And even more surprised when Neuro leaped from my arms and padded over to the golden-haired dog. I held my breath while they sniffed the air and two-stepped around each other. Mr. Persi gave a bounding leap toward Neuro, landing playfully on his haunches. The cat jumped back but then slowly initiated the dance again. I laughed aloud, and it felt good. Chaos all around and order in the strangest places.

I put Mr. Persi in the fenced-in backyard with cat food and water and loaded Neuro in her carrier for our daily trek, then paid a surprise visit to the police station before work to show John the Dear Pru letter. After he finished laughing, I tried to explain about Elliott and his girlfriend, but our very important chief of police left for a very important meeting, muttering something about "nosy women needing to learn to mind their own business."

If the police weren't going to do their job, that left only me. And Carly. Unfortunately, my sweet-tempered sis can morph into a mule at the oddest times. I cradled the cordless phone against my shoulder and sprayed window cleaner on the floor-to-ceiling mirror in the workout room. "C'mon, Carly. You know we've got to talk to him sooner or later."

We needed to ask Elliott some key questions—if we could think of any—to try to mark him off our so-called list of suspects. The attraction between him and Carly could be a wonderful breakthrough for her. Or it could be a disaster. I, for one, did not intend to let my sister lose her heart to a murderer.

"Doesn't it seem a tad bit strange to just walk in and accuse a man of murder?"

"We're not going to accuse anyone. You know better than that." I wiped the mirror with circular motions that reminded me too much of how this conversation was going.

"I know *I'm* not. You, I'm not so sure about."

"I promise, Car. I'm not going to be confrontational. It'll be a friendly little information-gathering visit."

"Fine! I'll go, but if you embarrass me, you'll pay. And I mean it, Jenna Stafford."

I grinned. When we were growing up, if I ever tattled on her or hid behind the couch and made kissy noises at her and her date, I could always be sure that she'd get me back. Greased shower nozzle, short-sheeted bed, salted toilet seat—she was the master of payback. I wasn't willing to take a chance on the assumption that she'd outgrown such stunts. I'd handle Elliott with kid gloves.

"I'll behave. Pick you up at lunch?"

"I'll be ready."

An hour later, she climbed into my car and I turned toward the country club. I glanced over at her. "How should we handle this? Should we act casual? Or let him know we're there for?"

"I called and told him we wanted to come by and talk about Hank's murder." She placed her hands primly in her lap and looked out the window.

My mouth dropped open. "You did?"

She shrugged one shoulder. "I figured he deserved to know up front what we were doing."

That would undoubtedly be more welcome than my surprise attack. "Good." I pulled up under the club breezeway.

Carly sighed. "I dread Zac's reaction when he finds out I told Elliott what he said."

"You could ask Elliott not to tell him."

"I could, but I won't." She looked over at me as we opened our car doors. "I didn't agree not to tell, and if this helps us get closer to the truth, it'll be worth hurting Zac's feelings."

I parked my car and asked directions to Elliott's office. The golf pro answered the door on the first knock and ushered us into a homey-looking office, complete with TV, coffeemaker, microwave, and couch. Even a small refrigerator. All the comforts of home. I might have looked a bit surprised.

"Sometimes, when I have an early lesson, I sack out here the night before." He gave us a sheepish smile.

"No wonder you're not married. Or are you? I mean, were you?" Not my most shining moment.

Carly glared, but I was too far away for her to kick, so I opened my mouth, fully prepared to insert the other foot in the name of seeing justice done.

"What my sister means, Elliott, is that if you have no one at home waiting, staying overnight here would be a sensible thing to do." Then she surprised me and took the type of breath I used to take before leaping from the high board at a swim meet. "Elliott." She leveled him with one of Mama's you'd-best-come-clean-I-know-all-about-it-anyway looks. I guess when you have kids, you inherit the ability to pull off that look as needed. "Zac told us about your fiancée breaking up with you. And that you blamed Hank."

"Zac didn't mean to—" I felt like I had to defend my nephew even if his friend was a murderer.

Elliott held up his hand to stop me. "It's okay. I don't blame Zac at all. I wouldn't have spilled my sorry story to him if I'd known what was about to happen." He motioned to the couch. "Would you ladies like to sit down?"

We settled in on the sofa, and he sat across from us in a wingback recliner. I mentally reviewed my list of questions.

Carly leaned toward Elliott. "Why did you blame Hank?"

Oh yes, question number one. We'd agreed that if he told us about the Dear Pru letter on his own, that would be a big point in his favor. What we hadn't discussed was Carly asking the questions. Suddenly I realized what was going on. In spite of my promise, she didn't trust me not to hurt Elliott's feelings, or perhaps alienate him forever.

"I don't know now." His face reddened slightly, and he looked out the window as if the answer were there.

Uh-oh. Not good. Carly obviously agreed, because she avoided my glance.

Elliott drew his gaze back to me, as if he knew that even though Carly was asking the questions, I was the one demanding answers. "My fiancée, Heather, wrote the *Monitor* and asked some advice columnist what to do." He ran his hand over his face. "Dear Pro, or something like that, told her to dump me and get on with her life. Heather left me a good-bye letter and put the advice column in the envelope with it. I'm embarrassed to admit it, but I stormed into Hank's office and threatened to sue him and his paper for interfering with my life." He shrugged. "I didn't mean it. Heather and I had been growing apart for a while. But I was so caught up in my dream of what life was supposed to be that I pushed all my doubts to the back of my mind. You know?"

Carly and I nodded.

"I was giving lessons early and late, focused on my goal of being able to afford a nice house and so forth, things I thought she wanted. But then I lost sight of the real goal. Having a life."

"That's easy to do," Carly said softly. "Sometimes I've felt that way about getting my kids grown. I concentrate so much on the end result that I lose sight of the journey."

"I can understand that," Elliott said, smiling at her. "And I imagine, with your kids, the journey is the fun part."

He obviously hadn't met the twins. But he was just as obviously besotted with my sister.

"So you didn't kill him?" Carly asked.

He jumped to his feet, towering over us. "No, Carly. Of course I didn't. But if I did, would I tell you? I understand your wanting to help Zac. But this is your plan? Ask anyone who might be involved?"

"Sort of," Carly squeaked.

Elliott sat back down, and his voice softened. "I didn't mean to scare you, but. . .that's a bad plan. Whoever killed Hank means business. The best thing you two can do is let the police handle this." He put his hand on Carly's and squeezed.

I cleared my throat and stood. "So we've been told."

Carly sat like a lump on the couch, holding hands with the suspect. I cleared my throat again, and she reluctantly pulled her hand loose and got to her feet. "Jenna thought that we should look into it on our own," Carly confessed.

Now that all the blame was on my shoulders, I decided to ask one more question. "No offense, Elliott, but where were you when Hank was killed?"

Wow. Who knew Carly could slug that hard? I'd sport a bruise on my shoulder from that.

I glared at her. "Ouch! Look, I believe you, too, Elliott. But we need some type of proof. I mean, anyone can say, 'I didn't do it.' We need to *know* you didn't."

Elliott threw back his head and laughed. "You're right, Jenna. But the police have questioned me extensively. I guess the golf club pointed them in my direction, too. If only the killer had used something like a baseball bat. Then maybe the high school coach would be the one getting all the attention."

"I know." I did feel bad for him. What if Hank had been killed with a pair of swim goggles? I could've been in Elliott's shoes.

"So you don't have an alibi?"

He shook his head. "He was apparently killed in the very early morning hours. And I don't give lessons before daylight. It's so hard to hit the golf ball in the dark."

We laughed. "Thanks for putting up with our questions. You're a good sport," I said.

"Well, that's my alibi, then. Normally, murderers are not good sports."

As we walked to the door, Elliott cleared his throat. "Carly?"

We turned.

"I don't see any need to mention this little visit to Zac, do you?"

Her smile was a little teary. "Thanks, Elliott."

"Anytime."

10

Friday, right after lunch, my boss walked in wearing a Hawaiian print shirt and khaki shorts. "Bob!"

"Jenna! Baby doll! It's good to see you." He held his arms out.

I gave him a side squeeze and smiled. "Good to see you, too. When did you get home?"

"Just drove in from the airport. Dropped Wilma and the luggage off at home and came over here to see what was going on." He released me and looked around the health club with a toothy grin. "Good to be home. Anything exciting happen while we were gone?"

Um, no, other than a violent murder, not a thing. But surely Wilma's sister had already told him all about that. She wasn't one to leave news left untold.

His gaze settled back on me. "That was sure too bad about old Hank, wasn't it?"

"Yes, it was." In so many ways.

"They have any idea who did it?" He walked over to the watercooler and filled a little paper cone with water, then turned back to me. "Or why?"

"I'm not sure." I leaned against the U-shaped counter. If he hadn't already heard about Zac, I wasn't about to tell him. And if he had and was fishing for more information, I certainly wasn't going to satisfy his curiosity. I pretended to be absorbed in the stretch exercise chart posted on the outside of the workstation.

"Doesn't surprise me, him getting killed. Guess he finally took a story too far, you think?" He walked around to the inside of the U and started flipping through the sign-in registry.

"I suppose that's what the police are trying to find out." No need to mention my own investigation, which, so far, wasn't doing anything but opening up more questions.

"You sent flowers from the club, right?"

"Yes. I figured you'd want me to out of sympathy for Marge and Theo." Hank had been on the zoning committee a long time. Thanks to him and a few others, Bob's dream of building his athletic club in the heart of Lake View's historic district had been squashed like a bug. He wouldn't have sent Hank flowers for his own sake.

"Well, Marge, anyway. I always heard Hank and Theo didn't get along too good."

"Really? I hadn't heard that." Okay, maybe I was getting carried away. Every seemingly innocuous statement struck me as significant.

"Yeah, I figure Hank wanted his boy to stay around here instead of gallivanting off all over the world." He held up the sheets. "So how's the club? Things pretty slow?"

What did he think? That everyone would suddenly stop working out because he was gone on a cruise?

"No, everything's been going great." Actually, if anything, we were busier than usual, but his ego was just big enough to be hurt by that coincidence, so I didn't elaborate.

"Nobody's gotten hurt or anything?" Bob always worried that someone was going to get injured at the health club and sue him. As far as I knew, no one had ever even threatened him. But go figure. Sometimes we worry the most about the things least likely to happen. And vice versa. When I started teaching, I never worried for a second that a student would die during one of my classes. But that didn't stop it from happening.

"Not so far, but you know the odds increase every year that someone will." Ooh, that was mean, playing on his fear like that. Still, he had promised me an option to purchase, and I was tired of him avoiding me. "So the sooner you sell the place to me, the less likely you'll get sued."

He dropped the sign-in registry as if it were a subpoena to court. "Well, I'd better go on home, hon. Wilma will be wondering where I've been. I'll see you tomorrow." He walked out before I could say another word. That man was seriously starting to annoy me. He avoided every mention of selling, and with nothing in writing, there was no way I could force his hand.

I slammed my fist on the granite countertop just as Byron Stanton strolled through the double glass doors. Perfect. A little casual interrogation of the mayor should use up the adrenaline left over from my nonconfrontation with Bob.

He swept through the foyer and surveyed the room like a king looking over his subjects. "Is Amelia here yet?"

Was the king speaking to me, a lowly peasant? Judging by the expectant way he was looking at me, I guessed he was. "I haven't seen her." I checked the sign-in registry. "Nope, she hasn't signed in yet."

"She's late, then. She was supposed to be here at four."

Oops. Let's throw her in the dungeon. "Why don't you have a seat in the smoothie bar, and I'll get you a drink while you wait." Not my job. And I normally wouldn't make an exception for the king of Lake View, but I wasn't about to pass up the opportunity to ask him a few questions.

"Thanks." He nodded as if bestowing an honor on me.

A few minutes later, I slid a tangerine smoothie onto his table and handed him a straw. "Mayor Stanton, I want to offer my condolences to your family. I know you and Hank weren't close, but I'm sorry for your loss." Maybe I was overdoing the sympathy here, but I wasn't sure how to start a conversation about murder with the possible murderer.

"Thanks. I'll pass that on to Amelia." Always politically correct, our mayor. I had hoped to get more of a response than that.

Maybe he needed a little more prodding. "Do the police know the motive?"

"Possibly someone was just trying to make our small town a better place to live." Byron looked over my shoulder as if this conversation was way too boring for him to give his full attention to it.

"I heard he was getting ready to write another editorial about you. Did you know that?"

"Where did you hear that?" His brown eyes flashed with irritation. I definitely had his full attention now.

"You know how things are. Word gets around."

"Jenna, it sure would be a shame if the police were to have to take your nephew down to the station again for more questioning, wouldn't it?" He smiled the coldest smile I'd ever seen.

"You don't have to get snippy. I was just curious."

"Hasn't anyone ever told you that curiosity killed the cat?"

I nodded slowly. "I've heard that." A hundred times, but no need to volunteer that information. "So if I don't butt out, you're threatening to have Zac hauled in for questioning again?" If this were a made-for-TV movie, I'd be wearing a wire. Unfortunately, it was the real world, and I just wanted to hear him say it flat out.

"Threatening? Me?" He smiled. I wished he'd quit doing that. It seriously creeped me out. "I'm a friend, looking out for your family's reputation."

"What family's reputation are you talking about?" Amelia appeared at my shoulder in white shorts and a T-shirt, wiping her face with the edge of a towel draped around her shoulder. How did she do that? Pop up with no warning?

I smiled sweetly. "I'll let Byron explain it to you." I spun on my heel and walked through the open area of the smoothie bar, outwardly calm, inwardly a gelatin mass. By the time I got to the doorway, Lake View's First Couple had their heads together in heated conversation. I'd stirred something up. I just had no idea what.

❖

I was still steaming over Byron's threats when I left work that night. That might explain why I snapped at the Price Cutter cashier. Or it could have been because she was extremely annoying. I didn't know Marita very well, since she'd been several years ahead of me in school, but when she rang up my frozen pizza, Dr Pepper, and dog food, she raised her eyebrows. "Big Friday night planned?"

Many retorts danced through my head. But the one that came out was "Actually, yes." Technically that was true, since I'd already put in a call to the video store next to the grocery store and the clerk was holding a new release for me.

She scanned my single-serving pizza and clucked her tongue. "Bless your heart, sweetie. By the way, how's Zac handling all this?"

Me being dateless? I knew what she meant, so I decided to play nice. "Fine."

"Do you think he did it?"

"Of course not!"

"I don't know. Teenagers these days can be pretty unpredictable."

Unpredictable? Last time I checked, *unpredictable* was missing curfew by ten minutes occasionally. *Unpredictable* was *not* beating someone to death with a golf club. I handed her my twenty and took a deep breath. "He didn't do it."

"That's what people on television always say, isn't it? The neighbors— you know how they say, 'He was the nicest guy. He couldn't have done it.' " She ran my twenty-dollar bill over the edge of the counter to smooth it out and slipped it into her cash register. "Then they start finding the bodies under the house. . ."—she nodded over my head at Mona, the other cashier, who'd stopped to listen to Marita's tactless droning—"in the freezer. . ."

"Yes, I know what you mean. Happens all the time." I took my change and groceries with a sweet smile. "Some small-town grocery-store clerk turns out to be a mass murderer. Say, Marita. . .where were you the morning Hank was murdered?"

Marita's eyes widened, and she clapped her hand over her mouth. At least she wasn't talking anymore. I stomped out to my car and deposited the groceries, then strolled over to the video store.

"Hey, Jenna! I already rang up your movie." Susan laid the plastic box on the counter by the door while I paid. "You'll love it."

"You said it was a comedy, and I'm in the mood for funny. That's good enough for me." I slid my change into my pocket and grabbed the movie.

As soon as I got home, I invited Mr. Persi in to play and let Neuro out of her carrier. While I heated my pizza, they batted one of Neuro's toys around the floor. I kept one eye on the big dog and wondered at his gentle spirit. The cautious way he moved around with Neuro reminded me of a giant of a man with a little girl. He was playful but mindful of his strength.

I hate to eat alone, so I gave both animals a piece of pizza before I settled into my recliner and pushed the PLAY button on the remote control. Susan had nailed it. The movie was a riot. Small-town murder and a bumbling amateur detective. She barely escaped the killer's vengeful plots over and over without ever being aware of them. Struck a little too close to home, though, and three-quarters of the way through, I'd enjoyed all of it I could stand. Neuro was asleep on my lap and Mr. Persi on my feet. "Time for bed," I muttered.

Later, after Mr. Persi was safely tucked into the laundry room, Neuro perched on the vanity and licked her paws, watching intently as I brushed my teeth and washed my face, still thinking about the movie. "Am I as clueless as that woman?" I asked her as we padded over to the bed. I snuggled under the comforter and looked down at her where she curled up next to my feet. "I failed in the Olympics, I failed as a teacher, I can't get Bob to sell me the business, and now I can't solve Hank's murder." I raised myself up partway, punched my pillow, and then lay back down. "Trouble is, everybody seems guilty," I murmured as the world as I knew it faded into oblivion.

A crowd was gathered around the health club receptionist's desk when I walked in. Amelia's neon-orange spandex workout clothes made me raise my hand to shade my eyes.

"There she is," she said, pointing an orange fingernail at me.

"What's wrong?" I peered over her shoulder, but the crowd blocked my view.

The man beside her turned around. Brendan Stiles, holding up a wallet. "Looking for this?" he snarled at me. How had I ever thought he was handsome?

"What are you talking about? I gave that to John."

John broke away from the group, the light off his badge glinting in my eyes worse than Amelia's neon. He walked toward me.

"John, I'm so glad you're here. I think you should question Byron. And Elliott. Or even Brendan. One of them killed Hank."

"That's your plan, huh? Take the heat off yourself by pointing a finger at them? Why'd you do it?" John dangled a pair of handcuffs in front of him, the clink-clink echoing in the high-ceilinged room.

My heart thudded against my ribs. "I didn't kill Hank."

"Who said anything about Hank?" John asked, shaking his head sadly. "Zac killed him."

I gasped. "He did not!"

Behind him, Marita, the Price Cutter cashier, wagged her finger at me. "Yes, he did, sweetie. Just like I said."

"Fore!" Elliott called and pretended to line up the perfect shot down the tile hallway. He swung away with his golf club at an imaginary ball. "And she had the nerve to accuse me," he said to a man next to him. I couldn't see his face clearly, but I was afraid it was Alex.

"I didn't accuse you!"

"You accused almost everybody, trying to hide the truth, I guess." Marge, with sorrow-filled eyes, stepped toward me. "Jenna, honey, I didn't believe it. You were always such a sweet little girl. But now I know it's true."

"It's not true!" I screamed.

I opened my mouth to say more, but Marge was no longer Marge, but Marge's friend Lois, the librarian. "Shh...this is a library." She held her finger to her lips.

"It is not! This is the health club."

Debbie, the waitress from the diner, appeared beside her, looking bored. She peered in her handheld mirror to apply a fresh coat of red lipstick, then smacked her lips. "Homicide must run in the family. To think I trusted you."

"Homicide? Is someone else dead?" I ran toward the crowd. What—or who—were they gathered around? John grabbed my arm.

I jerked away from him and crashed between Marita and Debbie, determined to see what they were hiding.

My pulse pounded in my throat, and I let out a low moan. My boss, Bob, in a Hawaiian shirt and khaki shorts, lay unmoving on the tile floor. My favorite swim goggles framed his unblinking eyes, and strands of thin black videotape wrapped tightly around his neck.

11

Lake View Monitor

The Monitor weather forecast for the Lake View area Saturday: 70% chance of rain with thunderstorms possible. Highs in the mid-70s and lows in the upper 40s.

So he actually said that? That Zac might get taken back in for questioning?" Carly's indignation came across the phone line loud and clear.

"Would I make something like that up?" I plopped down on the couch with my coffee. I loved the health club, but weekends were definitely my favorite part of the week. Saturday mornings at home rocked. I looked out the window. Even cloudy ones.

"Oh, I hope it's him," Carly growled.

"Huh?"

"You know, the murderer. I hope it turns out to be Byron." Then she sighed. "That's not fair to Mama and Daddy, though, with the cabins and all. Nothing puts a town's tourist business in the toilet faster than the mayor being charged with murder."

I stroked Neuro's back, still grappling with the fact that genteel Carly had said "toilet." She must be even more upset than I realized. "You're right. Let's hope it's a stranger. Someone we don't know."

"Not very likely, though, is it?"

"No, 'fraid not. And we've got to figure it out soon. You won't believe what I dreamed last night."

After I told her the morbid details of my nightmare, she laughed. "So you think you got so sick of him not selling you the business that you put your swim goggles on him and killed him with a videotape?"

"I guess. It was bizarre. But so real that when I woke up, I had to go check to be sure the tape was still where I left it."

"I told you to give up your dinosaur VCR and get a DVD player. Maybe this will convince you."

"It's doubtful. I've got too many VHS tapes to switch over now. You know how I am about change."

"Yeah, and you call John stubborn. By the way, you never told me what he said about the pills."

"*Ack.* I got so mad at him for laughing at me about the Dear Pru letter that I forgot to mention the pills. They're probably nothing anyway."

"You're right. Hang on, girl, I've got another call."

"Sure." I shoved myself to my feet and meandered into the kitchen. Mr. Persi followed me, his expression hopeful. "Hungry, boy?" I poured dog food into his dish, and he dug into it as if he hadn't been fed for a week. I could sympathize. I nuked a leftover piece of pizza and picked up my vitamin bottle. Empty.

I'd have to stop by the pharmacy and get some more. No wonder those empty bottles at the newspaper office were from the Lake View Pharmacy. It was the most popular drugstore in town.

Suddenly the silence of a dead line was broken by a sob.

"Carly? What's wrong?"

"That was John. He wants to bring Zac back in for more questioning."

Anger shot through me. "Thanks to Byron, of course."

"I don't know." Her voice shook. "He said, 'In light of some new evidence.' What do you think that means?"

"It means our chief of police is on the mayor's payroll. But I'll take care of that. Is Zac there?" I walked back into the living room and slipped on my shoes.

"Yes."

"Okay, call Alex and have him meet us there. Do you want me to pick you and Zac up?" I snatched my keys from the hook by the door.

"No, thanks. I can drive. Besides, Daddy will want to come, too."

"Good. Let John and Byron see that we're not going to let them do this to Zac. I'm going on over. See you there."

"Okay, thanks, Jen."

I may have broken the speed limit slightly on the way to the station, but I figured the cops in our town were too busy railroading innocent sixteen-year-old boys to be worried about a little speeding. As I got out of my car, I cast a glance at the overcast sky. It wasn't our big storm season, but I felt one coming on. Maybe it was my mood.

The sergeant at the front desk opened her mouth to speak to me, but I hurried past her and made a beeline for John's office. The door stood partially open, and that was invitation enough for me.

John looked up from his desk, and his face reddened. "Jenna. What are you doing here?"

"What's wrong? Easier to pick on teenagers than full-grown adults? I never figured you for a coward."

He held up his hand. "Whoa. What are you talking about?"

"I'm talking about our esteemed *mayor*." I spat out the word. "We both know he's the reason Zac was called in this morning."

John's brows knitted together. "Now you're confusing me. What does Byron have to do with this?"

"You mean besides using you to cover up the fact that he killed his brother-in-law?"

John stood. "That's a serious accusation. I think you'd better stop and take a deep breath."

I marched over to the desk, so tall in my anger that I could almost believe I towered over him instead of vice versa. "Believe me, I've had plenty of time for deep breaths ever since Byron threatened this very thing yesterday at the health club."

"Threatened to have Zac brought in? Why would he do that?"

"His reasons are clear. He killed Hank and wants me to stop trying to prove it. You're the one I can't figure out." I slapped my hand on the desk, and his Styrofoam cup of coffee sloshed.

"Jenna—" He retrieved his coffee cup and moved it to the windowsill. Out of the crazy woman's reach, obviously.

"Sure, we've disagreed a lot, but I thought you had integrity." Tears stung my eyes. "I can't believe you brought in an innocent teen just because I asked Byron a few questions he didn't like."

"Jenna—" John walked around the desk and reached out his hand as if to stave off an attack.

"How could you? I'm pretty sure Byron killed Hank, and here you are letting him tell you what to do."

"Stop it!" John yelled in my face. The vein in his neck bulged.

I didn't say a word. Even if he was a lowlife, if I caused him to have a stroke, Denise would kill me.

He followed his own advice and took a deep breath, then spoke softly. "Mayor Stanton didn't kill anybody."

"I think there's a good chance he did." I lowered my own voice as if the entire Lake View police station hadn't already heard our heated exchange.

"Look, I give you my word, he had nothing to do with me calling Zac in. I know you're upset and worried, but that's no excuse to go throwing accusations around. He's the mayor, for goodness' sake."

"And that means he's above the law?"

"No, and neither is your nephew. I had a reason for bringing Zac in, but it had nothing to do with the mayor."

"So I'm supposed to believe this whole thing is a funny coincidence?" I was practically foaming at the mouth now.

"Calm down and listen to me. This. Has. Nothing. To. Do. With. Mayor. Stanton." He said the words one at a time as if I were slow-witted.

"Okay then, Mr. Big Shot, tell me why. Why would you put Carly and Zac through all this?"

"Look, I know you're never going to shut up and go away unless I tell you, so you'd better keep this to yourself." He sank into his leather chair.

"Tell me." My heart pounded in my throat. I knew Zac was innocent, but I could see in John's eyes that he wasn't so sure.

He nodded for me to sit across from his desk, and I did.

"An eyewitness came forward. Someone who said they saw an old car, description matching Zac's, pulling out of the parking lot at the park. We have no choice but to ask Zac if it was him and if he was in the park that morning."

"I'm sure he wasn't. He said he was out driving around, remember?"

John nodded. "I remember. Let's hope you're right."

"So you're saying Byron Stanton didn't call you? Could he have been this Johnny-come-lately 'eyewitness'?"

"Definitely not. Byron didn't call me, and I personally interviewed the witness." John leaned back and retrieved his coffee.

"Who was it?"

John took a sip from his cup and shook his head. "You know I can't tell you that."

"But you think they're telling the truth?" That was the reason for John's obvious doubt concerning Zac's innocence? A trustworthy witness?

"They're not involved in the case and had no reason to lie that I could see. Look, let's wait and see what Zac says, okay? I promise I'll be as easy with him as possible."

"I still think Byron probably killed Hank." I pointed at his badge. "Are you too much under his thumb to investigate the possibility?"

"Please don't say that again. I'm not under anyone's thumb. But you have to stay out of this and let us do our job."

"Well, if you do your job, I will." I pushed to my feet.

"You know who you remind me of?" John tossed the half-full Styrofoam cup into the round trash can and leveled his gaze at me. "Hank Templeton. Always asking questions, always butting into other people's business. And look how things ended for him. Is that what you want?"

A tap at the door saved me from answering what I'm sure was a rhetorical question. Sergeant Betty Riley poked her curly head in the door. "They're here, Chief." She eyed me with a mix of sympathy and concern, so I was sure who "they" were. Carly and Zac had made it to the station.

Ever the professional, John stood. "Jenna, I have to go."

"I'll wait here for you to finish." I crossed my legs and relaxed in my chair, eyeing the clear polish on my fingernails with great interest.

John glared at me. "And go through my files? I don't think so. Let me rephrase. *You* have to go."

Heat rushed up my neck and into my face. John knew me too well. "Fine." I pushed myself to my feet. "I'll wait in the hall," I said over my shoulder as I shoved the door open.

John was right behind me. "You'll—" He stopped. My dad leaned against the wall beside the bench in the hall. "Hello, Mr. Stafford."

"John." Dad nodded. "You doing okay?"

"I'm sure sorry about all this."

I looked up at him. Why hadn't he told me that?

"I know you are. You'd better get on in and do your job. Carly and Zac are in there, with Alex, of course. Jenna and I will wait out here."

"Yes, sir." John didn't even glance at me as he walked down the hallway.

Dad pulled me to him and patted my back. "You okay?"

"Just tired of all of them trying to pin this on Zac. You?"

He nodded and released me, giving me a gentle nudge toward the bench. I sat, and he sank down beside me. "Do you know what's going on?"

I knew what John had told me, but often Daddy had an uncanny sense for the truth of the matter. "Do you?"

He smiled. "I know you've been asking questions."

I looked at him. How did he know that? I knew Carly wouldn't tell, and I hadn't told anyone else.

Behind the worry for Zac, I saw a little twinkle in his eye. He knew what I was thinking. "I heard it at the diner."

So Debbie was a tattletale. Or was it Brendan? Or Byron? Or Amelia? Or Elliott? Whew. Maybe I should slow down on the questioning or at least quit assuming that nobody knew what I was up to.

"Yeah, I've been trying to get a little information." I found myself telling him everything—except about my job as Dear Pru, since I'd only gotten permission to tell Carly and no one else.

"Sounds like you've been busy."

"So far nothing to show for it." I leaned back against the wall and closed my eyes. Here came the lecture. *Mind your own business. I don't want you to get hurt.*

"Maybe you haven't asked the right person yet."

My eyes opened, and I looked over at my dad. No lecture? "Who else would I ask?"

"Just so happens, I was at the diner the day Hank and Brendan had that argument." He stroked his chin. "Sitting in the booth right behind them."

"Really?" To think I'd been avoiding my parents because I didn't want them to find out I was investigating. I should have been questioning them.

"I tried not to listen, but some things I couldn't help but overhear."

"Like what?"

"Mostly the same things Debbie heard. Something about a bag."

"Oh." My heart plummeted. I'd imagined breaking the case right here and now.

"But I also heard them mention the word *pills* several times."

"Pills?" Pills. Bag. The bag of empty pill bottles. I gasped. "Dad, Brendan Stiles is the murderer." I jumped to my feet. "We've got to go tell John."

"Whoa there, sweetie." Dad reached out and touched my arm. "Sit down and let's talk."

I obeyed but shook my head. "You don't understand. Carly and I were at the newspaper in the break room," I said quickly. "For reasons too complicated to explain. And there was a bag. In the freezer. It had empty pill bottles in it from Lake View Pharmacy."

"So?"

"So it's obvious. Brendan was doing something illegal concerning medicine. Hank found out and threatened to expose him. And Brendan killed him." My heart thudded against my ribs.

"And you think if you tell John this, he'll arrest Brendan and clear Zac?"

"Yes!" Why was he acting so hesitant? Surely he wanted to clear his own grandson.

"But you've already accused Elliott to John, right?"

"Yes, but—"

"And Byron?"

"Yes."

"So what makes you think he'll believe you?"

"We'll tell him what you told me. Plus I saw the bag of pill bottles."

"What if Brendan isn't guilty?"

"He is!" How could Daddy be so calm?

He held out his hands palms up in that let's-reason-this-out manner I knew so well. "But what if he and Hank were arguing over some ad copy and whether or not to use certain pictures with it? And what if Brendan was saying, 'I gave you that bag of empty pill bottles so you could get some good shots for the ad, and now you're not going to use them?'"

I leaned against the wall again. "Do you think that was what they were talking about?"

"No. But I'm still not convinced Brendan killed him. And I'd think twice before I accused another possibly innocent man."

The door to the interrogation room burst open and Zac walked out. He looked at Dad and me for a second—unreadable emotions in his red-rimmed eyes—then stomped down the hall. We rose to our feet as Carly came out next, Alex right behind her. "Hey, guys, I've got to go talk to Zac." She looked at Alex grimly. "Would you fill them in?"

"What's wrong?" I asked, icy ribbons of fear braiding around my heart.

"Zac didn't tell us the whole truth about the morning Hank was killed."

Dad shook his head. "I could tell he was hiding something."

I remembered having that feeling, too, the first day Zac had told us about being fired, that all wasn't being said. "What was it?"

Alex glanced around the deserted hallway and lowered his voice. "When he told us he was driving around that morning, he neglected to tell us that he pulled into the Main Street Park parking lot for a few minutes then left."

"Oh no," I whispered. "What are they going to do?"

"John reminded him again not to leave town. But between us, I think if something else doesn't break in the next few days, they'll arrest him. I got the impression the DA may very well be preparing a case." He looked from Dad to me. "I'm sorry."

I hit my fist against the wall and turned to Dad. "Meet me in the car, okay? I'm going to talk to John."

Dad reached toward me then dropped his hand. "You have to do what you have to do. But remember what I said."

I nodded. "I'll be cool."

"That'll be the day," I heard Alex mutter as I walked toward the interrogation room door. I considered going back and giving him a piece of my mind, talking about me that way and especially to my own father. But I had to deal with John first.

The Lake View Police Department's interrogation room served as a break room when there were no dangerous criminals to question. So I wasn't surprised to find John scarfing down a doughnut and coffee. When he saw me, he picked up a napkin and started wiping at his sticky fingers. "Jenna," he mumbled around the remains of his pastry.

"You've got the wrong guy. I think Brendan Stiles killed Hank."

John swallowed quickly and choked. When he didn't quit coughing, I began to beat him on the back, but he held up his hand for me to stop. "Enough."

"I'm sorry. I was only trying to help." I waited patiently while he took a big gulp of coffee.

"That's your problem," he croaked. "Always trying to help. You come in here accusing everyone and his brother of murder. Next you'll be thinking it was me."

"But I have proof that Brendan and Hank weren't getting along—"

"Hank didn't get along with anyone. Can't you get that through your head?"

John threw his coffee cup in the trash and closed the doughnut box, then hurried from the room without a backward glance at me.

I guess I'd ruined his appetite. Well, pardon me. I followed him out of the room and stood in the hallway, watching his back disappear around the corner. "I'm trying to tell you who the murderer is. Can't you get that through your head?"

When I walked out of the station, I looked up at the dark clouds and a drop of rain hit me in the eye. I sprinted for my car but couldn't outrun the downpour. Lightning streaked across the sky as I jumped, soaking wet, into the driver's seat and nodded to my dad. I should have stayed home in my warm, dry pajamas.

12

Lake View Monitor

Thank You

The family of Hank Templeton would like to thank everyone for their food, flowers, prayers, and expressions of sympathy. May God bless each of you.

After Saturday's storms, Sunday morning in Lake View dawned bright and sunny. As I drove to church, I couldn't help but notice how full of promise the day seemed, the trees resplendent in their freshly washed, multicolored ponchos. After Alex's prediction that Zac might be arrested, I don't know what I'd expected. Maybe for the world to change overnight to grays and blacks, a dreary winter scene, more fitting to my family's mood. Instead, the changing leaves, Lake View's claim to fame, were at their most glorious. Unfortunately, the town was so abuzz with talk of murder and suspects, nobody noticed.

I had a couple of questions to ask Marge Templeton after services. Speed was essential if we wanted to save Zac the embarrassment of a false arrest, not to mention the anguish of a false conviction. But the way I looked at it, if we didn't take time out for the Lord, how could we expect Him to take time out for us?

Before I walked into the whitewashed building, I sent up a little prayer that He would help me to keep my mind on Him alone until worship was over. And when Alex squeezed in next to me right before we started, I repeated the silent petition more fervently.

Before we dismissed, Jack Thompson stood to recap the announcements. I shifted on the padded pew and allowed myself to look at Alex, clean-shaven and sharp in a gray suit. I'd studiously concentrated on forgetting he was there during the worship and had almost succeeded. But technically, announcements weren't worship.

Was it by pure accident that Alex had ended up beside me this morning? Or had he sought me out? Maybe with the new threat, since he was Zac's lawyer, he thought he should sit with the family. But Mama and Daddy were at the other end of the bench, and he'd have shown just as much support down there. Not that I was complaining.

Jack's last announcement pulled my attention to the front. "Oh, by the way, we're glad to have Marge Templeton back with us today. She asked me to thank you all for the food and prayers. Your dishes will be on a table in the fellowship hall."

I watched heads turn toward an area on the opposite side of the building. I'd have to hurry to get over to Marge before she left.

After the closing prayer, Alex turned to me, his smile crinkling the corners of his eyes. "Jenna, how's it going?"

"Fine." I watched Marge's permed curls bounce down the aisle toward the front of the building. *She must be getting the dishes from her car to take to the fellowship hall.* I looked back at Alex. "How are you?"

His smile was a shade less bright. "I'm okay. You looking for someone?"

"Me? No." Not anymore.

"I was wondering if you have plans for lunch?"

"I usually go over to Mama's on Sundays. Um. . ." Marge had left the building. If I let this chance to talk to her go by, who knew when I'd get another one that didn't feel forced? I felt a trickle of perspiration at the back of my neck.

I wanted to go out with Alex, but was I ready to open that Pandora's box and poke and prod at all the old hurts there? I turned to Carly, who was sitting on the other side of me. Her normally smooth face was drawn with worry. "Carly. Talk to Alex for a minute." I stepped deftly out into the aisle, leaving them facing each other looking puzzled. "We'll talk later, okay? I have to see someone. I'll be back!" I called.

Had I flipped my lid? Judging by the openmouthed look Alex gave me, he sure thought so. I'd have to worry about that later.

I speed-walked down the aisle, because one of Mama's firmest childhood rules had concerned running in the church building. And she might be looking. I reached the fellowship hall as Marge set the dishes on the table. I glanced at the doorway to the tiny kitchen but saw no one. Perfect. "Marge."

She spun around. "Jenna, honey. So good to see you."

I hugged her. "You, too."

"Did you come to get your bowl?" She reached for my bowl, and I took it and set it on the table in front of me.

"Thanks." I had my carefully rehearsed speech prepared. Lead with a couple of questions about Dear Pru and then ease into some delicate questions about Hank and the empty pill bottles we found at the newspaper office. Contrary to my reputation at the diner, I could be subtle. Deep breath. "Actually, I wanted to see how you were doing and ask your advice about the Dear P—"

"Lois is in the kitchen, washing up a few things. Do you want me to ask her for a bag for you to put your bowl in?" Marge actually wiggled her eyebrows and put her finger to her lips in a shushing motion.

"Um, okay. Sure." I guess she wasn't exaggerating about keeping the Dear Pru identity a secret, if even her best friend was kept in the dark. So much for my lead-in to the real questions.

Without waiting to be asked, Lois bustled out with a plastic grocery bag and handed it to me.

"Here," Marge said, taking the bag from me, "let me do it."

"Oh, thanks." I relinquished the bag, wondering how to bring up the pills.

I never thought I would be grateful to be the subject of gossip, but when Marge said, "I was over at Shear Joy for my weekly set yesterday, and Joyce said you had an argument with that boyfriend of yours at the bowling alley the other night." I'd have kissed the garrulous beautician if she had been there.

"Well, he isn't actually my boyfriend, but yes, we had a small tiff. Speaking of Brendan, do you know if Hank was doing any kind of investigation of him or the pharmacy?"

"I have no idea. Why do you ask?" Marge was still wrestling the bowl into the plastic bag, but her furrowed brow and pursed lips clearly said, *I'll handle this*, so I left her alone.

"What have you heard?" Lois leaned forward, obviously eager to hear the latest gossip. Guess she wanted to contribute her share at the beauty shop or pass along a little extracurricular knowledge at the library.

"Nothing specific, you know; you just pick up things here and there." Like empty pill bottles in freezers.

"If he was investigating, he didn't mention it to me," Marge said, finally getting the bowl in the bag.

"Well, do either of you know Anne Mansfield or Josephine Winston?"

Marge was handing me the bowl, tied up neatly in a plastic bag, but before I could loop my hands through the handles, it slipped from her hands and shattered on the floor.

"Oh, Jenna, I'm so sorry." Tears filled Marge's eyes, and she squatted down to scoop up the bag of broken glass.

"There, there, dear. Jenna knows it was an accident." Lois patted her friend's shoulder. She pulled a tissue from her purse and handed it to Marge.

"Don't worry about it. Honestly. It was a bargain-aisle special." I took the bag and tossed it into the trash can beside us. "At least it was all bagged up so we don't have to get the broom, right?" Marge looked unconvinced, so I figured I might as well press on. "Anyway, where were we? Oh yeah, Anne Mansfield? Josephine Winston?"

Lois tapped her lips with her fingertip. "Those names don't sound familiar to me at all. Do they to you, Marge?"

Marge swiped a tear away and arranged the dishes on the table to fill in the spot left vacant by my bowl. "No," she said thoughtfully, "but you know, our small town is growing so fast, all those big-city people moving to the country." She sounded depressed by the idea.

"I heard the other day that Harvey and Alice were thinking of putting the diner up for sale. I bet they won't have any trouble selling it." Lois was back to her gossip again.

By the time I finished talking to them, Alex was long gone. I couldn't decide if I was relieved or disappointed, but the heavy feeling in my chest didn't feel much like relief. I was almost to Mama and Daddy's before I realized that neither of the ladies had even asked why I wanted to know about Anne Mansfield and Josephine Winston.

I parked around back at Mama's and went in the kitchen door. When Carly was upset, nothing could keep her from cooking. Not even the fact that she was still wearing her Sunday dress.

"Where've you been?" Carly asked from the stove as she stirred a pot of something that smelled delicious. Mama's old KISS THE COOK apron was draped around her dress. "And what was with the disappearing act?"

"I had to talk to Marge." I looked around the empty kitchen and lowered my voice anyway. "I wanted to find out if she knew who those women were whose names were on the bottles."

"Did she?" Carly slid open the drawer, retrieved a teaspoon, and bumped the drawer shut with her hip. She dipped it in the pan and held the spoon of tomatoey-looking liquid up to me. "Taste this."

"She had no idea. Neither did Lois." I blew the spoonful gently, then drank it down. "Yum. Your spaghetti sauce is always perfect."

"Thanks. Bummer about the pills. Drain that spaghetti for me, if you don't mind."

I stretched on tiptoes and retrieved the strainer from the top shelf of the cabinet. "Where's Mama?"

"She and the girls are changing out of their church clothes."

"But you couldn't be bothered, right?"

Her wry grin didn't reach her eyes. "I had to get my mind off things."

"Daddy and Zac in the living room, I guess?"

"Mm-hmm." She sprinkled a little more garlic powder in the sauce.

"How's Zac holding up?"

"He's wishing he'd turned around somewhere else that morning rather than the Main Street Park driveway. Still, I don't think he thought it was a big deal not mentioning it the first time he was questioned. So he's pretty stunned. But he's counting on God and Alex to get him out of this mess."

"Speaking of Alex, what happened with him after I left?" I'd given her every opportunity to volunteer the information, but since she hadn't, I decided I'd ask.

"Daddy came over and invited him to come over for lunch. Bless his heart, I could tell he didn't know what to say after you ran off like that. Then Mama wandered over and invited him, too. Poor Alex stammered all over the place before he finally got out of lunch."

"Poor Alex? Whose side are you on anyway?"

"Side? Who said anything about sides? I thought you were enjoying seeing him again."

"I was at first. But he's taken his slow, sweet time about asking me out, don't you think?" An invitation extended to both Carly and me to go eat after Hank's funeral did *not* count. Nor did his agreeing to go play golf with us last Saturday.

"So you're pouting?"

Why'd she have to make it sound like that? "Let's just say that his hesitation has made me realize that I shouldn't jump into anything, either." I ran water over the noodles. "I don't want to get hurt again."

"Maybe he doesn't, either." She took the spaghetti from me and dumped it into a glass casserole dish. In seconds, she'd poured the sauce in, stirred it together, sprinkled the whole thing with Colby Jack cheese, and popped it into the preheated oven.

"I'm not the one who left town twelve years ago."

"Yeah, but you said he tried to call and you wouldn't talk to him."

"Oh, well," I huffed. "If he gives up that easy, I don't know how he ever made it through law school."

"And you say you never hold a grudge." She tsk-tsked me as she brushed butter on top of the rolls she'd made earlier.

The door from the living room swished open just as Carly said that, and Mama smiled a welcome at me. When we were growing up, we watched the Waltons, and Mama always reminded me of Olivia Walton. Her smile was as gracious as her voice was soft. "Hi, honey, glad you made it. Who's holding grudges in my kitchen?" Yet, like Olivia, she always managed her house, especially the kitchen, with a firm hand.

"Thanks," I mumbled to Carly. "Nobody, Mama. Carly's teasing."

"Oh, good." Mama bustled over to put the teakettle on to boil. Neither Carly nor I dared to make tea with Mama around. She's the master of sweet tea, and our family would tolerate nothing of lesser quality. "Hand me those tea bags, please."

I retrieved the box from the counter and passed it over to her. "Speaking of grudges, though, Mama, do you know why Hank and Byron fought all these years? Are they the only reason Marge and Amelia don't get along?"

"Hmm. I don't guess I know the specific thing that made them fight. If there was one. As far as Marge and Amelia, when their family first moved to Lake View, they were as thick as thieves. The sisters and Lois. Three beautiful girls—always together." She measured a liberal portion of sugar into the bottom of her tea pitcher. "Then not too long after I met them, something tore the sisters apart. I never did know what."

"I didn't know Lois was from here." Carly checked the broccoli with a fork.

"She moved here with their family after her dad died in a fire, sort of a foster daughter, I think."

"No wonder she always tries to help Marge out. You think Amelia got jealous of their friendship?"

Mama seemed to consider this then shook her head. "The men came in the picture about then. More likely it had something to do with them. There's been bad blood between Hank and Byron right from the beginning. I always figured it was because each was afraid the other would get more of the family money."

I leaned against the counter and breathed in the aroma of baked spaghetti and fresh rolls. Smells that made me think of Carly and always would. Did Amelia think of Marge when she smelled spearmint? And maybe Marge remembered Amelia when she smelled. . .tanning lotion? I couldn't imagine anything ever coming between Carly and me. Certainly not money. The sisters' estrangement was almost as big a mystery as Hank's murder. At least Zac wasn't being blamed for that one.

After lunch, the dishes were cleared, Zac took off for the golf course, and Mama asked the girls to go help her change the linens in the cabins to get ready for new guests. Carly and I offered to help, but Mama had that train-up-a-child look in her eye, so we finished up in the kitchen instead. When everything was done and Dad was snoring in his recliner, Carly tiptoed in and got the paper then ran back into the kitchen with it, grinning as if she'd completed a secret mission. Today was my Dear Prudence debut.

She flipped it open and began to read, " 'Dear Pru, I will be sixteen in two months and twenty-three days. My parents always told me I could date when I turned sixteen. Well, I met this neat guy and he asked me out, but my mom said no. I have begged and threatened, but she won't change her mind. I am very mature and have never given my parents any reason to doubt me, so why are they sticking to this dumb rule? I mean, what difference does two months make? Sixteen is just a number. So what can I say to make them see how silly they are being? Trapped Teen.' "

"Here's the scary part," I said, leaning against her chair. "My answer."

" 'Dear Trapped, You have begged and threatened? But you are mature? Sounds to me like your mom needs to extend the no-dating rule and give you a good dictionary. When you discover the real meaning of *mature*, you will understand why they don't think you are ready. Also, it might help if you don't refer to rules made by the rule-makers (in this case, parents) as "dumb" if you want them on your side. My advice to you is simple: Grow up.' "

She laughed and clapped her hands. "Jenna, you're a natural at this."

"Do you think it was okay?" The sense of responsibility I felt answering the letters had surprised me.

"Perfect." Carly had moved on to the next letter, one from a woman who started out asking advice about how she could convince her longtime boyfriend to propose, but who ended by saying, " 'Now that I have read my own letter, I see that he's not all that great anyway. So I don't care if he proposes or not—because I'm going to dump him. Thank you, Dear Pru, for helping me see what I need to do.' Signed, 'So Over Him.' "

I nodded. If only they were all that easy.

" 'Dear So Over Him,' " Carly continued to read, laughing. " 'You're welcome!' " She looked up at me. "You did great!"

"Yeah, but look at my life. Don't you think it's kind of silly for me to be giving advice?"

"Sugar, people need to know someone cares. Look at what you've already done for Zac—"

"You mean nothing?" I dodged as she elbowed in my general direction. "Well, nothing that has helped."

"I have a feeling it will. I know I was against it, but right now, knowing you're on the case—"

"*We're* on the case." I couldn't believe she was finally coming around.

She rolled her eyes. "Whatever you want to think. Anyway, knowing that you won't give up is the only thing keeping me from going nuts. And it proves you care. Which was my point."

I thought of Zac. He'd barely spoken at all today. Everyone else had tried to be cheerful, but even the twins seemed to know it was an act. How could I possibly give up?

Lake View Monitor

Dear Pru,
I broke up with my boyfriend, and now I regret it. I've tried to tell him, but he won't take my calls. What should I do?

Desperate

Alex, Jenna again. Give me a call when you get this." I slapped my phone shut and climbed out of my car. I'd been phoning Alex for two days to apologize for leaving him so suddenly after church Sunday. Apparently he wasn't ready to accept my apology.

And as if that weren't bad enough, Carly had forgotten all about our standing Tuesday night date at the creepy deserted *Monitor* building and had already promised the twins a movie. So here I was alone. At least the hallway light stayed on permanently.

In Hank's office I turned on the overhead light and quickly retrieved the new envelopes from the Dear Pru file. I placed my typewritten copy of this week's column in the manila folder. "No way I'm going to look around without Carly to back me up. I'm outta here," I muttered. I turned off Hank's light and started down the hallway. A noise on the opposite side of the building froze me in my tracks.

Every side of the *Monitor* office had an exit. I'd come in the back door. But the noise came from the east side. Nothing over there but the alley that wrapped around the building. Except the central-heating unit. *The heater. . .it was the heater,* I repeated to myself silently.

A doorknob rattled in the distance. Not the heater. Someone was obviously trying to get in. An employee who'd forgotten something maybe. Or a murderer come back to tie up some loose ends. *Should I call 911? Run for my car?* I looked up at the Women sign on the wall beside me. Hide in the bathroom? If I didn't calm down, I'd need to be near the bathroom.

I heard the door open before I could decide, so I quickly slipped into the ladies' restroom. After a minute of no noise, I stuck my head out the door and looked both ways down the hall. No one in sight. But with several empty offices on both sides of the hall, that didn't necessarily mean I was alone in the building. I ducked back inside and waited, back against the wall. I could hear a muffled sound, possibly footsteps. But they didn't sound really close. I stuck my head out the door again. Nose to nose with Brendan Stiles's shocked face.

I screamed, a short frantic cry, cut off by clapping my own hand over my mouth.

"Jenna, what on earth are you doing here?" Brendan's eyes were wide and his breathing shallow. I could tell he'd considered screaming.

"I work here. What are *you* doing here?" I tried to sound normal, but my voice trembled.

"Just looking for some papers I left with Hank." He held up a key. "A buddy loaned me his key so I could get them. So you work here. What are you, the night watchman?"

"Uh. I, uh. . ." I looked down at the manila envelope still clutched in my hands. It didn't say DEAR PRU anywhere on it, thankfully. "I got a part-time clerical job here. Marge hired me." *Whew. Almost forgot my cover story.* "Why did you say you were here?" I tried for casual, hoping he'd attribute the slight quiver in my voice to leftover surprise.

"I was getting advice on some investments from Hank not too long before he died, and I left some papers with him. Since they were confidential, I wanted to pick them up before anyone else read them." He gave me that wide grin that used to make me feel like I must be wrong about his personality. I've always been a sucker for a nice smile. And his was definitely above average. But after that night at the bowling alley, I was grin-resistant.

"Thought you said you weren't friends."

"Hank was a good investor. I didn't have to be his friend to ask for his advice." The smile stayed in place, but his eyes were cold.

Uh-oh. Time to back off. "Gotcha. Well, I hope you found them. Or do you want me to help you look?" My turn to force a smile.

"No, Jenna, that's okay. I'll go look around some more in Hank's office." He appeared to buy my helpful attitude. "There is one thing I'd like you to do, though."

"What is that?"

"I'd rather you didn't mention to anyone else that I was here." Brendan winked at me, and I forced myself not to shudder. "I don't want anyone else to know Hank was looking into those investments for me."

"Right. No one else needs to know." Except maybe John and Marge. But this was not the time to mention that. Who wanted to antagonize a killer? I just wanted out of there alive.

❖

"So you were at the paper last night doing some clerical job for Marge. . ." John regarded me with a skeptical expression I was getting too used to seeing on his face. "And your old boyfriend dropped by. And now you want me to arrest him. Is that about it?"

"Not even remotely close. In the first place"—I held up my fingers and counted one off with the other hand—"he's not my old boyfriend. Second, he didn't know I was there when he dropped by; he was looking for some papers that he'd given Hank."

"So he broke in and you didn't call the police?"

"He had a key."

"Hmm. . ." John shook his head. "Sounds like he had as much right to be there as you did, then."

"Did I tell you about the pill bottles?"

"What pill bottles?"

"The ones in the freezer at the *Monitor*."

A different look came in his eyes. The same expression he'd worn that day I was rattling on about the wallet. "No, you didn't mention that. What about it?"

Suddenly I knew that the police had found the brown paper bag in the freezer and left it there as unimportant. "You saw them, didn't you?"

"What I saw and didn't see is none of your business, Jenna." He thumped his desk with his fist. "This case doesn't involve you."

"Really?"

"Yes, really."

"Tell that to my nephew next time you bring him down here to the station."

The desk sergeant's voice blared over the intercom. "Chief Conner, you have a phone call on line 1."

John reached for the phone then looked at me pointedly.

I plucked a peppermint from a bowl on his desk and popped it into my mouth. "I'm leaving, I'm leaving."

As I climbed into my car, I instinctively looked over at the empty passenger seat. Normally on my way to work, Neuro was there, peeking out at me from her carrier. But today Mr. Persi had balked at going outside and Neuro had actually run the other way when I opened the carrier. I'd given in and left them alone in the house. We'd see if I ended up regretting it. Slowly, I was learning to take chances on commitment.

I picked up my cell phone and dialed Alex's office. Even though he hadn't returned my calls to his cell from yesterday, I still felt I owed him an apology.

"Tracey? This is Jenna Stafford. Do you think I could talk to Alex for a minute?"

"Sure, Jenna. I'll put you right through."

Surprise, surprise. Why hadn't I thought of phoning his office yesterday instead of wasting time calling his cell phone?

"Alex Campbell here."

His voice made my knees go weak, even over the telephone, and even though I was sitting down already. Not fair.

"Hi, it's Jenna."

"Hey, great to hear from you. What's going on in your corner of town today?"

Okay, too smooth. Besides the fact that I'd been calling and calling him? "Did you get my messages?"

"Messages?"

"On your cell phone?"

"Oh. No."

"You didn't get the messages I left you on your voice mail?"

"No, I haven't checked my messages."

Would it hurt him to expand a little? He didn't have to listen to a message to see on his caller ID that I'd called. He sounded terribly guilty, but why? "I was calling to apologize for Sunday after church. There's no excuse for how I acted, but I was trying to figure out some stuff about Hank's murder. I'm sorry."

"I accept your apology. How's your undercover investigation going?"

"Nothing so far."

"Be careful that you don't mess things up for the police."

"Have you been talking to John?" I gripped the phone tightly.

"No. . ." His voice was puzzled. "I'd just hate to see you tamper with the evidence or anything."

"I'd never do that." Unless finding the pill bottles from the *Monitor* and writing down the names on them counted as tampering.

"I know. Sorry for sounding lawyerly."

I laughed. "That's okay. It's your job. Well, I wanted to say again, I'm sorry."

Silence. Then he cleared his throat. "Thanks for calling."

"And if you'd still like to go out, that would be great." Where had that come from? I was just being a good Christian, calling to apologize to someone I'd offended. That surely didn't include soliciting a date. Besides, what if he said no?

"How about supper tomorrow night?"

Wow. An invitation for a Thursday night date. Unfortunately, I couldn't go, but Mama always said it's a sure sign a man likes you if he doesn't wait for the weekend to ask you out. "I'd love to, but I have to work late tomorrow night. How about Friday?" Unless he asked me out for Thursday night because he had a real date on Friday night? *Argh.* I had to quit second-guessing myself.

"Great! Dinner and a movie?"

"How about dinner and a walk along the river?" I guess my regular confrontations with John were making me pushy. But I'd missed Alex, and if we were going to do this, why sit in a darkened theater beside each other when we could spend that same time talking and getting to know each other again?

"Sounds even better. We've got a lot of catching up to do."

I hung up the phone, glad to have the apology off my chest and even gladder to have a real, honest-to-goodness date with Alex.

Bob came in three hours late, as he'd done every day since he got home last Friday. I only knew he was there because I saw him running on the treadmill when I walked by. Must be trying to lose the ten pounds he'd gained on the cruise. Whatever the reason, he didn't grace the office with his presence. We were going to have to have it out. But right now I had my hands full with life-or-death questions. I couldn't worry about silly little future-deciding questions.

I got off at four and didn't even try to find Bob. Instead, I flipped open my phone and called Carly. "Well, I called Alex and apologized for running off to talk to Marge on Sunday."

"I'm proud of you. Was he nice about it?" I nodded my head and realized she couldn't see me. "Well, he did act a little odd about my messages. I can't figure out why he ignored them."

I pushed the UNLOCK button on my key fob then slid into the driver's seat. A white envelope flapped against the windshield. "Hang on, Carly. There's something under my windshield wiper."

"Okay."

I clambered back out of the car and snatched the offending item. "I don't know who advertisers think they're going to impress. I know I'm dying to get out of my car after I'm already settled in."

"Who left it?"

Warm and comfortable again, I examined my find. "No idea. It's not an ad, though. Has my name on it." I ripped the envelope open and stared at the white card. "Carly," I whispered. "You won't believe this."

"What?"

I hit the LOCK button on the door. Letters, all different shapes and sizes, had been cut out of a magazine and pasted onto a plain white card. BUTT OUT BEFORE YOU GET HURT. I started the car and glanced around the deserted parking lot. Several vehicles, but not a person in sight.

I quickly conveyed the message to Carly.

"Are you sure it's for you?"

My hand trembled as I retrieved the envelope from the passenger seat. "It says JENNA right here on the envelope."

"Oh."

"Come on. I need a little sisterly reassurance." I tried to laugh as I put the car in gear. "You can do better than that."

"Are you by yourself in the parking lot?"

"Oh, see? That's so much better. Yes. But I'm getting out of here as quickly as I can." The motor revved as I pulled onto the road.

"Where are you going?"

"Home. I let Neuro stay home with Mr. Persi today. They're both inside. I don't think I have a choice."

"Maybe it's a good thing you have a dog now." Carly had teased me mercilessly about Miss Never Commit ending up with two pets. "Aren't you afraid someone might be waiting there for you?"

"I wasn't." I slowed down.

"Oh, sorry. Want me to meet you there?"

"Oh yeah, I can see the headline now. STAFFORD SISTERS SINGLE-HANDEDLY SUBDUE SUSPECT."

"Very funny. Seriously, though. I'll come on over right now."

"Thanks, but I'll swing by John's office and show him the note. Give him the thrill of having not just one but two visits from me in a day."

"Then what?"

"Then I'll go home."

"Alone?"

She didn't know when to quit, did she? Maybe I should name her Ms. Persistence.

"I'll call you when I leave the station, and you can meet me at the house." I slowed down at the city limit sign. The last thing I needed was a police escort to the station.

"Good. I might get Zac or Dad to come with me."

"And mess up our headline with its perfect alliteration? We're the Stafford sisters. We can handle it."

Ten minutes later, I walked into John's office, my shoulders back and my head high. I had a legitimate reason to be here. Let him try to throw me out this time.

"What are you doing here?"

I slapped the paper down on his desk and smoothed it out with my hand, then stood back.

John studied it for a second; then his dark eyes flashed to my face. "Where'd you get this?"

"My windshield. At the health club." I produced the envelope bearing my name and put it beside the letter.

He rubbed the stubble on his chin. "Did you ever think about doing what it says?"

"I get a threatening letter with a killer on the loose and you think this is an appropriate time to chide me about minding my own business?" My voice squeaked, and I took a deep breath.

"No, I'm going to investigate it, but in the meantime I think it's real good advice."

"You're going to investigate it?" I asked, trying not to screech. "The same way you've been investigating Hank's murder. I've tried to tell you—"

He jumped to his feet. "Tried to tell me? Tried to tell me that the mayor is the murderer, or wait." He put his hand on one hip and tapped his lips with his finger in an exaggerated feminine motion. "Is it the golf pro? No, no, that's not right. It's the local pharmacist."

"Well, maybe if you listened once in a while instead of making fun of me..."

He yanked up the letter he'd been so careful not to touch a minute before. "Did you do this?"

"What?" Could he be saying what it sounded like?

"Did you make up this letter to throw me off Zac's trail?"

"Did you kill Hank Templeton?" I knew he didn't, but it was no more ridiculous than his accusation of me. Fury rolled like a ball in my stomach.

"Get out." He pointed his finger to the door. "Jenna Stafford, I love you like a sister, but you've crossed the line from annoying to downright interfering with my investigation. I wouldn't believe you if you had a taped confession!" The vein in his neck was bulging again.

"But I—"

"The boy that cried wolf."

"Excuse me?"

"That's what you remind me of—the boy that cried wolf." He hitched up his pants by the belt loop. "So don't come crying to me anymore."

I spun on my heel and left without a word, hoping to get out before he saw the tears streaming down my cheeks. Being unjustly accused always made me cry.

John needn't worry.

I would never call on Lake View's finest again.

14

Carly and Zac were waiting in her van when I pulled into my driveway. I didn't for one second think someone was in my house, but it was ironic to see my nephew motion Carly and me to get behind him as he led the way with a baseball bat clutched in his hands. How quickly boys go from being the protected to being the protector.

As soon as Zac opened the door, Mr. Persi bounded toward us, wagging all over. Neuro hung back, in that way cats have, but I could tell she wasn't agitated. "It's all clear," I assured my nephew and took the Louisville Slugger from his hands. "Thanks."

"Cool dog." Zac scratched the dog behind his ears. "Aren't you, buddy?"

The golden retriever grunted.

"He agrees with you," Carly said.

I looked at the house—exactly as it was when I'd left it that morning. "I do, too." I patted Mr. Persi and scooped up Neuro. "Wanna take him out back, Zac?"

"Sure."

After they went out, Carly looked up at me. "You goin' to be okay?"

"I guess. Nothing a cup of hot chocolate won't cure, maybe." We sat at my bar and sipped our cocoa while I told her about my visit to the police station.

"I'm goin' over there and give him a piece of my mind." Carly's knuckles were white as she gripped my Krispy Kreme mug handle.

"You can't. That would only make things worse for Zac." We both watched out the kitchen window as the golden dog jumped to catch the Frisbee. Zac threw back his head and laughed.

Carly's eyes glistened with tears. "It's not fair."

I reached over and took her hand. "We both learned that a long time ago, Car. C'mon, who needs the police? With God's help, we can do it."

"I guess you're right, but it frustrates me to no end how pigheaded John's being." She waved her hand toward the window. "Do you think he sincerely believes that boy killed somebody?"

"I have no idea what he believes anymore." I finished my cocoa and put my cup in the sink. When she handed me hers, I set it beside mine and nodded toward the back door. "Let's go out and play." She needed some serious downtime, and maybe it would help me to quit gritting my teeth—something I'd noticed myself doing ever since I left the station.

"Does this mean you're going through your second childhood?"

"Hey, you're older than me. Always will be," I taunted as we hurried outside.

"Aunt Jenna, catch!" Zac spun the flying disc toward me. I reached up to grab it, but a golden blur leaped into the air and intercepted it.

Zac's dimples flashed. "Can you believe how good he is?"

I took the soggy Frisbee from Mr. Persi and had a sudden flashback to retrieving Hank's wallet from him that fateful Friday morning. All roads led to the murder these days.

I tossed it to Zac. "He's got talent, that's for sure."

"Anybody ever answer your ad about him?"

I shook my head. "The vet said most likely his owner had died or ended up in a nursing home and the family just let him go. Or someone got tired of feeding him and dropped him off at the park. But I'm still not sure why he adopted me."

"He knew a good thing when he saw it." Carly sank down on the yellow grass.

"Yeah," Zac said and draped his arm across my shoulders. "After all, you're my favorite aunt."

"Wonder why." We'd had the favorite-aunt, favorite-nephew thing going since Zac was tiny. "Maybe because I'm the only one," I growled and tickled his ribs through his T-shirt.

He ducked away from me. "Hey! I'm too old to tickle."

"That's a surefire way to know someone's not 'too old' for something," Carly drawled from the grass. "When they feel like they have to say they are."

Zac laughed. "Yeah, well. . .I don't think that made any sense, Mom." He threw the Frisbee to her, and it landed in her lap. He nodded toward Mr. Persi. "Wanna take him to the park for a while? We could go by and get the pipsqueaks."

"Sure."

"Sounds good. I'm sure Hayley and Rachel will be thrilled," Carly agreed and reached out a hand for Zac to help her up. "Since when do you want to go to the park with your family?"

Zac winked at me as he tugged his mama to her feet. "Since my aunt got a dog that's cool enough to be a chick magnet." He opened the door. "Come on, Mr. Persi—" He froze and looked over his shoulder at me. "Any chance he's up for a name change? 'Mr. Persi' is kinda weird-sounding."

It was so good to see Zac acting more like his old self. Maybe if we could clear his name, he wouldn't have any lasting scars from this ordeal. "You're more than welcome to call him by his full name—Mr. Persistence."

"Ooo-kay. Maybe I'll stick with 'Hey, dog.'"

Sadly enough, "Hey, dog" followed him into the house without complaint and stuck right to his side the rest of the afternoon.

◆

I clutched the intercom mic and made the announcement I make every Thursday night at 7:40. "Lake View Athletic Club will be closing in twenty minutes." One of the first improvements I made when I started working here, the announcement cut down on closing time.

"Night, Jenna!" Dave called. "Sure you don't want me to wait and walk you out to your car?"

"I'm sure." The personal trainer asked the same thing every week, but so far I'd managed to steer clear of Mr. Universe. The endless parade of blonds on his arm anytime I saw him after hours gave a pretty clear indication this was not a man who might help me meet my deadline. And I tried not to listen to locker room talk, but apparently when he was with the guys, he never shut up bragging about his conquests. He was cute, but I wasn't about to be another notch in his barbell.

"Night, Jenna. Everyone's cleared out of the locker rooms. Want me to wait on you?" Gail asked. She had her hands full with her college load and her job here, so sometimes she was kind of scattered, but she was a big help to me. And the members loved her.

"No, thanks, Gail. I'll be right behind you."

I flipped off the last light switch and let the door *whoosh* shut behind me, then stood with my key in the doorknob as I went over my mental checklist. Had I checked the pool area and all locker rooms to make sure there were no stragglers? With Gail's help, yes. Had I checked the coffeepot and smoothie bar area to make sure everything was turned off? Yes. Had I set the security alarm before shutting the door? Yes.

Satisfied, I locked the door. It seemed darker than normal tonight. *Must be a new moon. Or maybe just my nerves.* As I was walking across the deserted parking lot, Carly's nagging advice about making someone stay late to walk me to my car didn't seem so silly. Dave's bulging muscles were looking better every second.

As I buckled my seat belt, I squinted at the darker shadows at the other end of the parking lot. Was that a car parked over there?

I pulled out onto the highway and flipped open my phone. Talking to Carly would calm my nerves. I waited until the first curve was safely maneuvered then glanced down at my phone to hit Carly's speed-dial number. Headlights glared in my rearview mirror, and suddenly I felt a hard thump against my bumper. The vehicle behind me had come from nowhere. Had it bumped me? I slowed a little. If it had, it would surely back off now. *Bam!* The cell phone flew out of my hand, and I gripped the steering wheel tighter. The words of the anonymous letter flitted through my mind. Was the driver doing this on purpose? "Dear Lord," I murmured, "please, please help me."

I pushed the accelerator down, hoping to get away, but I felt a hard hit behind my door, and my car fishtailed. I had no idea whether to brake or speed up some more. Why hadn't I taken those defensive driving courses offered at the high school? I slammed on the brakes then screamed as my car hit the loose gravel on the shoulder of the road and the steering wheel spun out of my hands. "God, help me!"

I tried to hang on, but my body jerked against the seat belt as I bounced over terrain that was clearly not the road. When the swerving headlight beams showed a line of trees in front of me, I squeezed my eyes shut and braced for the impact.

15

I woke slowly, details of the strange room filtering into my sleep-fuddled brain. A television was suspended from the ceiling in the corner. My gaze slid sideways to rest on my dad, reading the *Monitor* and wearing a frown. My dad hardly ever frowned.

"Daddy?" I tried to say, but it was more like a croak.

He lowered the paper and jumped up. A smile spread across his face. "Jenna! How you doin'?"

"Hospital?"

He took my hand in his and caressed it with his thumb. "You had a little car accident."

"What happened?" Shadowy images flitted in and out of my semiconscious. Bright headlights. Then a hard bump from behind.

"We think maybe a deer ran out in front of you. Do you remember?"

I hesitated and felt my eyes close again. Sleep called me like a pied piper's song. "Sort of," I mumbled. "A car. Behind me. No deer."

"Okay, we can talk about it later, honey. You go ahead and rest."

The next time I woke, Daddy was gone, but Mama was there in the same chair, her gaze locked on my face, her brows knitted together with obvious worry. She smiled. "Hey, how's my baby?" She was using that hospital voice—almost a whisper but not quite.

"I'm okay."

"No, I mean how are you *really*?" She reached for my hand and squeezed. "You can tell me."

"I ache all over. My head hurts, and every time I breathe it feels as though someone is stabbing me." Well, that sounded whiney enough. I felt like crying.

"Oh, honey, I'm so sorry. You've got a lot of bruises and abrasions, but no concussion, at least. I'll call the nurse to give you some pain medicine."

"What I'd love is a Caramel Macchiato. Remember when Hayley had her tonsils out, we got one at the little coffee shop downstairs?" If she would go get me one, that would give me time to decide what to do about the memories that were rushing in like a river now that I was completely awake.

Mama's eyes lost some of their sadness and regained a little of their normal twinkle. "Good to see you're still yourself. And I'd be glad to go get you one, but I hate to leave you alone." She hesitated. "Do you remember much of last night?"

Leave it to Mama to get to the heart of the matter.

I nodded then immediately regretted it. My skull felt as though a little man with a big hammer had taken up residence inside. "Some. How did they find me?" Had the driver of the car behind me developed a conscience and called it in? Or was it a murderer with no conscience? I shuddered. I had to tell someone about being run off the road. But Mama, face already drawn with worry, wasn't my first choice.

"You called Carly. When she answered, she heard thumping noises and you praying aloud, then a scream. She called 911, and they headed out of town toward the health club, looking in all the ravines along the way with their spotlight. You'd gone down under a hill, but they found you within ten minutes, thankfully."

I closed my eyes. If I hadn't punched Carly's speed-dial button, I might still be in my car instead of safe in the hospital. "What about my car?" I loved that car.

"Sorry, baby, it's completely totaled. At least it's insured."

I closed my eyes against the tears that threatened to overflow.

"You can use my car until you get another one," Mama murmured. Her cool hand brushed across my head and a bandage I hadn't realized was there. "Go on back to sleep. You're going to be fine."

"I'm not sleepy. Just resting my eyes." *And thinking*. I stared at her and noticed something else behind the worry. Strength. Mama could handle the truth. "When I left the health club last night, I was calling Carly when I got to the second curve, and headlights came up behind me—fast. Then I felt a hard hit on my back bumper. Before I could react, the car pulled up beside me and rammed me."

She put her hand over her mouth but nodded. "That's about what we figured after what you said to your daddy earlier. He's gone to talk to John right now."

John? Great. Exactly what this day needed.

"Jenna, did you see who it was?"

"No, but there's more." I told her about the threatening letter.

She sank to the chair, her face almost as white as the wall behind her. "Honey, what have you gotten yourself into?"

"I'm doing it for Zac, Mama. And for Marge."

"Your dad and I would do anything to keep Zac from being arrested. But not risk your life. You've got to stop this snooping."

"I want to know." I stared at her eyes, so much like mine. How could she not understand? "I *need* to know."

She gave a half laugh. "You always have *needed* to know. Needed to know what would happen if you mixed vinegar with baking soda, needed to know where that butterfly had gone or where the falling leaf would land. When you were little, you kept me busy rescuing you from your need to know." The smile faded. "But it's time to outgrow that insatiable curiosity. It's too dangerous."

Tears burned my eyelids. "I'm sorry, Mama."

She reached up and touched my cheek with her palm, tenderness evident in her eyes. "Promise me you'll be more careful."

"I promise." That was easy. I didn't want to end up in the hospital again. . . or worse. Besides, I had a date tonight. I intended to live long enough to find out if Alex Campbell was as special as I remembered. Although we might have to rethink that long walk beside the river. "Now how about some coffee?"

"I don't know about leaving you."

"No one is going to bother me in broad daylight with all these nurses and doctors running around."

She shoved the call button at me. "You keep this close and push it if a stranger comes in."

"I will." Anything to get my caffeine. No need to add that if the murderer was the one who ran me off the road, I seriously doubted the person would be a stranger.

After she left, I closed my eyes again and thanked God for getting me out of last night alive. The door creaked open slowly. My heartbeat accelerated, but I kept my eyes closed.

"Jenna? Jenna, are you asleep?" Brendan Stiles's quiet voice sounded close to my face. I resisted the urge to open my eyes and kept my finger resting lightly on the call button. If I screamed and pushed it at the same time. . .

Before the scream materialized, Brendan whispered, "I hope you can hear me. I need to tell you, you were right about Zac. He didn't kill Hank. But

I think I know who did."

With no direction from my brain, my eyes flew open. Just like in the hall at the newspaper office that night, I was staring straight into Brendan's eyes. "Who?"

"Well, well!" A woman's voice echoed through the room. Brendan jerked upright, and I looked past him at Amelia, who had pulled her usual trick of entering a room with absolutely no noise. *Wonder if she'd teach me how to do that.* "I hope I'm not interrupting a tête-à-tête. I'd heard rumors that you two had a falling out. That should be a lesson to all of us not to listen to rumors."

I used the buttons on the hospital bed console to raise myself up to a semi-sitting position in the bed. "So, Amelia, what are you doing here?" That didn't sound right. Tact has never been my strong suit, but surely after the last twenty-four hours, I couldn't be expected to say everything perfectly. "I mean, how did you know I was here?" Well, that may have actually been worse given the circumstances. . .and the suspicions racing through my mind as I stared at my two surprise visitors. How *had* they known I was here? And had one of them tried to run me off the road?

Brendan began making those see-you-later noises, and I clutched his arm. I may not have been thinking clearly, but there was safety in numbers, and I was better off with both of them than one of them. "Stay here until Mama comes back. I'm sure she would love to see you."

"Well, I—" He looked at Amelia and paused.

I what? I can't kill you with her here? I'm still mad at you, so I don't mind if she bumps you off?

The door opened again before he could finish, and I let go of his arm. Marge bustled into the room, Lois in her wake, each with a vase of flowers. My hospital room was obviously the place to be in Lake View this morning. The recurring question was, how did they all know I was here?

Marge froze when she saw Amelia. The two sisters stared at each other without a word. Emotions flickered across both of their faces so quickly I couldn't begin to name them all. Then Amelia looked at me. "Darling, I must go. Sorry for barging in on you lovebirds. When Byron's whispering in my ear, I surely don't want to be interrupted." She gave an airy wave and swept from the room.

Lois frowned and plunked her flowers down on the windowsill. "*Humph.* What was *she* doing here?"

"She just dropped by to"—I actually had no idea—"see me. How are you ladies doing today?"

Marge seemed to snap out of the trance she'd been in ever since she saw Amelia. "We're doing okay, but what about you?" She set her floral arrangement beside Lois's, hurried to my side, and kissed my forehead.

"I'd better run, Jenna." Brendan had edged closer to the door without my realizing it.

"Okay." I gave him what I hoped was a private, meaningful glance. "We'll talk later."

He nodded, yanked the door open, and hurried out.

"How'd you know I was here?" I directed the question to either of the two women.

"Lois took me to breakfast at the diner for my birthday. Debbie told us a customer heard it on the scanner."

The scanner. Of course. Lake View's version of the town crier. Maybe I should get one.

"Happy birthday." My reply was instinctive. Sadly enough, Amelia had to have known it was her sister's birthday, yet she'd not said a word.

Marge nodded. "Did a deer run out in front of you and cause you to swerve off the road?" Concern laced her voice.

"That area out there sure is rife with deer this time of year," Lois offered before I could answer. "Last week, I had a huge buck dart out right in front of me." She shuddered. "Thought I was going to plow into it, but I was careful not to swerve."

"They taught us that in the defensive driving course we took over at the school last year," Marge said.

I knew I should have taken that course when they offered it this year.

"So is that what happened to you?" Marge asked again.

I had no idea what to say. Thankfully, Mama walked in right then with my Caramel Macchiato. Amid all the greetings, the question was apparently forgotten.

While they chatted, I closed my eyes and listened to the comfortable bedside chitchat. Sarah Hutchins had her baby. Little Joy Fields fell on the monkey bars at school and broke her arm. There was a time before Hank's murder when those things *were* the news in Lake View. Would we ever get back there again?

❖

Someone was watching me. Intently. I peeked through my eyelashes at Alex's well-sculptured face.

"Hey, water girl, you okay?"

I opened my eyes completely. "I think so. They're supposed to let me go home this afternoon." If he'd come to the hospital to cancel our date, he could forget about it. I wasn't letting him off that easily.

"I know you probably don't feel like going out tonight. . . ."

I couldn't believe it. He was ditching me in a hospital room. "Is this why you ignored my messages? Because you didn't want to go out with me?" Might as well find out now.

"Technically, I didn't ignore your messages; I just didn't get them." A sheepish smile spread across his reddening face. "Here's the thing. I washed my cell phone."

"In the washer?"

He nodded. "I admit I'm not much at washing clothes or keeping house. But I do have my redeeming qualities."

"Like what?" *A heart-melting smile?*

"It's been said that I'm not a bad cook. So, as I was saying. . ." He drew his brows together in mock sternness. "Since you're probably not up to going out tonight, I was wondering if you might want some company."

"That would be nice," I said, suddenly shy.

A smile spread across his face. "Do you mind if I come over a little early and make us some supper?"

Did I mind? What could be more decadent than reclining on the couch while a man cooked the meal? "Perfect."

"Okay, then, I'll see you about five." He leaned toward me, and I held my breath. I kept my eyes open, though, in case he was just brushing a speck of lunch off my face. At least they'd taken the little heart-rate thingy off my finger. Otherwise, I was sure the nurses would be rushing in to see why my pulse had gone off the chart.

In my limited experience, hugs over hospital bedrails are not usually life-changing. But as I returned Alex's gentle embrace and breathed in the familiar scent of his soap, I felt so blessed with second chances. A second chance to live after last night. And after all these years, a second chance to love.

"I'm glad you're okay," he whispered in my ear, then released me.

I shivered.

"Are you cold?"

"No, um—" How embarrassing.

His smile crinkled the corners of his eyes. "Good." He leaned in and brushed his lips to mine. "See you tonight."

I waved good-bye as he walked out the door.

When Carly came in a few minutes later, I was still smiling.

16

Lake View Monitor

Fun Quiz of the Week

Are You a Stiletto or a Sneaker?

1. *Your idea of a great time is to:*
   (a) *go to Chez La Troque for a scrumptious five-course meal and possible celebrity sighting*
   (b) *get a burger and fries from the local Dairy Bar on your way to a rousing game of putt-putt*

2. *The perfect guy for this date is:*
   (a) *Vin Diesel*
   (b) *Orlando Bloom*

Even another run-in with the chief of police couldn't ruin my mood. At least John hadn't accused me of forcing myself off the road. As a matter of fact, I'm pretty sure that beneath his gruff questioning was concern for me. A concern my family shared. Carly took me home with strict orders from our parents not to leave me until Alex got there. She was going to come back when he left. Although I don't know what they thought she'd do if someone came after me again.

I pushed END on my cell phone. "I still can't get Brendan to answer. I left him another message to call me."

Carly came out of my closet with a red T-shirt in her hand. "Here, try this one. If he knows who killed Hank, wonder why he doesn't go to John?"

"I don't know." I'd settled on jeans, but finding the perfect top was proving a challenge. It was hard to find something that coordinated perfectly with the bandage on my forehead.

As I tried on the shirt, Carly plopped down on the bed. "Does this remind you of when I used to get ready for dates with Travis? You'd watch me, ever ready to give your opinion."

"Yes, and even as a thirteen-year-old, I had no sense of style."

"You didn't need a sense of style. Still don't. Anything looks good on you."

"Yeah, right." I turned from the mirror to look at her. "Did I tell you I took a coffee quiz the other day online?"

"A coffee quiz?" Carly looked at me as if I'd lost my mind.

"Yeah, to tell you what kind of coffee you are." I smoothed down my red T-shirt over my jeans. "No big surprise I turned out to be a plain old cup of joe."

Carly nodded. "Well, you're in luck. Think about it. Most men prefer a plain old cup of joe."

"Uh-oh." I met her eyes in the mirror.

"Uh-oh?" She pushed off the bed and walked over to stand beside me.

I grinned at her reflection. "I took it for you, too. You're a cappuccino."

"Then I'll have to find a special man, won't I?" She blushed and ran her hand through her short curls.

"Carly Elizabeth. What happened to my man-hater sister?"

"I never hated men." She picked up a denim vest from the pile of discarded outfits draped across my chair. "I couldn't trust them. I'm still not sure I can. Put this on."

"But my shirt isn't tucked in."

She rolled her eyes. "Just put it on."

I slipped into it and turned back to the mirror. The red T-shirt was three inches longer than the open vest. Even though I'd never have considered wearing it that way, it worked. "Perfect. Casual but different. How do you do that?"

The doorbell rang, and my gaze flew to the clock. "It's five already. He's right on time."

"You look beautiful."

We started down the hallway, and I stopped. "I can't believe I'm this nervous. This is Alex, the boy who gave me a frog for my eighth birthday. What am I worried about?"

Carly studied my face. "That you might go out there and find a stranger in his place?"

"That's it. What if it's all been a schoolgirl fantasy, and we don't click anymore?"

"Then it's better to know and be done with it. I'm going to slip out the back door while you answer the front."

"Sure you don't want to stay?"

She laughed. "I'm positive. Call me when he leaves, and I'll be over to stay the night, though. I'm looking forward to our sleepover. Even if I am just playing the role of bodyguard."

We hugged carefully, being mindful of my bruised shoulder, and then she was gone.

I opened the front door to find Alex, his arms laden with grocery bags. "Let me help you with those."

"Thanks, but I've got them. Just show me the kitchen."

I led the way into my small kitchen. "Can I help?"

He unloaded his arms and motioned toward a bar stool. "If you'd hold that stool down, I'd appreciate it." He grinned. "Seriously, I'd love it if you want to talk while I cook. You need to be resting."

"I've been resting all day," I said, but I sat down anyway. It's amazing how a little car crash can sap your energy.

"Do you know what happened last night?"

"Did you eat lunch at the diner?"

He nodded.

"Then you probably know as much as I do."

"Is it true someone ran you off the road?"

" 'Fraid so."

He frowned. "Can you leave this alone?"

I shook my head.

"I was afraid of that."

I sighed. How many times could one person get the same lecture? I was going for the Olympic record. "Do you mind if we don't talk about this tonight? I've already promised Mama I'd be more careful. For now, I want to forget it."

"Sure."

For the next few minutes, Alex got acquainted with my kitchen and kept up a running commentary about the food he was preparing. He opened a bag of salad into a bowl and sprinkled shredded cheese, real bacon bits, and chopped tomatoes on top of it. "Ranch?" he asked.

"Do you have to ask?" We'd both always loved Ranch dressing.

"I was hoping you still felt that way. It's the only kind I brought."

When the oven was preheated, he popped the rolls in and placed the salmon on the indoor grill. "Hope you don't mind that we're keeping it simple tonight."

"This is simple?" I tried to raise an eyebrow but failed miserably. I might as well face it. At almost thirty, chances weren't good that I would suddenly be able to pull off that little feat. Especially with the bandage on my head. "For me, this is gourmet. When did you start cooking?"

"Right after college. I dated a girl who loved to cook, and I was fascinated by all the dishes she made. It didn't take long for me to realize I could save myself a lot of headache and learn to cook."

As soon as he said the words "dated a girl," jealousy seared through my stomach. It wasn't as if I thought he hadn't dated, but he'd said it so casually.

"So you left her brokenhearted?" My smile felt forced. Was this his normal way of doing business? Love 'em and leave 'em? Maybe I'd just been the first in a long string of women who started using his brand of soap after he left so they could still feel close to him.

He froze with the seasoning shaker suspended above the salmon. "Not hardly." He narrowed his eyes. "Is that what you think of me?"

"I don't know what to think of you," I said quietly, my stomach churning. Why hadn't I saved this conversation until after supper?

"Let's make a deal," he said as he seasoned the salmon.

"What?"

He plunked the shaker down on the table. "We'll enjoy the meal and each other's company. Then afterward, we'll sit down and talk." He extended his hand. "Deal?"

I hesitated. Could I do it? My heart desperately wanted this time with him. I put my own hand in his. "Deal."

While we ate, we reminisced, but by unspoken agreement, we limited our nostalgic journey to the years before we dated. As we finished up, he set his glass on the table. "How's Carly doing now, really? I can't believe she never remarried."

"She handles it pretty well, I think, but she has some trust issues." I thought of her sauna confession about Elliott, but I wasn't about to tell Alex about that.

"Remember how you cried when she ran off with Travis to get married?" he asked.

I nodded. "Almost like I knew what would happen, but in reality I was just fourteen and it felt like I lost my big sister. I couldn't believe she kept it a secret from me. She was afraid I'd feel like I should tell Mom and Dad."

"Which you probably would have."

"True. But I still felt betrayed. That's why I ran off to the tree house."

"I could hear your sobs before I even got up the ladder. But I'd have known where you were even if I hadn't." His voice was soft with memories.

"That day. . ." He'd held me while I cried. When I stopped, I must have been a sight, but he wiped the tears from my cheeks and looked at me as if I was beautiful. My best friend was suddenly much more.

He touched my hand. "Our first kiss."

So much for boundaries. I slipped my hand out from under his. "So now that supper's over, the deal is off?"

He sat back and blew out his breath. "I guess so. Where do we even begin?"

I stood and picked up my plate. He took it from me. "Why don't you let me clean up?"

"Don't you think you've done enough?" Oh, that was a classic Jenna-ism. "I didn't mean—"

He chuckled. "I know what you meant."

"We can just leave this. I'll clean it up later," I said.

"Let's deal with it tonight. It'll just be harder to face tomorrow."

I nodded. Why did everything have to have a double meaning? We'd been so relaxed earlier, but now tension crackled in the air. We worked in silence for a while, and when the dishwasher was running, he touched my arm. "I forgot to tell you—you look nice tonight."

"Thanks." Heat crept up my face. "So do you."

He laughed. "You don't have to say that."

"No, it's true. . . ." My voice faded off. Was I actually standing in my kitchen telling Alex Campbell I liked how he looked? "Let's go sit down for a minute—and relax," I added under my breath.

"Sounds good."

I led the way to the living room, where Carly had left an eighties CD repeating softly when we first got home from the hospital. Had she planned this? And figured I needed all the help I could get? Probably.

"Oh, man. It's been a long time since I heard that song." Alex sank onto the couch and patted the spot beside him.

I sat—not quite at the opposite end of the sofa but not right next to him, either. Distance made my mind work better, and I wanted to think as clearly as possible while we had the discussion I'd been dreading since I first heard Alex was back in town.

He laughed. "I don't remember your being this prickly."

I tossed him a quick, totally insincere smile. "Maybe I didn't have a reason to be prickly then."

"You?" He pushed back against the sofa back and crossed his feet in front of him. "Deep down, I knew our relationship always came second to your swimming. But I never realized you'd break up with me because you lost a swim meet."

"A swim meet?" I jumped to my feet then put my hand on my bandage. Whoa. No more sudden movements. He saw me and in a second was on his feet beside me, but I pushed him away. "It was the Olympics! Besides, I didn't break up with you!"

I walked over to the window and stared blindly out at the sunset. If I faced him, he'd see the tears sparkling in my eyes, and I wasn't ready to completely trash my pride.

"What do you call refusing to talk to me?" His voice sounded close behind me.

I steadied myself against the windowsill and kept my eyes fixed on the fading day. "I call it needing some time to come to grips with the fact that I let the whole nation down."

"What about letting me down?"

I turned around, amazed by his bluntness. He was less than a foot away. "You were included in the whole nation. And yes, you most of all. You believed in me. So did your dad. And I flubbed up."

"Dad said you had a bad cold."

I rolled my eyes. "Don't even try to make excuses for me. I wasn't good enough. I lost."

"Okay."

"Okay." I was obstinately pained that he gave in so quickly, but at least we knew where we stood now.

"So what if you weren't good enough? Did that give you the right to throw away our future?"

I'd thrown away our future? Had I stumbled into one of the endless strings of kids' movies where the main characters swap bodies? "I'm not the one who left."

"You knew I was going to college. I sent flowers, I called you, I even came over, but your mama said you weren't up to seeing anyone. I tried everything."

Suddenly I remembered the flowers. White daisies and red roses. I'd felt so unworthy that I'd thrown them out. Was Alex right? Had I overreacted? Was I partly to blame? I pressed my back against the windowsill, letting it support my weight. The thought made me dizzy. "Thank you for the flowers. They were beautiful."

His eyes widened, and he gave an incredulous laugh. "Why didn't you say that then?"

"I was ashamed."

He shook his head. "Until the other day when we were eating at the diner, I thought you blamed me because my dad and mom moved away and left you."

My turn to laugh. "We messed things up good, didn't we? I was so self-centered to think that the world revolved around the Olympics."

"I should have tried harder to get through to you. I let my pride get in the way."

"Is that why you never tried again to contact me once you went away to college?" I had to know. Deep down even then I'd realized the way I acted after the Olympics was wrong. But I never expected him to just forget about me.

"I didn't want to be rejected again. By the time I got over that, it seemed that it had been too long."

"I'm sorry." I didn't mind saying it first. Pride wasn't all it was cracked up to be.

"Me, too." He reached for me, and I didn't pull away. "I wish I'd tried harder."

He traced my lips with his thumb and kissed me on the cheek. "Do-over?"

"Yes," I whispered as he brought his lips to mine. The ghosts of the past had been laid to rest. There was no strong sense of the familiar, no reawakening of a childhood romance. There was just me—almost thirty but far from desperate—kissing a strong Christian man I could easily imagine spending the rest of my life with.

"Lucky you moved back to Lake View, or we'd never have known, I guess," I said a few minutes later.

He grinned and raised one eyebrow. "Luck had nothing to do with it."

Lake View Monitor

Advertisement

Find Freedom on Liberty Lane!

Ready Realtors have listings available in Liberty Lane Estates off Liberty Road. Enjoy country living at its best with all the conveniences of the city. Just one mile from the Lake View city limits, Liberty Lane Estates offers the best of both worlds. Call (870) 555-REAL!

A buzzing noise jarred me awake. I lay still in the dark for a minute, listening to Carly breathe. I'd been deeply engrossed in a vivid dream. Alex and I were on jet skis, racing each other across the lake. We were both laughing, when suddenly a big wall emerged from the water, and he went to the left of it and I went to the right. No matter how far I went, there was never a break in the wall or a place to cut over to him. Some dreams weren't worth analyzing.

I fumbled around on the nightstand and winked at the red numbers on my alarm clock—5:29 a.m.

Beside the clock, my cell phone was lit up. I picked it up and looked at the screen. One New Message. I held it in my hand as I relaxed back on my pillow. "Dumb phone." Sometimes it wouldn't show I had a new message until hours after the fact. Unfortunately, I never thought to check them until it buzzed.

"Um, Jenna. . ." Carly's sleep-blurred voice sounded beside me.

"Yeah?"

"You might be going a little overboard with the animal thing."

I raised myself up on one elbow and looked over at her. A shadowy figure I recognized as Mr. Persi was sprawled out on top of her, and Neuro was curled up on her feet. I laughed. "You wanted me to commit."

"Yeah, but I had something a little more human in mind," she mumbled.

"Well, don't start planning the wedding, but at least I'm working on that." I shooed the animals off the bed and sat up. Mr. Persi usually came and got in my bed when he needed to go out.

She kept her eyes closed, but she smiled. We'd talked until one thirty or so about my date.

"What about you?"

Her eyes opened. "What about me what?"

"Have you seen Elliott lately?"

She gave a negative grunt and turned her back to me. "I need sleep."

I pressed the phone against my ear as I stumbled down the hall, the dog at my heels. The automated voice said, "You have one message sent at 9:34 p.m." Of course, I'd left the phone upstairs while I was with Alex.

I opened the back door and listened to the message as Mr. Persi bounded into the backyard. "Jenna? It's Brendan. I still need to talk to you. It's urgent. Call me in the morning or just come by. I'll be up by six." Silence crackled on the line, then, "And, Jenna, please don't tell anyone I called."

I saved the message. A dreadful howl sounded from the porch, and I hurriedly opened the door. Mr. Persi shot in. Not long after I had allowed him into my house to stay, I solved the mystery of that first night's episode of horrible howling on the porch. The dog was highly attuned to sirens. Even when I couldn't hear them, he could. And they apparently inspired him to mock them. "You ambulance chaser, you," I grumbled as he padded down the hall to go back to bed.

Twenty minutes later, I'd showered and dressed. Carly, still dead to the world in Animal Kingdom, burrowed deeper into her pillow. I knew she'd be mad at me for not waking her, but if I let her go with me, Brendan might clam up. Not a chance I could afford to take. I scrawled a quick message explaining my departure and ended with—

If you don't hear from me by seven, come after me. And bring the cavalry.
Love, Jenna

I quietly set the alarm clock for 7:00 a.m. and put the note on my pillow.

In the garage, reality hit me. My wonderful old Volvo, my faithful friend since I bought it my first year of teaching, was now a totaled heap in a junkyard somewhere. I glanced at Carly's van. She wouldn't mind my borrowing it, once she got over being mad at me for going without her. But then she'd be stuck without a ride if she needed to come get me. The bicycle on the wall rack caught my eye. My body, still bruised from the car accident, flinched at the idea. *C'mon, Jenna, you can do it.* Brendan's house was less than two miles, especially if I cut through the park.

Visions of Hank lying motionless behind a bush flashed through my mind. On second thought, maybe going through the park before daylight was a bad idea. It wouldn't save me over five minutes.

I stretched my sore muscles for a minute then climbed gingerly onto the bike and pedaled down the dark road. The streetlamps lent an eerie glow to the neighborhood street. Not a soul in sight.

When I turned onto Liberty Road, I paused with my feet still on the pedals for a second. If Brendan turned out to be the murderer, I'd have no neighbor to yell for. Instead of next door to each other, houses were half a mile apart out here. Some, like the mayor's, were mansions, while others, like the up-and-coming pharmacist's, were more modest. I put all my energy into pedaling. An early riser had been burning leaves or something, and the acrid smell of smoke wafted to me.

Carly would wake up in less than an hour and come right over with the cavalry if I didn't call her first. If Brendan was the killer, which I'd stake my life he wasn't. . . Wait—I actually was staking my life that he wasn't. But if he was, I'd have to stall him until help came. And pray.

Almost there. I pumped hard to get up the last big hill. When I crested it, I tapped my brakes instinctively and gaped at Brendan's house. Or what was left of it, which wasn't much. Two fire trucks on each side of the driveway flanked John's police car. My mind spun as fast as my tires as I coasted down the hill and into the driveway.

John had his back to me, talking to a fireman, but the man motioned to me, and John spun around. "Jenna! What are you doing here?" His florid face was streaked with black, and his eyes looked as though he'd been up all night.

I braked to a skidding stop. "Brendan asked me to come. I needed to talk to him." I stared over his shoulder at the tiny tendrils of smoke curling up from the ashy remains of the house. "Where is he?"

His tired eyes filled with compassion as he put his hand on my shoulder. Oh no. Had the killer gotten to Brendan before I could?

"I'm sorry," John murmured. "He's dead."

My legs buckled. John lowered me to a sitting position on the cold driveway and squatted down beside me.

Hot tears splashed down my cheeks.

"I didn't know you were that close."

I shook my head. "He knew who the murderer was," I croaked, the smell of smoke suddenly choking me. "He wanted to tell me."

"No, Jenna, honey. . ." John smoothed my hair down with his beefy hand as I sobbed against his jacket. "He *was* the murderer. And he wanted to kill you."

18

LAKE VIEW MONITOR

Local Man Dies in Fire

A mysterious fire has apparently claimed the life of Lake View pharmacist Brendan Stiles. Firefighters were called to the residence at 1422 Liberty Road at 3:00 a.m. Saturday morning by an anonymous 911 call. By the time they arrived, the entire house was in flames. No further details are available at this time.

The sky lightened gradually as I sat with my back against a tree, praying about Brendan, praying for Marge, praying for practically the whole town, while I watched the crime scene crew gingerly pick through the coolest part of the ruins. John had gone to greet them and give them instructions, leaving me denying his accusations of Brendan.

"I'll prove it to you in a minute. Stay put!" he'd ordered.

"Jenna! Are you okay?" Carly collapsed beside me, her brightly colored Tweety Bird pajamas morbidly incongruous with the scene, her face blotchy and red. Tears streaked down her cheeks.

"Oh, Carly!" I fell against her. "I'm so sorry." I motioned toward the ruins. "I forgot to call you."

"I tried to bring the cavalry, but the desk sergeant said they were already here. Betty felt sorry for me and told me what happened."

"You're in your pajamas." She surely knew it, but I just couldn't grasp the fact that she'd rushed out without getting dressed. I was the sister who did that kind of thing.

"Surely you didn't think I'd take time to dress when the alarm went off at seven and you weren't there."

"I'm sorry," I groaned. "Did Betty tell you that Brendan's dead?"

"Yes." She lowered her voice. "And that he's the murderer. She could probably get fired for that, but like I said, I guess she felt sorry for me."

"That part we'll talk about later. John's got some harebrained idea that Brendan meant to kill me this morning, but if that's the case, why did he kill himself and burn his house down?"

She shrugged. "Who knows?"

"Who all did you call while you were driving over here?" I waved weakly at Daddy, who was walking toward us.

"Everyone on speed dial."

A familiar truck squealed to a stop in the driveway just as Daddy got to us. "Is Alex on your speed dial?"

She twisted around and watched as he jumped out of the truck. "'Fraid so."

Daddy hugged us both quickly. "You all right?"

We nodded.

"Let me find out what's going on, girls," he said and strode across the lawn to where John stood.

"That's Daddy. Take-Charge Stafford. Get answers and get 'em now," I said quietly.

"Humph." Carly looked from him to me. "Looks like someone's a chip off the old block."

"You make a habit of slipping out before daylight to go meet murderers?"

I spun around.

Alex's face was a study of puzzlement and pain.

"Only when they invite me."

He pulled me close. "You scared me to death."

"I'm sorry. It made perfect sense at the time." I relaxed for a minute against him then pushed back and looked at him. "Besides, I don't think he's the murderer."

"Then maybe you need to take a look at this." John's gruff voice cut into our conversation. He held out a note sealed in a ziplock bag. "We found this taped to the mailbox," he said grimly.

Alex took it and read aloud, " 'I'm sorry about Hank. It wasn't supposed to happen that way. And tell Jenna I'm sorry for what I almost did to her.'" He looked up at me bleakly. "It's signed 'Brendan Stiles.' "

John looked at the four of us. "This information isn't to leave this circle. Are we clear on that?"

We all nodded.

"The way we figure it, Hank got wind that Brendan was dealing drugs illegally. Hank's autopsy results came in a week or so ago. Turns out a drug overdose was the real cause of his death. The golf club was just an added bonus."

"So naturally that means the pharmacist did it."

John glared at me and waved the plastic bag at me. "When you have a signed confession, it does."

"Well, that's certainly convenient, isn't it?" I asked, and they all turned as one to look at me. "Brendan's dead. And he's the murderer. Oh, and he ran me off the road."

John nodded. "That about sums it up, the best we can figure it."

"Well, maybe you need to start refiguring. Mama always told me that when something looked too good to be true, it probably was." I picked up my bike and sat it up on its wheels. "Murderers don't normally tie themselves up in a neat little bow." I rolled the bicycle over to Alex's truck, leaving them to think whatever they wanted.

"You want a hand with that?" Alex asked.

I scrutinized his face. "You on my side? Or you think I'm crazy?"

"I tend to agree with you, but I think maybe you should use a bit more discretion. Try a little harder not to get yourself killed." He took the bike and put his hand over mine with the same motion. "There are people who'd be extremely disappointed if that happened."

"Like you?" I asked, and relinquished the bike as he lifted it effortlessly into the bed of the truck.

His eyes flickered back to where Daddy and Carly were locked in deep conversation, no doubt debating my sanity. "Among others. But yes, definitely me."

I could see the concern in his eyes. Underneath the banter, Alex needed me to reassure him. He was worried about me. That should have annoyed me, but it didn't.

"I promise, Alex, from now on discretion is my middle name."

"Good." He pulled me gently into his arms. I inhaled his clean soap smell, almost forgetting the horrific scene behind me and the danger that might lie ahead.

❖

Wednesday afternoon, I waited until I knew Amelia was in the pool, then turned to Gail. "I'm going to lunch. See you in an hour."

In the locker room, I slipped into a swimsuit and picked up a towel. At least three times a week, I swam in the mornings before we opened, but usually I avoided the pool during normal business hours. Too many people gawking to see if I ever had a chance at the Olympic gold.

I breathed a prayer of thanks when I entered the pool area. Other than Amelia swimming laps and a young mother with two little girls splashing in the far corner kiddie pool, the place was deserted.

I dove in on the opposite side from Amelia and swam a little underwater. *Discreet. Discreet.* I said the word over and over in my mind with each stroke. *Lord, please give me a natural opening.*

I surfaced and glanced around. No Amelia. Had she slipped out while I was swimming?

"Looks like someone's feeling better."

I turned, and she was perched on the side of the pool, her lemon yellow bikini showing off her trim figure.

I wiped the water from my face with one hand. "Amelia. Hi." Not brilliant. But discreet.

"Hi." Her makeup was apparently waterproof and quite possibly bulletproof. Other than her slicked-back hair, she looked as if she were ready to go out. "Glad you made it out of the hospital."

"Yeah, me, too."

"I'm sorry about Brendan." She actually looked uncomfortable. "I hope that wasn't too painful for you."

"Actually, in spite of what you thought at the hospital, we weren't involved."

She nodded. "Oh. Good. I found it hard to believe you were. Even before we found out he killed Hank, he didn't seem your type."

A shriek from the kiddie pool drew our attention. The two little girls in their ruffled two-piece bathing suits were pulling on a blow-up doughnut. "Mine! Mine!" they screamed in chorus.

Amelia rolled her eyes. "Some people need to learn to control their children."

"Well, you know sisters...," I said. "They don't always treat each other the best." The old me would have said something about not mentioning birthdays, but the new discreet me just left it at that.

"You wouldn't let anyone come between you and your sister, would you?"

I shook my head. "Not if I could help it." Who did she mean specifically? Hank? Or Byron? Or both?

To my amazement, a genuine smile broke across Amelia's face. "You're a scrapper, aren't you?"

I didn't know how to answer. Was I? And if I was, should I admit it?

"I like that about you, Jenna. A lot of people think you've settled, giving up on the Olympics then quitting teaching. Moving back home to work here." She waved a well-manicured hand at the pool area. "But I have a feeling about you. You're just preparing. Regrouping. When the time comes for you to decide your future, you'll know what to do."

I nodded. Had Obi-Wan Kenobi disguised himself as Amelia Stanton? Her words sounded like a fortune-cookie message, but oddly enough, I was touched. "Thanks, Amelia."

"Don't thank me. I know all about regrouping."

Discreet. "Really?"

"Yes." She slipped off the rim of the pool and into the water, then swam to the other side. I had little choice but to go back to swimming myself. Apparently along with discretion came baby steps and patience.

121

❖

I was alone in the locker room, tying my shoelaces, when she came in. Faced with now or never, I kicked my newfound diplomacy out the door. "I understand you and Byron have an alibi for Hank's murder."

Her laughter trilled through the air, and she pointed at me. "I was right about you. I knew I was." She whirled the combination lock on her locker. "What difference does it make? Everybody knows Brendan Stiles was the killer. Even though he wasn't your boyfriend, that was still a shock, wasn't it?"

"Mm-hmm."

She looked at me. "You don't think he did it?"

I shrugged. "I don't know."

"Byron and I have already given our alibis to John."

"Oh?"

Her smile faded, and her eyebrows knitted together. "Leave it alone, Jenna."

"I'm a scrapper, remember?"

"That's good. To an extent. But you need to learn to mind your own business, before you get hurt. . .or worse." She snatched up her clothes and her towel and sashayed toward the shower without another word.

I sat on the bench for a minute longer thinking about what she'd said. Those words sounded strangely familiar. What big secret were the mayor of Lake View and his charming first lady hiding? And more importantly, had Amelia just threatened to kill me?

19

LAKE VIEW MONITOR

Advertisement

Honest Larry's Car Sales

When you buy from Honest Larry, you get the best car for the best price. Our name says it all. Enjoy all the benefits of a late-model car without the high cost. If Honest Larry sells it, it's got to be good. Honest!

During my Friday inspection of the weight room equipment, my cell phone vibrated. A text message from Alex appeared on the screen. WANT TO GO CAR SHOPPING THIS AFTERNOON? A smile tilted my lips. Those words might not seem romantic to most people, but only someone who cared about me would realize how tired I was of driving Mama's Buick and how much I needed my own wheels.

SURE, I typed back. PICK ME UP AT 4:30 AT HOME, OKAY?

SEE YOU THEN.

With a lighter spirit, I went back to my inspection.

Bob stuck his head in. "Jenna, can we talk in the office for a few minutes?"

I'd been trying to have a private conversation with him ever since he got back from his cruise, but he'd avoided me like I was a persistent telemarketer. Now *he* wanted to talk to *me*?

In the office, he took one of the two chairs beside our desks and motioned me to the other. A good sign? If he'd wanted to make me feel inferior, he'd have surely sat in his own big leather chair and put me across from him in the job applicant chair. Maybe he was finally ready to treat me as an equal and sell me the business.

"The thing is. . ." He cleared his throat. "You know I've talked about selling the business."

Yes, you've talked about selling the business to me. *How could I not know?* I wanted to scream. But Mama always said you caught more flies with honey than vinegar. So I just said, "Yes, sir?"

123

He studied the chair arm and picked a loose thread from between his fingers. "I still want to sell it."

Okay, good. And?

"Remember my daughter, Lisa?"

I nodded. She'd been behind me in school, but while we were in college, she'd married a very wealthy older man. I hardly ever saw her, but I'd been by their house a few times, a big mansion with black wrought-iron gates, not too far from town. According to Bob, she did all of her business in Little Rock or Memphis. I'd often wondered why they even settled here, but that wasn't something you could just ask.

"She's"—he cleared his throat again and picked harder at the thread—"having some trouble."

"Trouble? Is it her health?" He looked positively gray.

"Marriage trouble," he whispered. "She's moved back home with Wilma and me."

"Oh. I'm sorry."

"Me, too." Bob shook his head. "The thing is. . .she wants to work here."

"Work here?" What little I remembered of Lisa made Amelia look like Ellie Mae Clampett.

He nodded. "She needs something to do. A chance to get out of the house for a while. I was hoping you might train her to do your job, take her under your wing. Just until she gets her bearings."

"My job?" I'd become a parrot, but this conversation couldn't have been further from what I'd expected.

He looked at my face, no doubt seeing the shock there. "Oh, she won't be taking your job. I just want her to know a little more about the family business."

"The family business?" Polly want a cracker? I could surely do better than that. "Correct me if I'm wrong, Bob, but didn't you promise to sell me this business?"

"Sure did, sure did. And I still will if you'll just hang with me. But in the meantime, this will keep Lisa busy. Give her a chance to feel good about herself." He winked at me. Actually winked at me. "When she's back on her feet, then we'll get your name on the deed to this place." He stood.

I jumped up. "Bob, I—"

I don't know what I was going to say. Probably something closer to vinegar than to honey. But before I could speak, he said, "I know you're in a hurry to buy this place. And I aim to see that happen. But just to show you that I mean what I say, I'm giving you a raise effective Monday."

"A raise?" If he thought that raising my barely-above-poverty wage fifty cents more would make everything okay, he'd totally lost it.

He named a figure.

"Could you repeat that?"

He did, and I sat back down. The bottom line—he'd just raised my income level to that of my former teaching salary. I remembered what I told John the day of Brendan's fire—*If something looks too good to be true. . .*" "Why would you do this?"

"You keep things going around here. And I use your name for advertising. That brings in a lot of business." He cleared his throat again and avoided my eyes. "Plus, I know you'll be real good to Lisa, and I want you to know in advance how much I appreciate that."

Oh brother. She must be even worse than I remembered if he was willing to cut into his profits to bribe me to be nice to her. But what could I say? I needed a new car.

❖

I'd just climbed into Alex's truck when my cell phone rang. I glanced at the caller ID and shot Alex an apologetic glance. "Sorry, I'd better get this. I don't know who it is, but it's a local number. Hello?"

"Jenna?" An unfamiliar female voice came over the line.

"Yes?"

"This is Debbie. Over at the diner?"

"Oh, hi, Debbie." I immediately felt guilty that I was with Alex. When she'd asked me about him at the diner, I *hadn't* been dating him. "What's up?"

"Remember how you asked me to call if I heard anything or remembered anything about Hank?" Her voice was low.

"Yes?"

"I know everybody's saying Brendan is the murderer, but are you still interested in information?" she whispered.

"Definitely. Tell me." I strained to listen.

"Today at lunch, I was carrying food to the Stantons' table. The mayor and his wife had their heads together, and before they knew I was there, I heard her say, 'Thought it would be over after Hank was out of the picture.' Then she said something so low I couldn't hear, but she finished with, 'Jenna Stafford nosing around.'"

I heard muffled voices in the background; then Debbie hollered, "Be right there!" And in a quieter tone to me, "I've got to go."

"Thanks," I said to a dead line.

As Alex and I drove into town, I told him word for word what Debbie had said.

"You think they did it?"

"A Bonnie and Clyde type deal?" I mused. "I don't know. They strike me more like Barbie and Ken."

He snorted. "Barbie and Ken? The dolls?"

"Yep." I thought of Amelia yesterday, sitting on the poolside, her makeup perfect. "Sort of plastic. But not necessarily all bad."

"Oh, something I've been meaning to tell you. . ."

"Yeah?" His voice sounded so serious that I dreaded hearing his words.

He waited until we rolled to a stop at the red light then turned to look at me. "I didn't say this the other day. But I'm sorry about Brendan. Since you dated him, I mean."

"Thanks. We weren't very close, but I appreciate it." I traced the *J* on my purse with my finger. "But I'm afraid he was killed because he was about to tell me who murdered Hank. I hate feeling like I'm somehow responsible."

He reached across the seat and took my hand in his. "Is that why you quit teaching?"

My gaze slid to his face. "You heard about that, huh?"

"Yeah, but I'd rather hear it from you." He caressed my skin with his thumb. "If you want to tell me about it." The light changed, and he let go of my hand. I felt the loss.

"One of my students had an undiagnosed heart valve problem. We were doing some simple calisthenics. Nothing strenuous. But his heart stopped." I pushed my hair back from my face and looked up at the truck ceiling, trying not to see fifteen-year-old Colton lying lifeless on the gym floor. "I did CPR until the paramedics arrived." Memories of never-ending compressions and breaths flooded over me. "He didn't make it."

Alex pulled into the first car lot and parked. "Jenna, I'm sorry that happened. But you weren't responsible."

"I know. At first. . .maybe I thought that. I was mixed up, mad at God, madder at myself. But I found a good Christian counselor, and that helped a lot. Logically, I know his death wasn't my fault."

He got out of the truck and ran around to get my door. When I was on my feet, he hugged me. "I'm proud of you for getting past that. I can't believe how strong you are."

I laughed. "Just wait until you get to know me better."

"I can't wait." He dropped a quick kiss on my mouth. "But for now, let's get you some wheels."

Unfortunately, that was harder than it sounded. After perusing several different car lots, we both were exhausted by the time we got to Honest Larry's Car Sales. "You sure you want to stop here?" Alex asked as we pulled in.

"Because of the name?" I shrugged. "Dad says he is an honest car dealer." I gave him a rueful grin. "Besides, we've looked everywhere else in town."

He raised an eyebrow. "And the fact that you're practically drooling over that silver Mustang out front has nothing to do with it, right?"

"Hey, cut a girl some slack, okay?"

He shook his head. "Gotta keep you on your toes."

Amazing how easily we'd gotten back into our old banter. He kept me on my toes all right. Every time I thought of him, my feet barely touched the floor. But I wasn't ready to tell him that yet.

Honest Larry walked out to meet us. We exchanged pleasantries with him, and I glanced around at the cars. The silver Mustang made all the others in the lot look like scrap metal. I'd bought my first car for safety, same reason I'd taken the teaching job. Now I was finally ready to step out on faith a little bit, take a chance. The Mustang was a step.

"Wanna drive her?"

"Hmm?" I looked at Larry. He and Alex were both watching me.

"What? The Mustang?" I smiled, trying hard for nonchalant, but I could tell by Alex's knowing grin I'd missed the mark. "Sure, I'll take her for a spin."

Less than two hours later, I drove away happy in my new-to-me silver Mustang.

Lake View Monitor

Support Your Local Mayor Fund-Raiser

A fund-raiser for Mayor Stanton's reelection fund will be held on Saturday, October 19, at the Main Street Park from 10 a.m. until 6 p.m. Mayor Stanton and his lovely wife, Amelia, will be on hand to meet everyone. Mayor Stanton will answer questions and discuss his views on issues of importance to Lake View. The Breckenridge Boys, a local band, will provide entertainment.

> *Come meet the mayor, listen to good music, and enjoy all the BBQ you can eat!*

I tucked my legs up under me on the couch and looked at the letter again.

Dear Pru,

> *My house is a mess, my kids are rude, and my husband doesn't appreciate me. But today for a few minutes, we were outside raking leaves and the love was as tangible as the cold rake handle. Should I take advantage of those times to talk about how awful it is the rest of the time? Or just leave well enough alone?*

Unsure

After we'd gotten the car, Alex had left his truck at my house and followed me over to Mama and Daddy's in Mama's Buick. Everyone ran out to see my new car, and we'd all teased Zac mercilessly for asking first thing if he could borrow it. When Alex and I were leaving, my parents and Carly and her kids stood on the big front porch for a few minutes, laughing and talking, enjoying one of those simple times that you want to freeze and replay over and over. I'd leaned against the porch rail and silently thanked God for the love He'd given us all.

I thought of that as I penned my reply:

Dear Unsure,

> *Sometimes, even in the midst of chaos, you have to grab little*

*moments of peace and happiness wherever you can get them. I'd find a
blank-slate time, like first thing in the morning, to discuss your problems.
Let life's joys be spontaneous and unhampered. Peace to you and yours.*

I picked up another letter. I'd started with an easy one, but they seemed
a little more difficult to answer this week. Maybe my mind was just too distracted. I reached for the folder of archive letters I'd brought home the first
week. A refresher in how the preceding Dear Prus answered might help. I
flipped through the questions and snappy answers. Snappy was cute, but sometimes it was too close to snippy. Besides, I wanted to develop my own style.

I started to close the folder when the bright yellow brochure that Carly
and I had seen earlier caught my attention. I picked it up.

Makeover for Couples!

*Two-for-One Special at the Luxury Spa in Memphis
Thursday, September 5, through Sunday, September 8!*

*Surprise your Special Someone with a spa weekend featuring Botox and
collagen injections in the privacy of your Luxury suite with your own
personal attendant.*

 *Tanning beds, permanent makeup, and elimination of spider veins
and unsightly age spots included.*

 *No need to grow old together gracefully when you can stay young for
each other forever.*

Something bothered me about that brochure. I just couldn't put my finger
on it. The dates were long past. I glanced at them again. Actually, the dates
included the day Hank was murdered. Had Hank considered doing this with
Marge and then not gone through with it? If he had, it might have saved his
life. Somehow I couldn't imagine him and Marge with tautly stretched skin
and full-lipped smiles. That was more up Byron and Amelia's alley.

Of course. Their stiff smiles at the funeral. Amelia's perfect makeup. My
thought that they were plastic. They must have been doing little procedures
here and there for a long time. Even Hank's upcoming editorial about the
mayor being up to his eyebrows in something was a clue. I touched the brochure. Hank must have figured out they were going and intended to rat them
out in the paper when they returned.

It wasn't worth killing someone to keep a few beauty secrets, though.
Then it hit me. This wasn't the motive. This was their alibi. And I knew John
well enough to know he'd checked their story out thoroughly. If I could

verify I was right, I could mark them off the suspect list and narrow the field considerably.

I glanced at the clock. Almost nine on a Friday night. John and Denise might have already put the kids to bed, but they'd still be up. I could call. Or I could just drop by and show them my new car. A lame excuse maybe, but at least it was an excuse.

Before I could change my mind, I sped down Liberty Road, past the ruins of Brendan's house, and peered through the darkness at the hulking shell. This case seemed to have more questions than answers.

At John and Denise's, I pulled into the driveway and ran up to the door before I changed my mind.

Denise answered the door. "Jenna, it's good to see you." She hugged me. "Come in."

"I wanted to show y'all my new car."

She clapped her hands together. "Oh, goody! We were finishing up the dishes, but that sounds like loads more fun. John!" she called over her shoulder. "Come see Jenna's new car!"

John actually had a dishcloth in his hand when he came to the kitchen door. Seeing him at home, out of uniform, made me realize how much I'd hated being on the outs with him. "Hey, John, how's it going?"

"Fine. What's this about a new car?"

I shrugged. "Well, it's new to me. Y'all want to come out and see it?"

We walked together out to the car, where I'd conveniently parked under a streetlight. They oohed and aahed over it and patted me on the back. When we got back to the house, Denise turned to me. "Wanna come in for a while?"

"Sure." They were bound to be wondering why I was here. As soon as we got in the foyer, I said, "John, I just wanted to talk to you about Byron and Amelia's alibi."

"Jenna?" John rubbed his hand down his face. "You know I can't answer any questions about that. I've told you a thousand times to butt out. Mind. Your. Own. Business." All of John's words seemed to start with capital letters these days.

"John," Denise gasped. "You can't talk to Jenna that way. You'll hurt her feelings."

"I don't have any questions. I have an answer." I shoved the Luxury Spa brochure into his unwilling hand.

One look at his face was enough to know I'd guessed right. Amelia and Byron had been living in the lap of Luxury the day Hank died.

21

Lake View Monitor

Crime Stoppers Neighborhood Watch

In light of recent happenings, the citizens of Lake View have started a Neighborhood Watch program. For more information or to start a group in your neighborhood, call Debbie at (870) 555-3111.

If Carly had known I'd even considered that Marge might be the murderer, she'd never have agreed to keep Lois occupied while I went to see the widow. But during my sleepless night after I left John and Denise's, my mind had run the gamut of theories. Maybe Hank was killed because of a land deal gone bad or so Marge could collect the insurance. Then I'd thought about Brendan. The only thing I could see that tied the two murder victims together was the pills. It just made sense to see what Marge could tell me about whatever story Hank was doing.

We split up with a plan. Carly would go visit Lois and keep her from showing up at Marge's. My smart-thinking sister even called ahead to make sure Lois stayed home. I, on the other hand, wanted the element of surprise on my side when I confronted Marge.

So I pulled into Marge's driveway, killed my motor, slipped quietly up to the door, and rang the doorbell. I wasn't going to break in. But as I stood on the porch, I had that feeling of déjà vu all over again. Hopefully the old saying about the third time being a charm was true.

"Jenna, honey, come in!" She looked genuinely happy to see me. Would she still be glad after she figured out why I was there?

"Hi, Marge. I just wanted to stop by and check on you." *See if maybe you killed your husband.* My throat was so dry I could hardly get my words out.

"I'm glad you did. I'm doing so much better. Come on in and have a seat."

I followed her into the living room and sat down again on the chintz sofa. "You look like you are feeling better."

"I really am."

"I have a question."

"About Dear Pru?"

Her words jarred loose another wild theory I'd had in the night. "Well, I do have a question about Dear Pru, actually. Is it possible that whoever was Dear Pru before me might have been angry enough about getting fired to kill Hank?"

"Oh my, no." Marge shook her head. "Why would you ask?"

"Well, it just seemed odd, him getting killed so soon after the turnover of Dear Pru. The police thought Zac was a suspect because Hank fired him. I just thought maybe this person might be a suspect, too."

"Definitely not."

"In that case, I'll get to the real question I wanted to ask."

"What is it, dear?"

"When I was at the newspaper, I found some pill bottles in a bag. They had women's names on them." She didn't say anything, and I wasn't sure if it was my imagination or if she'd gone a shade whiter. "Those names I asked you and Lois about at church the other day, remember?"

Marge's face crumpled. I'd hoped for some kind of reaction—an eyelid twitch, a facial tic, but I'd never expected this. She looked up at me, tears tracing through the wrinkle tracks of her face. "You know, don't you?"

"Know? About what?"

"About my problem."

Her problem? Her problem. Of course. I should have seen it earlier. Marge was an addict. "I'm sorry." I patted her on the back.

She shook her head and snatched a tissue from the box next to her. "I don't care, I don't care. I was terrified Hank would find out. But he did anyway right before he died." She blew her nose loudly. "I'd have checked into rehab after that, but Lois said it would look suspicious. She was worried that the police would arrest me because I didn't have an alibi."

"What about Lois's stomach bug?"

"Truth is—I was passed out from the drugs. That's why I didn't know Hank wasn't home. Lois made the other up to protect me."

"She's a good friend."

"Yes, she is. She cared for me after my back surgery, and when the pain was so bad, she understood that I had to have my pills. Since then, she's tried everything to help me quit the drugs, but I couldn't."

"Are you still using?" I asked quietly.

She shook her head. "I took myself off cold turkey after the funeral. It almost killed me."

I remembered the haunted look in her eyes on my second visit when she'd said she'd rather live with the pain than lose herself. She'd been speaking from hard experience. "I'm sorry," I told her. I paused for a few seconds. "So who were the women whose names were on the bottles?"

"Oh, they weren't real people. After my prescription ran out, Lois talked Brendan into selling me pills under fake names. Just until I could quit."

"I guess Hank was pretty mad at Brendan when he found out."

Marge nodded. "Listen, if Hank hadn't been dead when Brendan died, I'd have thought Hank killed him. That's how mad he was."

I stood and hugged her. "I'm glad you got it under control, Marge. I'll be praying you keep getting better."

"Thank you, Jenna. I'll be praying you get the answers you're looking for, too."

"Thanks."

As soon as I was in the car, I called Carly's cell phone. No answer. I wanted to ask Lois some questions anyway, so I headed in that direction. As I drove along the river road, I glanced out at the sparkling water down below. Saturdays should be spent kayaking or fishing, not interrogating sweet elderly women so I could find a murderer.

I breathed a prayer of thanks that Marge had broken free from the drug habit. It would have been so much easier on her if she'd only gotten help. I could understand her not wanting to while Hank was alive in case he found out, but it looked like Lois would have insisted after his death. If Marge had been honest with John about her alibi, he'd have understood.

I turned down the little lane that led to Lois's riverfront house. The alibi. It hadn't only been Marge's alibi; it had been Lois's, as well. Unless I missed my guess, Lois had hated Hank. He'd been talking to Brendan about the drugs. No doubt he'd discovered that Lois had gotten Marge the pills from Brendan. My mind whirled like the river currents below. According to Marge, Lois was the main one who dealt with Brendan. Had she dealt with him permanently?

This was my most unbelievable scenario yet, but what if I was right and Carly was entertaining a murderer? Carly's van loomed ahead in Lois's driveway. I picked up my phone and punched in Carly's number again. No answer. I hesitated then dialed John.

"John? It's Jenna." I started telling him about Marge and Lois, but he interrupted me.

"Jenna, I'm worried about you. I think maybe you should get some counseling."

"I—" The line was dead. I punched in 9-1 then stopped. Was I prepared to go into an innocent woman's house and have it surrounded by police within minutes? Did I really want to face that kind of humiliation?

I hit the END button on my phone and climbed out of the car, praying as

I walked up to the house. Carly's old van was parked in the driveway. And the front door was open. I could hear voices through the screen door. Suddenly Lois stepped onto the porch. "Jenna, come in, come in. I'm so glad to see you." She looked so innocent in her polyester slacks and oversized cardigan. Like everybody's grandma. But something in her eyes wasn't right.

I froze and weighed my choices. Run as fast as I could in the opposite direction or go in and join Carly in the black widow's web. Not very good options. But I wasn't about to desert my sister. "Hi, I just thought I'd drop by." I forced a smile that must have looked more like a grimace.

"Actually, I was about to call you. Carly's bored with me, I'm afraid."

When I entered the house, it took a few seconds for my eyes to adjust from the bright sunlight to the dim interior. But there was Carly at the kitchen table, a cup of coffee in front of her. She had her elbow on the tiled surface and her hand under her chin. "Hi, Shenna. Jenna," she mumbled. "Good to shee you." Her eyelids drooped.

I glanced at Lois, who was smiling. "Let me pour you a cup of coffee, dear."

"No, thanks. I just came to get Carly. Emergency at home." I walked over to my sister and nudged her. Her elbow fell out from under her chin, and she barely got it back under her before her face splatted against the table. I wanted to scream.

"I'm sorry to hear there's an emergency." Lois didn't move to stop me, just stood there smiling with her hands in her cardigan pockets.

"Emerg—emergensheee?" Carly slurred the word and shook her head.

"Yeah, Car, we have to get home." I grabbed her arm and tried to pull her up. "Now."

"You have to drink some coffee with me before you go, Jenna," Lois said.

"No, thank you," I said firmly.

Then she raised her hand from her pocket, and I found myself staring down the barrel of a lethal-looking pistol. "I insist." She motioned to the chair next to Carly. "Have a seat."

I sat down at the table. "Is this what you did to Hank? Held a gun on him and made him drink coffee?"

She laughed. "You've been reading too many mysteries if you think you can keep me talking long enough to escape. I'm a librarian, remember?" She plunked a dainty white and blue coffee cup in front of me then leaned in close to me. "I've read them all. There's no way out for you, Jenna. You've asked one too many questions. Even the chief of police thinks you're crazy."

She picked up the pot from the counter and poured my coffee, then kept her eye on me as she brazenly poured some white powder into it. "Drink."

"What's in it?" I eyed a small mound of open capsule containers on the otherwise spotless countertop.

"What difference does it make?"

"I'd rather know what kind of death I'm facing."

"I'm not into rat poison. Just something to make you relax."

Carly's arm gave way, and the weight of her head plopped onto the table-top. I reached for her, but Lois motioned toward the coffee with the gun. "Drink or die now."

I leaned toward Carly anyway and was quiet until I could hear her light snoring. Sitting up straight, I looked at Lois. "I'll drink if you'll tell me why you did it. Surely I deserve to know that much."

She narrowed her eyes as if to gauge my sincerity then nodded. "Take a drink."

I took a swig from the coffee cup and watched with a little satisfaction as her eyes widened. She'd been expecting ladylike sips, no doubt. "So talk."

She sat down across from me, gun above the table, trained on me. "Men are a problem, dear. In a way, I'm doing you a favor by keeping you from hav-ing to deal with them anymore."

"You'll forgive me if I don't thank you," I murmured, fury warring with pure fear inside my chest.

She laughed. "I learned early enough that when you have a problem with men, you have to get rid of them. It worked with my dad and then with my husband. Marge is the only one who ever understood me."

The woman was stark-raving mad. And the fact that John would feel terribly guilty at my and Carly's double funeral gave me no comfort at all. I looked around the room for a sharp object, even a blunt object. If I could distract her for a second. . .

"Take another drink." She was staring at me intently. No doubt she knew exactly what I was thinking. I picked up the cup and drank. Black coffee. Yuck. But whatever she'd put in it was tasteless.

"Did Hank know the coffee was drugged?"

She shook her head. "He had no idea. A nice cup of fresh-brewed coffee—my little way of making it up to him for threatening to keep Marge away from me. The golf club wasn't necessary, but it helped me feel better about his firing me from Dear Pru."

I gasped.

She laughed. "You didn't guess? See? I was good at it. If the golf pro hadn't been such a big baby. . ." She shook her head and clucked her tongue. "Hank had to die."

"What about Brendan?"

She looked at me and tilted her head.

I faked a yawn and was rewarded with a big smile from her. "How'd you get him to drink coffee with you?" My words were slurred. Not too much, but enough to buy me some time.

"I thought Brendan was different at first. One of those rare good men. He didn't seem to have a problem helping Marge with her pain medicine as long as the payments kept coming. But then he started figuring things out after Hank's death. And you kept asking questions. So I held a gun on him and he wrote the note, then drank his coffee just like you are." Her smile was gone. "Only he went out fast like your sister."

I shuddered and looked at Carly's cup. Hers was barely touched. Mine was half gone. How much more could I take?

"It was painless. He was unconscious when the fire started. Take another drink." Her voice had changed and the smile was gone. Should I pretend to pass out on the table? Or was her idea of painless death to knock us out with drugs then put a bullet through our skulls? I couldn't chance it.

I reached for my cup but missed on purpose and yawned again.

She pushed to her feet. "Good. It's finally kicking in." She waved the gun at me, and I braced myself for the shot. "Come on and help me with your sister while you can still stand."

She put one arm under Carly's, but I remained seated. No need to make it easy for her.

The gun barrel shifted to Carly. "She's deadweight anyway. Doesn't matter to me if she's just plain dead. Nobody will notice the gunshot by the time her body washes to shore."

I stood quickly but then remembered the drugs should be affecting me. I moved to Carly's other side, stumbling as I went. "To shore?" I asked, slurring the words.

"Yeah, you're going to have another little car accident. Only this time your dear sister is going to drive you into the river." She heaved Carly up, and I helped. Our chances of getting away would surely be better outside. And had she forgotten I was a swimmer? It would be tough, but I had a better-than-average chance of rescuing us. *If* the pills didn't kick in.

I knew from past experience that when the pills took effect, it would happen all at once. In my mind, I kept a stream of prayers going up, asking for that moment not to be too soon. Carly had conveniently parked the van facing straight toward the river bluff. Nothing would stop two sleepy sisters from plunging to their death. And how long would it be before anyone even knew we were missing?

Too soon we were at the van, and Lois leaned Carly against the side and opened the driver's door.

"Lois!"

Startled, Lois turned. Marge stood there in the driveway. I threw myself against Lois. Her gun went flying, and she tumbled to the ground with Carly and me in her wake. Thankfully, Lois landed on bottom. I looked up to see Marge holding the gun.

Lois scrambled to her feet, knocking Carly and me into the grass. "What are you going to do? Shoot me?" she taunted Marge.

"Try me," Marge said grimly. "Just try me."

Lois's eyes widened. "Hank was going to keep us apart. He was so mad at me for helping you get pills. He said I'd never see you again."

"I wouldn't have let that happen." Tears trickled down Marge's face, but the gun in her hand never wavered.

"I did it for you, Marge. I did it all for you."

Sirens sounded in the distance.

"Save it for the judge," Marge said then looked down at me. "You all right, honey?"

"I'm sheep—sleepy." I fought to get up but couldn't lift my head.

"It's too late for her. She's had enough roofies to kill a horse." Lois laughed. "At least I'll have the satisfaction of knowing I took care of Miss Nosy before they got me."

The world was fading to black, but I had time to breathe one more prayer. *Dear God, please let her be wrong.*

22

LAKE VIEW MONITOR

Help Wanted

Lake View Library seeks stable, easygoing librarian to fill immediate opening. Send your résumé ASAP to P.O. Box 183338, Lake View, AR 72001.

Beyond the intense beam of light, everything was white. I could hear. . . singing? No. More monotonous. *Beep. Beep.*

A cool hand touched my forehead. If I could just keep my eyes open long enough to focus.

"She's waking up." Mama sounded happy.

My dad's face floated in front of me. "Jenna, Jenna, honey, how do you feel?"

"Are you in heaven with me?" Even to me, my voice sounded strange.

"Honey, you're in the hospital, not in heaven." Mama's laugh sounded like a sob.

"Hospital?" That explained the tiredness.

She looked at Daddy. "Do you want to go out and tell the others she's awake?"

He nodded then gave me a big hug. Then right there at my bedside, my quiet dad took my hand and closed his eyes. "Dear Lord, thank You so much for giving us our baby back." When he opened his eyes, tears were glistening there.

Whatever happened to me, I must have been at death's door. After he went out, I said as much to Mama, who was bustling around, getting me some clothes to put on and laying out my toothbrush and toothpaste.

"We had some scary times, sweetie. The whole church family has been praying for you around the clock, though."

"What happened to me?"

She walked over to my bedside and used the arrows to raise me to a sitting position. "How much do you remember?"

Remembering was a strain, but the events of that Saturday came back to me slowly. "Lois drugged me."

Mama nodded.

"And Carly!" I looked around the room. "Where's Carly? Is she okay?" I threw the covers back and started to swing my legs down.

"Wait, wait!" Mama put her hand on my legs. "Carly's fine. She slept for about twelve hours and woke up. You've been out of it for three days. But Carly has no memory of anything once she got to Lois's."

Relief sapped me of any desire to get up. I sank back against the mattress. "Why do I remember?"

"We didn't know if you would or not. Your reaction to this drug isn't typical." Her smile was watery. "But then, you've never been typical." She nodded toward the hairbrush on the bedside table. "A lot of people want to see you. Why don't we get you freshened up a little?"

Why don't we not and say we did? All I really wanted to do was just go back to sleep.

"Alex is in the hall, waiting his turn to come in."

In that case. . . I slid my legs around again, and this time she let me.

A few minutes later, my breath minty fresh, I sat in the blue vinyl chair next to the bed while Mama brushed my hair. "Your daddy and I have been so worried. Jenna Marie, promise me you won't ever pull a stunt like this again. Confronting that crazy woman. And it's not enough that you go, but to get Carly to go, too! You girls could've been killed!" When she noticed the tears streaming down my cheeks, she stopped. She buried her face in my hair and wrapped her arms around me. "Jenna, honey, you girls are our lives. If we lost you. . .well, it's just unthinkable. I didn't mean to upset you; I'm just so thankful you're okay."

I twisted around to meet her hug. I felt so safe in Mama's arms. But, I guess partly because of the lingering effects of the drug, I couldn't stop crying. Face buried in Mama's shoulder, I mourned everything, from losing the Olympics to losing Colton. And for misplacing Alex. I cried for my inadequacies. I had messed up enough for someone twice my age. When I thought of what a blessing it was to have a Father in heaven who forgave my inadequacies, in addition to earthly parents who loved me for who I was, I cried some more. After the tears were gone, I pushed back and patted Mama's soggy shoulder. "Sorry."

"This old thing?" She motioned toward her turquoise blouse. "Don't give it another thought. Do you feel better?"

I nodded. I really did. "Think I've got time for a shower?"

"You've got all the time in the world, honey." That was good to know. I looked forward to heaven. But I was happy living the life on earth God had planned for me. Including the twists and turns.

After my shower, Mama settled me back into the blue chair.

"Knock, knock." I looked up to see Alex standing in the door, unshaven and wrinkled but, I had no doubt, still the best-looking man in the hospital.

"Hey."

"Hey, water girl." He dropped a light kiss on my brow. I hurried to unpucker my lips before he saw me. *Somebody let me out of the hospital!* We were regressing. "How you doing?"

"I'm doing okay. Slowly putting the pieces together."

He took my hand. "We thought we were going to lose you for a while there."

I reached up with my other hand and rubbed the stubble on his cheek. "Have you been staying here?"

"Yes." He shrugged. "They had to sneak me into ICU." He shot me a wry grin. "Since we don't have an official relationship."

"Leave it to a lawyer to worry about legalities. Official or not, I missed you."

In my mind, I interrogated him. *Counselor Campbell, did you mean you want an official relationship with the patient? Or not? If so, what constitutes an official relationship in your mind?*

"Jenna? Did you hear me?"

I looked up to see a worried look in Alex's eyes.

"Sorry. I was just thinking. What did you say?"

"I said I missed you, too." He bent down and hugged me as if I were made of spun glass. Yes, it was definitely time to check out of the hospital. "I'd better go and let the others come in."

I reluctantly let go of his hand.

Carly was my next visitor. When I told her all the things Lois had said, she was disappointed that she'd slept through it. "I barely remember that Saturday at all," she said, shaking her head.

"Car?" I threaded my fingers through hers.

"Yeah?"

"I'm sorry for getting you into this mess."

She laughed. "Are you kidding me? I wouldn't have missed it for anything." She squeezed my hand. "You bring out the best in me, kiddo. I can't believe I was brave enough to help solve a murder."

"I couldn't have done it without you." I looked over her shoulder. "Who's got the twins?"

"Zac's watching them." She smiled. "Here's a news flash. Hayley and Rachel have hardly been fighting at all since Saturday. Something about almost losing us must have made them appreciate a little more what they have."

"I'm so glad, Carly."

"Me, too. Not that I necessarily expect it to last." She hugged me. "I've got to go. Marge has been sitting out there waiting to talk to you ever since Daddy called and told her you woke up."

"Oh, okay." I clutched Carly's arm. "Is she mad at me for ruining her life?"

Carly gave me a you-must-be-crazy look. "Honey, don't develop a phobia about sweet little ladies, okay?" She smiled. "She's not mad at you." She kissed me on the cheek and left me to face Marge alone.

"Jenna, honey. I'm so sorry." Marge hugged me, tears streaming. "Are you sure you're okay?"

"I'm okay. And I'm sorry, too." I patted her back. How could she be thinking of me when she'd gone through so much? "I'm so thankful you showed up at Lois's."

"I couldn't really believe it was true. But I had to find out for myself."

"Marge, this must be awful for you."

"It's been tough. But Amelia and Byron are staying with me a few days."

I must have looked as stunned as I felt, because she actually laughed through the tears.

"She and I are working things out, believe it or not. Come by and see me, and I'll tell you all about it."

"I'll do that." If I hadn't been so tired, I'd have made her tell me right then.

"Thanks, Jenna. I appreciate your getting to the bottom of all this." She hugged me again, in a cloud of spearmint.

I relaxed my head against the chair back and closed my eyes.

"How about a nap?" Mama said from the doorway.

"Sounds good."

She tucked me in and sat down beside me. I drifted off to sleep, safe in the knowledge that, as crazy as this world gets, I have a place in it.

Over the next twenty-four hours, visitors poured in the door, some out of concern, some out of just plain curiosity. Between Mama, Daddy, Alex, and Carly, I hardly had to talk to anyone. They just said, "The police have asked us not to share any details." Bob brought me a box of chocolates, but it didn't take him but a minute to ask me when I could come back to work. To hear him tell it, the place was falling apart without me there.

The king and queen of Lake View stopped by for a short visit. While Byron was talking to Daddy, I asked Amelia about Marge. "Byron and I have been staying with her ever since Lois was arrested. Come by and visit her when you get out." I was dying of curiosity to get to the bottom of that. Guess I hadn't learned my lesson. Let's hope this cat has nine lives.

John and Denise came, with flowers, and I half expected an apology. Instead, I got the usual speech about minding my own business and staying out of police investigations. But when, at the end of the speech, they both hugged me and John said, "I'm so glad you're okay, Jenna," I could tell he really meant it.

He even grudgingly shared some information with me. Lois was spilling her guts to anyone who would listen. Evaluations were under way, but it looked like she might not be mentally competent enough to stand trial. She did say she felt bad about trying to kill Carly, but she apparently had few regrets about "Miss Nosy." If I hadn't had such a close brush with death, I'm pretty sure John would have smiled when he told me that. Before I could remind him that if not for me, a murderer would be walking free, Doc Brown stuck his head in the door, and John and Denise left.

"Young lady, you need to try and stay out of trouble. I don't want to see you back here again for a long time." Doc Brown had been my doctor for as long as I could remember and still talked to me as if I were a child. "It doesn't look like you're going to have any long-lasting effects from those drugs." After shining that bright light in my eyes one more time, he sent me home. "I think you're clear to resume your normal activities." He winked at me. "As long as that doesn't include trying to catch a murderer."

◈

The day after I got home from the hospital, I was on Marge's front porch—again. Grief covered her like a mantle, but along with it was a quiet strength I'd never seen in her. "Oh, Jenna, honey, come in. I'm so glad you came over." I gave her a hug and was relieved to feel her ribs weren't as prominent. Maybe she was slowly getting her life back together, too. "Is Amelia still staying with you?"

"No, she and Byron went back home. They wanted me to move in with them, but I'm not ready to leave my house yet. So many good memories here." She glanced around the living room.

"I'm sure there are." I hoped I sounded comforting, like Mama.

She gestured toward the sofa, and we both sat down. "I blame myself for all of this. If I had only known about Lois's feelings, maybe I could have helped her." Marge's eyes were full of gut-wrenching sadness. "But after my back surgery, I was in such pain. She moved in for a while to help me. Then I got hooked on pain medicine. . . ." She gave me a wry smile.

I could easily imagine Lois subtly encouraging Marge to become dependent on the pain meds, but I saw no purpose in sharing that suspicion with Marge.

"And after that, things were pretty much a blur. I relied on her for everything." She shook her head. "I had no idea her mind was so. . .twisted."

I patted her on the shoulder. "No one could tell anything was wrong. She seemed normal."

"So you and Amelia have worked out your differences?" I didn't want to sound like a gossip buzzard waiting to swoop down, but I just had to know.

She nodded. "After Lois was arrested and I began to realize the depths of her deception, I called Amelia. We had our first heart-to-heart in decades." She patted my hand. "When I tell you this, you'll just have to forgive me for being so gullible. I'd been friends with Lois since childhood. That's my only excuse."

"You trusted her. That's to be expected." I hated to see her feel guilt on top of everything else. She hadn't been to blame.

"When Byron and Amelia were newly married, Lois told Hank and me that Byron had made a pass at her. I know you young people may find it hard to believe, but Lois was a beauty in her day." Marge's voice grew distant, as if she were looking way back into the past. "We were both furious and wanted to tell Amelia, but Lois didn't want to cause trouble in Amelia's marriage. Hank never liked Byron after that, and he didn't want me around him, either."

"I can understand that." Hank may have been cranky, but he had morals.

"Over the next few years, Lois would mention that Byron tried to get her to go away with him for a weekend when he went out of town on business. Or that he tried to get her into a secluded area at a public get-together." Marge shook her head. "Of course I told Hank every time. Eventually Hank would use his power in town to fight Byron on every corner. After that, Hank and Byron were sworn enemies. I wanted to tell Amelia, but she was obviously so much in love with Byron that I was afraid it would destroy her. I kept waiting to hear rumors about him being unfaithful to her, but in all these years I haven't heard a thing." She closed her eyes. "That should have told me something."

"You couldn't have known."

She opened her eyes and looked at me as if she'd forgotten I was there. "It was all lies. Did you know that? Every bit of it. They let me go see Lois the other day, and she couldn't wait to confirm that she'd made the whole thing up. She also bragged that every time it looked like Amelia and I might make up, she'd invent something that she'd heard Amelia said about me."

"Oh, Marge, I'm so sorry." I couldn't imagine losing all those years with Carly. "But you've got each other now."

Marge smiled, a little of the haunted look gone from her eyes. "Yes, we do. And we intend to make the most of that." Amelia was picking her up for lunch in a few minutes, so I hugged her and left, with a promise to visit often.

Marge and Amelia weren't the only ones who were making up for lost time. I had to get ready for a date of my own.

DROP DEAD
DIVA

Who in the world would name a child Holly Wood?" I glanced over at Carly, who was engrossed in her tattered copy of *Holly Wood: The Queen of Country Music.*

For that matter, who in the world would read Holly's autobiography? But I wisely kept my hands on the wheel, my eyes on the hills and curves of the highway before us, and that last question to myself. My older sister, Carly, was a big fan of Holly Wood, country music's female performer of the decade. Especially since Holly was originally from our hometown of Lake View, Arkansas.

Carly looked up from her book and rolled her eyes. "Gracious, Jenna. Everybody knows that story."

My mouth twitched at her exaggerated drawl. We were born and raised in Arkansas, and our native language was definitely "Southern." But Carly's decade in the Deep South—Atlanta—apparently made her a master at the art of all things below the Mason-Dixon Line.

"Not everybody, I guess."

She sighed. "When Holly was born, her parents were worried about sibling jealousy, so they let Ruth, her ten-year-old sister, name her."

I snorted. "Brilliant parenting strategy. They probably read about it in some article written by Dr. I-Give-Child-Rearing-Advice-Even-Though-I've-Never-Actually-Had-Kids. Then they thought it was a great idea, until they were stuck with that ridiculous name."

"You know, that could be considered the pot callin' the kettle black. You offer advice about kids in your Dear Pru column all the time."

I cranked up the air-conditioning one notch. She had a point. Taking over the advice column in our small town's local paper had started out as a way for me to gather information in an amateur murder investigation. But after the murder was solved, I'd found myself reluctant to give up the position. So in addition to my day job as manager of the Lake View Athletic Club,

I moonlighted as sage advice columnist, Dear Pru. And occasionally I did have to answer questions that dealt with raising children.

"True, but I always confer with you about those letters." I nodded toward the backseat where Carly's preteen twins, Hayley and Rachel, were engrossed in a DVD, and her sixteen-year-old son, Zac, was listening to his MP3 player with his eyes closed. Even though her husband had left her for a stick-figure model when she was pregnant with the twins, as far as I was concerned, Carly had done an amazing job of raising the kids alone. "My own personal parenting expert."

Carly followed my gaze. "Yeah, at least I didn't let any of my kids name each other." She tossed me a sideways grin. "Unfortunately, neither did Mama and Daddy. Let's see. I think I was in my Sesame Street stage about the time you were born."

"Oscar the Grouch Stafford? Believe me, I'd have changed it as soon as I was old enough." I crept past the city limit sign behind a long line of traffic. If Marta hadn't been having her grand opening now, I wouldn't have chosen to make this trip in June, but even now during its peak season, I liked to think of Branson, Missouri, as the city that's worth the wait.

"But Holly's *sister* named her," Carly protested. "How could she change it?"

I snorted. I didn't buy that sentimentality. "It still amazes me that anybody would—oh, forget it." Talk about wasted breath.

Carly closed her book. "Forget what?"

My sister and I are different in a lot of ways, but neither one of us will ever let a "forget it" slide. So I knew the discussion wasn't over yet. With my hands still on the steering wheel, I shrugged. "You'd think she'd have used marriage as a way out of a bizarre name, but no. . .five marriages later, she's still Holly Wood."

"Actually, she did take Maurice Seaton's last name the first time they were married, but that was before she was famous. After that, her stage manager thought her career had a better chance if she kept Holly Wood, so when she divorced Maurice and married Carl, the stage manager, she went back to—"

"She's what? Thirty-seven or so? And she's been married five times already? Don't you think that's overkill, even for a celebrity?" I wasn't jealous, but I was thirty and hadn't even been married once. There was a minute there on Valentine's Day when I thought Alex was going to propose, but he was just bending down to tie his shoe. After eight months of dating, I'd finally decided that just as I'd gotten over my commitment issues, he'd apparently developed some.

"Ah, don't be so hard on her, honey," Carly drawled. "She's had a tough time of it. Even back in high school she was all mixed up. I'm prayin' she'll straighten her life up someday."

Back in high school? Back in high school, Carly had barely been on the same planet as Miss Popularity Holly Wood. When Holly had risen to the top of the social ladder at Lake View High in tenth grade, Carly and her best friend, Marta, were impressionable eighth graders.

I was guessing that Holly figured she already had her life about as "straightened up" as it could go. "Who would have dreamed back then that Marta would open her own theater in Branson and Holly would be the opening act?" How many times over the years when we watched the CMA awards had I heard Carly and Marta brag about saving Holly a seat on the bus every day? Of course, they glossed over the fact that neither of them actually ever got to sit with her. She shooed them away as soon as her size-zero designer jeans slid onto the torn vinyl seat.

"You're right, sugar, nobody saw that one coming. Marta and I had a different dream—*we* wanted to be the opening act." Carly laughed. "Even though I had absolutely no talent whatsoever. I guess every teenage girl wants to be a star."

Everyone but me. I just wanted to swim. As a young Olympic star, the attention came as an unwelcome part of the package.

"So Marta sounded pretty desperate on the phone, huh?"

Carly grunted. "Let's just say that Holly's reputation for being difficult must be justly deserved. I've never heard Marta so rattled." She pointed to a road sign, and I obediently turned. "Or so grateful as when I told her you were taking some vacation days and we could come earlier than we planned."

I held up a hand to shade my eyes from the sun glinting off the Branson Country Paradise Theater. I pulled into the circular drive and parked then smirked. "I hope you told her that I hadn't had a vacation since I started working at the club. Just so I don't look like a total flake."

"No worries. She knows how dependable you are. Thanks for throwing some stuff in a suitcase and coming with me so fast."

"I needed a distraction." I slapped my hand on the steering wheel and opened my door. "Let's go meet Holly Wood."

The combination hotel/theater was being remodeled, and even though the work was only half done, it was an impressive plantation-style building. John and Marta were convinced this place was the deal of the century. And since they'd invested their life savings in it, I hoped they were right.

"Cool place." Zac took out his earbuds and stuffed them in his pocket as he climbed out of the backseat.

"And it's not even finished yet," I assured him as we all got out and started walking toward the entrance.

"Wow!" Rachel pointed to the giant guitar beside the gate.

"Wow, what?" Hayley asked. "What's so great about Paul Bunyan's guitar?"

The twins are identical and used to enjoy their "alike" status. But lately, although they still got along, they'd been trying to be as different from each other as possible.

"It's huge," Rachel said defensively as they reached the shadow of it.

"Watch out! I think it's falling," Hayley yelled and dodged out of the way.

Rachel jumped then glared at her sister. "Mom!"

"The drama tweens strike again," Zac muttered as he walked past me into the building.

Carly led the way to the door with the OFFICE sign above it. I spotted Marta's dark no-nonsense haircut across the foyer. She had her back to us, arranging a display case of pamphlets.

"Anybody home?" Carly called.

Marta spun around. "Oh, girl, it's so good to see you." She enfolded Carly in a hug, and the twins wrapped their arms around her, too. In spite of her cheery smile, dark circles shaded the area under her eyes. Whatever the Country Paradise Theater was offering, a good night's sleep must not have been on the program.

We chatted for a few minutes, carefully avoiding the topic of the head-liner act. Finally, Marta motioned toward our bag-laden arms. "Let me show you where you'll be staying." We followed her down a long hallway. "We only have the performer's wing open next to the stage." She glanced back at us and wrinkled her nose. "Holly and her people are taking up most of the available rooms. But we saved one of the larger suites for y'all."

Zac's eyes widened. "Sweet. A suite."

We grinned and Marta glanced at Carly. "No kitchen, though. But we live in a little cottage right behind the Paradise. You can use my kitchen while you're here. I've got it stocked for baking. Just for you."

Carly beamed. "Thanks."

I didn't say anything, but the offer really didn't bode well for our stay. Those of us who know Carly, including Marta, know that she bakes when she gets upset.

Marta unlocked a door. "We aren't opening the rest of the hotel until after the grand opening of the theater. So Holly and her entourage are the only ones here now. And a skeleton staff."

"Thanks for inviting us," I said as we walked into the room, unsure whether she wanted to talk about the reason we were here.

"Oh, don't thank me yet. You'll both earn your keep. That woman has enough demands to keep a small army hopping. You may be sorry you came before it's all over." She hugged us again. "I'm going to leave y'all alone until morning though. We'll get together then and figure out the best plan of attack."

Attack? Sounded like battle lines had been drawn. And she *had* mentioned an army. . . . I let my duffel bag strap slide off my shoulder and put my hands to the small of my back. "Is it okay if I use the pool in the morning?"

Her face fell. "Oh, I'm sorry, Jenna. Our pool isn't ready yet." She brightened. "But I made arrangements for you to swim at the health club down the street. It's just a block away, and they were thrilled to have the great Jenna Stafford as an honored guest." She waved and headed back up to the front office.

Carly dumped her suitcase on the luggage bench. "She means well, Jenna. She just doesn't realize how hard that whole Olympic thing was on you. People who haven't experienced it don't realize fame isn't all it's cracked up to be."

"It's okay." I wished I felt more gracious. It was bad enough that my boss, Bob, had insisted we capitalize on my notoriety as a past Olympic swimmer. But when I wasn't on official business of the Lake View Athletic Club, I tried to forget my brief turn in the spotlight when I was a teen. Maybe if I had a medal to show for it, I'd feel differently. But I'm not sure.

The twins came bursting out of one of the bedrooms. "Awesome room," they sang in chorus and then ran back to their newly discovered play area.

Carly and I shared a look. Simultaneous talking—something we'd always taken for granted with the two of them—hadn't happened much lately. Maybe this trip would restore a little bit of their unique twin-ness.

"Twin beds," I murmured as I glanced in the doorway. "Fitting."

Carly smiled. "Blue and yellow. Their favorite colors. I'll have to thank Marta." She stepped to the door of the second bedroom and motioned to me. Zac was sprawled across the red comforter on his double bed, earbuds stuck in his ears, seemingly dead to the world.

"Is he asleep?" I whispered.

"Who knows?" She closed his door gently. "How about pizza delivered in for supper? Since we're all so tired, I thought we might make it an early night."

"That's the best thing you've said all day."

While we waited for the pizza, we explored the other two rooms. "You can have the one with the Jacuzzi tub in the bathroom," Carly offered. "Since you're part fish."

"I'll take you up on that. But only if you promise to use it anytime you want."

"If you're going to twist my arm, then what choice do I have?" she drawled.

Five minutes later, we met back in the spacious living area. Carly settled into an overstuffed rocker and turned back to her book. "Want me to read some of this aloud? So we'll be better prepared to help?"

I shook my head, probably too quickly. "That's okay. I'll look at it later." Truth was, I'd already learned more about Holly Wood than I'd ever wanted to know. Unless I ended up as a contestant on *Jeopardy* and she was one of the categories. Which could happen, I guess. At least the part about her being a category.

Thirty minutes later, a knock sounded on the door, and I jumped up to look out the peephole. Instead of the pizza deliveryman, Marta stared back at me.

I yanked the door open. "Come in."

"I know I said I wouldn't bother y'all tonight, but I need a breather. I think I need my head examined." Marta ran her hands through her thick short hair. "Why did I ever dream it would be wonderful having her here?"

"Holly?" Carly asked softly.

"Who else? She's only been here three days, and it feels more like three years."

Carly shook her head. "Bless your heart."

I motioned for Marta to sit down. "What can we do?"

"Right now she wants smoked salmon and a salad. John's gone to get it." She shook her head. "You know, he's easygoing, but I don't know how much longer he'll put up with this. As soon as he left, she called me and said she needed a manicurist. Apparently she broke a nail while she was impatiently tapping them on the table, waiting for her food." She grimaced. "Okay, I'm kidding about that. But her nail is broken."

"Glad to see you've still got your sense of humor." Carly patted her on the shoulder. "I think I can fix her nail. I do manicures for the twins and their friends occasionally."

"Thanks." Marta started to push to her feet, but Carly gently shoved her back down.

"Here's a deal for you. You stay here with the kids and wait for our pizza, and Jenna and I will take care of Holly."

I'd have raised an eyebrow if I was able. But that wasn't a talent with which God had blessed me. Almost as if she were reading my mind, though, even without the raised eyebrow, Carly shot me a stern look over her shoulder that said, "We came to help."

Marta leaned her head back against the chair and closed her eyes. "You two are angels in disguise."

Guilt niggled at me. Why couldn't I just be gracious like Carly?

We turned to leave, but Marta called after us. "Wait. You need to wash off your makeup and put your hair up."

"Huh?" Even Carly, Miss I-Know-Everything-about-Holly-Wood looked stumped.

Marta shook her head. "Says she's allergic to shampoos and cosmetic smells, except her own. Between us, I think she just doesn't want anyone

152

around who might be competition."

Wordlessly, Carly pulled a bandanna from her makeup bag and tied it around her short dark curls. She dug deeper into the bag, found her makeup remover pads, and started swiping her face.

I opened my mouth to protest, but the pleading look in my sister's eyes silenced me. I secured my long red curls high on top of my head with a bear-claw clip. "I just have moisturizer on; do you think that counts?"

No answer. "Fine. I'll let my skin dry out." I used a washcloth from the bathroom to scrub my face until it tingled.

Out in the hallway, though, I got my voice back. "Can you imagine any-one being so self-centered?" Even my boss's daughter, Lisa, with her ridiculous demands couldn't top this.

Carly was already bouncing along three steps ahead of me, and in spite of Marta's warnings, I was pretty sure she was *excited*. Sure enough, she looked over her shoulder at me and grinned as wide as a beauty queen. "We're about to see Holly Wood, Jenna. Up close and personal. How can that be a bad thing?"

I remembered the defeated look in Marta's eyes and shuddered at my sis-ter's naïveté. But I forced my feet to keep walking. Someone had to look after Carly in her innocence.

When we reached Holly's suite, I tapped on the door. Carly, never shy, but apparently feeling especially forward at the moment, rattled the handle. As she shoved on the door, it opened. Not latched, I guessed, but the low lights and the shadowy vastness of the interior lent a creepy aura to the place. We stared in the open doorway at the elegant colonial furniture. So this was the Presidential Suite. It made our four-bedroom suite look like a child's playhouse.

"Hello?" Carly called softly into the cavernous room. We took a few steps inside and froze beside the fireplace when we heard a familiar voice.

"It's a disaster and only you can fix it. I need you here now, CeeCee. It's urgent."

Facing the floor-to-ceiling window, Holly, cell phone clutched to her ear, was holding her offending nail up to the light, apparently calling her own per-sonal manicurist. Her signature blond curls cascaded halfway down her back. "Saturday? I can't wait that long."

As if she sensed our presence, Holly spun around. Whoa. The last time I saw a top that tight and short was when I pulled a dry-clean-only sweater from the dryer. Even then I hadn't thought to pair it with an elegant silver-hoop belly-button ring. Another missed opportunity. Or not.

Holly's perfect features broke into a scowl, and she spoke quickly into the phone. "Fine. I've got to go. Come by as soon as you get into town." She flipped the phone shut and glared at us. "Who are you, and what are you doing in here?"

2

For the lips of an adulteress drip honey,
and her speech is smoother than oil.
PROVERBS 5:3

I stepped forward. "I'm Jenna Stafford. No relation to Jim." I couldn't count the number of times I'd been asked in Branson if I was related to funny guy Jim Stafford. But judging from Holly's answering grunt, she wasn't wondering anyway. I rushed on. "We're here to help with your fingernails. You remember my sister, Carly. From Lake View High School."

I was hoping my phrasing would save Carly any embarrassment if Holly didn't remember her. But Carly grinned. "Don't be silly, Jenna. I'm sure she doesn't remember me. She's met so many people since then."

"But when someone saves you a seat on the bus every day, it seems to me like that should forever imprint her in your memory," I deadpanned. Maybe it's my near brush with being one, but something about celebrities makes me slightly irreverent of their status.

Carly glared at me. But before she could give me a piece of her mind, Holly pasted on a smile as artificial as her, um. . .fingernails. . .and floated toward my sister. "Of course I remember you, darling. . . ." She stretched out her hand.

"Carly," I supplied, just in case.

"Carly," Holly repeated and waved toward the other room. "Now be a dear and fetch my emergency nail kit from the dresser."

Carly had been about to take Holly's hand, but she realized her faux pas in time and jerked her own back. "Okay." She hurried out, and in just a few seconds she was back with a little white kit. "Want me to give you a whole manicure? Or will your own manicurist be arriving soon?"

"My own manicurist?" Holly's voice had a naturally haughty tone, sort of like a spoiled child. Condescending.

"CeeCee?" I reminded her. Apparently my role in this little production was to fill in the blanks in her memory when it came to names.

"CeeCee?" she repeated. Then she laughed. "CeeCee does many things for me, but nails are not among them."

"Oh, sorry," Carly muttered. "We just thought. . ."

154

"Yes, well, eavesdropping is never a good idea, is it?"

"Right. Sorry." Carly's embarrassment and apology annoyed me. I'd had enough.

"Look, we just came to help you. If you don't want our help, we'll be happy to leave." I didn't want to be snippy, but it had only been twelve hours since I escaped from one demanding diva, and I wasn't ready to go back to being bossed around by another one. I guess Holly realized I meant it, because she backed down.

"No, of course I don't want you to leave." Her smile would have melted butter. "Please fix my broken nail." She waved her hand in Carly's face. The glitter of her rings nearly blinded me. "I keep them short to play the guitar, but they're still important to me."

As she and Carly sat on the elegant sofa, I wandered around the room and listened to their muted conversation as I examined an arrangement of framed photos on the end table. Most of the photos were of Holly receiving awards. I had to admit she was a gorgeous woman with her perfect figure, beautiful smile, and glorious hair.

"You have no idea how hard it is to be in the spotlight all the time, Carly. My fans are everywhere." Holly sounded tearful. "I'm even afraid to go out to eat for fear of being mobbed."

Poor girl. Probably cried all the way to the bank. But sucker Carly was buying every word. I guess my experience with my boss's daughter, Lisa—aka prima donna and the sole reason I was in desperate need of a vacation—had made me just a little bit cynical. Okay, a lot jaded probably.

"My husband, Buck, has been a rock, though. He's wonderful," Holly gushed. "He's so tolerant of the paparazzi and has even agreed to do some interviews."

"Is he here?" Carly carefully applied clear polish to Holly's nail.

"He's my personal trainer, too, so he's probably at the gym working out. Ruth's around somewhere, but she's never in here when I need her."

Carly made a noncommittal sound in reply and put the brush back into the bottle then closed it.

"I let my personal assistant have a vacation while I came here. I knew Marta would take care of me." Then her tone switched to petulant. "But she's been so busy with this place, that she. . ." She looked at us as if weighing her words. "Well, let's just say, it's a good thing you came to help me, or I don't know what I'd have done."

Oh, boo-hoo. I didn't know how much longer I could stomach this. If it weren't for Marta, I would have just told Holly to fix her own nail and then gone for a swim.

But my sweet sister smiled and patted Holly's hand before releasing it. "I know we'll enjoy being here. I can't wait for the show Friday night." Carly stood and I headed for the door. Just as I reached for the knob, a dour-faced woman pushed it open. She had her arms full of clothes, and without a word, she walked past me and headed for the bedroom. As Carly shut the door behind us, we could hear their raised voices.

Carly glanced behind us. "That's Ruth, Holly's older sister."

"Sounds like she's a little irritated."

"Probably just something to do with the show. She takes care of Holly's wardrobe and makeup."

"Oh, as opposed to her vacationing personal assistant, who takes care of everything else." Oops. Was my disdain showing?

Carly smiled. "Right."

Was there anything my sister didn't know about the queen of country? I opened my mouth to suggest she try out for *Jeopardy*, but my cell phone rang before I got the words out. I glanced at the caller ID. Apparently Alex finally remembered my number.

"Hey there, water girl."

Even after all these months, his deep voice still made my heartbeat accelerate. "Hey."

"How's it feel to be hanging out with the stars?"

I smiled into the phone. If he only knew. "Tiring."

"Running from the paparazzi?"

"Something like that. How's work?"

"It's going great. But I was thinking of coming up there this weekend." Stop the presses. Considering he'd worked every Saturday for the last month and a half, this was big news.

"To Branson?"

"Unless you're really in Vegas. Yes, Branson."

I laughed. "Well, yeah. Can you really come?" He'd been working so hard for the last two weeks, I'd barely seen him even before I left town.

"If it's okay with you, I'll try. I miss you, Jenna."

"I miss you, too."

We chatted a few more minutes, but when we hung up, my mind wandered back to his unabashed confession—he missed me. And he was willing to drive several hours to see me. Maybe his commitment issues were working themselves out.

❖

The next morning, I left Carly and the kids sleeping and slipped out to the breakfast area to get us something to eat. While I was surveying the continental spread, a blond hunk sauntered in. He scanned the room, and his gaze settled on me. All over me, actually. Ick.

He sauntered over with a wolfish grin and stuck out his hand. "You must be one of Marta's friends. I'm Buck Fisher."

Holly's earlier gushing came back to me. Buck Fisher. Holly's personal trainer and husband. An unexpected pang of pity for the diva hit me.

"Jenna Stafford." I returned his greeting then tried to figure out how to extricate my hand without yanking it away.

"Any relation to Jim?" He grinned big, clearly getting quite a kick out of his little joke.

I was tempted to say, "As a matter of fact. . ." but thought better of it. Those kinds of lies always come back to bite one on the proverbial behind. "No." Abrupt answer, but I had a feeling I'd better not encourage this guy or I'd be fighting off his massive hands every time I was near him.

I glanced over Buck's shoulder, trying to avoid his roving eyes. A beautiful girl with long black hair and flashing green eyes was headed toward us, and it didn't look like food was on her mind. I recognized her from the posters as Reagan Curtis, Holly's opening act. "Buck."

He dropped my hand and whirled around.

I wiped my palm on my pant leg. It looked like things could get ugly, but I was just grateful for the interruption.

"I've been looking all over for you." Her voice was possessive, and she ignored me completely as she wrapped her long silver fingernails around his arm. "I need breakfast."

Guess I'm wrong about food not being on her mind, I thought facetiously.

Buck gave me a quick wink and followed her out the door. Apparently they breakfasted elsewhere.

I loaded a tray and slipped back into our suite, where silence greeted me. I ate a couple of orange slices and grabbed a swimsuit. I could easily be back before they knew I was gone. If not, they'd forgive me once they found the food.

When I pushed open the double doors to the health club, I immediately felt at home. The zip code might be different, but the slight smell of chlorine in the air remained the same. And I loved it. I had the pool all to myself, which was even better.

In the locker room, I changed into my swimsuit and twisted my long curls up into a tight bun. Just like always, I couldn't wait to get in the water.

Halfway through my swimming routine, the door opened and a tall, muscular man came in. His black hair included almost as much salt as pepper, but his dark eyes were sharp as he glanced at me. Just as quickly as he noticed me, he ignored me and dove into the pool. His long arms sliced through the water with ease as he rapidly swam several laps.

From all my years of training, and more recently my job at the health club, I've grown spoiled to swimming alone. But this guy swam with a precision that was a pleasure to watch. When he took a breather, I nodded. "Nice form."

"Thanks," he grunted then dove back in.

I climbed out and slid a towel around me then hurried to the women's shower. When I finished and dressed, I came back out just as the dark-eyed man was reaching for a towel.

"Do you swim professionally?" he asked.

"I might ask you the same thing."

He shook his head. "Exercise only for me."

I hesitated. "Me, too." Which was totally true. And I wasn't ready to dredge up the agony of my Olympic defeat. Certainly not for a total stranger.

"Really? You've never had professional training?"

His hawk nose was distinctive, but his eyes were what grabbed my attention. They seemed to pierce to the marrow to get the facts.

"When I was younger—," I found myself saying, then stopped. I heaved my swim bag onto my shoulder and spun on my heel. The faster I got away from this man who seemed to demand the truth the better.

Out on the street, I headed back to the suite, unsure what it was about Hawk Man that had upset me so much. Once I reached our hallway, a door nearby opened, and muted voices drifted toward me. I instinctively glanced over just in time to see Buck step out. Reagan, wearing a short white silk robe, was framed behind him in the doorway.

Buck's smile faded as soon as he saw me. He glanced back over his shoulder where Reagan stood frozen.

"This isn't what it looks like." He jerked his head toward the door. "She just spilled juice on her clothes."

"Believe me, if you're Marta's friend, you're better off not mentioning this," Reagan piped up. "If Holly gets upset, the show *won't* go on."

Buck shot her a glare then hurried away.

Carly might claim that I'm never at a loss for words, but even Dear Pru didn't know the proper etiquette for a situation such as this. Before I had time to think of something to say, though, my cell phone rang.

I didn't even glance at the caller ID. Anything would be better than this. Reagan took the opportunity to slam the door, so apparently she agreed.

"Hello?"

"Jenna! How's Branson?"

"Bob?" I'd noticed a missed call from my boss, but I'd been in no hurry to return it.

His hearty laugh sounded forced. "Forgot me so soon? Girl, I'm hoping you're about done with vacation and ready to get back to work."

I stopped and leaned against the wall. Considering what I'd been putting up with from his daughter-turned-manager, he should be glad I was taking vacation days and not permanently quitting. "I'm sure Lisa can handle things. After all, you put her in charge, right?"

"Lisa misses you terribly."

I closed my eyes. That was reaching, even for Bob. "Explain to me again how I went from being just about to buy your business—a promise you've been making to me for a long time, I might add—to waiting on your daughter hand and foot while she pretends to do my job."

"She's been through so much with her marriage troubles. I just wanted you to help her get her self-esteem back."

Lisa and her husband had split, and she'd moved back to town a few months ago. Now Bob and Wilma couldn't do enough for their spoiled daughter. Which was exactly why I'd come to hate my job. Lisa had her daddy wrapped around her finger, and Bob was in denial. I'd tried to quit numerous times, but I always felt too sorry for him to go through with it. But if something didn't give, I'd forever be fetching juice drinks for the spoiled socialite and working long hours to fix her mistakes. It was time for Bob to get a taste of Lisa's management skills without me. "Like I told you, I'll be back in two weeks."

I hit the END button before he could reply. Holly and I had something in common. We were both being deceived, and our hopes and dreams lay in the balance.

When I opened the door, the girls were bouncing up and down with excitement. "Zac and Danielle are taking us to Whitewater!" they chorused.

"Good." I had a feeling that for once Zac would be glad to have his sisters along. He'd been friends with John and Marta's daughter his whole life, but now that they were teens, I'd noticed an awkward silence in the air between them.

Carly and I tag-teamed the kids with warnings about not talking to strangers, looking both ways before crossing the street, and my personal contribution, probably because of my red hair and tendency to freckle—wearing sunblock.

When they were gone, I filled Carly in on my phone conversation with Bob. After she sympathized, I told her about Buck and Reagan's hallway drama.

She shook her head. "Like Mama says, 'Life gets so messed up when people throw out their Bibles.'"

Guilt hit me in the gut. I'd started a study of Proverbs a few weeks ago. But lately, with things so bad at the athletic club and Alex breaking our dates in order to work, I'd gotten distracted. Instead of turning to God, I'd been trying to handle it all myself. No wonder my prayers felt like they weren't going above the ceiling these days.

So when Carly left to check in with Marta, I dug out my Bible and spent a little time catching up. By the time Carly came back with our marching orders, I felt like God and I were on speaking terms again.

My newfound pity for Holly made me more understanding as Carly and

I played servant all day. Midafternoon, Marta caught us in the hall. "You girls take the rest of the day off. Let your hair down. You deserve it."

I grinned. "In that case, the red roof is calling my name. And the blue one is echoing it." That's another thing I love about Branson. With their brightly colored roofs, its malls are easy to find. "I'm going to get a quick shower and shop 'til I drop." I glanced over at Carly. "How about it?"

She shrugged. "If it's okay with you, I think I'll just stay and help Marta."

I couldn't imagine why anyone would prefer waiting on Holly hand and foot to Branson's terrific outlet malls, but I was just glad she didn't ask me to stay, too.

❖

I returned to the hotel tired and hungry but halfway done with my Christmas shopping—and it wasn't even July yet. While I was gloating over my finds, Carly stumbled in and collapsed on the bed.

She moaned, bandanna askew and eyes closed.

"What happened to you?"

"Can't walk. Can't talk. Too tired," she mumbled.

Poor girl. I offered to get dinner for us all—or to take the kids out and bring Carly a plate. But she dozed off while we were discussing it.

When the kids bounced in a few minutes later, slightly sunburned—in spite of all my sunblock warnings—and more than slightly filthy, I made an executive decision. They stayed in and washed up, and I made a run for ribs, one of my favorite Branson foods. After everyone was showered, Danielle came back to join us for our feast in the room. When we finished eating, Carly stretched out on the couch with a blanket and pillow. Zac looked at me. "Is it okay if we put a movie in?"

Carly snored softly. I nodded. "Sure, if you keep the volume low."

Dani and Zac pulled their chairs up toward the TV.

The twins followed me into my room. And while I got ready for bed, they regaled me with drama-filled stories of getting lost and nearly drowning at Whitewater. So ended another day in Paradise.

Pride goes before destruction, a haughty spirit before a fall.
PROVERBS 16:18

When Alex called midafternoon Friday and said he had to work after all, I felt like having a prima-donna fit myself. After two days of observing an expert, I was pretty sure I could pull it off. But there was room for only one diva at the Paradise. Maybe if I'd told Alex that for the second day in a row I'd met a mysterious man for a swim, he'd have come anyway. But the way I figured it, we were a little old for silly games. Besides, Hawk Man had totally ignored me this morning, and I'd returned the favor.

So I squashed down my disappointment and ran to the nearest grocery store to get Holly some more Evian. She dismissed us around five, and Carly and I hurried back to the room to shower and dress for the show. Thankfully it didn't take us long to get ready. John called an hour before showtime and begged us to go to Holly's dressing room to stop a shouting match that Marta couldn't handle.

"Fine, but I'm not messing with my face or hair," I muttered.

To my surprise, Carly nodded. "Me neither."

As we rounded the corner to Holly's dressing room, we could hear Holly screaming through the closed door. We almost bumped into a guy Marta had introduced to us earlier as Joey from the band. In his midtwenties, "Joey from the band" looked as if he wished he were "Joey on another planet." He shrugged and shook his head then brushed past us.

Carly tapped on the door, but when no one answered, she pushed it open. We walked in to see Holly shaking her finger at her sister.

"You deliberately made this smaller so it won't fit me. You'd better quit trying to make me look bad and remember who supports you."

Holly's blue-sequined dress did look like it had been glued onto her. But I wasn't sure it looked any tighter than her normal attire.

Ruth shrugged. "Maybe you should train more and eat less. Assuming your trainer is willing to spend time training you instead of. . ." Ruth clamped her lips together at this interesting juncture. I knew what she was implying, but did Holly?

161

Carly managed to get the brush out of Holly's hand before she threw it, but it was a close call. My amazing sister even convinced Ruth to let out a seam so the dress would fit. But as Ruth left with the dress, she leveled a look at Holly I would never give my sister. Or anyone else. Holly didn't appear to notice. Instead, she turned her attention to another offender.

"You sneaky, ungrateful beast." Holly's voice was shrill, and I spun around, ready to attack if she was talking to Carly.

Buck filled the doorway, an embarrassed grin playing across his handsome face. She heaved a shoe at his head. Fortunately, or maybe unfortunately, she missed. "Now, Hol..."

"Don't you 'Hol' me. I keep you in the lap of luxury, and this is how you repay me?"

He nodded at Carly and me. "Preshow nerves." But he backed out with his hands up to ward off any more tossed items. Apparently he'd been this route before.

"That's right. Get out! No one understands me!" She turned on us. "I just want to be alone. Is that too much to ask?" An almost tangible relief washed over the room. Marta mumbled an excuse and sprinted out as if she'd been practicing for the hundred-yard dash. Carly and I didn't exactly linger, either.

But we hadn't been in our room too long before Carly's cell phone rang. She looked at me, cringing.

"Surely you didn't give her your number?"

"Hi, Holly." Carly listened to the frantic voice even I could hear.

"Carly, can you come back? I just go a little crazy before a show."

Carly murmured a soothing "yes" and shut the phone. "Go ahead and shoot me, but I'm going to go back."

For some reason, Carly had decided it was her Christian duty to be there for Holly. I most certainly didn't share her mission, but I couldn't stand to send her into the lion's den alone. "Wait, I'll go with you. You may need me as a shield in case she starts throwing things again."

Holly was pacing in her room when we entered, but she was alone. The offending dress fit beautifully.

"You look great, Holly." I heard the relief in Carly's voice.

Holly snorted. "Naturally, the dress looks fine now that my so-called sister fixed it back to normal size."

"Is there somethin' else we can do for you before the show?" Carly asked.

"Bring me a glass of cold water. And I need a throat lozenge from the bag on the dressing table." Poor Holly had nearly had to pour her own water. Good thing we'd gotten there in time. Carly patiently handed her water and unwrapped a lozenge.

"Anything else?"

Yeah, should we breathe for you? But Holly inclined her head graciously.

"No, I really must be alone now. I have to get centered before I go onstage so that I can give my all to my fans. Do you realize that some of these poor people have waited years, and seeing me in person is their lifelong dream?"

I felt my eyebrows shoot up into my hairline. Did she really believe that? She sat down at the dressing table and examined her face in the mirror. "It's such a responsibility. Sometimes it's almost too much even for me." She smoothed an imaginary wrinkle. "My one unbreakable rule is that no one enters my dressing room for the thirty minutes before I go onstage. I delve deep into myself and get my psyche ready so I can pour my whole being into my performance."

Okay. We got it. Her whole self and psyche had to get ready so she could fulfill the lifelong dream of her fans. Could we go now? Carly must have been reading my mind again, because she nodded and pushed me toward the door.

"We'll see you after the show, Holly. Break a leg."

Now there's an idea.

In the hall, I turned to Carly. "Can you believe the total conceit of that woman? 'Back off, lowly one. My one unbreakable rule is that none of the peasants get near me without express permission. It's bad for my delicate psyche."

"She doesn't realize how she sounds."

"More than likely, she doesn't care," I whispered as we entered the packed auditorium where Reagan was already in the middle of a song. The audience clapped along with her, but I got the feeling they were waiting for the main event. I glanced around the crowded room. Was Holly right? Had some people waited forever to see her in person? That crossed the line from fan to fanatic in my book.

When Reagan and her band finished, I had to admit that even though she didn't seem to have much in the way of morals, she had talent and a certain amount of stage presence. Apparently the audience agreed, or at least some of them. During the fifteen-minute intermission, she lingered in front of the stage signing autographs.

When the emcee announced Holly and she walked out, the crowd went wild. She offered a self-effacing smile and drawled, "Well, hello, y'all. It's great to be in Branson." People screamed and stomped their feet. Holly glowed. No other word for it. She seemed likeable, even to me, and I knew better.

After the show, Holly, gracious smile still intact, signed autographs for several minutes. Once the crowd dispersed, Carly dragged me over with her to tell Holly how much we enjoyed the show.

Reagan appeared behind us. "Did you notice how much the audience loved my opening number?" she said loudly. "I had to pull back a little after that to keep from stealing the show."

As I remembered Buck leaving Reagan's hotel room, I couldn't keep quiet. "I don't think the crowd needed much encouragement to adore Holly." I couldn't believe I was defending the honor of the most hateful, shallow person I'd met in years.

Holly ignored Reagan.

Reagan shrugged. "Well, they were mostly senior citizens. More her age group."

Carly gasped, but again, Holly seemed not to hear the venomous words. Maybe her psyche was still centered. Or maybe she recognized Reagan's jealousy for what it was.

Out in the hall, Marta turned to us, excitement shining on her tired face. "A sold-out show! Can you believe it? What a grand opening!"

Carly hugged her. "We're so happy for you."

"We couldn't have done it without you both. Let's get the kids and go somewhere and celebrate."

Carly nodded, and I smiled. "I've got some work I need to do back in the room. I'll have to count on Carly to bring me a doggy bag."

"You got it."

After they had collected the kids from the room and were gone, I settled in at the computer. I had an agreement with my editor—I could stay away as long as I stayed on the job, so to speak. I snagged three Dear Pru letters from the stack I'd brought with me and began typing away. Before I fell asleep at the wheel—or in this case, keyboard—I managed to answer all three with a modicum of good sense. As I drifted off to sleep, though, I wondered if I was a little too vehement in my response to the woman who suspected her husband of cheating. While I was advising her to find out the truth at all costs, a picture of Buck and Reagan flashed across my mind.

❖

I swam thirty minutes earlier Saturday morning and avoided Hawk Man. When I got back, Marta insisted Carly and I take the kids to Silver Dollar City. We invited Danielle and enjoyed a few carefree hours scaring ourselves silly on rides like Wildfire and Powder Keg. But by midafternoon the kids were so tired they didn't even argue when Carly said we needed to get back to the hotel.

At the suite, I came out towel-drying my hair to find Carly already dressed and relaxing in the recliner.

"Want me to find John and Marta and see if they want to eat with us?"

"Sure." Carly was nearly asleep, so I left her to grab a few minutes' slumber and headed down the hall. I hadn't taken three steps away from the door when my cell rang. I flipped it open. "Did you change your mind about supper?"

"Jenna? What are you talking about? Are you girls okay?"

"Mama. We're fine. I'm sorry. I thought you were someone else. How are you and Dad?"

"He's a little grouchy, but I think that's just because he's worried about you suddenly deciding to take vacation days then hightailing it out of town with your sister and the kids."

"Things haven't been good at the club lately." Which she knew but refused to acknowledge. "Tell Dad not to worry. My job will still be waiting for me when I get back." *If I want it.*

"That's what Alex said. Your dad talked to him at breakfast yesterday. Honey, I don't mean to pry, but do you think it's wise to go off for so long and leave Alex here?" She made it sound like I forgot to pack him when I was loading my suitcase.

How wide could one generation gap get? "Alex is a grown man, Mama. If he wants to come to Branson, he's perfectly capable of getting here. I have let him know he's welcome." But he'd let me know he had to work. "What else can I do? Go back home and drag him here?" My voice might have risen a little as I finished that question. I know my blood pressure did.

"You don't have to get huffy."

She was right. They don't call something a "sore" subject for no reason. "I'm sorry. It's just that this is one of those issues Alex has to work out for himself. He knows how I feel. Now the ball's in his court. Besides, you know what they say about absence making the heart grow fonder."

"They also say absence makes the heart go wander." Job's Old Testament friends could take lessons from my mother. "Jenna, darling, I don't want you to be *forward* or anything. But you *can* be subtle about it."

Apparently she heard what she said and remembered who she was talking to. "On second thought, maybe your dad will kind of feel him out and see how he responds. No use risking embarrassment."

"Mama." I wasn't shouting. Exactly. Okay. Maybe I was. But I was thirty years old, and my mother was offering to have my dad ask my boyfriend if his intentions were honorable. "Please—do—not—tell—Daddy—to—ask—Alex—anything."

"Jenna Stafford, don't use that tone of voice with me." I felt fifteen again. Only I was not the one Mama talked to like that usually. Carly had been the wild child in our family.

"I'm sorry. Really I am. But I was serious about not wanting Dad to mention me to Alex."

"Okay, honey. You're right. This is between the two of you. I just want you to be happy."

My irritation melted away. I knew she meant it. Sometimes it was just hard to remember that fact when she started trying to work things out for me.

"I *am* happy. I have a great family. If I end up marrying Alex, fine. If not, then God must have something else in mind." I sounded so trusting. Maybe if I said it aloud often enough, I'd really feel that way.

"That's the right attitude, sweetie. Tell Carly and the kids hello for me. I'll call Carly when I get a chance. The cabins are full right now." My parents own resort cabins, and I know from experience that when Stafford Cabins are full, Mama has little time for anything else. "Oh, and of all things, Harvey says he and Alice are very serious about selling the diner or quitting business altogether. If they do that, what will our guests do?"

I started to remind her that there were other places to eat in town, but then I realized she'd transferred her worry to something besides me. Without waiting for an answer, she finished with, "Your daddy just came in. Take care. Love you."

"You, too. I've got to go find Marta—," I started to say, but I was talking to dead air.

A few seconds later, I found Marta without any trouble but immediately wished I hadn't.

"You can't do this to me!" Marta's voice escalated to a near scream, drawing me toward Holly's suite. "We've invested everything in this hotel. You'll ruin us!"

"Oh, come on, Marta. Grow up. I can do whatever I want. I'm the star, remember?"

"Grow up? That's a joke coming from you. You're still as self-centered as you were when we were in school. You haven't grown up at all."

"Me?" Holly's mocking laugh chilled me. "You're still a groupie just like you were in junior high."

"You signed a contract." Marta sounded rather desperate now.

"With an exemptive clause about illness." Holly's voice took on a saccharine quality. "I really can't help it if I develop a bad migraine. And I won't perform if I can't give my best to my adoring fans."

I glanced behind me. Should I go back to our suite? Or try to rescue Marta?

"So help me, Holly, you will be on that stage when the curtain goes up, or. . ." Marta's voice was as tight as clenched fists.

Holly's voice turned hard. "You'd better leave now."

As the doorknob turned, I impulsively ducked into the janitor's closet across the hall. I stood there, surrounded by mops and brooms, my heart pounding, until all was quiet then returned to our room without trying to follow Marta. I woke Carly and told her what I'd heard and that I didn't end up asking the Hills to eat with us. I motioned toward the kids, glued to a movie. "Hey, let's fling the kids a purse of gold and let them pick up dinner. We'll feel a lot better after we eat."

"Sounds like a plan."

"Here, slaves. Earn your keep." I waved several bills in front of them to get their attention. It worked. Kids are so easy.

A little while later, Carly's cell phone pealed out the first few bars of Holly's first number-one hit, aptly titled "What's Wrong with Me Is You." My sentiments exactly.

"Calm down, Holly. Jenna and I will be right there." Carly flipped the phone shut and hustled me out of the room. Before we knew it, we were in The Presence again. And the country queen was not pleased. Surprise.

"Reagan had better be out of the main auditorium when I'm introduced tonight or she'll be sorry. She hung around signing autographs last night, trying to upstage me. If it happens again, Buck will have to remove her using all the force he needs to." I smothered the thought that neither Buck nor Reagan would probably consider that punishment. "That is, if Buck happens to appear for the show. Who knows where he's been all day?"

I knew it was a rhetorical question, but I could have offered an educated guess.

"If he knows what's good for him, he'll remember that airtight prenup—" She stopped as if she just realized we were still there. "I hope Ruth didn't mess up my dress for tonight."

"You looked great last night, and I'm sure you'll look even better tonight." This from Carly—the pourer-of-oil-on-troubled-waters.

"Yes, well, not if you all stay here and gab all night."

I almost laughed out loud at the pointed look Holly gave us. Had she forgotten that she called us here? I shook my head as Carly and I made our way back down to our room. Considering the show was supposed to be starting immediately, we were the ones in danger of not getting any supper, thanks to Holly's summons.

"I'd rather miss part of Reagan's performance than not eat," Carly said, as if she read my mind.

"Me, too." I opened the suite door and hurried in. "I thought the kids would have been back by now."

The words were barely out of my mouth when they burst in, bringing with them the wonderful aroma of burgers hot off the Mcgriddle.

While we ate, the twins launched into a tale about almost getting run over in the hotel parking lot. Zac shrugged. "They ran ahead of me, and some guy squealed his tires braking for them to walk by. He stopped in plenty of time, though. No big deal."

When Carly didn't scold the kids for running in the parking lot, I glanced over at her. She was staring off into space. "Carly? You okay?"

She gave me a rueful grin. "I feel guilty that we weren't there earlier to calm Holly. What if she ruins things for Marta tonight?"

"Look how well she did last night once she got onstage. And she seemed okay just now. It's all going to be fine." I dipped my last french fry in Ranch dressing and popped it into my mouth.

Carly reminded the kids not to leave the suite or let anyone in. We opened the door and followed the sound of blaring music the short distance to the auditorium entrance. We handed our tickets to the usher and walked in just as Reagan belted out the last line of a classic woman-done-wrong song.

When we were seated, I glanced at the aisle directly beside my seat. How hard would it be to slip out to see the Presleys or Yakov Smirnoff and make it back before anyone realized I was gone? A laugh would have been nice. Wishful thinking. Maybe Marta would let us come back sometime when she had a comedian headliner.

A low-maintenance comedian headliner.

A few minutes later, Carly leaned over to me. "She's more nervous than she was last night."

I nodded.

Reagan finished out the set with professionalism, if not pizzazz. When she sang the last notes of her closing song, she exited the stage to polite applause. And she didn't appear to sign autographs, so Holly must have gotten her point across.

A minute or two later, a disembodied voice proclaimed, "Ladies and gentlemen, please welcome to the Paradise Theater stage. . .Holly Wood!"

The lights flashed up and down, the drums rolled, and—nothing. No Holly. The audience went wild. After several minutes of cheering finally subsided to loud complaints, the emcee cleared his throat and tried again. "Ladies and gentlemen, direct from sold-out performances all over the USA, greet four-time CMA Entertainer of the Year, Ms. Holly Wood!"

The audience erupted into even louder cheers, but Holly still didn't show.

"Ladies and Gentlemen. . ." The emcee was definitely nervous himself by now and apparently taking direction from someone backstage. "Holly has been delayed, but Reagan Curtis will sing one more number while we're waiting."

I turned to Carly in horror. "Do you think Holly decided to show Marta she meant what she said about not showing up?"

Carly shrugged. "When we left her, she sure sounded like she was planning to sing tonight, so I don't know."

Reagan bounced back out, a little disheveled but all smiles. "Just remember, anything worth having is worth waiting for." The audience twittered, and she launched into a cheerful upbeat song.

Marta hurried down the aisle toward us. She leaned across me and hissed, "Carly, would you go get Holly, please? I'll stay here in case we need crowd control, but hurry."

I put my hand on Carly's arm. "I'll do it. I may not be Gandhi, but I can keep peace when it's necessary. Be right back."

Like the athlete I used to be, I fairly sprinted down front and flashed my backstage pass at the row of security guards. Once in the hall, I made a beeline to Holly's dressing room and knocked lightly. If her psyche wasn't centered by now, she'd just have to go onstage and take her chances. Taking a deep breath, I opened the door. Holly—decked out for the show—was almost reclining in her chair in front of her mirror.

"Holly, you're late! You've missed your cue. Hur—" I broke off as nausea slammed into my gut.

Holly's unfocused eyes were bulging in a blue face.

4

The righteousness of the blameless makes a straight way for them,
but the wicked are brought down by their own wickedness.
PROVERBS 11:5

I've never seen anyone look so. . .blue. A slender plastic thread was draped across Holly's neck and down the front of her red bangled dress. I quickly averted my gaze to her hands. At least they were normal color.

Even though I knew she was dead by her eyes, I touched her wrist to feel for a pulse. The fingernail Carly had fixed was broken again. Holly would have a thing or two to say to my sister about that, no doubt. Except she wouldn't be able to speak. Not with her face blue like that. My feet felt like lead bricks, and hysteria bubbled up in my throat. There was no pulse.

I clutched my stomach and bolted from the room. Which way? The stage area or the private section? Maybe I wasn't as calm as I should be. The decision was taken from me when Buck turned the corner coming from the suite hallway. Before I could say anything, he accosted me. "They said Holly's not onstage. Have you seen her?"

Boy! Had I ever. I stifled a nervous sob. "She—she's—call 911."

"What?" He looked at me as if I were crazy and reached for the door-knob. "Holly?"

He had the door opened a scant inch when I finally came to my senses. I pulled it shut and grabbed his arm.

"Buck," I said, fast and low. "Holly's dead."

"Wha—? Is this a joke?" Buck must have seen the truth in my face. He backed up uncertainly. "Are you sure? Maybe we can help her."

I shuddered as I remembered her face. "I'm sorry. She's definitely dead. We need the police." I dialed 911 on my cell and pulled Buck toward the nearest security guard.

The tall blond guard looked at me as if I were crazy as I babbled to him and the 911 operator at the same time. His partner, older and obviously more experienced, took my cell phone and barked out a clear assessment of the situation. When he finished the call, he narrowed his eyes and put a seemingly friendly hand on Buck's arm. "Why don't you go with us to check this out?"

Buck frowned but nodded. They started down the hall to Holly's room, and the older guard looked back at me. "Be sure you're available to talk to the police when they get here."

I nodded numbly and walked into the auditorium. A faint buzzing echoed in my ears, but I was pretty sure that was shock. Could someone be in shock and know it? I surveyed the scene, trying to get my bearings.

Reagan was up on the stage, singing her heart out to a restless audience. Marta came scurrying down the aisle, with John right on her heels. "Where's Holly?"

I motioned to the double doors, and we stepped outside, where I broke the news as gently as possible.

"I don't believe it," Marta said, but the tears that spilled down her cheeks said otherwise. John wrapped his arm around her shoulders.

She looked up at him. "We have to go see what's going on."

He nodded, and they left, whispering furiously.

I watched them go and then glanced down at the marble-tiled floor of the lobby. If I could just rest for a while, I'd feel better. The double doors opened behind me and Carly stepped out. "Jenna? What's wrong? You look awful."

I nodded. "Awful."

She put her arm around me. "Honey, what happened?"

The sympathetic tone in her voice melted the wall I'd erected when I found the body. Hot tears splashed onto my cheeks.

She eased me over to a bench and helped me sit down, then sat beside me. "Tell me."

When I finished, she gasped. "You poor thing."

I cried for a few minutes while she patted my shoulder. Then I sat up straight and swiped my eyes. "Poor Holly."

"Yes, poor Holly. A person can only make so many enemies without making the wrong one." In spite of her matter-of-fact tone, I could see her own eyes were moist with tears.

"I'm sorry." I slipped my hand into hers and squeezed. "I know you really cared about her."

She nodded. "I did. I thought I could make a difference."

"You gave it your best shot, Carly."

"Who do you think murdered her?" Carly whispered and glanced back at the double doors, where we could still hear Reagan singing.

I shrugged. "She had even more enemies than Hank did."

For a few seconds, we didn't speak, remembering, I'm sure, the horrible murder of the newspaper editor in our hometown a few months ago. Zac had been a suspect, and Carly and I had eventually solved the murder, but we'd almost gotten ourselves killed in the process.

"Promise me something," Carly said softly.

I looked over at her. "What?"

"We're going to stay out of this murder investigation, right?"

My legs still felt like noodles, and every time I closed my eyes, all I could see was Holly's blue face. I was ready to pack and leave as quickly as possible. "Definitely."

She sighed and pushed to her feet. "Good. Do you feel up to going with me to see if we can help Marta? I suppose the police will be here soon."

I stood, and we wove our way around the corridor to Holly's dressing room. When we rounded the last corner, we stopped. A shiny yellow crime scene ribbon stretched across the hallway. Several armed policemen milled around. Two were in deep conversation with the security guards I'd told about Holly's death. The tall blond guard looked up at us and pointed. "There she is. She's the one."

❖

"Remind me to send John a basket of fruit or something when we get home," I muttered as I trudged into our suite two hours later.

Carly looked up then glanced over to where Zac, the twins, and Danielle were engrossed in a TV DVD game. "Marta's John?"

I shook my head. "The Lake View chief of police John."

"Why?"

"He may be a pain, but at least he never suspected me of murder." I sank down beside her on the couch and kicked off my shoes. "Those officers must have made me repeat my story twenty-five times. They were obviously hoping I'd get it wrong one time—then they'd have their murderer, before the detectives even arrived."

The phone rang and I stretched out to snag it off the end table.

"Miss Stafford?"

I frowned at the deep voice. For some reason it sounded vaguely familiar. "Yes?"

"Chief Detective Jamison here. We need you and your sister, Carly Reece, to come downstairs."

"You're kidding." I slipped my feet back in my shoes even as I said the words. "Why?"

"We have some questions for you."

"You do know I've just told about finding the body several times, right?"

"We'll expect you in the breakfast area shortly."

"Fine," I muttered.

"Miss Stafford, all exterior exits and entrances are sealed with a police guard."

"Do you think we're going to bolt?"

"Why would you say that?"

"You were warning me."

"Warning you? I just wanted you to know that it's safe to walk down here."

"We'll be right there."

Carly looked at me with a bemused expression on her face. "It didn't take long for you to develop an antagonistic relationship with the local police. How do you do that?"

"You heard, huh?"

She nodded. "Let me get my shoes on."

When we got down to the breakfast area, police were everywhere. Carly motioned to the small dining area where the booths gave the illusion of privacy. "Apparently they're questioning everyone in the hotel. There's Buck."

I glanced over at Holly's wayward husband who sat across from two policemen. He'd lost a lot of his swagger. "Wonder what they told the crowd?" I glanced toward the auditorium. "Surely Reagan's not still singing?"

Carly nodded to a corner where two detectives were sitting with the young woman. "She looks like she's singing, but I'm not sure what the tune is."

I couldn't hear what Reagan was saying either, but she gestured wildly. One of the men said something, and she tucked a strand of hair behind her ear and cast a nervous glance toward the opposite corner where Buck pushed to his feet. He said something loudly, but all I caught was the word "lawyer." The police nodded and escorted him away. To where, I wondered. Jail? His suite? His lawyer would surely have to come from Nashville. So at least he was buying himself some time.

"Miss Stafford, Mrs. Reece?"

We spun around.

A tall dark-haired man stepped toward us, and I gasped. "You."

Carly looked at me as if I'd lost my mind. "Hawk Man," I whispered. "From the pool."

She nodded and stepped forward to extend a gracious hand. "Carly Reece."

He glanced over her shoulder at me, no recognition showing in those piercing eyes. "You must be Jenna Stafford. I'm Detective Jamison."

He motioned to a uniformed woman near the coffeepot and nodded to Carly. "Mrs. Reece, Detective Mayfield is going to ask you some questions. Miss Stafford, if you'll come with me. . ."

Carly left with the woman, and Detective Jamison looked at me.

"Small world, huh?" I quipped.

Without speaking, he led me to a small closet.

"You're kidding. You're going to interrogate me in a closet?"

"Desperate times," he said and waved a hand at one of the chairs that had obviously just been put there.

I sat. And went over the whole story again of how I found Holly. I must have gotten every detail consistent with my previous recital of events, because he didn't ask me any questions about it. He just nodded then looked up at me. "Do you know anyone who disliked Holly Wood?"

I snorted then tried desperately to make a cough out of it.

"You find that question amusing?" he asked, those truth-seeking eyes honed in on mine.

For some reason, when I'm confronted with people who won't show emotion, I want to force them to. I don't know why I'm that way, but I am. "I'm not sure I'd call it amusing, but if you'd known Holly, you'd know a better question might be, 'Who liked her?'"

"You mean besides her thousands of fans?"

I grimaced. "Well, yes, there are the fans. But in real life, most people clashed with Holly. The question was just to what degree."

"So you had a problem with Ms. Wood?"

See? Why couldn't I have just left well enough alone? "No, not really. I didn't know her well enough to have a problem with her."

"But you did notice other people 'clashing' with her. What did you know of her relationship with Reagan Curtis?"

I took a deep breath. "I'm sure Reagan didn't kill Holly. She was performing on the stage." I squashed down the memory of a robe-clad Reagan telling Buck good-bye the other morning. The last thing I wanted to do was incriminate someone falsely.

Detective Jamison stared down his hawk nose at me. And waited.

The silence stretched until I finally had to say something. No doubt just what he had in mind. "Holly and Reagan had a lot of jealousy issues. Professionally."

He made a note on his pad and looked back up at me. "Just professionally? What about personally?"

Another deep breath. Buck creeped me out and Reagan's self-centered personality irritated me, but did that mean they were murderers? "They had some personal issues, too, I imagine." I quickly told him about my first meeting with Buck and his subsequent rendezvous with Reagan.

He made a few notes while I squirmed in my chair.

"What about Holly's relationship with her sister?"

"Ruth?"

"Do you know of another sister?"

"No." For a split second, I considered offering him Carly's tattered copy of Holly's autobiography. "Ruth tried to do whatever Holly wanted. At times that was harder than others."

"Did you ever hear them argue?"

Poor Ruth. No way on earth she'd killed Holly, but I couldn't lie. I nodded.

When I finished telling him about the silly argument about the dress, he sat back in his chair. "Besides the band members, do you know anyone in the hotel who plays guitar?"

"Guitar?" Suddenly I remembered the slender plastic thread at Holly's throat. Of course. "A guitar string," I whispered.

The detective's normally implacable face flashed a hint of dismay. He obviously hadn't realized I didn't recognize the murder weapon.

"Please answer the question."

"No, I don't know anyone else who plays the guitar."

His gaze was stony now. "Do you have any idea who might have killed Ms. Wood?"

I shook my head. "No clue."

He handed me his card. "We'll need you and your sister to stay in town for a few days. I trust that won't be a problem."

"I guess not."

"Call me if you think of anything else."

❖

When everyone was settled into bed and the kids had finally quit talking about the murder and fallen asleep, I tiptoed into Carly's room. The bathroom light gave enough illumination for me to see she was in her bed, with the navy comforter pulled up under her chin.

"I'm awake," she said. "That was pretty weird, Hawk Man and Detective Jamison being the same man, wasn't it?"

"Weird doesn't even begin to cover it. But I should have known he was a cop. He's a natural."

She raised up on one elbow. "Are you attracted to him?"

"Not really. But his ability to get immediately to the truth fascinates me."

She chuckled. "I can see why you'd envy that."

"Is this another dig at my curiosity?"

"Me? No way. You can be as curious as you want as long as we don't get drawn into this murder investigation."

"I'm pretty sure Detective Jamison can handle it without our help."

"Good. Did you get in touch with Alex?"

"No. I left a voice mail." He'd heard the news, because he called during the police interrogation and left me a message to call him. I'd wrongly assumed he'd be waiting by the phone when I finished. "Did you talk to Elliott?" The local golf pro had given Zac golf lessons, but I think Carly had been the one who'd ended up learning that she was ready to give love a second chance. They were taking it slow, but there was definitely something there.

"Yeah, he called right after I hung up with Mama and Daddy. He offered to come."

"Did you say yes?"

"I told him to wait until tomorrow and let's see what happens. If they find the murderer overnight, we may be on our way home."

"True." But it would have been nice if Alex had called and offered. Our relationship, though not exactly new, was complicated. Except for a decade of not talking, we'd been close since we were very young. It had been easy to slip back into sharing everything important with him. And I thought vice versa. Apparently with me out of town, I'd dropped down on his list of priorities.

Carly rolled over, facing me, and punched her pillow.

"Trouble sleeping?"

"Yeah, I was thinking about poor Ruth."

In the semidarkness, I squinted to see my sister's face. "The truth is, she might be better off without Holly around."

"Except that I heard someone say that Holly left a large trust fund in her will for Ruth."

"Really?" I was amazed. Had there been a tiny bit of sisterly love lurking beneath Holly's heart of stone?

"But with the stipulation that every penny be used to set up and operate a large Holly Wood Museum. With Ruth as the permanent curator."

I sighed. So much for sisterly affection. "In other words, even in death, she made sure Ruth remained her faithful servant. Sneaky."

Carly groaned. "That's exactly what I thought. Speaking of sneaky, I have a confession."

"Should I call Detective Jamison?"

"Very funny. The way I knew about the museum is I heard part of Ruth's police interrogation."

My natural curiosity pushed the question out of me, even though I hated to ask. "What else did you hear?"

Carly pushed the thick down comforter back and sat up in the bed, resting against the walnut headboard. "Something about a man, but I didn't hear enough to understand. I just caught bits and pieces. The detective who was questioning me got called away, and while she was gone, I could hear Ruth."

"Sounds like they thought she might have a motive to kill Holly."

Carly nodded. "I know, but Ruth was so humble. And when she told the policewoman that she'd always love Holly no matter what she'd done, I felt myself tear up." She reached over and snagged the extra pillow then pressed it to her abdomen. "I really don't see why they have to dredge this all up. Some bum off the street probably wandered in and killed her."

"You think?"

176

"Do any of the people here seem capable of murder to you?"

I shook my head. "Not really. But we surely learned our lesson about that with Hank's murder." I shrugged and patted her foot through the comforter. "Still, it might have been a stranger."

I decided to wait until tomorrow to tell her I feared it was an inside job. But I'd been thinking about it the whole time we were getting the kids settled in. The back entrance could only be accessed with a key unless opened from the inside. Holly wasn't likely to open the door at random, and, even though it was almost directly across the hall from her dressing room, I didn't think she could have heard someone knocking on it. So either she or someone else from inside the hotel let a stranger—a murderer—in, or the killer was already inside.

It seemed a little far-fetched that a stranger would make a trip to the Paradise, knock on the door at the exact time Holly would be in the room alone, she would let him or—chilling thought—her in, and then the mysterious visitor would strangle her. Ergo, the killer must be someone we knew. Someone who was already in the hotel.

"You don't think it was a stranger, do you?"

I jerked a little, startled out of my reverie by her words. "It could have been." I stood and sighed. So much for not sharing my bad feeling until morning. "But I don't think so."

"We'd better get some sleep. We've got church in the morning."

"Yeah. Don't forget to say your prayers."

Even in the dim light, I could see her smile. How many times had we said that to each other right before bedtime growing up? Something about the familiar words gave me comfort, as well.

I was almost out the door when her voice stopped me. "Jenna?"

I turned back. "Yeah?"

"Did you. . .um, did you tell the detective about Marta arguing with Holly?"

My stomach lurched. "Actually, I'd forgotten all about it. Did you?"

"No. But she never asked me directly." The anxiety in my sister's voice spoke volumes. Her uncharacteristic quietness since the murder interrogation hadn't been so much from all of the chaos. It had been from a guilty conscience.

"I'm sure Marta told them."

"Yeah. Surely. I wish I knew what it was about."

I started to slip out of the room but then hesitated. When Carly was in junior high, she went through a period of bad dreams. She'd come in my room right before bedtime and say, "You know, squirt. . .if you want to crash in my room tonight, you can." I'd gather up my pillow and blanket and run into her room, while she followed at a cooler pace, as if she'd done me a big favor.

I cleared my throat and stepped completely back into the room. "Carly?

Why don't I crash in here with you tonight?"

"Sure." She tossed the pillow back over to the other side and slid down into the bed. "If you want to."

Big sisters. They never change.

5

Better a little with the fear of the LORD than great wealth with turmoil.
PROVERBS 15:16

L
ook at this! We're on TV."
I hopped into the main room, one sandal on and one in my hand.
"Where?"

Carly motioned to the flat screen on the dresser. "Okay, not us, but the Paradise Hotel. Marta called and told me. She and John just finished making a statement to the press. They'll pick us up at the back entrance in twenty minutes for church."

On the screen, a well-known national news anchorwoman glanced at a small picture of the Paradise over her left shoulder. "As most people know by now, popular country singer Holly Wood was apparently murdered at this Branson, Missouri, theater last night. Now, reporting live from the Paradise is our own Colby Bell. Colby, tell us about the crowd behind you, but first, are there any new developments in this tragic event?"

I sank onto the couch and fiddled with the buckle on my sandal. "Wow. Look at all those people."

The camera zoomed in on the young man's appropriately solemn expression. "Thank you, Bridgett. We have an unsubstantiated report that Holly Wood's widower, Buck Fisher, arrived at the police station early this morning with his lawyer. It doesn't appear that any charges have been filed at this time, but we are here in Branson to keep you apprised of all the latest developments in this breaking story."

"I guess whatever time Buck bought himself last night is up now," Carly said.

I narrowed my eyes. "If he did it, why would he have come from the opposite direction when I went to Holly's dressing room last night?"

"Who knows?"

We turned our attention back to the TV. Colby Bell had moved closer to the crowd. "As you can see, an impromptu memorial has been started here in front of the Paradise. Fans have gathered here, many who have been here since last night, to pay their last respects to the beloved star." The camera panned the crowd of mourners around the candlelit memorial.

I shook my head. "It's sad that on Sunday morning they're all here paying homage to Holly."

Carly looked up from the mirror, where she was applying a light touch of lip gloss. "Do you really think they've been here all night?"

For a split second, the camera zoomed in on one woman's anguished face. Her hair askew, her T-shirt rumpled, she stared at the candles.

I shuddered. "She definitely looks like she has." Even though Holly was dead, passion still burned in the woman's eyes. "It's kind of creepy, isn't it?"

"That she was right? That to many people, she was their life?"

The news cut to a commercial, and I hit the MUTE button. "Yeah. What would it be like to inspire that kind of devotion in just one person, much less thousands?"

"He'll call," Carly said dryly.

I laughed. "You know me too well."

My cell phone rang just as I finished speaking.

"Told you," she muttered.

I snagged it from my purse and glanced at the caller ID. Alex had finally managed to fit me into his busy schedule. "Hello?"

"Jenna? Are you okay?" His voice sounded warm but tinged with exhaustion. My irritation faded away. He truly was working hard to get his practice off the ground.

"I'm fine. You sound tired."

"Just worried about you."

Then why didn't you call sooner? "We're okay. We're going to leave for church in a few minutes, but I can call you back after. If you're going to be around."

A knock on the door echoed through the room. "Hang on, Alex."

"I'll get it." Carly hurried toward the door. "It's probably Marta and John."

"Don't forget to look in the peephole," I whispered.

Carly nodded.

"Good to see you're being cautious," Alex said.

Carly put her eye to the tiny hole then gasped.

"What is it?"

She shook her head as if speechless and yanked open the door.

I hurried toward her. "Alex, I'm going to have to go." Clearly, from Carly's reaction, it wasn't John and Marta, but who else would she let in?

"Okay, I wouldn't want to keep you from your company," his deep voice boomed through the room.

I glanced at the phone, wondering for a brief second if I'd accidentally hit the SPEAKER button.

"Hey, water girl. You fall into the deep end without even trying, don't you?"

I looked up into his gorgeous blue eyes and smiled, sympathizing with Carly's speechlessness.

Carly cleared her throat. "I'm going to go check and see if the kids are ready for church." She hurried out of the room.

Alex closed the door behind him and stepped toward me. "When I couldn't get in touch with you, I threw some things in the truck and drove up here. I hope that was okay."

"More than okay."

He folded me into his arms. "I was worried about you," he whispered against my hair.

Tears sprang to my eyes as I listened to his steady heartbeat. "Thank you for coming."

"Nothing could have kept me away. It was so late when I got in town last night, I was afraid you were asleep. And I couldn't get within a mile of the Paradise. So I booked a room at a hotel down the road. This morning I decided to surprise you with an escort to church."

I pushed back and looked at him, still having a hard time believing he was really here. "How did you get past security?"

"I got here right after Marta's press conference. I introduced myself, showed her some ID, and she let me in." He motioned toward the TV. "That's even scarier live. I was thankful she was there."

The fans were still singing and swaying, holding candles and roses. The woman I'd noticed earlier was still in the front row. I stepped over to the couch, snagged the remote, and hit the POWER button.

Hayley and Rachel came barreling into the room. "Hi, Alex," they chorused.

Zac ambled in behind them. "Hey, man." He and Alex touched knuckles in greeting.

"Marta called again. They're waiting at the back." Carly grabbed her Bible and purse from the desk and grinned at me. "She seemed to think you had another ride."

She waggled her fingers and shepherded the kids out. "See you there," she called over her shoulder.

I glanced up at Alex.

He raised an eyebrow. "That's assuming you trust me to drive you."

"If I remember correctly, you did assure me that your NASCAR-wannabe days are behind you. So I guess I'm safe."

As he rested an easy hand on the small of my back and escorted me into the hall, I admitted something to myself. I not only felt safe with Alex, I felt as if I was exactly where I belonged.

I opened my mouth to try to tell him what I was thinking, but just then

I saw a figure step away from the doorway of Buck and Holly's suite and start in the opposite direction.

"Hey!" I called instinctively. The man glanced back for a split second, but it was enough time for me to recognize him as Holly's guitar player, Joey. I started toward him, but he broke into a sprint and soon was out of sight.

A hand on my arm made me turn around. "Jenna? Is something wrong?"

I nodded. "I think he just came out of Buck and Holly's suite."

Alex raised an eyebrow. "Is he a stranger?"

I shook my head. "He's in the band."

"So he was probably paying his respects to the widower."

"Except that Buck is at the police station with his lawyer."

He sighed. "Jenna, I'm sure he had a legitimate reason for being in the room. Besides, we didn't even see him come out the door for sure; he could have just dropped something and picked it up."

Men and their logic. "I guess, but why did he run?"

"Because you sounded like you thought he was a criminal."

"What if he is?"

Alex frowned. "You're going to try to solve this murder, aren't you?"

"Not necessarily."

He looked harder, worry lines deepening between his eyes.

"I can't just ignore something like this, can I?"

For a second he didn't speak; then his words came slowly. "I'd like to think you could. You definitely should." He blew out a pent-up breath. "But I know you won't."

"Does that bother you?"

He stopped and faced me. "It hasn't been that long since your curiosity almost got you killed. Do you honestly think I could not be worried about you getting involved?" He pushed my hair back from my face and looked directly into my eyes. "I—"

My heart slammed against my ribs. He was finally going to say it.

"You're very important to me."

◆

After church, the kids talked us into going to the Uptown Café. The twins, along with Zac and Danielle, commandeered the soda counter. The rest of us crowded into a retro booth, with me sandwiched between Carly and Alex.

As soon as we ordered, Alex looked at John and Marta. "You two okay?"

John nodded. "We're going to be fine. As sad as Holly's death is, the Paradise will make it through."

Marta's eyebrows knitted together. "You're being overly optimistic, honey."

"We can reopen by the first of next month if the police will hurry and clear this up." John sounded bone tired but determined.

"Yeah? And who will want to perform where the star got killed? Especially with the murderer still on the loose." I could tell Marta had repeated this sentence or a variation of it several times. This was obviously an ongoing discussion. "We might as well admit it, John—this is the end of our dreams. I should start looking for a job."

My eyes widened. In all the years I had known her, Marta had never given up on anything she set her mind to. She'd bounce back from this. "You can't quit."

Carly leaned forward and covered Marta's hand with hers. "Maybe we can help you find the murderer, at least."

Alex stiffened beside me. I elbowed Carly. What had happened to us staying out of this investigation?

Marta gave Carly a teary smile. "We'd better just let the police do their job, but thanks."

"Wonder where the funeral will be?" I asked, hoping the subject change was subtle enough not to be obvious.

Carly jumped in to help. "Nashville, I'm sure. With a huge monument and eternal flame."

"That would be one way of guaranteeing our place's success," John said dryly. "We could offer to build a mausoleum in front of the Paradise."

Marta gasped. "John!"

He put his arm around her. "I'm just kidding. I promise."

The waitress brought our burgers and passed them out. She clutched the tray to her chest. "Did you folks hear about Holly Wood?"

We nodded.

Tears sprang to her already red-rimmed eyes. "It's sad that's what people will always remember Branson for."

Now it was Marta's turn to cry. John tightened his arm around her. "Murder can happen anywhere."

The waitress shrugged, obviously not picking up on his gruff voice. "I guess."

She left, and Marta turned her face into John's shoulder.

"Marta," Carly said softly. "Holly's death wasn't your fault."

"I'm so selfish," Marta said, her voice muffled. "I only thought about it ruining our business. I didn't even think about us taking Branson's reputation down with us."

John motioned to the full restaurant. "It doesn't look like we've single-handedly destroyed Branson's good name yet. Think about that pile of teddy bears and flowers out in front of the theater. It sounds callous, but the truth is, tourist trade may go up. People will come here just to be near where Holly died." He squirted ketchup on Marta's plate and even dipped the first french fry for her.

She obediently took the fry and popped it into her mouth. "It all depends on the murderer being caught quickly."

"You know, John," Alex said quietly, "Your idea of a memorial for Holly at the Paradise isn't all that crazy."

I jerked around to look at him. I knew he was desperate to get us off the subject of finding the murderer. But was he seriously suggesting that John and Marta build a mausoleum at their theater?

"What about hosting a memorial concert? In a couple of weeks. After the funeral."

Carly clapped her hands together softly. "That's a wonderful idea!"

Marta fiddled with her cheeseburger. "Don't you think people would think that we were capitalizing on tragedy?"

I shrugged. "We can't control what people think, but if I were a fan, I'd love a memorial concert. Let's face it. There won't be room for the world at Holly's funeral. This would give people closure."

John wiped his mouth. "She's right, honey. Plus we could recoup a little of our loss from last night's concert."

She drew back and stared at him in horror. "We are *not* charging people to come to Holly's memorial concert."

"But expenses. . ." John's voice faded away.

"God will take care of the details," Marta said.

See? I knew it wouldn't take long for the old Marta to return.

"And we're not about to profit from her death," she finished.

"Fat chance of that," John mumbled, but he reached over and took his wife's hand. "We'll give them a few days then talk to Buck and Ruth about it."

"Assuming the police don't arrest Buck," I murmured.

Marta ignored me and grabbed an ink pen and a napkin. "Buck, Ruth. . ." She scrawled names as she talked. "What about Maurice Seaton? I wonder if he'll come to Branson?"

At Alex's confused expression, I whispered, "Holly's first husband and her longtime financial advisor. Oh, and he's from Lake View."

Marta continued, "He loved Holly so much. I bet he'll be grief stricken, but he could help us." She added his name to her list.

She looked so much more hopeful that I resisted the urge to remind her that she was going to let God take care of the details.

"Didn't Holly say she had a personal assistant?" Carly offered. "Maybe she could help."

Marta shook her head. "Cindy Cunningham. I called her last night. Turns out Holly didn't give her time off. She fired her."

"Why would Holly lie about it?" I couldn't see the logic. "Did Cindy say why she got fired?"

"No. But she didn't seem terribly upset about Holly's death."

Carly pursed her lips. "Was she surprised?"

"She didn't say, and I couldn't decide. I think she'd probably already heard it on the news."

"Did you call her home phone?" I asked quietly.

Marta frowned. "No, it was her cell."

"So she could have been anywhere."

Carly grabbed my arm. "Like in town getting revenge."

Alex cleared his throat. "Y'all don't have any trouble jumping to conclusions, do you?"

I grinned at him. "We're athletically inclined like that. But the good news is, we do rein it in sooner or later."

"More sooner than later, I hope."

The twins came running over to us. "Zac and Danielle said they'd take us to ride the go-karts!"

Marta and Carly exchanged a look, and I could read it as clearly as if they'd spoken aloud. Not with a murderer loose in town.

"What if we all go?" I asked them quietly.

They both nodded. The kids bounded off to tell the teens, and John and Marta stood.

"If it's okay with you," I added to Alex.

He grinned at me. "Looks like I'd better hang around close to keep you from getting in over your head."

"Don't worry. I know how to swim."

"Everybody gets a cramp now and then and needs a buddy."

Carly rolled her eyes. "Would you guys just say what you mean?"

I laughed. "Did you forget he's a lawyer?"

Alex put his hand to his heart. "Are you implying I don't say what I mean?"

"If the Italian leather loafer fits. . ." I threw over my shoulder then hurried out before he could cross-examine me.

6

Anger is cruel and fury overwhelming, but who can stand before jealousy?
PROVERBS 27:4

Alex and I watched the kids ride for a while, but then I noticed in between laps, he'd close his eyes. "You must be worn out," I said softly during one of those times.

His eyes flew open, and he looked over at me. "I'm sorry I wasn't here."

"You had to work. I understand that." In spite of my momentary diva lapse when he called Friday and canceled, I was adult enough to get the concept of needing to work. Of course, I was also adult enough to know some people use work for an excuse to avoid personal commitment.

"I should have been with you when you found the body." He reached over and knitted his fingers through mine.

"Alex, you can't protect me from everything."

"I can try," he said, the quiet words almost lost in the roar of the go-karts passing by.

"You drove half the night. If you're going to be Superman to my Lois Lane, you'd better get a nap first. I'm ready to go if you are."

He smiled. "I do feel like I've been a little too close to kryptonite. What if I go back and rest for just a bit then take you to a show tonight?"

I gave him my best cheesy grin. "Sounds super."

We said our good-byes to John, Marta, and Carly then walked out to the parking lot.

Alex opened my door and gave me a hand up into the four-wheel-drive truck.

On the road to the hotel, I grabbed my cell phone. "I meant to ask Marta about getting you in a room."

He shook his head. "Marta's got enough on her mind. As much as I'd like to be closer to you, I'm already settled in where I stayed last night."

"You sure that's okay?"

He nodded and pulled into the Paradise entrance. I stared at the huge mound of teddy bears, flowers, candles, and letters.

Alex let out a low whistle. "Will you look at that!" Even more fans were

186

crowded together in the hot sun. Police officers milled around the crowd, and while we watched, a young blond collapsed onto the concrete. A female cop bent down to her, talking on her radio at the same time.

"Talk about pandemonium."

"I'll walk you in," Alex said.

"If you don't mind just driving me around to the back, I think I can slip in by myself. I didn't get much sleep last night either. I might try to catch a nap, too."

When we got to the back entrance, there was no one in sight. Alex got out and held the truck door open for me. He pulled me toward him and dropped a light kiss on the top of my head. "Stay out of trouble."

I laughed. "Always."

He raised an eyebrow. "I wish. Call me after your nap."

"What if you're still asleep?"

He brushed my hair back from my face. "Some things are more important than sleep. Call me."

I slid my key into the slot, pulled open the door, and stepped into the cool hallway. What kind of loyalty would persuade people to stand for hours out in the hot June afternoon sun? As I passed Holly's dressing room, I noticed the yellow police tape sagging low in front of the door. I looked both ways and carefully turned the knob. It opened easily.

A little frisson of nauseous déjà vu skittered in my stomach as I looked at her chair. But there was nothing to indicate that a dead body once sat there. As I stepped over the tape and into the room, the sliding closet door, slightly ajar, caught my eye. Detective Jamison's men weren't as tidy as they should have been. I walked over to close it and glanced in at the shimmering materials and jewel-bright colors of Holly's wardrobe. Poor Holly. She'd always dressed so vibrantly. It was still hard to believe she was dead.

I shut the closet door firmly. I needed to get out of here. Some places aren't meant to be snooped in. I was almost to the door when a soft, swishing sound came from the closet. My first impulse was to dash from the room and padlock the door. But curiosity moved my feet toward the noise. Just before I touched the handle, the door slid open with a *bang*. A body erupted from the closet, pushing me backward by pure momentum.

"Don't you ever close a door on me again," the blur of motion said. "I can't stand to be in a small space." Reagan caught her balance and advanced on me.

I took another step backward. "I'm sorry," I said instinctively in the face of her fury.

"What are you doing in here anyway?" She glared at me. "Going through Holly's stuff? Maybe trying to find something to sell on eBay? Some people have no shame." She moved to go around me as I took in the insults she spewed at me. I came to my senses in time to block the door.

"More to the point, what were *you* doing in Holly's closet?" I gave her the look Carly gives the twins when they're trying to pull one over on her. But Reagan was made of sterner stuff. Instead of wilting and confessing all, she pushed me out of the way and grasped the doorknob. I closed my hand over her hand on the knob and held it still. We were both huffing and puffing like two kids fighting over the same toy. Reagan must be guilty of something or she wouldn't have gone on the defensive so quickly.

"Reagan," I panted. I paused for a deep breath and voice control. "Reagan," I tried again, and thankfully, it came out sounding a bit more mature. "Why *were* you in Holly's closet? If you don't want me to call Detective Jamison immediately, you have to tell me." I shot her a nervous look. I could hear Alex's voice in my head. I don't think this is what he meant by staying out of trouble. Had I just threatened a murderer? I tightened my grasp on her hand.

She grunted. "Good grief. Don't get your panties in a wad. I was just"—she paused and her eyes darted around as if searching for inspiration—"looking for a scarf Holly borrowed from me." I followed her gaze to the coat rack and saw a blue scarf.

"Come on, Reagan. Tell me the truth." I tried to sound tough.

She bit her lip. "Actually. . ." Her hand on the doorknob relaxed. I loosened my grip in response.

She yanked open the door and dashed out.

"Well, that went well," I muttered to the empty room.

Adrenaline still pumping, I leaned against the door to catch my breath. What had Reagan been doing in the closet? I tiptoed back to the rows of glittery clothes, half afraid that a left-behind cohort would jump out at me. I wasn't sure whether to be disappointed or relieved to find nothing out of the ordinary. I chose relieved and hurried from the dressing room.

As I approached Holly and Buck's suite, the door started to open. I stopped and took a deep breath. Had Joey not finished with his business in there this morning? I stared at the doorway and waited.

I blew out my breath as Buck Fisher stepped out of his room, a suitcase in his hand and a hanging garment bag across his arm. His eyes were red-rimmed, and overnight his face seemed to have aged. Either he was truly sad or a fantastic actor.

I nodded and started to move on by.

He touched my arm with his free hand. "Jenna, right?"

"Yes."

He reached in his pocket and pulled out a turquoise money clip bulging with green. He peeled a hundred dollar bill from the stack. "Would you have someone pack up Holly's things and send them to our Nashville address?"

He pressed the money and a business card into my hand, along with a room key.

"I'll be glad to do it. You don't have to—"

He shook his head. "It's worth it to me not to have to handle them right now."

His voice rang with sincerity, and I was overwhelmed with a crazy sympathy for this man who had undoubtedly cheated on the queen of country music. "I understand." I took the card and the key, but I shoved the money back to him.

"Please keep it," he said.

I shook my head. "No, but thank you. I'll let you reimburse me for shipping. Where are you going?" Okay, I knew I was pushing it, but I hoped he'd answer anyway.

He sighed as he added the bill back to his stash. "The cops gave me permission to go to Nashville and take care of business there. Make funeral arrangements."

"Oh, don't forget to let someone in Lake View know what date you pick." Lame, but totally normal for me in these kinds of situations.

He gave me a blank look.

"Holly's from my hometown. And we're all so sorry for your loss."

"Oh, thank you. I'm sure the funeral arrangements will be well reported." His smile was a shadow of his former cheesy grin. "So Lake View will know along with the rest of the world."

My cheeks grew hot. He'd certainly put me in my place.

I went back to our suite to wait for Alex to wake up from his nap, all the while feeling a little like Alice in Wonderland. Maybe I'd fallen asleep and dreamed of Reagan in Holly's dressing room closet and Buck giving me carte blanche to their suite. I lay back on the bed and ran my thumb over Buck's business card. Holly's body hadn't been a figment of my imagination, and neither was the fact that there was a murderer among us.

This was the real deal. And my pounding heart every time I thought about crossing that police tape proved that Alex was right.

I was in over my head.

❖

"I haven't laughed that much in so long," I said, as we exited the comedy theater. "Thanks for taking me."

Alex hooked his arm through mine and leaned in close to my ear. "You have a beautiful laugh. I've missed hearing it."

I shivered. "I've only been gone for a few days."

"Seems like longer."

"It does, doesn't it?" Even finding Holly's body last night seemed so far away. So much had happened.

When the double doors opened, the blast of hot air hit me. At ten o'clock at night, the air was still sticky hot. Alex held my hand as we walked out to his truck. He hit the UNLOCK button on the key fob then opened the door for me. His parents had raised him right. He's a throwback to a more gentlemanly generation, and I loved it.

When he slid into his own seat, he started the motor and turned the air on but didn't put the motor in gear. "You know, Jenna, unless you really need me to stay, I have to be in court Tuesday morning."

I swallowed against a sudden lump in my throat. It wasn't as if I'd thought he could stay forever. But I wasn't ready to say good-bye. Even for a short while. I nodded, not trusting myself to speak.

"So I guess I'll head home tomorrow afternoon."

So soon? *Keep it light*, I coached myself. "Well, Counselor Campbell, as much as I'd like for you to stay, I know your clients are counting on you to play Superman for them. Will we be able to do something together in the morning before you put on the cape?"

A boyish grin flashed across his face. "I was hoping we would. If I won't be hindering your investigation."

I stared up at him. I hadn't wanted to keep my "investigation" secret from him, but I hadn't trusted him not to overreact. Was he giving me tacit permission to look into the murder? "Any 'investigating' can wait until Tuesday," I said, part seriously and part tongue-in-cheek.

"Want to tell me what you've found so far?"

I tried to read his eyes.

He laughed. "Even in the moonlight, I recognize that you-can't-handle-the-truth look. Lay it on me, Stafford. I'm tougher than you think."

"More powerful than a locomotive. I know, I've heard." I made a split-second decision. It was time for me to commit. Not by saying "I love you" first, because there was nothing wrong with me waiting to hear it from him, but I needed to commit by trusting him. Trusting him to keep my secrets and respect my decisions. "Well, you know what happened in the hall with Joey, the guitar player, this morning. Which may or may not be anything."

"Right. And?"

I quickly told him about finding Reagan in the closet.

"You crossed the police tape?" His voice didn't squeak, but it definitely rose in tone.

I should have stopped while I was ahead. I nodded without speaking.

He took a deep breath. "That took a lot of nerve."

"Thanks."

"And was completely illegal."

Now it was his turn to learn to stop while he was ahead.

"Well, it was sagging and looked almost like they'd just forgotten they put it there. You could tell lots of people have been in and out of there." I cringed. "Okay, I admit it. I shouldn't have gone in. I didn't stop and think before I stepped over that tape. I've felt awful ever since. Does that count for anything?"

He reached over and touched my shoulder. "Don't beat yourself up. Your natural curiosity is one of the things that makes you so special." He pulled slowly out onto the highway. "So why do you think Reagan was in there?"

"I have no idea. She and Buck were . . .kind of close. . .before Holly died." I gave him a quick rundown on the morning I found them with Reagan in her robe. "But it also seemed like Holly was Reagan's standard—the one singer she compared herself to. She could have gone in her dressing room to get closure."

Alex frowned. "Or tamper with evidence."

"True. But we left Holly's room the first time at seven sharp. Exactly the time Reagan took the stage. And during the break when Holly was supposed to come out, Reagan was only gone five. . .maybe ten minutes."

"Long enough to commit murder," he said flatly as we pulled into the hotel entrance.

I motioned to the candle-holding group still lingering around the make-shift memorial. "Then come back out and sing to a packed crowd?" That seemed cold—but then, I guess if she were a killer. . .

He shrugged as he drove around back. "The show must go on." Instead of pulling over to the hotel's door, he backed the truck into a parking place and let the engine idle. He turned slightly in his seat to face me and locked his gaze with mine. "Make no mistake, Jenna. This isn't a game. You are dealing with a killer who is capable of anything. Including killing again."

"I know. I'm being careful."

He sighed. "I hope so. I'd hate to lose you."

"I'd hate that, too." I half laughed, a feeble attempt to lighten the mood.

He smiled. "So we're on for tomorrow?"

"Definitely. What do you have planned?"

"Oh, I think I'll just keep our itinerary a mystery. That way I know you'll show up."

"You're a very funny guy. Tell me."

"Here's a clue. Dress outdoor casual. And be at the back entrance at seven."

"Are you serious? You're not going to tell me what we're doing?"

He leaned toward me and brushed my hair back.

"Is this a plan to distract me from my questions?" I whispered.

"Maybe," he whispered back, his face close to mine.

"It's working."

"Good." He dropped a light kiss on my lips, but before I could respond, he put the engine in gear and pulled up to the hotel back entrance.

Without a word, he jumped out and came around to hold my door open.

He walked with me to the door and waited while I slid my key. But as soon as I stepped inside, I glanced back, and he was standing by his truck, watching me.

So much for long good-byes.

7

A hot-tempered man stirs up dissension,
but a patient man calms a quarrel.
PROVERBS 15:18

You have no idea where you're going?" Carly squinted against the morning sun and sat on the edge of her bed, blanket nubbies marking the side of her face. She sleepily watched me put on my socks and tennis shoes.

I shook my head and pulled my shoe up to tie it. "None. Just 'outdoor casual,' whatever that means. What are you doing today?"

"I think the kids and I will just hang out within walking distance. Dani will probably spend the day with us."

"Keep an eye out for Reagan, Car."

She cocked her head at me. "Why?"

I quickly told her about my closet encounter. "And Joey, too."

"Holly's guitar player is on your suspect list?"

I nodded and tied my other shoe. "I think I saw him coming out of Holly and Buck's suite yesterday morning while Buck was at the police station."

"So thanks to the news report, he would have known that Buck was gone."

"Exactly. And we know the murder weapon was a guitar string. Which could actually incriminate either of them."

"That settles it. We'll steer clear of Reagan and Joey, I promise. You forget all this and enjoy Alex's last day in town."

Something in her voice made me do a double take. Why did I have a feeling she was thinking about her golf pro and wishing she was enjoying Branson with him? "Are you sorry you told Elliott not to come?"

She shrugged. "A little. But I'm not ready for that kind of commitment."

As I walked down to the back entrance to meet Alex, I thought about Carly's words. I wondered if Alex still would have come if he'd realized his Branson trip constituted commitment.

❖

We rode in silence for a while; then Alex whipped the truck into a parking lot and killed the motor.

I nodded toward the big white letters on the side of the building. "A day at Wal-Mart. I can see why you kept this such a big secret."

"Funny girl. Let's go."

"Good thing you told me to dress casual," I murmured as we got out of the truck.

He put his arm around my shoulders. "If I could have done this part without you, I would have."

I looked up at him. "That's so romantic."

He winked. "Just wait."

Inside, we said hello to the door greeter, and Alex guided me toward the back of the store.

"If you tell me where we're going, you won't have to hold on to me."

He grinned. "I don't mind."

Truthfully, neither did I. The big johnboat suspended from the ceiling and the rows of camouflage gave it away. "What are we doing in sporting goods?" I whispered.

Alex turned to the white-haired man behind the counter. "We need a couple of out-of-state fishing licenses."

"We're going fishing?" Alex and I used to fish together when we were young. Since he'd moved back to Lake View, we'd talked a lot about it but never done it.

"Shh. . ." he said out of the side of his mouth. "It's a surprise for my girlfriend."

At least he knew I was his girlfriend. Unfortunately, I was looking for a little more assurance for the future.

I handed the clerk my driver's license and looked over at the brightly colored lures hanging on a display. "Won't we need fishing tackle?"

Alex grinned. "I've got it all taken care of. Trust me."

Believe me, if I didn't, I wouldn't still be hanging around. . .waiting.

❖

An hour later, all my cares had melted away with the heat of the sun reflecting off Lake Taneycomo. I could lose myself in the soft sloshing of the water. Even the distant motor sounds created a sort of white noise conducive to forgetting everything. My contention with Lisa at the health club. . .a distant memory. Even Holly's murder and all Marta's troubles took a break from the forefront of my mind. I looked over at Alex, kicked back in his boat chair, his fishing pole stuck in the holder beside him. His eyes were closed and the bill of his cap shaded his face.

"Are you letting it all go?" he asked without opening his eyes.

"Yes. Thank you." I watched the water for ripples or other evidence of fish. "Are you?"

He reached and still without looking grabbed my hand. "I'm not thinking about letting go."

I shivered. "Good."

His eyes popped open, and his gaze met mine. "Cold?"

I shook my head. "This was the perfect idea."

He sat up slowly. He pointed toward a cluster of buildings on the far shore. "See that campground over there? I spent some great times there with my folks when I was a kid." Suddenly his rod bucked. He snatched it loose from the holder and began to reel.

I grabbed the net just as the fish broke the surface of the water, still attached to his line. Its fins sparkled like a treasure trove. "Easy to see why they call it a rainbow trout, isn't it?"

"It's a nice size. Think Carly will want to cook trout for y'all's supper?"

I nodded. "If Marta's not using her kitchen, then she definitely would."

He undid the hook and dropped the fish into the live well.

We sat down again, our lines drifting across the peaceful water.

I laid my head back. "I'd love to come out here at night. I bet there are a million stars."

He nodded. "When Dad and I used to night fish out here, we'd play amateur astronomer and try to name all the constellations." He pointed toward the shore. "The North Star comes up right over the campground."

"I'm glad you and your parents did things together. In my distorted memory, it seems like I took all of your dad's time with my swimming."

He laughed. "You worry too much about the past. I had a normal childhood. You, on the other hand. . ."

"Hey!" I slapped at him. "My childhood was normal. Except for the twenty hours a week I spent swimming."

"If you ever have kids, do you think you'll encourage them to do something so demanding?"

I squinted into the sunlight, hoping that any moisture in my eyes would be attributed to that. If *I* ever have kids? Not if *we* ever have kids, but if *I* ever have kids. . . I'd let this relationship get out of balance. I seriously needed to reevaluate what I was doing with Alex. If this is what I wanted for the rest of my life—a boyfriend—then I had it made. But if I was looking for more, then I probably needed to move on.

"I mean. . .not that there's anything wrong with your childhood. I just wondered. It seems like a lot of pressure for a kid."

I cleared my throat and fiddled with my reel. "I guess that would just be a decision my husband and I would have to make based on what's best for our child." Whoa. Did the day suddenly get colder, or was it just me?

"That makes sense."

This time my pole buckled. Relieved, I stood and reeled in a good-sized trout. Alex netted it and took it off my hook, then dropped it in with the other one.

For a while we fished in silence. What was Alex thinking? Did he know I was hurt, or was he so unaware of my feelings that he didn't even realize?

Thankfully, we caught a few more fish right in a row, making conversation not impossible, but unnecessary.

Alex grinned. "You hungry?"

I'd lost my appetite back when he asked me about if *I* had a child, but I wasn't going to tell him that. "Are we going to the shore for lunch?"

"You'll see."

He started the motor and puttered due north to the campground he'd shown me earlier. When he lifted a blanket and retrieved a wicker basket from the back of the boat, my jaw dropped. "You made us a picnic lunch?"

He ducked his head and shot me a wry grin. "I ordered it from a local deli. But it's the thought that counts, right?"

"Right." I let him help me out of the boat.

He spread the blanket out on a small spot of green grass and set the basket down next to a scraggly pine. We had a perfect view of the lake.

The sub sandwiches were delicious, complete with fresh, crisp pickles and chips. Alex proudly poured me some cold lemonade.

It was hard to stay upset when he was so kind, but I had to remind myself of my earlier epiphany. Did I want a life of spontaneous fishing trips and surprise picnics? Or did I want home and hearth? Or both? "This is great, Alex. But I bet it was a lot of trouble to arrange."

"Nothing's too much trouble for you."

Aww. Now see? Every time I thought about walking away, he'd do or say something sweet like that.

◈

Carly looked up from her chair as I walked in. "You look tired." She took a second look. "But happy. And sunburned. Didn't you wear sunblock?"

I touched my hot face. "I did actually. I forgot to reapply it, and then I fell asleep for a while."

"Oh Jenna. I'm sorry."

"I haven't pulled a stunt like that since college. But the time just flew."

She grinned. "It does that when you're having fun. Did he finally say it?"

I shrugged. "In words? No. But in every other way that counts, yes. He even let me bring you the fish we caught, cleaned and ready to cook." I lifted the tiny cooler for her to see.

Her face lit up, and she jumped to her feet. "How did you know I needed to cook? I already called Marta and told her I'd be fixing supper for all of us."

"Why? Is something wrong?"

"Not really wrong. But I found out something a little odd while you were gone." She glanced toward the sitting room where the kids were playing a rowdy game of Cranium. She lowered her voice. "I think you might be right about Joey."

"Oh?" So she *was* serious about investigating? This was a new Carly. "When did you go all Miss Marple on me?"

She looked pleased but shook her head. "This info fell into my lap, actually. At lunch we were talking about Holly's band, and Danielle said that Joey hated Holly."

I leaned toward her to catch the last words. "Why?" I mouthed.

"Seems Holly took his dad away from his mom."

"So at one point she was his stepmom?"

Carly shrugged. "I'm not sure if Joey's dad was one of the husbands or not. Dani didn't mention that."

"It really doesn't matter. His father ditching his mother for Holly gives Joey the perfect reason to hate her."

"And kill her? So should we tell Detective Jamison?" Carly asked.

"Not yet. All we have at this point is hearsay. But it's enough for me to have a talk with Joey."

"You're just going to march down to his suite?"

"Don't be silly. I'm going to meet him in the lobby. Wanna come?"

She held her hands out as if they were scales. "Let's see. . .cook. Or confront a possible killer." She took the cooler from my hand and started for the door. "If you need me, I'll be in Marta's kitchen at her cottage. Supper will be ready at 6:30."

❖

I used the house phone in the lobby to be connected to Joey's suite, and after the second ring, I heard a gruff, "Huh?"

Clearly I'd awakened the sleeping beauty from his afternoon nap.

"Hello," I chirped. "This is Jenna Stafford, the Hills' assistant, and I need to talk with you. Please meet me in the lobby." Hopefully that sounded professional enough that he wouldn't ask any questions.

"W–h–y should I?" He sounded like a particularly touchy bear prematurely awakened from hibernation. This should be fun. And so much for my professionalism.

"W–e–ll." I drew the word out in a drawl Carly could be proud of. "We can just skip our talk, and I can go straight to Detective Jamison with the information I've obtained. I just thought you might want to hear it first. Maybe clear things up a bit?"

"I don't know what you're talking about." The bear voice sounded slightly quivery now. Like maybe he'd accidentally put his paw in a beehive. "But I'll meet with you if I have to. Give me a few minutes."

I'd barely fixed a cup of coffee from the lobby pot when Joey appeared wearing a black shirt with a guitar played by skeleton hands emblazoned on the front and some gray army-style pants. His stand-straight-up hair and five-o'clock shadow completed the scruffy rock star look. Since I was the only person in the large open area—so much for my great plan of safety in numbers—he walked right over to me. "You the one who called me?"

I stood. "Yes. I'm Jenna Stafford."

"Congratulations. What's this about the police?" The venomous look in his eye caused me to back up a little. Maybe this wasn't such a great idea after all.

"Why don't we sit down?" I motioned toward the two chairs that framed the table with the coffeepot.

He growled. "No."

"Er, how about a cup of coffee?" He'd obviously gotten up on the wrong side of the bed. Maybe caffeine would soothe the savage beast. I poured another cup of the steaming stuff and shuffled it across the table toward him, the angry bear analogy still fresh in my mind. He gave the cup a contemptuous look, which he then transferred to me. I decided to cut to the chase.

"I. . .I. . .heard that maybe Holly was your stepmom." I cleared my throat. That wasn't quite as emphatic as I had intended it to be. "Is that true?" At least I had quit talking about coffee and sitting and had gotten down to why we were here. That was a start.

"What business is that of yours?" He seemed to tower over me as he shoved the coffee to one side.

"Joey, you need to tell the police if there's a connection between you and Holly. If someone else tells them, you'll look guilty."

"So what are you saying? You're the one that's going to tell them?" If looks could kill. . .Holly wouldn't be the only victim.

"Well," I temporized. "Someone will. If I found out about it, obviously others already know. It would be better for you if you give them all the facts yourself. That way they won't get any twisted story."

"Twisted? You don't know nothin' about my life." He clenched his fists and glared at me. "So what if Holly shacked up with my old man? My life is none of your business."

"No, you're right, it isn't my business. I was only trying to help."

"I don't need your help. So butt out." Before I could reply, Joey slammed both hands on the table, and the coffee cup crashed to the floor, splashing hot coffee everywhere. With a mocking smirk, he turned and strode from the room, leaving his inept questioner—aka me—to clean up his mess.

❖

While I was still on my knees swiping up the last of the liquid, my cell phone rang. I fished it from my pocket and flipped it open. "Hello?" I tried to sound upbeat instead of nearly beaten up.

"Jenna? This is Gail." If she hadn't said my name, I'd have thought it was a wrong number, because this woman sounded beyond agitated. The Gail I knew was a sweet-tempered college student who worked part-time at Lake View Athletic Club.

"Hey, Ga—"

"When are you coming home?"

"I—"

"If you don't hurry, there won't be anything to come home to. Lisa is ruining the club. Half the members have threatened to quit. Do you know what she's doing?"

"Well, not ex—"

"I'll tell you what she's doing."

I had a feeling she would. I clambered off the floor and onto a chair. I probably needed to be sitting for this one.

"For starters, she didn't gather towels to send to the cleaning service. Do you know how happy people were when they got out of the hot tub and pool to find they didn't have anything to dry with? And guess who they got mad at? Me."

I barely had time to grunt before she continued. "And do you know what else she did? I'll tell you." She was off again. "She didn't measure the chlorine when she serviced the pool. She just dumped it in. A lot. Amelia's new hot pink bikini turned as pastel as a baby blanket. She threatened to sue. Sue! Over a bikini. Can you believe it?"

Maybe if it was a designer bikini. Which, knowing Amelia, it probably was. "Unfortunately I can believe it."

"Well, that's not the worst. Some people burned their eyes so badly they had to have eyewash right then."

I gasped. Surely she was exaggerating.

"Only guess who took the medicine kit home with her and forgot to bring it back? But naturally, she wasn't on duty when all this happened. I was. So who do you think got chewed out? I'm telling you, Jenna, if you don't come home soon, this club will be closed. The only running Lisa's doing is running it into the ground."

She took a deep breath.

"Gail, I'm sorry, but the truth is—"

"Amelia said to tell you they're getting up a petition, and if things don't get better, they're all quitting."

Ouch. One thing I knew about the first lady of Lake View. She didn't make idle threats. I waited a second to be sure Gail was out of steam before I attempted a reply. "Have you talked to Bob? He's the owner, after all. He won't want the place to fall apart."

"All Bob says is that we have to give Lisa time. And that you'll be back in a few days."

That figures. Same old scenario. Bob assuming I'd feel sorry for him and cut my vacation short.

"I'm sorry to dump on you like this, Jenna, but I don't know what else to do. We'll all lose our jobs if the club closes."

I sighed quietly. As much as I had a right to be mad at Bob for how he'd treated me—promising me the health club at a good price then bringing in Lisa instead for me to "train," or what I call "wait on hand and foot"—I couldn't let all my coworkers lose their jobs. "I'll talk to Bob."

"Thanks, Jenna. And hurry back!"

I hung up and shook my head.

"Jenna?" A trembling voice behind me made me spin around.

Holly's sister, Ruth. And a male friend. "I'd like you to meet Maurice Seaton."

I nodded. Holly's ex. Twice, actually. No wonder he looked so sad.

"Maury, Jenna Stafford. She's from Lake View, just like we are. Though she's a little younger, of course."

"Oh?" Maurice gave me a blank look from red-rimmed eyes. "Hello."

His grief was so real that shame almost overwhelmed me. My main emotion over Holly's death, other than shock, had been dismay on behalf of John and Marta.

"I'm so sorry about your—Holly." Oops. Almost said "your wife." I don't know how long I stood there with my mouth open, trying to think of just the right word. Where was Ms. Social Graces Carly when I needed her? "Holly. About your loss." How lame. No wonder, with one foot in my mouth. "It's nice to meet you." I started to edge away, but Ruth stepped toward me, and Maurice obediently followed.

"Jenna was an Olympic swimmer."

Maurice nodded, but I didn't really see any recognition on his face.

"Well, I bet you remember her older sister, Carly." Ruth seemed to be trying desperately to bring the man to life. "They saved Holly a seat on the school bus every day."

A gleam flickered in those dull eyes. "Little girl with black curly hair? I remember her. There were two of them. Twins, weren't they?"

"Just good friends." Ruth patted his shoulder as if giving him points for trying. "They're here, too—both of them. In fact, Carly's friend, Marta, owns this theater."

"Yeah?" Uh-oh. She'd obviously lost him again.

"Yes, remember I told you that Marta wants to have a memorial concert for Holly?" She turned to me. "I think it's a wonderful idea and so does Maury."

He nodded absently.

"Nice meeting you," I tried again. "I'd better get to. . ." I couldn't think of an excuse. I hated when my brain went on vacation and left my body in a delicate social situation. Ironically, Ruth saved me.

"I was just seeing Maurice out. He's staying at a condo down the street." She practically pushed him out the door. "Remember what we talked about, Maury. I'll see you tonight." He obediently left, and Ruth turned to me as if we were best buds.

"I need to talk to you," she said in a low, riveting voice. My ears stood at attention. "I called Maurice." She waited for my response. I had no idea what she was after. Thanks? Congratulations? A medal? It seemed a normal thing to me. Her sister died, Maurice was an old friend and ex, so she called him. Where's the mystery? I must have looked blank—not difficult, since I was.

She frowned as if maybe I was a little simple. "To help me figure things out."

"Things?"

She nodded emphatically and leaned toward me, her no-nonsense salt-and-pepper bob covering her face slightly. "Buck did it," she whispered.

8

A fortune made by a lying tongue is a fleeting vapor and a deadly snare.
PROVERBS 21:6

I pulled back and looked into Ruth's swollen eyes. "Have you told the police?" First Joey then Ruth. My friend, John, who also happened to be Lake View's police chief, would have been so proud of me for encouraging everyone to take their information to the police.

"Oh yes. I told them that Buck killed her, and they know about the life insurance, but as far as the other, what's to tell until we have proof?"

Life insurance I understood. But "other"? I felt as if I were in a cell phone commercial. Talk about a bad connection.

"But when Maurice checks it out, we'll take the information right to the detectives. The important thing is I know Buck is the murderer."

She could be right, but my gut feeling was that—even though he was a slimeball—he wasn't a murderer. For one thing, he was coming from the other direction right after I found Holly. So unless he killed her, left the scene, then wandered back by, my money was on Reagan. I wanted to be diplomatic, but judging from her remarks when she and Holly were arguing, Ruth was aware of the relationship between Reagan and Buck.

"What about Reagan? Do you think it's possible she did it?"

"You mean because she was having an affair with Buck?" So much for being subtle.

"Well, they weren't very discreet, were they? Even I could tell they were close, but did Holly know?"

"She never admitted it if she did. You know how she is—was. It would have been nearly impossible for her to believe that her husband could prefer anyone over her." She looked so miserable and wrung out, my heart twisted.

"Do you want a cup of coffee?" I asked and motioned toward the two overstuffed lobby chairs near the smaller fireplace. I had nowhere I had to be for another couple of hours. If I couldn't spare time for someone who was grieving, what kind of person was I?

After ten minutes of listening to Ruth talk about Holly, I almost regretted my impulsive invitation. Now that she was dead, Holly had suddenly transformed into Mother Teresa to hear her sister tell it.

"She did have a certain presence," I said gently.

Ruth seemed to realize that she'd been canonizing her sister. "Well, I know she had flaws, but that wasn't really her fault. When she was growing up, we always treated her like a fragile princess. Because to us, she was. She was so beautiful and perfect that we felt like she deserved whatever she wanted. So she took it as her due, whether it belonged to someone else or not."

"I can see how that could happen." The Bible warned against spoiling children for a reason. Because if you did, they were. . .spoiled. Like something ruined.

Ruth leaned forward. "She made enemies, you know," she whispered.

I made a noncommittal sound and bit back the "You don't say?" that desperately wanted to pop out.

"But she was so gullible," Ruth continued. "She couldn't ever see possible evil. Like her stalker."

Curiosity kicked in. Hard. "Stalker?"

Ruth nodded, still staring off into the distance, as if I were invisible. "He came to at least ten shows every year—for the last three years. He sends—sent—her letters planning how they would go away together."

"Did the police know?"

"I tried to get her to go to the police when she got the first letter, but she laughed in my face. Still, there was something about those letters that gave me the creeps. Holly said he just wanted attention."

"So she encouraged him?"

Ruth frowned, and I thought I'd gone too far. But she slowly drifted back into her lazy monologue. "One show, after about a year or so of the letters, he described what he would be wearing. When Holly spotted him in the audience, she waved at him. Thought she was being cute." She pursed her lips, obviously remembering Holly's reaction. "I told her she was playing with fire. But she said if he was gonna do something, he would have done it by then. I guess she was right."

"Umm, when did she get the last letter from him?" Casual tone, but my heart was thumping.

"Just before we left Nashville. That was odd, because he usually sent the letter to the show location. But this was really just a note. It said something like, 'I've always wanted to see Branson. Maybe we can see it together.' And that was it."

"Did you tell the police about that note?"

Suddenly Ruth seemed to come out of her trance. She straightened and gave me a hard stare, almost as if she were accusing me of forcing her confidence. "I told them all they need to know. I mentioned the stalker, but I know

Buck did it, and that's what I told them." She stood, her back as straight as if she had a rod for a backbone. The slumped, helpless woman was gone. I had a feeling that was the last information I would get from Ruth.

As she strode out of the lobby, I remained where I was, transfixed by the extreme sudden change in her. One thought gripped me. Was there really a stalker? Or was he just a made-up scapegoat in case Buck managed to prove his innocence? Ruth obviously loved her sister, but she also had plenty of reasons to hate her. What if she'd pulled the same Dr. Jekyll/Mr. Hyde Saturday night as she had just now and killed Holly?

◆

"Poor Ruth. It can't have been easy living in Holly's shadow." Marta took a sip of her tea.

"The bane of talentless sisters everywhere," Carly intoned dryly as she leaned forward to offer John another piece of grilled trout.

"Tell me about it." I held up my last bite of fish. "I'm not the one who made us a gourmet meal out of a morning's catch."

"Now that you mention it. . . ," she drawled. "You're looking a little pale. Must be all that time in my shadow."

I touched my sunburned face. "Make fun of me, why don't you?"

Hayley looked up from her plate. "Aunt Jenna, why didn't you wear sunscreen?"

"Yeah," Rachel piped up. "You're always telling us to."

I smiled. "Extenuating circumstances."

She gave me a puzzled glance then looked at her mom.

Carly pursed her lips and shook her head. "Aunt Jenna got distracted. But see how she paid for it?"

"So who all is still staying in the hotel?" I asked, partly to divert attention from my sunburned face and partly because I was curious. "I know Buck left Sunday." I'd told Marta and Carly about his request. Unfortunately, every time I started to clean out the room, something kept me from it. There was no telling what clues were in there. Waiting. "And Ruth left today, didn't she?"

"Yes, she went to Nashville for the reading of the will," Marta said. "Joey and Reagan are still here."

"Really?" Carly's brows drew together. "Wonder why?"

"Apparently the police aren't quite ready for either of the guitar players to leave town, so I told them they could stay for a while longer." Marta must have seen the surprised look we exchanged, because she hurried on. "Both of them offered to work for their room and board. As a matter of fact, Reagan got wind somewhere of the memorial concert plans and volunteered to sing."

Carly snorted. "I can just see Ruth going along with that."

I nodded. "It doesn't seem very likely."

The twins pushed their empty plates away, apparently bored with the adult conversation. Rachel looked at her mom. "Supper was great."

"Can we go, please?" Hayley asked.

Carly hesitated, and again I thought of how differently we reacted since the murder. When we first arrived, Paradise Theater and Hotel seemed like the safest place in the world. "You may be excused from the table, but you can't go back to our suite without us," Carly said firmly.

They shoved to their feet, and Zac and Dani did the same.

"Hold it right there." They turned to look at Carly. "Plates in the sink."

They groaned, but all four of them carried their plates and silverware into the kitchen before disappearing into the living room.

Marta looked at Carly. "I guess we know who needs to be in charge of getting the memorial concert together."

"Me?" Carly squeaked. "Not unless you're havin' the concert in a kitchen, sugar."

"If that's the only way you'll help, we might consider it," John deadpanned.

Marta cut her gaze to him. "I thought we were going to ease into it."

He chuckled. "That's as subtle as I could be while begging for help, honey."

Marta blew out an outraged breath. "John! I never said to beg—"

Carly and I exchanged a quick look. "Y'all don't have to beg us. We'll help any way we can," she said.

Marta set her napkin on the table and pulled a sheet of paper from her pocket. "I agree that Ruth would never go along with letting Reagan sing, so I need you two to call these country singers and see if any of them are willing to perform at the tribute."

Carly took the paper. "Y'all asked Buck about speaking?"

"Yes, he agreed *and* offered to let us use a short video montage he's having done of Holly."

"What about Ruth? Will she say a few words?" I couldn't imagine her onstage, but based on what I'd seen earlier, there could be a superstar personality lurking inside her mousy exterior.

"She asked if Maurice could speak in her place. Buck wasn't thrilled about it, but he couldn't really say no. So that's what we're doing."

"That's great, Marta." Carly handed me the sheet.

I glanced at the list. These were the biggest names in country music. "Did you decide to charge admission?"

John cleared his throat. "Well, I—"

"No!" Marta jumped to her feet. "I told you I don't want to profit from her death."

John dropped his fork onto his plate. "Listen, honey—"

Her eyes flashed. "Don't you 'honey' me."

"Marta," he said softly. "Believe me, we're not going to 'profit' from her death. I was just hoping we could make back a little of what her death cost us."

Tears sparkled in her eyes and she sat back down. "I'm sorry. I just wanted to do something nice for Holly." She nodded toward the list. "I know it's a long shot. But I was hoping someone on that list might sing Holly's songs just as a tribute to her. Not for the money."

"If we could find a singer who would do that," Carly mused, "then you could take donations at the door and recoup some of your losses." She gave Marta a shrewd look. "*Without* charging admission."

"It's really short notice, though." I hated to be the voice of reason, but the chances of any of those names not being already booked for two weeks from Friday were slim to none. Marta's lips tilted down. "But we'll try."

Marta sighed. "How much longer can you stay?"

Before Carly had a chance to commit us to hanging around Branson until the concert, I spoke up. I had a cat and a dog, not to mention a lawyer, who missed me. "We should probably head home Friday afternoon. That way I can go back to work on Monday and take more time off when we come back for the concert."

"Sounds perfect," John boomed.

"It does." Marta pushed to her feet. "Thank y'all so much. Who wants coffee?"

"Definitely me." Carly started clearing the table.

"I'd better not. I've got. . .things I need to do." I said good night to John and Marta. "My compliments to both the chef and the hosts."

"Dear Pru?" Carly mouthed as John and Marta carried things into the kitchen.

I nodded.

"See you back at the suite later, then."

As I stepped out into the hot, humid night, a strange noise drifted to me. I followed the stepping-stones around to the sidewalk in front of the hotel and suddenly realized what it was.

Singing.

Holly's fans. I slowly walked toward them, drawn by the a cappella singing and the sea of candles swaying in the darkness. Were these the same people who had been out here since the murder? Or were they taking the vigil in shifts?

As I eased up to the group, the first thing that struck me was how normal they all looked. A mother wearing a T-shirt proclaiming, GOD NEEDED A PERFECT ANGEL SO HE TOOK HOLLY, clutched her preteen's hand. I frowned. Several others were wearing the same shirt. As conscientious as Marta was about not making money off Holly's death, others obviously had no such compunction.

A college-age boy stood behind his tearful girlfriend, his arms wrapped around her as she waved a candle. She glanced at me and pressed her lips together as new tears poured down her face.

Her grief pained me, and I turned away. Into a face distorted with rage. His hate-filled gaze burned into mine, and his lips were drawn into a snarl.

I stumbled back. A group of middle-aged women shifted into the gap between us. Without looking back, I sprinted for the front door of the hotel. I ignored the startled desk clerk and continued to run until I reached our suite.

Behind the safety of my locked door, I collapsed against the wall and slid down to the floor. I picked at the gray tweed of the carpet, my heart pounding in my ears. I'd seen people angry before. And the man didn't seem to be mad at me personally, but just filled with rage. So why had his anger chilled me to the bone? Before the question formed in my mind, I knew the answer. I was afraid I'd stepped directly into the path of a murderer.

9

A gossip betrays a confidence; so avoid a man who talks too much.
PROVERBS 20:19

I sat on the floor and prayed for at least ten minutes. When I stood, I was considerably calmer, but I still knew that if hate had a face, that man's was it. I wanted to call the police. But what would I tell them? That I had a bad feeling about one of Holly's fans? That he seemed to be disproportionately angry? That didn't even make sense. I might as well just tell them a good joke. I'd get the same laughs.

Just as I reached for the Dear Pru files, my cell phone rang. For a split second, I was afraid to look at the caller ID and even more afraid to answer it. I shook my head and looked at the number. Alex.

"Hey!"

"Hey, water girl. Or should I say Detective Stafford?"

I laughed. Shakily. "I'll just stick with Jenna. The last thing I'm interested in tonight is investigating Holly's murder."

"What happened?" His voice grew quickly serious. "Are you okay?"

I told him about the man outside, relieved to be able to share my fear with someone I knew wouldn't think I was crazy.

"Come home."

That was love in his voice, wasn't it?

"I can't. We promised Marta and John that we'd help with the memorial concert. It's in two weeks."

"You're planning on staying for two weeks?" He sounded panicked.

I felt better. "No. Just a few more days for now. We'll be home Friday night."

"Why don't I come back up there until then?"

"Alex, listen. I promise to be careful. If this man is the murderer, the police will find him. He's right out in the front of the hotel. He's probably been out there since the news broke about her death. Maybe he's just hurt and angry that she's gone and isn't a threat at all."

"Maybe. But you still need to be careful."

"I will, Alex." I tossed the Dear Pru files onto the bed. "I'm glad you made it home. I've got some things I've got to do, so I'd better go."

"Okay. Will you be home in time for us to go out Friday night?"

"Sure, I'd love to."

"Good." He hesitated. "Well, I'll let you go. Take care, Jenna."

My lips twisted in a bittersweet smile. "You, too."

I flipped the phone shut and picked up the first Dear Pru letter.

My boyfriend of two years is the man of my dreams. Really. But I think he's become obsessed with me. He frequently tells me he loves me and gets upset if I don't respond. My best friend says I should be grateful that he's open about his feelings. But I'm not so sure. What do you think?

I tossed the letter onto the bed and grabbed my gown from the drawer. Maybe tomorrow I'd feel like giving this poor soul some sound advice. Right now I just wanted to give her a sound whack on the side of the head with a verbal two-by-four. Just because someone needed to hear "I love you" didn't mean she was obsessed. Did it?

❖

The next morning, I was half finished with my swim when Detective Jamison walked in. I wasn't in the mood to be scared off this time, so I completed my laps, studiously ignoring him.

After I finished, I quickly showered and dressed. I thought I'd be sitting at Starbucks working on Dear Pru letters before the detective got out of the pool. But when I came out of the women's locker room, he was coming from the men's, fully dressed. Either he'd cut his workout short or I'd taken a longer shower than I thought.

A loud *crash* outside drew my gaze to the floor-to-ceiling windows around the pool. Lightning flashed. Rain suddenly pounded down, blowing hard against the glass.

No way I was going out in that downpour. Starbucks and Dear Pru could wait. I plopped my gym bag on the small table, sat down in a white plastic chair, my back to the floor-to-ceiling windows, and stared at the concrete block wall.

"Olympics, huh? That must have been pretty exciting." A crash of thunder punctuated his bombshell.

He slid into the chair next to me as if I'd invited him.

"If you consider letting down your hometown and possibly your whole country before you're even old enough to vote, then sure. It was a bundle of excitement." I slipped my fingers through my gym bag handle and scooted it toward me.

"So you're embarrassed? That's why you lied to me about having professional training?"

"I didn't lie! I said I'm not in professional training now. Two entirely different things."

"I see."

My knuckles whitened on the gym bag handle. "And I'm not embarrassed. I'm just being realistic about the experience."

His smile seemed genuine, not snarky like I'd have expected. And it softened his whole face. "Isn't it funny how we always focus on the negative and forget the good parts?"

"What good parts?" The loudness of the rain threatened to drown out my voice.

He leaned forward. "I'm sure there had to be a great feeling of accomplishment when you made the Olympic team."

I shrugged. But as soon as he said it, I did remember how excited I'd been.

"Maybe you've forgotten how great you must have felt just knowing you'd made it there?"

Tears pricked at my eyes. I blinked. "Maybe." If I was honest with myself, I knew I had. The end result had seemed so catastrophic that I had blocked out the thrill of going. But I wasn't going to admit it to a stranger. "Did you want to be in the Olympics? You're a very good swimmer."

He frowned and motioned toward the pool. "I took up swimming after my wife died five years ago. So I was way too old for Olympic aspirations. Unless there's such a thing as the Senior Citizen Olympics."

"I don't think you qualify for those, Detective." My best guess at his age would be forty-five.

"Call me Jim."

I looked up, startled that he'd want to be on first-name basis with me.

As if he read my mind, he said, "May I call you Jenna?"

I nodded. "So you preferred to get your fame by solving murders?"

He laughed. "Not everyone wants fame. Was that really why you wanted to be in the Olympics?"

"Actually that was my least favorite part."

"That's what I would have guessed." He looked out the window as if fascinated by the rain. "Your friend Holly seemed to thrive on her fame."

"She did. But she wasn't my friend. It was more of a servant-master relationship." I kind of laughed then stopped when he looked at me intently. "I mean, Marta asked us to come here to help her take care of Holly." But he already knew that.

"Ah, yes, Marta and Holly were high school friends, weren't they?"

I snorted. "Holly wasn't the type to have female friends."

"Really? I would think all the girls would want to be her friend. Unless they were jealous." For someone who was so perceptive a minute ago, he didn't seem all that intuitive now.

"Like I said, Holly didn't make friends. She made groupies." I tried not to sound negative, because I didn't want to be at the top of the suspect list.

"Well, Marta and your sister were close, weren't they?"

Finally, a subject I was more comfortable with. "Yes, they've been best friends as long as I can remember. They stayed friends even after they married."

"The Hills seem to have a good relationship."

"Yep. Marta always says they're the perfect balance. He's easygoing, the voice of reason, and she's impulsive and quick-tempered."

"Really?"

Had I lost my mind? I just told the chief detective in charge of Holly's murder case that Marta had a bad temper.

"Well, not quick-tempered maybe. Just impulsive, and sometimes she gets a little aggravated then quickly gets over it."

He was staring at me as if he were reading my thoughts again. I wanted to add, "She would never kill anyone, though." But even I had sense enough to know that would make things worse.

"Have you ever seen her do anything violent when she was mad?"

I frowned. "No. You can forget Marta. She didn't kill Holly."

"And you know this because. . . ?"

"Because she wouldn't hurt a fly. Maybe you should find out why Joey hated Holly. And what he was doing in her suite Sunday while Buck was at the station. And while you're at it, you might consider that I found Reagan hiding in Holly's dressing room closet. Marta is the least—"

His eyes bored into mine. "What were you doing in Holly's dressing room?"

Too late I remembered the crime scene tape. Me and my big mouth. I clamped my lips together and resisted the urge to turn an imaginary key and throw it away.

The only sound was the pounding of rain.

Finally, he leaned toward me. "Jenna, I get the feeling you've taken an interest in this crime. My guess is you read mystery novels, and now you think you're the next Miss Marple. But you'd do well to remember those are books. In real life if you mess with a murderer, you'll probably end up dead."

I dropped my gaze to the table.

He cleared his throat, and I looked up.

"And that would be a real shame."

I jumped to my feet.

"I can't wait any longer. I've got things to do," I stammered. "'Bye." I clutched my bag to my chest and dashed out into the torrential rain. I was reminded of my sprint to get away from the fanatic last night. Considering my innocence, I sure did seem to spend a lot of time running away these days.

❖

I'd dried out completely by midafternoon. Fueled by white chocolate lattés, I'd even finished the Dear Pru letters. When I got back to our suite, the first thing I saw was a note on my bed.

> *At Marta's. Come over when you get in.*
>
> —C

I made my way to Marta's via the back entrance this time. I didn't want to go near the mourners out front. Not after last night. I knocked and waited then knocked again. Finally, Zac opened the door. "Mom's in the kitchen." He disappeared into the living room, where I could hear a DVD trivia game playing. I stood in the foyer for a minute and breathed in the spicy aroma of cinnamon rolls mixed with the warm nutty smell of banana nut bread. Yum. But uh-oh.

I rushed into the kitchen. The empty kitchen. "Carly?"

She popped up from behind the work space. "Jenna, I'm so glad you're here. I didn't want to call you, because I knew you needed to work."

Flour spotted her face, but it was easy to see her eyes were swollen and red. "What happened?"

"They've taken Marta away."

Okay. They. The little men in white coats? Aliens from outer space? The city zoning board? Well, my boss had been having trouble with our zoning board, so it's not as far-fetched as it sounded. I waited for enlightenment.

"They think she had something to do with the murder." Carly looked at me as if I were obtuse, which I probably was. But I finally knew who *they* were.

"The *police* took her?"

"Yes. That's what I've been telling you."

"Why did they take her? What did they say?" Suddenly I remembered what I'd said to Jim—Detective Jamison just a few short hours ago. Was I responsible for Marta being arrested?

"They just said they needed her for more questioning. She asked what it was about, and they said they'd discuss it at the station."

"Did John go with her?"

"Oh yeah. He had to. Marta was so upset when she called me." She looked toward the living room. "The kids were at our suite when it happened. They think John and Marta just went to town for something." Her voice broke. "Poor Dani."

212

"Wait. She wasn't actually arrested, right?"

"Not officially. They let John drive her. But who knows what's happened by now?"

The *click* of the front door opening drew us both out of the kitchen. Marta looked at us bleakly. Behind her, John's always-pleasant face was a thundercloud. Not good signs.

"Marta," Carly whispered, glancing toward the living room where the kids thankfully had the volume on their game set to loud. "I can't believe they took you in for questioning. They should be able to tell by looking at you that you wouldn't hurt a flea."

I waited for Marta to explode the way she often did when I made her mad as a kid. No explosion. She just walked toward the kitchen looking defeated. What was going on?

"John?" Carly said, her voice trembling.

He ran his hand over his thinning hair and motioned for us to precede him into the kitchen. "Marta and Holly had a fuss. Someone overheard it and reported it to the police."

Marta was sitting on a stool, elbows on the bar, chin in her hands. "Holly started being difficult," she said softly.

Apparently she wasn't out of it enough not to see the look that Carly and I exchanged, because she sighed. "Okay, *more* difficult. She got more and more demanding—insisting after the first night that we cut the intermission." She glanced up at us, indignation flaring in her eyes. "Do you know how much we make on concessions? But we had no choice but to go along with her or she'd leave."

"I don't understand," Carly said, sinking onto the stool next to Marta. "Didn't Holly have a contract?"

"Yes, but her agent called the day of the opening show to tell her she had an offer to play a huge venue. They were offering twice as much as we were. She wanted out of her contract. I refused. From that moment on, I think she set out to make me want to get rid of her."

Her face paled. "Not get rid of her, get rid of her. I mean let her out of her contract." She leaned closer to Carly. "At that point I would have loved nothing better than to see the last of her." She gasped. "No wonder the police suspect me. Nothing I say comes out right."

Carly patted her shoulder. "With Buck and Ruth both in Nashville for the reading of the will, the detectives probably just had some time on their hands. We know you didn't kill Holly. And I'm sure they do, too."

"I hope you're right. We'd have been ruined if she left. It was too late to line up another act, and we had sold tickets." She looked at John then took a deep breath as if she'd decided to tell the whole truth. "We'd already used the money to refurbish the theater. I knew we'd be knee-deep in trouble if Holly left." Marta gave a bitter laugh. "I was sure right about that."

"But for that very reason, it makes no sense that they'd suspect you," I said. "You had the most to lose by Holly being out of the picture." Unless they thought she did it in a fit of temper. Guilt churned in my stomach. Why hadn't I just stayed completely out of that conversation with Detective Jamison? I'd let my guard down with him because he'd been so insightful and understanding about the Olympics. But at what cost?

❖

Thursday morning, I went late to the pool, with one purpose in mind. My timing was perfect. I'd barely walked in the door when Detective Jamison came out of the men's locker room, fully dressed.

"Good morning," he said, his deep voice cheerful.

I glared at him.

"Or not?"

"Yeah, right," I snarled. "You don't have a clue why I might be in a bad mood."

He raised his eyebrows.

"You used me. You took advantage of our relaxed conversation to get me to say something against my friend then brought her in for questioning."

He stepped toward me. "Actually. . ." He lowered his voice in a very cloak-and-dagger way. "Marta was already on the list to be brought in based on that overheard argument between her and the victim. Our conversation had nothing to do with it."

"Honestly?"

He nodded.

My sigh of relief was cut short when he chuckled. "Not that I'm above using information from any source to solve a case."

"I see. Thanks for the heads up." Forewarned was forearmed, so I'd be keeping my mouth firmly shut in the future.

"Jenna, don't you want the murderer brought to justice, even if it is your friend?"

Did I? I frowned. "Marta didn't kill her."

"Unlike amateurs, real investigators start out with no preconceptions." He swept out the door without another word.

But he'd planted a seed that I couldn't unplant, no matter how much I wanted to. The whole time I swam, unwelcome memories tumbled through my brain. Marta telling Holly that she'd be on that stage Friday night or else. Marta adamantly refusing to profit from Holly's death. At the end of my workout, I was no closer to answering the terrible question—was the very person we were trying to help actually the killer?

10

A gentle answer turns away wrath, but a harsh word stirs up anger.
PROVERBS 15:1

When I got back to the suite, Marta was waiting in our sitting room.

Guilt hit me hard when I saw her. What had I been thinking?

Marta smiled and held up a bag of black garbage bags. "You're gonna kill me."

I ignored her unfortunate turn of phrase and smiled. "What's up?"

"I'm here asking for a favor again. I was hoping you and Carly would help me gather up the teddy bears and candles the wind scattered all across the front of our property. Thankfully, the Branson chapter of Holly's fan club took most of them right before the storm yesterday morning, but I think it must have started raining before they finished."

I remembered the fanatic from the other night. "Are the mourners gone?"

She nodded.

"Sure, I'll help."

"I knew I could count on you. I don't know what we'd have done without you and Carly."

Carly came bounding out of the bedroom in tennis shoes, jeans, and an old T-shirt. "We've had a good time."

I cut my gaze at her. A good time?

She shrugged behind Marta's back with a "What was I supposed to say?" expression.

"It's been an adventure," I said. "And we're always up for an adventure."

"Did you tell Jenna the news?" Carly asked.

I glanced at Marta. "What news?"

Marta looked back over her shoulder as she started out the door.

"I called Buck to see if he could be here tomorrow night for a planning meeting for the memorial concert. He said he'd be here for the concert and help any way he could in the planning, but that he wouldn't be at the meeting."

I pulled the door behind us with a *click*. "He must have his hands full, getting things ready for the funeral."

Carly shook her head. "Not according to him. He said that Ruth is in charge of the funeral. And everything else."

I lowered my voice as we passed the other suites. "Everything else?"

Marta nodded. "Apparently Holly left Buck out of the will."

That wasn't such a surprise, really. "I remember Ruth saying he signed a prenup, so maybe—"

Carly butted in. "So then Marta called Ruth, and she's going to be here tomorrow night. But you'll never guess where the funeral is going to be."

Apparently not in Nashville or it wouldn't be a surprise. How many times had Carly and Marta tag-teamed me with their guessing games? Too many to count over the years. Personally, I think they just liked to see me guess wrong. "Here?"

"Hardly." Carly pushed open the outside door. "Ruth chose a venue much more intimate."

"You might want to press your little black dress, Jenna," Marta said as she tossed me a garbage bag. "The funeral is in Lake View."

I skidded to a stop. "Lake View, Arkansas?"

"I know. Can you believe it?" Carly waited for Marta to tear off a black bag for her. "Our little hometown won't know what hit it."

We spread out and began to gather the soggy stuffed bears and bunnies, along with candles and wet, unreadable notes of devotion.

As I stuffed my bag, I was suddenly seized by a deep pity for Holly. She'd had so many admirers, but she hadn't gotten along with her sister, couldn't hold a husband, and, even with constant positive reinforcement, hadn't been happy.

Carly wasn't far away, and I looked over at her. "Why do you think Ruth set the funeral in Lake View?"

She looked up at me. "Just a guess, but maybe she's passive-aggressive and thought she'd finally get back at Holly for all the mean things she said and did to her?"

"Maybe she really thought Holly would prefer to be buried near their parents," I mused, hoping I was right.

"Ha. You and I both know Holly would have wanted a giant tombstone right in the middle of Nashville. Maybe with an eternal flame and plenty of room for the fans who would make their annual trek there to pay homage to the late queen."

"Yeah, you're probably right." I snagged a letter plastered against the base of Paul Bunyan's guitar. Somehow the rain hadn't defaced it enough to make it illegible. "I love you, I love you, I love you" was written on every inch of the page.

I rested for a second on the stone base and stared at the words. Which was better? Those words repeated mindlessly? Or an obviously caring action like driving to Branson to check on me? Had I gotten so hung up on hearing Alex say those three little words that I'd lost sight of what love really was?

"Have you seen Marta?" Carly yelled.

I shook my head, and we both turned toward the area near the building where Marta had been cleaning.

"She was there a minute ago," I said.

Carly frowned then ran around to the other side of the building. I followed her at a slower pace.

"Turn her loose!" Carly screamed as I rounded the corner. Like a minitornado, she headed toward the man who was pulling a struggling Marta into the woods.

"Back off if you want her alive," a harsh voice snarled.

I froze, my heart pounding. His hair was dank and twisted, and he looked as if he hadn't slept or eaten in days, but the burning eyes were the same. My nightmare from Monday night's crowd was back. And he had his arm locked around Marta's neck.

"She hasn't done anything to you." Carly's voice, though a little trembly and out of breath, was that of a mother soothing a frightened child. "She won't hurt you. We're just cleaning up so it will look nice. That's what Holly would want."

He didn't relax his hold.

"I don't care what you do. It's too late to help my sweet Holly. We had such plans." He shook an already shaking Marta, and I was afraid he'd snap her neck. "But thanks to you, we'll never get to carry them out."

It hit me as surely as if Paul Bunyan's guitar had fallen on me. This was the stalker Ruth had told me about.

"I didn't do anything," Marta croaked.

"You own this place, don't you?"

"Yes," she admitted.

"If you'd had good security, no one could've gotten to Holly. You didn't even have a security camera up. Anyone could get in without being seen."

"How do you know that?" I wondered aloud.

His brow wrinkled as if the distraction puzzled him. When his face wasn't distorted with anger, I could see that at one time, he'd been fairly nice-looking. But despair and grief had taken their toll. Not to mention a touch of craziness. It had been just two days since I ran into him Monday night, and he looked so much worse than he had then.

"I have security cameras. They're just not up yet. Holly wouldn't let me have them installed," Marta stammered. "She said they made her nervous.

I begged her to allow it, but that was one of her stipulations."

"Trying to blame someone who's not here to defend herself?" His dirty hair hung in his eyes. He slung his head back and pushed Marta onto her knees. "You had the most precious person in the world to guard and you failed."

"How can you say that? Marta did everything a person could do to make sure Holly was safe and happy." Carly was no longer trying to soothe. She was furious.

I put my hand on her arm, because for a second I thought she was going to take her chances and tackle him.

"Everything except take the precautions anyone with sense would take." He shifted his weight but never loosened his death grip on Marta's neck. "Saturday morning, Holly let me in and assured me no one would know. I asked her then about security cams, and she said you were too cheap to install them."

He sounded like he was telling the truth. And if this was the same stalker, Ruth had said Holly was convinced he was harmless. "Holly let you in?"

"You got a problem with that?" He glared at me. "For your information, Holly and I were like that." In front of Marta's face, he twined two fingers together. "I would have taken care of her. She knew that. Not like El Cheapo here."

"He's right." The words were whispered, the tone defeated.

He loosened his grip a little, and Marta pushed to her feet, craning around to look in his face. "You're right. I should've had security cams in place, no matter what Holly said. But she barely allowed me to have guards. And she wouldn't let me put them anywhere close to her room. She said it made her feel trapped." For the first time since the ordeal started, tears coursed down Marta's cheeks.

The stalker relaxed his grip some, and Marta turned completely to face him.

"She did tell me that." Something in his voice had changed. I looked closer. His own eyes were filled with tears.

Marta stepped back out of his grasp, seemingly without a struggle. "I'm so sorry. Nothing you can say can make me feel worse than I already feel."

Sobbing, the man turned and walked into the trees without a backward glance.

Marta collapsed into Carly's arms, and I quickly called 911.

Branson's finest arrived almost immediately. I'd been worried that they'd doubt our story since Marta had just been taken in for questioning, but the officers obviously took the threat seriously. They were still combing the woods when Detective Jamison arrived. The officer nearest me filled him in on the situation.

"Are you ladies okay?" he asked, concern evident in his voice.

We nodded. He asked us a few more questions, and with each of us filling in the blanks, we were able to tell him the whole conversation verbatim. When the security cameras were mentioned, a glance passed between him and Marta that told me this topic had come up before.

An officer came out of the woods and approached us. "We found tire tracks on a back road where a car had apparently been parked. Our guess is that the suspect parked there and walked over."

"Then ran back to his car to make his getaway," Detective Jamison added, nodding. "He's long gone by now."

He handed us each a card. "If you think of anything you haven't told me, please call."

"We will," Marta said shakily. She didn't seem to have any hard feelings over his questioning her yesterday.

Carly put her arm around her friend and guided her to the front door.

I turned back to Detective Jamison. "I appreciate your department responding so quickly. And thanks for taking the threat seriously."

He smiled. "It's like I told you this morning. A good investigator doesn't have preconceived notions about who's guilty and who's not."

"Yeah, I'm keeping that in mind."

"Actually, I don't want you to worry about that. I just want you to call me if you see or hear anything suspicious. No amateur sleuthing. Just call me, okay?" I didn't say anything, and he touched my arm. "That old saying about curiosity killing the cat has more than a grain of truth."

I couldn't believe it. My mama had used that saying against me my whole life. Now a cop in another state was doing it. "It's lucky a cat has nine lives then, so he can live to be curious another day."

His jaw tightened. "Stay out of this murder investigation, Jenna. Consider that an official warning."

❖

My hand shook as I slid the key card down the slot. The green light flashed and the door opened smoothly, but in my mind it creaked mysteriously. I closed it firmly, and yes, quietly, behind me, letting the scent of expensive perfume settle over me like a mantle before I turned and surveyed the territory. I slid the key back into my pocket. Sanctioned snooping felt so odd.

I easily found the suitcases and bags at the back of the walk-in closet. The rows of hanging clothes astounded me. How many outfits could one person wear? I filled one garment bag after another with hanging clothes then slid them into a tall suitcase, obviously made for that purpose.

Holly's custom-designed luggage made it easy to see which one was for shoes, and it didn't take me long to get the seemingly endless collection stored away. One thing about it: If Bob didn't sell the athletic club to me soon, I could always look into a new career as personal assistant to the stars.

By the time I finished the closet and prepared to tackle the drawers, I'd changed my mind. I'd stick to Dear Pru and look for something similar if my day job fell through. Buck was a smooth operator. I would have earned every penny of the Benjamin Franklin I'd refused and possibly more. And so far I'd found nothing but a few notes from fans. Nothing beyond the usual "You're my favorite singer" or "I'd love an autographed picture" and a startling number that were variations of "Will you marry me?"

A loud knock on the door made me dive behind the bed. I admit I even lifted the comforter up to see if I could climb under the bed if I needed to, but there were boards going all the way to the floor. Another knock.

"Jenna? Are you in there?"

My sister. I jumped up and ran to open the door. I grabbed Carly's arm and pulled her inside. "What are you doing here?" I hissed.

She narrowed her eyes and gave a little shake of her head as if I were crazy. "I came to help you. I told you I would if Marta was resting."

"I thought you'd call me. Not bang on the door and scream my name."

"I didn't scream your name!" she screamed.

"Shh. . ."

"What's your problem? Correct me if I'm wrong, but didn't Buck ask you to pack this stuff up and ship it home?"

"Yes." I sank onto the couch.

"And didn't you call Ruth this morning and ask her if she wanted you to and she said yes, please?"

"Yes."

"You seriously need to get a grip. Every errand isn't a covert operation."

"Fine," I said tight-lipped, but I knew she was right. "Let's get to packing."

She tossed me a saucy grin. "You're welcome, sugar. It was my pleasure to come help you."

A smile tipped the corners of my mouth. "Thank you."

"That's more like it."

I opened the top drawer, and Carly said, "Whoa, baby."

Holly apparently owned stock in a lingerie company.

Carly reached in and with two fingers lifted out a tiny black nightgown. She shook her head and dropped it into the suitcase. Then she carefully extracted a red one that was mostly lace.

"That'll take all day." I scooped out the contents of the drawer and transferred the whole armload to the suitcase. "There. That's settled."

She pulled the next drawer open. "Oh, my goodness. I bet she only opened this drawer when Buck was out and the door was dead-bolted."

"Oh, no. I'm afraid to look." In spite of my apprehension, I peeked over her shoulder. The second drawer was filled with sweatpants and hoodies.

I emptied the drawer and stacked them neatly in the suitcase. "These make Holly seem more like a real person, don't they?"

"Yeah. I bet she had a hard time ever being able to relax." Carly's eyes looked moist.

I quickly opened the third drawer. In Holly's almost compulsively neat system, the tangled pile of pantyhose stood out like a punk rocker in Branson. Especially since the pantyhose box was underneath the pile with pantyhose sticking out the opening. Weird," I murmured.

"What?" It was Carly's turn to lean over my shoulder.

"Oh, nothing." I started to stuff the hose that were lying loose in the drawer back into the pink box. My fingers touched the edge of a paper in the bottom of the box. I pulled all the nylons out and retrieved a few folded sheets of paper. I unfolded them and stared at the official bank logo at the top of each one.

I sat back cross-legged on the floor. "Why would Holly bring bank statements with her on tour? And even more importantly, why would she hide them so carefully?"

Carly plopped down on the floor beside me. "Inquiring minds want to know."

"I know mine does." I skimmed the figures, some of which were circled. "It looks about like my own bank statement, only with bigger numbers."

I handed the first page to Carly.

She nodded. "Much, much bigger numbers."

"Rub it in, why don't you?" I skimmed the second page and stopped. "Look at this."

"It looks like someone withdrew twenty thousand dollars three times that month."

"I'd think that was normal star spending, but look at the tiny question marks beside each of these transactions." I did a quick check of the other three pages and found them to be similar. The amounts withdrawn during each month varied from ten thousand to fifty thousand, but each appeared to be a cash withdrawal and each had a question mark beside it. A few times the letter *B* appeared with a question mark after it.

"That looks bad for Buck, doesn't it?" Carly said, then went to work in the bathroom without waiting for an answer.

I put the papers back into the box and set it on the dresser. The whole rest of the time we were packing up, my mind raced. Who should I give the bank statement pages to?

When Carly came out of the bathroom with a satchel packed full of toiletries, I was sitting in the Victorian armchair holding the pantyhose box.

"Snooping with permission isn't all it's cracked up to be. I have no idea what to do with these."

She gave me a sympathetic nod.

"I can't imagine giving them to Buck, considering the *B* scrawled out beside half the question marks."

"No." She looked at the stuff we'd just packed. "Actually, I'm not sure any of this should go to Buck now since we know what the will said."

"Great. Another dilemma."

"I didn't make it, I just pointed it out."

"Well, since Ruth is the heir apparent, I guess it all belongs to her, including the bank statements. But what if she's the killer?"

"She surely wouldn't kill her own sister." Carly looked genuinely shocked.

"Not everybody has as good a sister as you do," I joked. "Maybe if I give them to Ruth, she'll pass them on to Maurice."

"Oh, that's good thinking. As Holly's financial advisor, he should know what to do with them. Or. . ." She grinned. "If you're feeling really brave, you could take them to Detective Jamison."

"I'm not afraid of him." Not much anyway. "But he'd just accuse me again of butting in on his investigation. I'll just give them to Ruth at our planning meeting tonight." I looked at the packed suitcases. "And talk to her about the rest of this stuff before I have it shipped to Buck."

"In that case, let's call it a morning and go get some lunch." Carly headed for the door. She looked back over her shoulder at me. "Speaking of Detective Hawk Man, should Alex be worried?"

"No!" I blurted instinctively.

She turned around and pinned me with her gaze. "That sounded a little defensive."

"It did, didn't it?" I considered the two men. "Honestly, for me, no one holds a candle to Alex."

"That's what I thought." Carly pulled the door open and motioned me to go ahead of her.

"What if the reason Alex won't commit is because he's just not that into me?" My voice sounded scared even to my own ears.

She popped me on the arm with the back of her hand. "That does it. From now on, you're banned from self-help books. He loves you. And eventually he'll gather the courage to tell you that."

I wished I could be so sure.

11

Couldn't you have put that in a bag or just brought the pages?" Carly whispered, as we followed the wafting scent of coffee down the hall to the lobby.

I glanced at the pink pantyhose box in my hand. "Sorry. I didn't even think about it."

"People will stare."

"In case you haven't noticed, there are almost no people here. We're living in a huge hotel with fewer than ten guests."

We rounded the corner just in time to see Maurice and Ruth sit down on the small couch next to the unlit fireplace. Our hosts were nowhere to be seen.

Carly groaned. "I knew it. We shouldn't have sent the kids to Marta and John's house so early. I bet she had to fix them something to eat before she could come."

I rolled my eyes. "Marta's more like me than you in the cooking department. She might have microwaved potpies for them. How long can that take?"

"I'm goin' to leave you to your box and go check on them. Just to be sure everything's okay."

I didn't even get a chance to respond before she was gone. Ruth looked up and waved me over.

"Hi. John and Marta should be here in just a few minutes." Carly was right. They were both staring at my pink box. "Oh, I brought this to you." I thrust it in Ruth's lap, and for a second, I thought she'd let it fall to the floor.

She put one hand on top of it. "Thank you, Jenna."

"It's not a gift." Where was I when social graces were being passed out? "I found it in Holly's room when I was packing up her things. There are bank statement pages inside."

"Oh." A frown puckered her brow. "That's odd." She started to set them on the couch beside her.

"I noticed there were some notations in the margins." The second I saw their mouths drop open, I knew how it sounded. How it was, really. Mama was right. I was nosy. "I thought Maurice might know if something was wrong. I'm sorry. I didn't really mean to look at them. But when I pulled them out of the box, I instinctively. . ." I should have just mailed them anonymously to Detective Jamison. "I'm sorry."

Maurice reached over and took the box from Ruth. "I can understand your curiosity. It's not every day someone gets to find out how much money goes through a superstar's bank account in a month, is it?" He smiled. "I know we can trust you not to run to the tabloids with this information."

"You can trust me not to run anywhere with it."

"Just so you don't worry, you should know that Holly asked me to look into the withdrawals. She seemed to think Buck had his hand in the cookie jar without permission. Before I had time to really explore the possibility"—he blinked quickly and looked down at his lap—"she was gone." When he looked back up, his eyes were red-rimmed and watery. "I'll take these to Detective Jamison now that this has turned into a murder investigation."

"Wow. So Buck had a good reason to want Holly out of the way." I didn't realize I'd spoken aloud until Ruth answered.

"I told you Buck killed her. No one will listen to me, though."

"But they are watching Buck, aren't they?" If I knew the husband was the most likely culprit, surely the police did, too.

"They let him go back to Nashville." Ruth sounded bitter, and I didn't really blame her.

"Maybe they sent someone to keep an eye on him?" My question was rhetorical. How would we know? But Maurice surprised me.

"Yes, they did."

How did he know?

"I asked them point-blank about letting him go. He could be halfway to the Cayman Islands by now." The thought obviously bothered him. He clamped his mouth shut and shook his head.

John, Marta, and Carly appeared before he could expound. No one mentioned the pink box resting on the couch beside Maurice's leg. And I hoped no one ever did again. I'd embarrassed myself enough to last a lifetime.

Carly sank down next to me on the love seat. "You okay?" she mouthed as John and Marta were standing in front of us, greeting Ruth and Maurice.

I nodded. "It was a little hard to explain," I murmured, for her ears only.

"To an accountant?"

"I mean, why I looked."

"Oh." She winked at me. "Imagine that."

"Are you girls whispering about how many big stars you've lined up for the tribute?" Ruth asked.

We both looked up to see that John and Marta had each settled into a wing chair.

"Well, to be honest," Carly said, "we didn't get any firm commitments." I noticed she didn't address the whispering issue.

I stepped in before it came back up. "We spoke to a lot of personal assistants. And most all of them said, 'We'll see.' Or some variation of that." By the end of the afternoon, we'd considered just sending out a mass e-mail, but we'd promised Marta we'd call, so we'd gone through the whole list.

"We'll just plan the program, then, and fit the stars in as they RSVP." Ruth looked less upset by the setback of having no entertainers than she had by me looking at Holly's bank statements.

"There's always Reagan," Marta said softly.

"Unfortunately, that's true." Ruth scowled. "But she isn't going to be singing at my sister's memorial concert. Not after how she treated her when she was alive."

John leaned forward. "If the police catch the murderer soon, I think the stars will be more receptive to performing at the Paradise."

"Not that it's about the Paradise." Marta stumbled over her words in her hurry to get them out. "We're not going to charge admission for the memorial concert, of course. The last thing we want is to profit from Holly's death."

John sat back in his chair, shoulders slightly slumped.

Ruth narrowed her eyes. "We most certainly will charge admission."

We all snapped to attention.

"But," Marta started, "I—"

"It's not open for debate. If you were to open this up free to the public, it would be mass pandemonium. Tickets will be one hundred dollars each."

Marta's eyes widened. "A hundred doll—"

Ruth raised her hand. "Half will go to the Paradise to make up for the money you had to reimburse for Saturday night. And half will go to St. Jude's Children's Hospital—Holly's favorite charity."

Maurice's brows drew together. "Holly had a favorite charity?"

"She does now," Ruth said dryly.

He nodded. "That sounds perfect, actually. Good idea." He patted her on the shoulder, and she lit up like downtown Branson at Christmas.

Well, well. Wouldn't it be wonderful if those two found a happy ending in the middle of all this trouble? I glanced at Ruth, so commanding seconds before, once again timid and meek. A happy ending would be very nice. Assuming Ruth wasn't a psycho killer.

❖

"If you left anything, don't worry about it. I'll just hold it for you until you get back." Marta leaned in and gave Carly a hug. She tapped on the back window and waved at the girls, who were already settled in their seats. Then she came to the driver's window and hugged me, too.

"Where's Zac?" I looked over my shoulder at the twins.

"He said he and Dani were going for a walk before we had to leave."

I looked at Carly and started humming "Young Love."

She and Marta grinned. Why did I get the feeling they were already thinking about planning weddings and spoiling grandbabies together?

Carly shrugged. "Honk the horn and maybe they'll hear."

Just as I reached to tap the horn, a black and white patrol car pulled in the drive. Two uniformed officers got out. For a minute I had a flashback of when Zac was taken in for questioning about his boss's murder. I looked over at Carly. Her face was white.

"What are they doing here?" she whispered.

"I have no idea," Marta said. "But I guess I'd better find out."

She started toward them.

Zac and Dani rounded the corner of the theater holding hands. Zac froze in his tracks and pulled Dani to a stop. They watched the cops enter the hotel, Marta right behind them. They didn't move until I motioned Zac over.

"What's that all about?" he muttered as he and Dani approached our car.

I shrugged. "Nothing to do with us."

"But if I know your aunt, we're not leaving until we find out," Carly piped up from the seat next to me.

"Like you wouldn't be curious all the way home, too."

Girlish giggles erupted from the twins in the backseat as Zac leaned toward Dani. He glanced at them then dropped a lightning-quick kiss on her cheek. "See ya."

She waved, her face red, and went into the hotel.

A couple of minutes later, the officers came out of the building escorting a handcuffed and struggling Joey.

We stared at each other. "Do we need to go back in and see why they arrested Joey?"

"No, let's just go on home. We can call Marta later and find out. Or. . ." She gave me an evil grin. "You can always call Detective Jamison and ask him what happened."

I ignored her attempt at wit and pulled out of the driveway. On Highway 76, I headed toward home. Carly watched me drive in silence for a couple of minutes. "You're dyin' to go back and see what's goin' on aren't you?"

"Admit it. So are you."

Carly laughed. "I admit it. But let me just call Marta and see if she knows anything. We don't want to be late getting home. You have a date with Alex tonight, remember?"

"You're right. And it seems like we've been gone forever. Mr. Persi and Neuro will have forgotten what I look like." I forced myself to keep driving away while Carly dialed Marta.

She talked for a few minutes then hung up and turned to me. "They didn't really come to arrest him. They just wanted to take him in for more questioning."

I frowned. "Then why the handcuffs?"

"Apparently Joey took exception with how one of the officers acted."

"And?" Carly can never get right to the point of a story.

"And Joey gave the cop a fat lip."

"Ouch. That looks bad for him."

"Yes, but look at Marta. Having a temper doesn't make him a murderer."

"I know." But like it or not, in the last ten minutes, Joey had moved past Reagan, Ruth, and Buck to the top of my suspect list.

◆

When the doorbell chimed, Mr. Persi ran in front of me, barking. The golden retriever had latched on to me the day of newspaper editor Hank Templeton's murder, and up until our trip to Branson, he'd been my constant companion. A tradition he apparently wanted to continue. Every step I took toward the door, he put himself directly in my path, barking nonstop. "You don't want me to leave you, do you, pal?"

Neuro, my somewhat neurotic cat, rubbed against my leg, as if to do her part in the "Keep Jenna home" campaign. "Come on, guys. Don't act like you weren't spoiled rotten at Stafford Cabins." According to Mama, the guests had all fallen in love with both my dog and my cat.

By the time I actually got to the front door, weaving in and out of the feline/canine obstacle course, I was laughing. I opened the door and gave Alex a rueful smile. "I think they missed me."

Alex grinned broadly. "Do we need to order in?" he yelled over Persi's sharp barks and loud whines.

"No, but maybe after supper we should just come back here and watch a movie."

"Sounds perfect."

On the way to the diner, I told him about Joey's arrest. "I'm impressed that you didn't ditch me to stay there where the excitement was," he joked.

I laughed. "Excitement isn't all it's cracked up to be. I'm glad to be home."

"I'm glad you're home, too."

"Thanks."

When we settled into our table, Debbie, bleached blond and single again, honed in on Alex like a heat-seeking missile. "What can I get for our favorite lawyer to drink tonight?" She giggled at her own non-joke.

"Lemonade," he said, keeping his gaze fixed on me. "Jenna?"

"Dr Pepper for me, please."

Debbie grunted and wrote it down. She'd been mad at me ever since she'd given me information about Hank's murder investigation in exchange for my promise that I wasn't dating Alex. How could I have known we'd start dating right after that?

She went to put in our drink order while we looked at the laminated menu. "I think I'll get the Friday night special." Alex tucked his menu behind the napkin holder and nodded toward the dry erase board on the wall.

"Fried catfish does sound good. And Alice's hush puppies. . .mmm. . . Carly offered her money for that recipe, and she still wouldn't fork it over. No pun intended."

Alex laughed. "I'll slide one in my pocket, and maybe you can get it analyzed for an ingredient list."

"Ohh, culinary espionage. You'd do that for me?" I drawled.

He leaned forward, a shadow of the laugh still on his face. "There's not much I wouldn't do for you."

"I bet I could think of some things."

"Oh yeah? Like what?"

Like say you love me? Like ask me to be your wife? I grimaced. "Like giving Mr. Persi a bath. Or clipping Neuro's toenails?"

"Couldn't I just pay a good groomer?"

"Some things can't be passed off for someone else to do."

His brows drew together. "I really think Persi and Neuro would prefer for me to call a groomer."

Did he really think we were talking about groomers?

"Hard to believe Holly's funeral is going to be in Lake View, isn't it?" Alex said.

Before I could answer, Debbie reappeared with our drinks. "So do you think any big Nashville stars will be in town for Holly's funeral?"

I shrugged.

"You don't know?" Debbie put her hands on her hips. "Aren't you the one who found her body?"

"Yes."

"And you don't know what stars are coming?"

I tried to raise my eyebrow, but I can't, so I ended up squinting with one eye. "There wasn't a funeral guest list next to the body."

"Oh." She dropped her arms down by her sides and just looked at me. "Oh. I guess not."

Alex put his hand up in front of his mouth but not before I saw the ghost of a smile. I kicked him under the table.

Debbie shrugged. "I heard it was invitation only. Is that right?"

I resisted the urge to point out again that finding the body did not equate to making funeral plans. Instead, I just nodded.

"So I guess you're invited."

I nodded again.

She looked at Alex. "And you?"

He pulled his hand away from his mouth and shook his head.

She smiled at him as if he were staying away from the funeral just so she wouldn't feel left out. "Me either." She raised her order pad, pencil poised, her gaze fixed on him. "What can I get you tonight?"

For a minute, I thought I'd have to do without food, but Alex said, "We'll both have the special."

She winked at him and scrawled a few words on the page. "Two catfish plates coming up."

Her hips swung like the pendulum on a clock as she sashayed over to the window and slapped the order pad sheet down.

Alex wadded up his straw wrapper into a little ball and flicked it at me.

I caught it in my hand, with an expertise born of years of practice.

He grinned as I tossed it back. "Good to see you haven't lost your touch. So have you ever been to an invitation-only funeral?"

"I've never even heard of one until now. I guess Ruth had no choice. Holly had a lot of fans."

Debbie hurried toward us. "Your food will be right out." She balanced an empty round tray against her side. "So do you think it's just family, or will there be like a raffle or something for tickets for her fans?"

I was speechless. "You know, Debbie, it's not a concert. I think Ruth will just invite people who knew Holly."

"Well, that seems kind of selfish." She huffed off as if I'd made the rules.

Alex picked up the saltshaker and examined it carefully, then did the same with the pepper. He reached for the napkin holder.

"What are you doing?"

He leaned forward. "Looking for the mic. Our table has to be bugged."

I laughed. "She does seem to come in right on cue, doesn't she?"

And just like that, she was back. "Alex, my mama's havin' some legal trouble."

"Really?" Alex was cool but polite. "Well, tell her to come on into the office, and I'll see what I can do."

"I already told her. You helped me so much when I had trouble." She leaned forward, and I thought she was going to plant one on him. Instead, she just smiled and gazed deeply into his eyes. "I'm eternally grateful."

His face grew red. "Glad I could be of service."

A ringing bell dinged across the room. "Debbie!" Harvey barked. "Order up."

"I'll be bringin' my mama in to see you real soon," she called as she headed up to the window then promptly came back and set our supper on the table. Another bonus about ordering the special. No long wait for food.

After Alex blessed the food, I glanced across the room at the blond waitress. "So Debbie's a client?" I don't know why I was so surprised. His practice is in Lake View. Who did I think made up his clientele? "Oh, never mind. Lawyer-client confidentiality, I remember."

He smiled. "You handle that really well, considering." He took a bite of fish.

"Considering what?" I knew what he meant, but after Debbie's big pass at him, I was feeling a little defensive.

"Your natural. . .curiosity."

I picked at my own food. "Because I'm nosy, you mean?" Did I sound huffy?

"I don't think of it like that. Honestly. That's one of the things I love about you—your inquisitiveness about everything. In this day and age of mindless apathy, it's refreshing."

Okay, he had no problem proclaiming his love of my curiosity. And apparently from his phrasing there were other things he loved about me, as well. I wish I found comfort in that, but even though I *loved* my mailman's punctuality and friendliness—and he didn't look half bad in his uniform—I had no desire to profess my undying love for him.

He touched my hand. "You okay?"

Debbie bustled up to the table. "You two need a refill?"

"No, thanks," Alex replied without even looking up, still holding my hand.

I gave a quick shake of my head.

"Is something wrong with your food, Jenna?" Debbie pointed at my almost untouched plate.

"No." I slid my hand out from under Alex's. Obviously she wasn't going to leave as long as we were touching.

She turned back to Alex. "You just holler if you need anything. Anything, okay?" Wink, wink.

"Thank you." He answered as if he really thought she was just being a good waitress.

Finally, she was gone.

He covered my hand with his again. "Now as I was asking before we were so rudely interrupted, are you okay?"

I nodded. I wanted to ask him where we were going in our relationship.

But in my mind, commitment is like loyalty and respect—if you have to ask for it, you probably aren't really going to get it.

"Dread going back to work tomorrow?"

"I don't know. I've missed the athletic club actually." I just hadn't missed certain employees, but no need to dwell on the negative.

"I heard it's falling apart without you." He rubbed the back of my hand with his thumb and gave me a slow grin. "I can believe it."

I smiled. He might be a commitment phobe, but he was a sweet one. "I doubt it. I guess I'll find out tomorrow how true the rumors are."

We talked for a few more minutes while we finished our food; then Debbie waltzed over and tucked the check under the edge of Alex's plate. If I were a betting woman, I'd have laid odds that she'd written her phone number on it. I couldn't imagine him using it, but there were no guarantees.

When we got back to my house, the animals welcomed us at the door.

Two hours later, the credits rolled to the sweet romantic comedy, and Alex grunted and rolled over on the couch, almost knocking Mr. Persi onto the floor. Neuro raised her sleepy head as if to remind her bed to be still. She yawned and snuggled back down into the bend of his leg.

Halfway through the movie, I'd gone to fix popcorn. And when I came back, I found this Dr. Doolittle scene asleep on my couch. I didn't have the heart to wake him.

But now that the movie was over, so was naptime. "Alex," I whispered as I shook his shoulder gently.

"Hmm?" he grumbled and opened one eye then the other one. "Oh, hey. Sorry." He sat up, and Persi and Neuro both jumped down. Alex stretched, adorable with his five o'clock shadow and sleepy expression. "I've been working overtime some while you were out of town."

"You work too hard."

He ran his fingers through his hair. "No such thing right now."

"Big case?"

"Every case is a big one when you're starting a practice."

"You're doing great. The whole town loves you." I offered a hand and helped him to his feet. "Look at Debbie."

He winced. "You could have talked all night and not said that."

"And here I was trying to help."

"I bet you were." He hugged me. "I've seen opposing attorneys more helpful than that."

"Well, fine then. If you want to slam my efforts to build up your self-esteem."

He kissed me on the forehead. "All kidding aside, you're the greatest." He jangled his keys. "Good night."

"Good night." I turned the dead bolt behind him.

"You know. . ." I said to Persi and Neuro. "It doesn't do any good to find Mr. Right if he doesn't have sense enough to know he's it."

I stood in the window and watched Alex's truck lights go down the driveway. The truth was, this wasn't about finding Mr. Right. Or even Mr. As-Good-As-It-Gets, as I'd joked to Carly a few years ago when I'd promised to try to find "the one" by my thirtieth birthday. I'd passed thirty a few months back, and the world didn't come crashing down around my ears. My reasonably-happy-with-my-life card hadn't expired at the stroke of midnight. I had good friends, a wonderful family, and an amazing church congregation.

Unfortunately, this was more personal than finding a husband. I'd committed dating's cardinal sin when I let myself fall in love with someone who might not feel the same way about me.

12

The simple inherit folly, but the prudent are crowned with knowledge.
PROVERBS 14:18

The only good thing about working Saturdays was that Lisa wouldn't be caught dead here on a weekend. Mostly because of that, I'd been glad to volunteer to work today so I could be off Monday for the funeral. An hour after I opened, Bob walked into the office we shared.

"Jenna. Glad you finally made it back from vacation."

"Looks like y'all had a few problems while I was gone." I didn't mention the gossip about members walking out due to poor management.

"Yes. I told you Lisa wasn't ready for you to take a vacation. She tried her best, I'm sure. But she just wasn't ready." He shook his head, and I expected him to wipe a stray tear any minute.

Well, you should have thought of that before you put her in my position. I bit back the words. "Bob. . .I'm not sure she's ever going to be ready. She really hasn't learned much in the months she's been here."

"A student is only as good as her teacher."

I *know* he didn't just say that. "Are you implying that I don't know my job?"

"Oh, no. No, no. I didn't mean that. I just mean, if you'd been more patient with her. . ."

"Patient?" I counted to ten, and the last few numbers I didn't even try to hide what I was doing. "For months, I've been her built-in servant. She hasn't listened to me because you brought her in and let *her* tell *me* what to do."

"I told you, I wanted to help build up her self-esteem."

"By bossing me around?"

"Aw, now. . .she wasn't the boss."

"Well, she didn't get that memo, apparently."

He pointed at me. "You should have made it plain to her."

I pointed back, instinctively. "No, Bob, *you* should have made it plain to her. She's your daughter."

"You're right." He hung his head. "But she's had it so rough lately. I just didn't want to hurt her any more." He looked so beaten down. "Wait until you have kids. It's not easy being a parent. Especially to a delicate girl like Lisa."

"I'm sure it's difficult. But you're going to explain it to her, right? That I'm the manager and she's an employee."

"Your assistant," Bob said, his expression switching from hangdog to bull-dog in one fell swoop.

"Okay, my assistant." Even that would be an improvement, because it had seemed like vice versa before.

"You mentioned taking more vacation time. Is that going to be soon?"

I nodded. "I have three more days, and that's just this year's vacation days. You know I haven't had a vacation since I started."

"I appreciate how dedicated you've been. But three more days is all I can spare you right now. We've got to get things back to normal around here."

With that parting shot, he walked out.

Normal? I glanced down at the nameplate on my desk. JENNA STAFFORD, MANAGER. Right beside it was Gail's list of irate members I needed to call. If I was going to spend all my time cleaning up someone else's mess, maybe I should change that title to janitor.

Midafternoon, I was checking the chlorine level in the pool when Amelia strutted in. She slipped off her terrycloth robe and did a little pirouette as if to show me her white bikini.

"I wore white today, just in case." She nodded toward the pool. "Did you get it all straightened out?"

"Yes, the levels are fine. I'm so sorry that happened."

"Yes, well, me, too." She slid into the water, and I slipped from the room. If the first lady of Lake View was willing to forgive, maybe our other members would be, too. "As Amelia goes, so goes Lake View" might not be entirely accurate, but it was close.

Later that afternoon, I was washing my hands in the restroom when she came in, hair damp but fully dressed.

"So, Jenna, tell me. What was it like being around the great Holly Wood? Was she still as hard to get along with as she used to be?" Amelia carefully traced her lips with coral lip liner. "I know you aren't supposed to speak ill of the dead, but she was the most egotistical person I've ever known." The mayor's wife examined her face in the mirror.

"Really? I didn't realize you knew her that well." Way back in my more naive days, before I got to know Lisa or Holly, I had thought Amelia was self-centered.

"I didn't know her that well, but I did know Ruth."

"You were friends with Ruth?"

Amelia glanced at me.

"Let's just say she helped me get through some subjects that were too boring for me to spend time on."

If anyone else said that, I'd assume that Ruth tutored her. But with Amelia, I felt sure it meant Ruth did her work.

"Poor Ruth." Amelia filled in her lips with the coral lipstick.

"Poor Ruth?" I watched Amelia in the mirror. Maybe if I knew how to apply makeup like that, I wouldn't be wondering about Alex's feelings. On second thought. . .I'd rather be me. "Because her sister died?"

"Well that, too. But mostly because Holly was her sister." She dropped her lip liner and lipstick into her Prada handbag. "Ohh. I wonder if Ruth killed her." She raised a perfectly arched eyebrow at me. "You do know that Holly ran off with Ruth's husband, Cecil?"

"You're kidding. Her own sister? Now that's cold." If I could have raised an eyebrow in return, I would have. I was surprised. But knowing Holly, I guess I shouldn't have been.

"I can't believe you didn't know that. Ruth and Cecil were married and had a little boy. Holly didn't keep Cecil long, though. He came crawling home with his tail between his legs and wanted Ruth to take him back."

"Did she? Where is he now?"

"I'm a little fuzzy on the details. After all, I *was* busy with my own life." She picked up her bag and gave me a little wave.

For some reason, the name Cecil seemed so familiar.

"Amelia!"

She stuck her head back in.

"If you figure out where Cecil is now, let me know, okay?"

She shook her finger at me. "Snooping again?" She grinned, her straight white teeth gleaming. "As long as I'm not your target, I'm happy to help."

❖

Alex called mid-Proverb. I slid my bookmark between the pages and closed the Bible then flipped open my phone. "Hey."

"Hey, Jenna. How'd your day go?"

"Long." I'd come home at six and waited an hour for Alex to call before I finally broke down and ate a single-serving microwave panini. After that, a long bubble bath, then bed and Proverbs.

"Were we going to do something tonight?"

I eyeballed the clock by my bed. "It's nine o'clock."

He sighed. "I'm sorry. I just finished working. Are you already tucked in for the night?"

All the way down to my Mickey Mouse nightgown. "Yep. Sorry. Mom invited us to eat with them after church tomorrow. How about that?"

Silence. "Actually, I need to go over some documents right after church. If I get hungry, I'll probably just grab a bite downtown and eat while I read."

"I understand." Sort of. Although the saying about all work and no play did jump into my mind.

"How about we get together Monday night after the funeral?"

"That sounds great, Alex. I'll see you then."

When we hung up, I turned back to Proverbs. I ignored my marked place and flipped over to chapter 31. All my life I'd heard people talk about being a virtuous Proverbs 31 woman. But it was hard. My eyes fell on verse 26. "*She speaks with wisdom. . . .*" *I could sure use some wisdom*, I thought sleepily.

I'm cleaning the tile around the pool with a toothbrush when Ruth and Cecil walk in. He actually looks just like Bob, but somehow I know he's Cecil.

"So you're the janitor here," Ruth says, tightening her grip on Cecil's arm. "You'll never get voted Most Virtuous Woman if you dress like that, you know."

I look down and gasp. Why am I wearing a white bikini? I stumble to my feet and grab a terrycloth robe from the stash of clean robes we keep for members only. With it wrapped tightly around me and cinched at the waist, I walk over to Ruth and Cecil. "Are y'all here for a swim?"

Suddenly the door opens and there stands Holly, looking vibrant in a blue evening gown. "I'm here for a manicure," she says, haughtily stepping toward us like she's walking down a runway.

Cecil drops Ruth's arm and runs to escort Holly to a poolside table. While Ruth and I look on, he sits down across from her, pulls out a manicure kit, and takes her hand in his. Wait, that's not Cecil. It is Bob. And the woman I thought was Holly is Bob's daughter, Lisa. The sparkling crown on her head should have been a dead giveaway.

I turn to explain the crown to Ruth. "She's Daddy's little princess, you know."

She nods. "She always was."

I frown. Is she talking about Lisa? Or Holly?

Before I can ask, Alex walks into the pool area, dressed for court and carrying his briefcase. "Hi," I call. "Want to go get something to eat?"

A frustrated look crosses his face. I see his lips move, but a sudden loud buzzing makes it impossible for me to hear what he's saying. Panicked, I look around for the source. The buzzing grows louder and I jump.

I sat up in bed, my heart pounding, and stared around my dimly lit bedroom. No Cecil, no Ruth, no Bob or Lisa. And especially no Alex. Just Neuro perched watchfully on my antique armchair and Mr. Persi snoring at the foot of the bed. And my alarm going off. Time to get up and get ready for church.

❖

As soon as the closing prayer was over, Mama turned around in the pew in front of me. "You and Alex coming for dinner?"

I grimaced. "I am." Alex had come in late and sat in the back pew. I glanced around the building and didn't see him.

"Did y'all have a fight?" Mama looked concerned. "I warned you about going off on vacation and leaving him here."

"And I told you then, he's a grown man. Besides, he came out to Branson, and we had a great time."

"Then why isn't he coming to dinner?"

"He has to work."

She clucked her tongue against the roof of her mouth in that age-old sign of shame. "I was just telling your daddy the other day, that boy works way too hard."

"That's not really our business," I said, hoping to gently remind her that Alex was not family. "I have to run by the house and let Mr. Persi out. See you in a few minutes."

"Hurry. The pot roast should be ready soon."

Well, that was some consolation. If I had to go solo to Sunday dinner, at least we were having my favorite.

Twenty minutes later, I parked around by the kitchen door at Mama's and hurried in. "That smells amazing."

Carly shoved a basket of rolls at me. "Put these on the table, and we'll be ready to eat." She picked up a pitcher of tea and led the way into the dining room.

Mama looked up from over by the buffet where she was putting ice in the glasses. "Your dad invited one of our cabin guests to eat with us."

Carly and I exchanged a look. Not that we had anything against hospitality, but all through the years, if a guest was alone and had interesting stories to tell, Daddy invited him or her for lunch. Sometimes it could get awkward.

The dining room door pushed open and the twins scurried to their seats, followed by Zac, who maintained his cool but hurried. Bringing up the rear was Daddy and...

I blinked my eyes. I *must* be seeing things.

"This is Detective Jim Jamison." Daddy introduced him to us all at one time. "I think you girls already know him."

Good thing I was already halfway into my chair. I think my knees gave way.

Jim nodded toward Carly and me.

"What are you doing here?" It just popped out even though I knew it was rude, especially when Mama gasped.

Mama threw me a look that plainly said she'd raised me with more manners than that. She motioned the detective to sit next to me then turned her attention back to her impolite daughter. "He's investigating Holly's murder."

Of course. I knew he hadn't followed me home. At least I was pretty sure of it.

After Daddy blessed the food, Jim looked at me. "I came in a little early to talk to some of Holly's childhood friends." He grinned. "And you've read enough murder mysteries to know the killer always goes to the funeral, right?"

I nodded, even though I knew he was making fun of me.

He smiled. "I can't take a chance on that being true and me not being here, can I?" He passed me the bread basket.

"I guess not." I buttered my roll, and for the next several minutes, I let the conversation swirl around me while I concentrated on pot roast, carrots, and potatoes.

"Fran LeMay told me Tom had to put off Joe Harrison's visitation and Sally Bearden's, too. They're going to use all the rooms tonight for Holly's."

As I bit into my roll, I thought about how Joe Harrison and Sally Bearden's families must have felt. The ninety-year-old baker and seventy-year-old wife and mother had been more a part of this community than Holly had. But fame demanded first place. Even in death.

I heard my name and looked up. "What?"

Daddy frowned. "I was just telling Jim that you'd probably be glad to show him the church building where the funeral is going to be before you head down to LeMay's for the visitation. And maybe take him over to the diner so he can meet some people."

That would teach me to pay more attention to what was going on. In my family the motto is "You snooze, you get volunteered." "Sure."

Carly coughed, and I glared at her. If she wasn't careful, I'd volunteer her.

When we walked out the front door, Jim led me to a little silver sports car parked by the cabin closest to Mama and Daddy's house.

"This is your car?"

He jangled the keys and grinned. "What? Were you expecting a Crown Victoria?"

Heat flooded my face. Actually I *had* been looking for a policeman-type car. But I wasn't about to tell him that.

He held the door open for me, and I sank down into the low-slung car. Amazing how spoiled I was to an SUV. Luxury aside, I felt as if I were going for a ride in a go-kart.

"Go up there to that big oak tree and take a right."

He looked over at me and raised an eyebrow. "What happens if the tree dies and falls down?"

I shrugged. "We'd say, 'Go up there to where that big oak tree used to be and take a right.' And in the meantime, we'd plant a new one."

"Of course you would. That makes perfect sense." He put on his right turn signal and made the turn. "In Lake View."

"You've only been in my hometown a few hours, and you're already making fun. That's not a good sign."

"I'm just kidding."

"Good. Go to the bottom of the hill and make a left."

"Why do you guys even name your streets?"

"It's just a formality."

"I can see that."

"The church building is on the right around the next curve."

He whipped the car into the parking lot and stopped in front of the old white clapboard building, its steeple almost as tall as the building was wide.

"Small," he murmured.

Was he talking about the building or his car? I'd seen lockers that looked roomier. Our faces were inches apart. Okay, maybe a couple of feet, but still. . . it was close quarters.

"The funeral is invitation only, plus a few press passes." Which of course he knew. Tell me again why he needed a tour guide? "So I guess Ruth figured it's big enough. It's where they attended as children."

"That makes sense."

I was tired of beating around the bush with men. Sometimes a little bluntness can go a long way. "Jim, why am I here?"

He stared at me for a few seconds, as if weighing his answer. "Because I thought it might give us a chance to get to know each other better. You'll be back in Branson, but only for a few days, then who knows if we'll ever see each other again?"

His eyes bored into mine. And just like always. . .read the truth.

"Which doesn't bother you a whole lot, right?" He gave me a self-deprecating grin. "I've been deluding myself, haven't I?"

My face burned, and I could only imagine how red it must look. "Jim, your ability to see straight to the marrow of the truth fascinates me. And I think you're a really nice guy. But. . ."

"I'm too old for you?"

If I'd been interested in him, fifteen years wouldn't have mattered. "Not really, but. . ."

"There's someone else."

"Yes. Maybe. At least for me— Oh, forget it." I ducked my head. "I'd love to be friends with you."

"Thinkin' it might be nice to have a detective consultant when you play Nancy Drew?"

"Have you been talking to our chief of police?"

"For quite a while this morning, now that you mention it. What was your first clue?"

We were still joking about John's opinion of my nosiness when we walked into the Lake View Diner and almost ran into Alex, who was holding a Styrofoam take-out container in one hand and his briefcase in the other.

Suddenly I remembered my dream. "Alex, this is Detective Jim Jamison. He came down from Branson for the visitation and funeral."

"Jim, this is my. . ." Now there was a stumper.

13

With his mouth the godless destroys his neighbor,
but through knowledge the righteous escape.

PROVERBS 11:9

This is my friend, Alex Campbell."

Jim offered his hand, and after a moment of hesitation that I may have completely imagined, Alex shifted his briefcase under his arm and accepted Jim's handshake. "Nice to meet you," he said softly and just stared at us, his brows drawn together.

Jim nodded. "You, too." He put his hand loosely on my forearm as if to guide me out around Alex.

"Good luck with your work," I said as I passed him.

He didn't answer. Did he think I was on a date with Jim? Was that why he looked so funny? I turned around to explain, but the door was already closing behind him.

For the next hour, I sat at the counter while Jim struck up conversations with locals. While I played with a straw, my bizarre dream drifted into my mind. Out of all the weirdness, the thing that puzzled me the most was why Cecil had been giving Holly a manicure.

As quickly as the question went through my mind, my breath caught in my throat. Cecil was CeeCee. That first night we met Holly, she'd been on the phone with CeeCee. Cecil. Of course. And she'd said that she'd see him Saturday. Yet no one mentioned Cecil being there. As far as I knew, the police hadn't questioned him. I looked over at Jim who was getting an earful from Debbie. I bet he didn't even know about Cecil.

I fidgeted until he finally came back over to me. "What are you dying to tell me?"

The words tumbled out as I told him about CeeCee and my discovery about Cecil. "Undoubtedly, he killed her."

"How many people have you thought were guilty since Holly's death?"

"What does that have to do with anything?"

"Just wondering if your muscles get sore from all that jumping to conclusions."

241

"So you aren't even curious about Cecil?"

He shrugged. "I'll look into it."

"So will I."

He shook his head. "Playing Nancy Drew is going to get you in serious trouble someday."

❖

Photos of Holly flitted across the huge screen at the front of the viewing room. I stood toward the front, mesmerized by how normal her life appeared. Holly as a baby. Just like all babies, she was precious. Toddler Holly holding the hand of her older sister, looking up at her as if she hung the moon. Holly at her sixth grade graduation, with her proud parents on either side of her. Then Holly on stage as a teenager, playing her guitar. And Holly beside Ruth, who cradled a baby in her arms.

A few slides later Holly and Ruth were each holding a hand of the young boy standing between them. With the next shot, Holly and Ruth by a Christmas tree while the same boy, only older and more sullen-looking, opened a huge wrapped box. That boy looked very familiar to me. I nudged Carly. "Is that Joey?"

She glanced around the room and lifted her hand in greeting to John and Marta who were talking to someone by the door. "Where?" she asked me distractedly.

"Never mind. He's gone now."

"Where did he go? What part of the room is he in?" Carly craned her neck.

I shook my head. "It was a picture. On the screen."

"Oh. I'll watch." Carly stood with her eyes glued to the screen until those snapshots came back around. "It sure looks like him."

"But if it is. . ."

"You said Holly ran off with his dad. That would explain the big Christmas present."

"Holly also ran off with Ruth's husband, Cecil, remember?"

"How could I forget—" Carly said a little sarcastically. "Cecil. Your numero uno suspect now."

"Do you also remember that Cecil left her *and* their little boy?"

Carly gasped. "Joey is Ruth's son."

"Nice detective skills, my dear Watson."

"So do you think he and his dad are in it together?"

I shrugged. "Stranger things have happened."

We walked over to Ruth. Thankfully, Carly led the way and stepped up to hug her. "I'm really sorry for your loss. Holly will be missed by so many people."

Ruth dabbed at her red-rimmed eyes with a handkerchief and looked out at the crowd behind Carly and me. "Yes. Everyone loved her."

Well, obviously not everyone. . .

Carly nudged me without even turning around.

I glared at her back. Making sure I said the right thing wasn't enough anymore. Now she was monitoring my *thoughts* in social situations.

I followed her lead, though, and hugged Ruth. "You chose beautiful pictures."

Her smile was teary. "Thanks. There were so many to choose from, but I wanted some that showed her private life as well as her public life."

Hard not to notice that none of them included Buck. But he'd have his day with the video montage he'd volunteered to have done for the memorial concert.

No sooner had the thought crossed my mind, than Ruth, glancing over our shoulders, stiffened. Fury played across her face. I knew without turning. But my curiosity wouldn't let me rest without seeing it for myself. I shifted toward the crowd and saw Buck coming straight toward us.

"That low-down hypocrite. How can he have the nerve to come up here and act all heartbroken when I know he's the one who killed my baby sister?" Ruth's voice rose on the last few words. Enough to draw the attention of the people nearest us.

Carly patted her on the arm, "Ruth, sugar, I know you're upset. This is a really hard day for you."

For a hopeful minute I thought it was going to work. Ruth seemed to relax just a little.

But Buck seemed unaware of the minefield he was about to enter. "Ruth, we're going to miss her so much." He actually reached out like he was going to hug her.

Ruth jerked back and narrowed her eyes. "How dare you. Don't you even pretend that you cared about Holly. You murderer!" Every head in the room turned to look at the drama being played out in front of them. I saw Maurice making a beeline for her from the back of the room, but I knew he wouldn't be in time to stop the drama.

"Get a grip, Ruth. You know I didn't kill her." Buck dropped his hand. "Why would I? I loved her."

"You loved the lifestyle she kept you in." She glared at him. "And that five-million-dollar life insurance policy you had on her."

My ears perked up. Ruth had mentioned a life insurance policy before, but I never knew how big it was. Five million dollars was a pretty good motive for murder. I looked at Buck again and wondered how good an actor he was.

"She didn't even include me in her will." He sounded hurt that Holly had left him out.

"That's right. She didn't." Her voice dripped venom. "And no wonder with you running around with that floozy right under her nose." Ruth was doing the Dr. Jekyll thing again. From bereaved sister to attacking tiger.

I could practically feel all the cell phones with cameras pointing toward us. "Can't you do something?" I hissed to Carly.

"Divide and conquer?" she whispered.

"Buck, come and let me show you some of the floral tributes to Holly." I reached out and took his arm to lead him away.

But apparently he wanted to have the last word, because he shrugged my hand away. "You have a lot of nerve acting all righteous. You were so jealous of her I wouldn't doubt if you killed her yourself."

Ruth's face whitened and she looked faint. "You mark my words, I'll see you behind bars before we're done." Maurice pulled her away, and she sobbed on his shoulder.

I looked across the room where Chief Detective Jim Jamison was watching and listening attentively. He lifted his chin at me, and I nodded. Even Nancy Drew would have a hard time sorting out all the drama in this case.

❖

Carly and I flashed the cards that Ruth had given us at the two security guards standing inside the foyer of the church building. We walked through the open double doors, and I stopped. The smell of roses hung over the packed auditorium like an almost sickeningly sweet fog. An usher showed us to two seats halfway down the outside aisle. We kept our heads down, but a couple of times I glanced around to see if I recognized any stars. I didn't want it to look like Carly and I were paparazzi, or worse, stalkerazzi. Carly nudged me with her elbow as we sat down. "See that blond at the other end of our pew?" she whispered.

I leaned forward subtly then turned back to Carly. "Yeah?"

"Is that Carrie Underwood?"

I frowned. "No."

"Taylor Swift?"

I shook my head. "It's Rachel Jones."

Carly looked one more time and sat back. "What does she sing?"

"She's Mrs. Jones, the librarian's, granddaughter."

"Oh." Carly slouched down in the pew.

A familiar profile caught my eye. "But I do think that may be Brad Paisley four rows in front of us and toward the middle."

Carly squeezed my arm. "Really?"

Just then he turned all the way around to speak to a woman behind him, and we both sighed. "That guy works at the post office," Carly said.

I nodded. "He sold me stamps yesterday."

The music started. I don't know what I'd expected, but maybe I'd thought that Ruth would have Holly's songs played. Instead, a haunting tenor solo of "Amazing Grace" echoed through the room. Traditional hymns like "Beulah Land" and "Never Grow Old" followed.

Understandably, I expected a preacher to opine about Holly's passing, but when the last note of "Time Is Filled with Swift Transition" faded away, tradition ended abruptly. Maurice made his way up to the microphone and did a brief bio of Holly, presumably in case anyone had wandered into the wrong funeral. Then he asked for those who knew Holly well to feel free to say a few words about her.

He sat back down by Ruth as several people lined up for the microphone. An old man in creased khakis, a crisp blue shirt, and a fedora talked about being Holly's parents' neighbor since before she was born. He told stories of how when she was tiny everyone thought she would be the next Shirley Temple. And he reminisced about how proud her parents had been of her right up until their deaths.

Ruth sat at the front on the opposite side of the aisle from us. If I looked between the Brad Paisley look-alike and the woman behind him, I could see her profile. Best I could tell, she was stone-faced and dry-eyed.

Several people shared little tidbits of praise about Holly. Painted with the forgiving brush of death, Holly became perfect and untouchable. When Buck walked up to the microphone, I saw Ruth stiffen. Would she make another scene today? Or would grief and respect for her sister keep her quiet? From the look on her face, it was anybody's guess. I saw Maurice put his arm around her. Maybe so he could make her behave.

Buck stepped to the microphone, looking suitably mournful in his black suit and muted tie. He addressed the audience with a somber face, and to me it seemed clear he was purposely downplaying his natural exuberance. Or maybe it was just me. With the obvious exception of Ruth, everyone else seemed enthralled with him. "Holly was a wonderful person and a talented performer. She was the best wife a man could ever wish for." His voice quivered, but he got control. "She was warm, loving, and caring." The image of her screaming and throwing things at him in her dressing room jumped to the forefront of my mind. "I could never do enough for her, nor she for me. We were soul mates, and I'll cherish her memory forever." He paused to wipe his eyes.

"He might as well cherish it. I heard her memory is all he got," a gray-haired woman in front of us whispered loudly.

"Huh?" her equally gray companion said.

"She cut him out of the will."

245

Buck walked back to his seat as an embarrassed silence fell over the crowd.

Reagan, wearing a glittery little black number that looked like it belonged at the CMA awards instead of a funeral, carried her guitar up to the microphone. "Holly was my hero. She set the standard for every country music performer in America." Ruth started to stand, but Maurice pulled her back down. "With that in mind, I wrote a song especially for Holly that I'd like to sing in her honor."

Maurice, still with his arm tightly around Ruth's shoulder, whispered in her ear.

Reagan put her guitar around her neck and adjusted the mike. "For Holly," she said softly.

She strummed the opening notes, and with a teary smile, started to sing.

A deep voice across the aisle from us yelled, "Killer!"

My head whipped around. Where had that come from? I jumped up just as two loud explosions sounded in rapid succession. Carly screamed and tugged on my arm. "Get down."

A man stumbled into the aisle brandishing a gun.

14

Chaos erupted. The woman beside us dove under the pew and pulled her husband down with her. The gray-haired couple huddled together. He put his arm around her and shielded her with his body.

The security guards converged on the shooter, but he waved his gun threateningly in their direction, and they backed away. "She deserves to die!" he screamed. He ran out the back doors with the guards right behind him.

As soon as he was gone, I pulled Carly toward the front of the auditorium. Buck and a couple of security guards bent over Reagan, who lay on the floor like a bundle of rags—sparkly rags. Before we could get to her, John Conner, the Lake View chief of police, stepped in front of me. "Jenna, y'all please just sit back down."

I didn't move. "Did they catch him?"

"Is she dead?" Carly whispered.

"Sit down," John growled, but then he looked at Carly and gave an almost imperceptible shake of his head.

A security guard stepped to the microphone.

"Is there a doctor in the house? We need a doctor up here. Everyone else, sit down, please."

Carly and I eased back to our seats as several people answered the call for medical personnel. A teenager in a miniskirt stomped back to her seat, apparently furious that they had doubted her medical credentials.

For a few seconds, the clicking of cell phone cameras was all that could be heard. Then Tom LeMay, the funeral director, walked up and stood next to the rose-draped casket. His face and even his bald head were almost as red as the roses.

"If he doesn't loosen his tie, we're going to have another casualty," I whispered to Carly, and she nodded.

"Ladies and gentlemen," Tom began, slightly stammering. "Please remain calm." He pulled a white handkerchief from his pocket and wiped his face.

"The. . .um, assailant has been apprehended." In the distance, the whine of an ambulance siren grew louder. "We're going to clear the building in an orderly manner to allow the EMTs room to work." He nodded toward his suit-clad assistant, who stood by the back row directing people outside. "Please get in your vehicles, and we'll continue to the burial at Eight Mile Cemetery as planned."

In that unique way that funeral directors have, he had the auditorium cleared within five minutes.

Outside, I blinked against the sunshine, unaccountably cheery and bright. "Do you think John was saying that Reagan's alive?" Carly asked.

I motioned toward Marta, who was standing near her vehicle in the lineup to go to the cemetery. "Maybe Marta knows."

We started across to her but stopped as an ambulance squealed into the parking lot. Two EMTs jumped out and ran into the building.

"At least they're in a hurry," I said.

Carly nodded. "Always a good sign."

When we reached Marta, she hugged us both. "I'm so glad y'all are here. Do you think one of you could go with Reagan to the hospital?"

"I will," I said.

"Is she alive?" Carly asked.

"She was earlier. I'm praying she still is."

I nodded. "So are we. Do you know how to get in touch with her family?"

"From what she told me, she was a foster child."

"Bless her heart." Carly wiped her eyes.

Marta's eyes filled with tears, too. "Yeah. She's twenty-two."

I thought about the sometimes pouty, sometimes sultry singer. "Just a kid, really."

Carly shook her head. "And no mama or daddy."

"I know it." Marta looked toward Ruth and Maurice sitting in the limo behind the hearse. "I hate not to follow the ambulance, but I don't want to leave Ruth."

My heart went out to Marta. She was going to be the perfect innkeeper. With all her guests' foibles and faults and even knowing there might be a murderer among them, she'd taken them under her wing like a mother hen with her chicks.

"Did she come with you?" Carly asked.

"No, Reagan did." Marta looked worriedly toward the building. "Ruth rode with Maurice." She motioned toward a low-slung red car in the parking lot. "But Ruth was complaining about not having any leg room. She might want to ride home with me, now that Reagan. . ."

I touched her arm. "Don't worry about the hospital. I'll be there if Reagan needs anything."

She hugged me again. "Thanks. Carly, will you ride with me to the cemetery?"

"Unless you want me to go with you, Jenna?"

"No, you go on and help Marta with Ruth. I'll probably spend all my time sitting in a waiting room anyway."

As white-faced as Marta already was, I hated to bring it up, but I needed to know. "So did you hear anything about the shooter? Who it might be?"

She stared at me. "Didn't y'all see him?"

"Only for a second from the back. Was it someone we know?"

"You could say that," Marta said. "It was the stalker."

Of course it was. As I remembered the things he yelled, I wondered why I didn't realize that immediately.

❖

The Lake View Hospital ER was packed when I walked in. I smiled at the receptionist. "My. . ." I paused. What was Reagan to me? I'd come mostly out of pity and out of a desire to help Marta. "Reagan Curtis was brought in earlier. A gunshot wound? Where is she now?"

The harried woman glanced up at me. "What's your relationship to Ms. Curtis?"

"I'm as close to family as she has nearby." Unless you counted the man she was having an affair with when his wife was killed. But in terms of giving information, sometimes less is more.

She shoved a clipboard of forms toward me. "Fill these out, please." She turned away from me.

"In order for you to tell me where she is?" I knew paperwork had almost taken over the medical world, but this was ridiculous.

A puzzled expression crossed her plump face. "We have to have these filled out, and you said you were her next of kin."

"I'll answer what I can. And what I can't, maybe I can get the answers for you. Okay?"

"Okay." Her tone indicated that she thought I was one page short of a complete document.

"I'll take these with me and fill them in. But right now, I need to know where Reagan is and how she's doing." First rule of negotiation. Get something for each concession you make.

She considered my offer for a few tense seconds then gave in with a sigh. "She's in surgery right now. After that, they'll move her to the ICU. You can wait in the ICU waiting room, and the surgeon will come out and see you when they're finished."

She quickly gave me directions. "Bring those forms back to me when you get them done," she called as I bolted down the hall.

I waved at her over my shoulder.

In the ICU waiting room, I glanced at the huddled groups of people and sat on a padded chair away from the others. I smoothed down my black skirt. I should have gone by the house and changed, but I'd been in too big a hurry to check on Reagan. I turned my attention to the clipboard. Name. Got that covered. Birth date. Uh-oh. This farce had gotten me into the waiting room, but if I went back up and told the receptionist that I didn't know Reagan's birthday or her address, would the surgeon still keep me posted on her condition? Somehow I doubted it.

I called Marta.

She answered on the first ring. "Jenna? How's Reagan?"

I groaned quietly. "I don't know. And I'm not likely to find out if you don't help me."

"What do you need?"

"Who has Reagan's purse?"

"I do. Why?"

I explained the information I needed, and within minutes, the three of us—Marta, Reagan's purse, and I—had the forms completed.

"Carly's here. She said she'd bring Reagan's insurance card by in a while."

I quickly took the paperwork back to the receptionist then rushed back to the ICU waiting room. And waited.

After a seemingly interminable time, a man in surgical scrubs appeared at the door. "Is anyone here with Ms. Curtis?"

I followed him to a small room where he gestured to a chair. I dropped into it. He sat across from me. "One bullet grazed Ms. Curtis's skull. Thankfully it didn't penetrate. The other one lodged in her thigh. We removed it, and I think we have the blood loss under control."

I nodded, processing the fact that Reagan was alive. A little of the tension drained away.

He continued, "In about an hour, you'll be able to see her for a few minutes. A nurse will let you know when you can go in. Ms. Curtis will be in ICU at least overnight."

I thanked him. On my way back to the waiting room, my phone vibrated in my little black purse. I fished it out. "Hello?"

"Jenna. Are you okay?"

We were supposed to go out after the funeral. I'd completely forgotten. "Oh, Alex. About our date—"

"Jenna, I'm not worried about that." He almost sounded irritated with me. "I heard about the shooting. Are you okay? Where are you?"

I told him about Reagan.

"I'll be right there."

"As much as I'd love to see you..." As I said the words, I was overwhelmed with a longing to feel his strong, safe arms around me. But there was nothing he could do here. "I wish you could go by and let Mr. Persi out and check on Neuro instead."

Silence.

"Alex?"

"Sure. I'll go check on the animals. So you don't want me to come out there?" There was something indefinable in his voice.

"I guess not. I should get to see Reagan in a little while. Then I'm not sure what I'll do."

"You sound tired."

"I am. Today's been pretty stressful."

"I know it has." His tone softened. "I want to hear all about it. About that date... Can we reschedule for tomorrow night?"

As much as I wanted to see Alex right that second, I felt like I could sleep forever. And I knew how busy he was. "Why don't we just get through the workweek and make it Friday night?"

Silence again.

Was he upset that I'd been at the diner with Jim? I considered explaining. But why should I, really?

He cleared his throat. "Friday night's fine."

"We can just go to the diner then get a video after or something," I said, anxious to take the pressure off him.

"Actually, I—" he started.

A nurse stuck her head in the waiting room door. "Is anyone here with Reagan Curtis?"

"Alex, I've got to go. They're going to let me see Reagan now. Thanks for taking care of things at my house."

"You're welcome."

" 'Bye." I flipped the phone shut as I followed the nurse out into the hall. We almost bumped into Carly, who was coming in.

"Hey, you're just in time. We're going to go see Reagan."

Carly held up a little bag. "Let me leave this in the waiting room and I'll be right there."

I nodded and almost ran to catch up with the nurse. "Is she awake?" I asked.

She shrugged. "That's a matter of opinion. She's still really drowsy. So she may not remember much about this visit."

"Maybe that will keep her from wondering why you and I are the ones visiting her," Carly murmured in my ear.

I jumped and shushed her. The nurse looked back at us and frowned, but she pushed the round silver button on the wall and directed us into Reagan's cubicle.

I bit back a gasp. Carly put her hand over her mouth, her eyes wide. Reagan had bandages around the top of her head. Her face white, her eyes closed, she looked like she belonged in a morgue instead of a hospital. Except for the tubes everywhere. How could this be the same woman who'd looked so vibrant this afternoon?

Carly reached out and gently touched her arm. Reagan's eyes fluttered open and she moaned. Carly started to move her hand away, but Reagan grabbed it. "Don't leave." Her confused gaze darted from Carly to me. "I'm scared."

"We're here," I murmured. "Do you want us to pray for you?"

"Please," she whispered. She moaned again then drifted back to sleep. Or out of consciousness. I wasn't sure which.

We stood over her bed and prayed. Then we stayed, without talking, until the nurse gave us the signal to leave.

Out in the hall, Carly glanced at me. "Is she going to be okay?"

I told her what the surgeon had said. We went into the ICU waiting room, and Carly nodded toward the bag. "I brought some extra clothes in case you had to wait longer to see her than you thought you would."

"You're a lifesaver."

She shrugged. "A little late, though. You can just go home to change now."

"I'm not leaving."

She smiled at me. "You're way more tenderhearted than you let on, you know it?"

"How do you know I'm not just staying to see what I can learn?"

"Because I saw your eyes when we were in there with that girl. You were thinking about how awful it would be not to have any family to stay with you."

"And thankfully you feel that way, too." I picked at an imaginary piece of lint on my skirt then raised my gaze to hers. "Because I have to go to work tomorrow."

She laughed softly. "If you want to stay tonight, I'll take over in the morning in time for you to get home and get ready for work."

"Thanks, Car. That would be perfect."

"Now go change and I'll wait so we can visit at least until time to go see her again."

She didn't have to tell me twice. I slipped into the restroom and changed into the sweatpants and sweatshirt from the bag Carly had packed. I was so glad she'd taken into account the cool year-round temperature of hospital waiting rooms.

Dressed and comfortable finally, I plopped down beside Carly. "Thanks again."

"You're welcome. So I don't guess you've heard any news, huh?"

I looked around the deserted waiting room. "The rumor mill is very close-mouthed around here. Do you know anything?"

"Apparently the stalker pretty much surrendered in the church parking lot." She pulled her leg up under her and got comfortable. "Oh! And get this. Guess how he got in?"

"By invitation?"

"Nice guess, wise girl, but he used a press pass to get by the guards."

"Stolen?"

Carly ran her hands through her hair and fluffed out her curls. "No! Apparently he's a reporter for one of the lesser-known country music fan mags. So he had a legitimate pass."

"No wonder Holly was so nice to him. My guess is she's dominated that particular magazine's content for the last few years."

"Exactly."

"But talk about stalkerazzi. Sounds like he invented the term." One thing was still bothering me. "Why did he shoot Reagan?"

"Seems his mag had gotten a 'scoop' about Reagan and Buck having an affair. In the end, he said he thought the two of them had killed Holly."

"Wonder if John and Detective Jamison believe him?"

She shrugged. "He's been arrested for shooting Reagan. So far that's all I know about that."

"Do you think Reagan killed Holly?"

Carly frowned. "No."

"Why not?" I tended to feel the same way, but I needed someone to verbalize reasons.

"She's so young." She looked up at me, and I know she could see I was about to start naming all the young killers in history. She sighed. "I just don't think she did. She's childish and flighty and didn't use the best moral judgment, but I don't think she's a murderer."

"I agree. Plus she wouldn't have used a guitar string. And anyway, I think she really did hero-worship Holly, and it just seems unnatural to kill your hero. But if she didn't, who did?"

"Buck?" Carly offered.

"He had motive," I said thoughtfully. "Even though he signed an airtight prenup agreement, remember what Ruth said at the funeral home—he had that huge life insurance policy on Holly."

Carly rummaged in her purse and pulled out a pen and a Wal-Mart receipt. She flipped the receipt over and wrote, "Buck—life insurance." Then she looked at me. "And even though he was coming from the opposite direction, he could have easily killed Holly then doubled back."

She scrawled the word "Opportunity" beside his name and motive.

"You're right. And don't forget Cecil."

Carly frowned. "I know I teased you about making a man we've never seen your main suspect. But what *do* we really know about Cecil?"

"We know Holly was talking to him the night we walked in on her. And she told him she'd see him Saturday."

"But no one saw him Saturday."

"Maybe because he slipped in and killed her then slipped back out. Never to be seen again."

She wrote, "Cecil—the Phantom Killer" on the receipt.

It did sound a little silly when she put it like that.

Pen poised, she twisted her lips. "Motive?"

I shrugged. "Who knows? Leave that blank for now." I pointed at her list. "You need to go ahead and add Reagan. We can't eliminate people based on gut instinct."

She put Reagan's name under Cecil's. "Motive?"

"Jealousy?"

She jotted it down. "She had the opportunity, I guess, during that ten minutes before she had to come back out and sing again."

"I wonder where she ranks on Detective Jamison's suspect list."

Carly held up the scribbled-on receipt. "Think he'd do a temporary trade so we could see?"

I laughed. "Somehow I doubt it."

The ICU waiting room door swished open.

Buck, his black suit rumpled and his face drawn, stepped into the room.

15

Hatred stirs up dissension, but love covers over all wrongs.
PROVERBS 10:12

Carly's face paled, and she stuffed the receipt into her purse.

He nodded to us. "Am I interrupting?"

"No, not at all." Carly's voice was nervous. I looked at her. Was she thinking the killer had come to finish us off for suspecting him?

"Have you seen her?"

"Yes." What was he doing here? Even in the best of times, his presence was in bad taste.

"How is she?"

"They think she's going to be okay." I thought about her bandaged head and tubes. And especially her pale face. "She looks pretty bad, though."

He flinched. "It's all my fault." Without being asked, he slipped into the seat directly across from us and put his head in his hands.

Carly and I looked at each other. Then she cleared her throat. "You didn't cause her to get shot. . .did you?"

He raised his head, and for a minute, I thought he'd forgotten we were even there. "I should have left her alone from the beginning. She was just a kid who wanted to be a star. And I took advantage of that."

If he was about to tell us the intimate details of his relationship with Reagan, I'd rather not know.

"Holly was different than any woman I ever knew." He met our gaze, and his eyes were hollow. "She was like a rare butterfly that would fly into your world briefly"—he reached out his hand and closed it on thin air—"but could never be held on to for long."

I wasn't sure how we'd jumped from Reagan over to Holly, but he obviously needed to talk, so Carly and I both just nodded.

"I fascinated her. Especially as long as I played the field. She was so used to total adoration that a little challenge went a long way."

I bit back a snort. "So you cheated on her to keep her from leaving you."

He sat back in the chair and nodded as if I'd answered the final *Jeopardy* question. "Exactly."

Twisted and crazy, but I could see his logic. "And Reagan was available."

Sadness flitted across his face again. "Yeah. She was."

"So after Holly's death, you two could be together, right?" Carly's brows were drawn together.

He frowned. "What was the point after Holly was gone?"

"So you both were trying to get Holly's attention?" she said thoughtfully.

"I guess you could say it like that."

No one spoke for a minute, and he stared absently over our heads at the muted TV up in the corner.

"Why do you feel responsible for Reagan getting shot?" I didn't want to leave this awkward conversation without finding that out, at least.

Still looking at the television, he answered slowly. "Even though I knew it would be tacky, I went along with her bringing her guitar to the funeral and singing that song she wrote for Holly."

"Why?"

He brought his gaze back down to me. "She said I owed it to her. To help her make atonement. And I decided she was right."

Were we about to hear a confession? Suddenly the waiting room seemed very deserted. "Atonement? For what?"

Carly nudged me with her elbow. I knew she was thinking I should quit asking questions.

"Not for killing her, if that's what you're thinking. Even the police know neither one of us did it." He squirmed in his seat. "Well, at least they know Reagan didn't. I guess they think I could have before I went to meet her."

"You went to meet her?"

"The night Holly was killed, Reagan sent me a note asking me to meet her in her dressing room after her set. So I did. She told me that she hated what we were doing. And that she wanted to stop. I tried to talk her out of it. But she wouldn't have it any other way."

"We were still there arguing when the stagehand came to tell us that Holly hadn't shown up and Reagan needed to go back out to stall."

"So she went back out, and you went looking for Holly."

"And ran into you in the hall."

Mentally I drew a big black line through Reagan's name on our suspect list and a thinner, more tentative one through Buck's.

He rubbed his hand over his face. "I never should have let her sing. Then that crazy stalker wouldn't have shot her."

"She's going to be okay," Carly said.

I nodded, pity overriding my extreme distaste. "Visiting time is in thirty minutes if you want to go in and see for yourself."

He shook his head and pushed to his feet. "I'm heading back to Nashville.

Hopefully Reagan can forget she ever knew me."

"Will you be at the tribute concert for Holly a week from Friday?"

He nodded. "I wouldn't miss it." He opened the door then turned back. "I know it's hard for people like you to understand. But I did love her."

People like us? I guess he meant people who didn't live in a world where a man cheated on his wife in order to keep her.

The door swished shut behind him, and Carly slumped in her seat. "For a minute, I thought we were going to hear a murder confession."

"Me, too."

She slapped me on the arm. "Don't sound so disappointed. The reason murderers are talkative is because they're going to kill the person—or should I say people—they're spilling their guts to."

I rubbed my arm. "So get your list out."

She fished it from her purse and read over it. "If we believe Buck, then that just leaves Cecil."

"That's just because we're not done yet. Don't forget Joey. And Ruth."

"And the personal assistant Holly fired," Carly drawled.

"Oh, you're right. We could call her about the tribute preparations and maybe figure out if she was mad enough to kill over losing her job."

Carly grunted. "We filled in as Holly's personal assistants for a few days. Would you have been mad about losing that job? That woman probably drove home singing, 'Hallelujah,' at the top of her lungs."

I smiled at the image. "Good point. Leave her off the list for now."

Carly and I hashed out suspects and motives for a while, then she put the list back into her purse. "So did Mama tell you that Harvey and Alice are probably going to sell the diner?"

I nodded. "She's all worried about it. Afraid that their guests won't have anywhere to eat. But there are other places. Besides, maybe whoever buys it will be a great cook."

"Yeah." She fiddled with her hair. "Maybe."

"Carly? What's going on?"

"I don't know. Since I found out they wanted to sell, I can't quit thinking. . ."

"Oh! You're thinking about buying it?"

"No!" She ducked her head. "Yes. Maybe."

"Glad to see you've made up your mind."

She blushed. "It's crazy for me to even think about it. Imagine me, running the diner."

"Pretty easy to imagine, actually. I think you'd be a natural."

"Thanks, Jenna. Even though it'll probably never be more than a dream, it's fun to talk about it." She pointed to the clock on the wall. "It's almost nine.

Time to go see Reagan. Then I have to get home."

Reagan, sound asleep, looked marginally stronger, but she still didn't appear to be out of the woods.

"She's been crying," Carly whispered and pointed to the moisture glistening on her cheeks beneath the plastic tubing.

I nodded and covered Reagan's hand with mine. Who wouldn't cry?

She shivered.

I pulled the blanket up over her shoulders and looked across the bed at Carly, who had her head bowed and her eyes closed. I joined her in a silent prayer for this young woman who right now looked more like a lost little girl.

◈

Sleeping—or trying to—on waiting room chairs tended to make the next day seem long. And Tuesday didn't need much help to seem like the longest workday ever. By the end of the day, my muscles ached and my head hurt, but at least Lisa's lack of supervision at the athletic club was no longer so evident. Except in my office, I noted sourly, glaring at the art deco prints she'd hung in place of the beach scene prints Bob and I had agreed on when we first started sharing this office. I'd run across my pictures behind a shelf in the pool supply closet when I'd gone to check on a filter. Along with various other items Lisa had apparently stuffed out of the way. Such as pool maintenance schedules.

As Mama always said, "Least said, soonest mended," so I'd kept my mouth shut. Now as I stretched and strained to get the pictures exactly back where they had been, I was thinking it might be worth a little mending to rip something.

Lisa had steered clear of me so far today, which was all good. Club members were getting back on their normal schedules, and most complaints had been cleared up. I was still doing all the work Lisa was supposed to do, but it was such a relief to have things running smoothly, I could live with that. As long as I didn't have her underfoot.

"Jenna." I heard her voice calling from down the hall, but before I could reply she opened the door and walked into my office without so much as a knock. "Oh. Here you are. I've looked everywhere for you."

I gritted my teeth. "Here I am. In my office." I adjusted the last picture and turned to face her. "What do you need?"

"One of the customers wanted a GET IN THE SWIM WITH JENNA STAFFORD T-shirt in blue. All I can find are pink ones. Where are the blue ones?"

She sounded so disgusted with the thought of my name being on a T-shirt that I smiled. "We only have pink ones." Bob had insisted on pink ones for a reason that only he knows. I begged for another color, especially considering that my hair is red, and pretty-in-pink for redheads is really just a movie gimmick. But no, he'd insisted on pink and pink only. I didn't have to wear them, he'd said. Just sell them.

"Well, that's not very smart, is it? Why didn't you order blue ones? Not everyone likes pink."

Deep breath. "I didn't order the shirts. Your dad did. And I don't know why he chose pink. Why don't you ask him?"

"Well, you don't have to get huffy about it." Lisa shot me a venomous look. "Place a new order."

She snapped her fingers at me. I blinked. Did she really just do that? I was going to hyperventilate from all the deep breaths I needed if she didn't get out. "Lisa, I don't order shirts. That's Bob's department. You need to talk to him if you're not happy with the selection."

"I don't need to talk to Dad about anything. You work for us. Now order blue shirts." Lisa turned on her heel and walked out without a backward glance.

After she was gone, I paced. It really had been a long day. And if I did something hasty like quit on the spot, I'd probably regret it. Possibly. Maybe Carly would let me waitress at her imaginary diner. I envisioned myself taking orders and balancing five plates on my arm. That would be good, honest work, and I might not be half bad at it. But what would happen when I started wanting to sprint from table to table and do calisthenics in between orders?

Poor Carly. I could just see her having to install a pool in the dining area to keep me happy. Might not be bad for business, but I don't think she'd like it.

Instead, I'd just thank God that the workday only had another few minutes of life left in it and get things ready to close. As I went through my checklist—a list, I might add, that remained untouched while Lisa was in charge—I thought about how mad she'd be when she found out I didn't order the shirts.

"Tomorrow is another day," I muttered to the empty office. "Just call me Scarlett."

Right now what I wanted was a good book and a long bubble bath. *And a slightly less active conscience,* I thought wryly, as it reminded me that I needed to get back to the hospital. I'd checked with Carly a few minutes ago, and they were getting ready to move Reagan into a regular room. So I'd have to settle for saying "hi" and "good-bye" to my animals and taking a quick shower.

❖

Carly met me in the main lobby. "They should have her in a room up on the second floor when you get up there."

"Good. How is she?"

She shrugged. "She's slept most of the day. The last time I went in to see her, she was a little more alert."

"That's good."

"I'm glad you think so, because she asked me about who shot her."

"What did you say?"

"The nurse came in right then to ask me to leave so they could get her ready to move. So I said you'd tell her all about it when you got here."

I laughed. "You did not. . ." My voice trailed off as I noted Carly's abashed grin. "You did! You dumped that on me?"

"I sure did. And don't act like you wouldn't have done the same, sugar. I was afraid I'd say the wrong thing."

"What about me saying the wrong thing?"

"Well, this way you've got time to think it over."

"True." I gave her a hug and waved. "I'll take the stairs and think while I walk."

"If you don't want to tell her, just turn on the news. I'm sure it's all over the television," she called back over her shoulder.

"Thanks for the tip," I muttered and headed up the stairs.

I beat Reagan to the room, but within seconds they wheeled her in, bed and all. She gave me a weak smile while the nurse checked her vital signs and filled out her chart. I waved but stayed quietly in the corner until the nurse and attendant had both gone. "How're you feeling?" I asked.

"Like somebody shot me."

"Ouch." I stood and moved to a chair closer to the bed.

She started to nod but stopped and raised her hand to touch the bandage on her forehead. "Who did this?"

I didn't answer immediately.

"Who shot me?" she clarified.

"Did you know Holly had a stalker?"

"Yes. Buck—" She stopped. "I heard she did."

"Well, apparently her stalker came to the funeral and shot you."

Her brows drew together. "Why?"

What could I say? Maybe it would have been easier just to turn on the TV and let the anchorwoman tell her. "He's a freelance writer for a fan mag, and he heard you and Buck were having an affair."

She flinched. "So why shoot me now? Holly is dead."

Might as well get all the tough questions over with. "He claims that you killed Holly."

I didn't think it was possible, but her face grew whiter. "I didn't."

I covered her cold hand with mine. "I know. Buck told me you two were together."

"I was breaking it off with him."

I nodded. "He told me."

She raised her hand to her forehead and covered her eyes with her fingers. "You must think I'm an idiot."

"I think we all do stupid things sometimes."

She peeked at me between her fingers, and a ghost of a smile flitted across her pale face. "You're tactful."

I grimaced. "Compared to my mama and my sister, I stomp in like an elephant in a dollhouse."

She started to laugh then groaned. "Hurts my head to laugh."

"Oh, I'm sorry."

"Don't be." She nodded toward the TV up in the corner. "Do you think we could watch the news?"

I hesitated, trying to exercise the tact she thought I had.

"Don't worry. I know what kinds of things they'll be saying about me."

"We can turn it off if you change your mind." I clutched the remote clipped to the bedsheet and hit the POWER button then switched the channel to an entertainment news station.

After a little of the latest celebrity gossip, a split screen of Holly and Reagan popped up behind the blond anchorwoman. "In breaking news, freelance writer Rick Clarkson, who was charged earlier with the shooting of singer Reagan Curtis has now been charged with the murder of beloved queen of country music, Holly Wood."

I gasped. "No way."

The blond finished, "We'll bring you live updates of this case as we get them."

Reagan glanced over at me. "You don't think he did it?"

"No. And I can't imagine why they do."

She pursed her lips in a pout. "Because he said I killed her?"

I shook my head. "It's complicated. Maybe he did do it. But I just didn't think so." I slipped my cell phone wallet from my purse. "Would you excuse me for a minute? I need to step out and make a phone call."

"Sure." But her voice was tinged with worry.

"I'll be right back," I assured her.

"No problem."

Out in the hall, I fished out Detective Jamison's card and punched in his cell phone number on it.

"Detective Jamison here," he growled.

"Jim? It's Jenna Stafford."

"Jenna? How are you?"

"I'm fine. But you didn't seriously charge the stalker with Holly's murder, did you?"

For a second, I thought the cell phone had dropped the call. But finally he spoke. "Yes, we did. Do you have a problem with that?"

I lowered my voice. "Is this some kind of trap for the killer?"

"No," he whispered. "We have the killer."

16

What kind of proof do you have that he murdered Holly?"

"Not that I'm required to share my proof with you, but we matched those unknown prints at the murder scene to his."

I slapped my forehead with my hand. "Of course you did. He told us that Holly let him in Saturday morning, remember?"

"Well, that's his story. But even when you told me about him saying that, I wondered if he'd been in there Saturday night instead."

"Did he confess?"

"I'm not at liberty to discuss this any further with you, Jenna."

"Fine. Some tabloid will have all the details by tomorrow anyway."

He chuckled. "Be that as it may, those details won't have come from me. Oh, by the way. One consolation for you being wrong. With the killer behind bars, your friends' upcoming tribute concert will be a huge hit."

"Bye."

"See you in Branson." His cheery voice got on my last nerve.

Back in Reagan's room, she was talking on the house phone. When I walked in, she said, "I've got company. I'll talk to you later," and hung up.

"Hey."

"What did you find out?"

I hit MUTE on the remote control. "What do you mean?"

"On the phone. You went out to get your own scoop on the shooter being charged with Holly's murder, didn't you?"

This girl was far from an idiot.

"Something like that. I didn't find out much. They really did charge him."

"But you still don't believe he did it."

I shrugged. "If the police think he's guilty, who am I to argue?"

She considered my words for a moment then gave me a feeble smile. "I'm glad they think so. I hope they're right."

"Why?"

She nodded toward the house phone. "That was Joey, calling to check on me."

"Oh?" I hadn't pictured Joey as the solicitous type.

She bit her bottom lip. "You know it was his string."

"His string?"

"His guitar string."

"Guitar? Oh, *the* guitar string." Around Holly's neck, of course. "How do you know that?"

"All I know is he and I use the same kind of guitar strings. According to the cops, that's the brand that was used to kill Holly."

"So if it wasn't yours. . ."

"Exactly. It must have been his. Besides, he broke a string that night and went backstage to get another one."

"Did you tell the police?"

She stared over my shoulder at the window. For a minute, she didn't answer. Finally, she met my gaze. "I didn't want to. But I had to. Because what if he did it?"

"You had no choice," I agreed.

A tear slid down her cheek. "I'm so glad they decided it wasn't him."

"Yeah." I didn't say any more, but my mind raced. What if Joey had killed Holly? Had the good detective been so eager to wrap up this case that he'd charged the wrong man with the crime? I couldn't help but wonder.

Dear Pru,

I love my job, but I dread going to work because of one coworker. She's an obnoxious, bossy know-it-all, and I can barely stand to be in the same room with her. I know I'm not the only person who feels this way, because I've heard others talking about her. Should I quit my job?

In a Dilemma

Dear In a Dilemma,

Minimize direct contact with this person as much as possible and still do your job. Make use of e-mails, voice mails, and even sticky notes if you must. Hang in there and bite your tongue. Coworkers come and coworkers go. Jobs you love aren't easy to come by.

Midafternoon Friday, Mama called me at the athletic club.

"I just have to know." Her voice was so quiet I could barely hear her.

"Mama?" After an exhausting week of working during the day and visiting Reagan at night, I wasn't up to a guessing game. "Know what?"

"Did you write that Ear-Day U-Pray letter?" she whispered.

"What are you talking about?" My pig Latin wasn't so rusty that I didn't recognize the words *Dear Pru*. But how could Mama possibly know I was Dear Pru? Carly was my only confidant, and we'd both been really careful.

She sighed. "I just got the paper. And I always read Dear Pru first, of course. Especially in the last year or so, it's gotten to be really good."

Her praise rendered me speechless. I finally opened my mouth to thank her and confess, just as she hissed, "So tell me the truth. I won't breathe a word. Are you in a dilemma?"

"Well, maybe a little." What kind of question was that? I'd promised never to tell anyone but Carly that I was Dear Pru, so with Mama asking me straight out, that definitely put me in a bit of a dilemma.

"What do you mean, 'a little'? Did you write the letter about not liking your coworker or not?"

Ohh. "No!"

"Are you sure?"

"Yes, I'm sure."

I could hear the paper rattling in the background. "Well, then you need to read this. Dear Pru gave In a Dilemma some wonderful advice that you'd do well to take to heart."

"Jenna!" Lisa yelled down the hallway.

I rolled my eyes. "I will, Mama. I promise. I get off work in five minutes, so I need to go get ready." And see if I could make Lisa see the wisdom of Dear Pru's advice. An e-mail yell would be much easier to take. Surely.

She burst into my office. "Some big shot is parked out on the curb. You need to go tell them we're closed."

I walked over to the window. A sleek black limo with dark windows was pulled up to the sidewalk in front of the club entrance. I glanced at her. "No one has gotten out of it?"

"No."

"Is Amelia here? Or Byron? Maybe this is a new perk for Lake View's first family. Being picked up from the health club by a limo."

Lisa tossed her brunette hair over her shoulder and crossed her arms in front of her. "Humph. In this hick town? I don't think so. Anyway, no one's here. It's closing time."

"Fine. I'll grab my things and handle it on my way out." Gail—supposedly with Lisa's help—was doing the actual closing routine since I had a date tonight. Assuming Alex remembered to show up. We'd barely talked all week.

She watched me as I dropped my cell phone into my purse, put the strap on my shoulder, and grabbed my keys. I wanted to make a smart remark about her taking inventory or being sure I didn't steal anything, but I took my favorite advice columnist's advice and kept my mouth shut.

As I walked down the sidewalk toward the limo, my curiosity almost made me run. Had some of Holly's Nashville friends stayed in town after the funeral? For three days? I mentally scoffed at myself.

The limo driver had a chauffeur's uniform on including the hat. He stared straight ahead as I approached his window. But when I tapped on the glass, he rolled it down immediately.

"Sir, I'm sorry, but we're closing." I craned my neck to see who was in the back of the car, but the partition was up.

"Yes, ma'am. I know. Are you Jenna Stafford?"

I jerked my attention back to him with a snap. "Yes." As soon as I said yes, I realized I should have been more coy. "Why do you ask?"

He held out a white envelope. "This is for you."

I clutched my keys in my hand, with the sharp point facing outward. "What is it?"

He waved it a little, but I still didn't take it. "I don't know what it says, but my best guess would be that it's a letter."

"Who from?"

His professional facade slipped enough for me to see he was getting irritated with my suspicion. Which only made me more suspicious. "Read it and you'll know."

I smiled because I knew it was crazy before I said it. "What if it's a bomb?"

A slight grin edged his lips upward. "Do I look like a kamikaze limo driver to you? Would I hand you a letter bomb to open three feet away from me?"

I grimaced and took the envelope. "I guess not."

My hands trembled as I slid my finger under the flap and tugged it open. I pulled the folded letter out and looked at the chauffeur. "It didn't blow up."

He tapped his fingers on the steering wheel. "I noticed that."

I unfolded it and gasped. The letterhead read, ALEX CAMPBELL, ATTORNEY-AT-LAW, followed by his address and phone number. The handwritten note was short:

Hey, Water Girl,
Get in the limo and see what happens. Trust me?

—Alex

My heart slammed against my rib cage. In spite of the hot sun, I shivered. I knew this note was from Alex. Besides the obvious, his letterhead, he wouldn't divulge his crazy nickname for me even under torture. And as far as the "Trust me?" that's my favorite line from my favorite Disney movie,

Aladdin. When they were about to be caught by the guards, Aladdin held his hand out to Jasmine and said, "Trust me?" and she took his hand. Later, she recognized him when he was disguised as a prince because he said it again— "Trust me?"

Alex knew these things about me. Things no one else did. And the truth was, I did trust him. Totally.

I started toward the backseat door of the limo, but before I could reach it, the chauffeur jumped out and opened it. I climbed in and forced down a giggle. At least he didn't bow.

He closed the door behind me. Just as we eased away from the curb, Lisa and Gail walked out. What would they think about my car still being here? I quickly rolled the window down and waved. "I'll get my car later," I called, feeling "hick" as Lisa would say, but not caring.

They gaped at me, and Gail nodded.

I hit the button to roll the window back up as we pulled out of the parking lot onto the road. I glanced over at the seat next to me, and there was a piece of paper with a single word printed on it. *Relax.*

I laughed out loud, even though no one could hear me, then settled back against the leather seat and let the cool air blow gently on my face. So this was luxury. Not bad, but more than anything I couldn't wait to see where we were going.

Out the window, familiar scenery flew by. No surprise that we were going into Lake View. But when we turned down my street, I was surprised. I guess I never thought about a limo just taking someone home. At least not without taking them to an event first.

As we pulled up in my driveway, the partition between me and the driver slowly descended. "I'm to wait here while you get ready." He held up a paperback book. "Take your time."

"Ready for what? How am I supposed to dress?"

"Comfortably."

I met his gaze in the rearview mirror. "Did you make that up, or were you told to say that if I asked?"

"That's what I was told to say." He glanced around as if making sure no one could hear. "My wife said if she was you, she'd dress like she was going to an outdoor barbecue at the governor's house," he said over his shoulder.

I grinned at him in the mirror. "You told your wife about this?"

He ducked his head. "Not your name or anything. Just about the plan."

"The plan?"

He zipped his lip with his forefinger and thumb then got out and opened my door. "Take your time."

"Tell your wife I said thank you." I clutched the letter in my hand and ran up to the door. As soon as I got in, Mr. Persi crowded against me. I patted his head and waved at Neuro up on the couch arm. She blinked her sleepy eyes at me. I called Alex. He didn't pick up. I hadn't really expected him to. I punched in Carly's number on my way to the back door to let Mr. Persi out. Thankfully she answered.

"Carly. Quick. What would I wear to an outdoor barbecue at the governor's mansion?" I let Mr. Persi out and watched him run around.

"You're going to the governor's mansion?"

"No." Gulp. "At least I don't think so."

"What does that mean?"

I held the door open for Mr. Persi to come in then locked it behind him. "Can you come over?" I asked as I walked into my bedroom.

"Now?"

I threw myself backward on the bed. "Please."

"I'll be right there."

I took a shower while I was waiting, towel-dried my long red curls, and threw on an old T-shirt and shorts. When the doorbell rang, I ran down the hall and opened it.

"I wouldn't wear that to the governor's mansion even if I didn't like him," Carly said, apparently by way of greeting.

"Thanks for your valuable fashion advice." I grabbed her arm and pulled her into the house.

She hitched a thumb over her shoulder. "What's the limo doing here?"

I showed her the letter and told her what little details I knew.

She reread the short note. "Wow. This is romantic. Are you sure it's Alex?"

I punched her on the shoulder. Even though I'd asked myself the same thing more than once since this adventure started.

She rubbed her arm. "What? I just asked a simple question."

"Yes, I'm sure it's Alex. Now come help me find something to wear. It's getting dark, and if this plan was for something outdoors, I'm pretty sure I'm late."

"Alex knows what he's doing, I'm sure. So don't worry your pretty little head about it."

I laughed. "You're a very funny girl."

"Thanks, sugar. I try." She pushed me into my walk-in closet. "Now let's get you ready to meet the governor."

"Cracking me up here."

She snatched a pair of flared denim capris off the hanger and laid out a red top and a white short jacket. "It's almost the Fourth of July. Why not go patriotic?"

I considered the outfit then shook my head. "I'm pretty sure I'm not really meeting the governor."

"You're right." She hung the jacket and top up but kept the capris. She added a light green long tank with a brighter green polo shirt over it. With a quick swoop, she snatched my green sandals from my shoe rack and put them with the clothes. "Perfect."

She was right.

When I came out wearing the outfit, she whistled. "I have great taste."

"And such modesty."

She handed me a necklace and earrings. "Just to dress it up a little."

I lifted my hair, and she moved around behind me to fasten the silver chain. As she worked on the clasp, I quickly slipped the small silver hoops into my ears.

Carly circled me as if I were a prize cow at the county fair. "Wonderful. Now turn around."

"Bossy, aren't we?"

She quickly swirled my hair up and secured it with a set of chopstick-style hair sticks.

"What kind of hairstyle is that?"

"It's called a messy bun."

I eyed it in the mirror. "I can see why." The effect was odd but not awful.

"It makes you look casually elegant. Like Cinderella going to the ball."

"In denim capris?"

"It's all in the accessories. And the attitude."

I grinned and hugged her. "Thanks for being my fairy godmother."

"I wouldn't have missed it for the world. Now let's get going before your carriage turns into a pumpkin." She hooked her arm in mine and walked me down the hall. "You'd better call me when you get home tonight. Oh, and before I forget. If you're up for it, ask the prince if he wants to play tennis with Elliott and me tomorrow morning."

"I'd love to. And I'll ask. But you know how much he's been working. I can't believe he's taken time off to plan something like this. . ."

She laughed. "This whatever-it-is?"

"Exactly."

17

For wisdom is more precious than rubies,
and nothing you desire can compare with her.
PROVERBS 8:11

By the time I got back to the limo, it was dark. I couldn't help but be concerned. I'd taken less than an hour to get ready, but what if Alex had something planned that required daylight? I guess then he would have instructed me to hurry. So I would just do what the note said and trust him.

"I think my wife gave good advice and you followed it well," the chauffeur said as he held the door open for me to get in.

"Don't forget to tell her I said thanks."

"I already did." He adjusted his hat and pulled his cell phone half out of his shirt pocket then dropped it back. "She wanted a play-by-play of my part in this... plan. Hope you don't mind."

I laughed. "Not at all." I thought back to Alex falling asleep on my couch during the movie last Friday night. I really didn't mind. And I loved that he was comfortable enough with me to do that. But who would have thought then that our romance would be worthy of a play-by-play?

❖

I didn't even try to relax as the limo turned off my street onto the main highway. I tapped on the partition. It slowly lowered.

I smiled at the driver in the mirror. "Do you mind me asking your name?"

He didn't look at me. "You can call me James."

"As in 'Home, James'?"

He chuckled. "I'm Trevor."

"That I believe. Trevor, where are we going?"

"You *are* curious, aren't you?"

"Alex told you I was curious?"

The partition started to slowly rise.

"Or did he say nosy?" I flounced back against the leather seat. My pouty reflection in the window caught my eye, and I started to laugh. I didn't even really care where we were going as long as Alex was at the end of the journey.

When we started winding around the lake road, I shook my head. There was no place to go out here. Was he taking me to the lake in a limo? I looked down at my outfit. Even in denim, I was overdressed for a fishing trip. As the limo eased into the marina's parking lot, I reached up to slip off the earrings and necklace. But just when he pulled sideways at the end of the dock, I dropped my hand to my lap and stared down the plank walkway. Tiny white lights outlined the small pavilion at the end of the walkway. And a few brighter lights illuminated the inside of the wooden structure. I opened my door and stepped out as Trevor was getting out of his seat.

He grabbed the handle and bowed low. "Good evening, mademoiselle."

I gave him my sauciest grin. "It sure is." I took a few steps onto the wooden planks and turned back. "Is that a waiter?" I whispered.

He shrugged and shooed me forward.

I tiptoed toward the bright lights.

A wooden podium stood at the entrance of the oblong pavilion, and behind it was a tuxedo-clad man with a napkin across his arm.

When I reached him, he bowed. "This way, please."

"Wait."

He stopped and looked at me. But I had to have time to gawk. To the left, inside an open booth with counters on all four sides, a man and a woman dressed in white and wearing chef's hats were working furiously. Before I could see what they were working on, the waiter positioned himself between me and them.

"I told you she was curious," a deep voice said from behind me.

I spun around just as Alex stepped out of the shadows. He looked fantastic in jeans and a blue shirt that just matched his eyes. And his slow grin. The one that still made my knees go weak even after all these years of knowing him.

The waiter discreetly stepped away, and in a few seconds, muted classical music filled the air.

Suddenly I felt shy and unsure. "Hi."

"Hi." He stepped toward me, and I instinctively took a step back.

He held out his hand. "Trust me?"

"What?"

"Trust me?"

I put my hand in his. "Totally."

He pulled me close. "You look beautiful," he whispered in my ear.

"Thank you. For all of this," I whispered back.

"Thank you for trusting me and going along with this." He kissed me on the cheek and released me. "I hope you're hungry."

I put my hand on my stomach. "I think I have too many butterflies to eat."

He laughed. "I knew the curiosity would drive you crazy. But now that you're here, you'll be fine. Let's sit down."

He led me to the table covered with a delicately filigreed white cloth. A bud vase with a single red rose was in the middle. Alex held my chair for me then sat down beside me. Within seconds, the waiter set a crisp green salad in front of each of us then disappeared again.

"Let's pray," Alex said simply.

I bowed and he gave thanks for the food. And for me.

When he finished I met his gaze. "Thank you."

He shrugged. "I thank God for you every day, Jenna."

Soft music filled the silence. I closed my eyes and swallowed against the lump in my throat. It had been a crazy few weeks. And for tonight at least, it seemed like everything had finally fallen into place.

He covered my cold hand with his warm one. "Relax and enjoy tonight. I wanted everything to be perfect, but I didn't mean for you to be nervous."

Me? Nervous? Just because any lingering objectivity I'd had about him was being whisked away with the warm summer breeze? Just because I was being forced to admit to myself that I'd fallen deeply and irrevocably in love with a man who may or may not love me back? Nah. No nerves here. I nodded. "I know. I'm having fun."

"Let's just pretend we're at the diner," he said.

I laughed. "So that's Harvey and Alice over there getting food ready?"

"Yep."

I nodded toward the waiter. "And this is Debbie?"

He leaned forward. "I wouldn't call him that to his face if I were you."

"I'll keep that in mind."

❖

"The fettuccine Alfredo was amazing." I dropped my fork on the empty plate and sat back with a sigh.

"Does that sigh mean you want to take dessert to go?"

"Sure. We can take it back to my house and watch a movie."

He ran his thumb over the back of my hand. "Do you have your heart set on a movie?"

I grinned. "Definitely not. But let's face it." I waved my arms toward the pavilion extraordinaire. "Anything is going to seem like a letdown after this."

He pulled me to my feet and into the shadows. "Even a trip around the lake to look at the stars?" He pointed to a pontoon boat tethered to the dock.

"Really?"

"The cheesecake is already on board."

I cut my gaze to him. "Race ya." I took off like a shot. Within seconds I could hear his feet right behind me, slapping against the wooden planks. I laughed and ran harder. Just as I jumped onto the boat, he caught me, and we collapsed onto the back bench seat together, laughing. His face was inches from mine, and the laughter died on my lips. He stared into my eyes for a long moment then gently kissed me on the forehead and stood.

I twisted sideways on the seat, with my back to him, and looked out at the dark water while he started the engine and puttered us away from the dock. If this had been a scene in a movie, it would have ended in a romantic kiss. Not a brotherly peck on the forehead.

Had Alex planned tonight as a way of letting me down easy? Tears stung my eyes. I closed them and let the lake breeze cool my hot cheeks. He drove without speaking. When I felt the engine slow, I sat up just as he pulled into a small cove and killed the motor.

"Are we going to put down anchor?" My voice sounded husky.

He nodded. "Drifting isn't as much fun as it sounds."

I shivered. Was it my imagination, or were we not talking about boating anymore?

The boat rocked as he stepped to the front and flipped up the bench seat to retrieve the anchor. Once it was in place, he came back and sat by me. I was still turned sideways, and he tugged me gently around to face him. "Hey. You okay?"

Define okay. I nodded and stared up at the stars. "The stars are beautiful."

"Yet you still manage to put them to shame."

I jerked my gaze back to his face. In the shadow of the running lights, I couldn't see his eyes clearly. But he reached up and cupped my cheek. "I'm sorry."

Sorry? Sorry for how you've been acting, or sorry for what you're about to say? I felt sure he could hear my heart beating out a skittish but loud rhythm in the quiet of the night. "Sorry for what?"

"For making things so difficult."

I pressed my hand to my stomach. "Alex, for a lawyer, you're not getting your point across very well. What are you trying to say?"

He dropped his arm around my shoulders and rested his head against the seat. We sat in silence for a few seconds, looking up at the stars. "Last Sunday at the diner. . .when you were with that cop. . ."

"I wasn't—" I couldn't believe that jealousy had been the motive behind this wonderful night.

He leaned up slightly and put his finger against my lips. "Shh. I know. You weren't *with* him. And before you think all this tonight was brought on by jealousy. . ."

I smiled. When did he start reading my mind?

"When you introduced me to him as your friend, I wanted to correct you. But I knew I had no right."

"You could have."

"I know. But what could I have said? That I wanted you to be more than my friend, but I was trying to get my practice up and running before I told you, so keep it hush-hush."

I blew out an exasperated breath. "I don't care about your practice— Wait. That didn't come out right."

"I know what you mean. And ever since you told him I was your friend, I've been rethinking my plan."

"Really?"

He sat up and ran his hand through his hair. I sat up, too, because the whole relaxed-and-looking-at-the-stars thing had just been a front for me anyway.

"When I was fifteen and you were thirteen, you and I went fishing in my little johnboat. In this very cove, actually."

"Really?" We'd fished a lot, but how could he remember what cove we'd been in? And this was an odd time for a fish story.

"You snagged a big trout that day." He pulled his arm out from around me and held his hands out to show the size. "When you pulled it out of the water, you jumped up and almost turned the boat over. You were laughing and your face just glowed. I looked at you and thought, *I'll never love anyone else like I love her.*"

My breath caught in my throat. "Oh."

"And I was right."

"Really?" What a stupid word. But the only thing I could seem to say.

He touched my cheek with his thumb. "You're crying."

Really? I didn't say it at least. But I thought it.

"You may not feel the same way I do," he said softly. "But I'm in love with you. And I always will be."

"Me, too." I shook my head. "I mean—"

He interrupted me. But not with a brotherly peck on the forehead. This was an "I'll love you forever" kind of kiss.

◆

The next few days flew by in a blur. Tennis with Carly and Elliott, Sunday dinner at Mama's with Alex by my side. Then visiting Reagan in the hospital and working.

We didn't tell anyone about our new commitment, but Mama pulled me over to the side and congratulated me. I joked about her best wishes being premature, but the truth was, I knew it was just a matter of time now. And not too much time.

Tuesday afternoon, I was at my desk writing out a last-minute reminder list for Lisa when Amelia popped her head into my office. "You're taking more vacation days?"

I nodded. "Just three days. I'll be back before you know it."

"That's what you said last time and look what happened."

I looked back at the list. "Barring murder," I clarified, "I'll be back at work Monday."

"Oh, don't even say that. Byron and I are coming up for the tribute concert, and we don't need that kind of excitement." She floated over to the mirror on my wall and tilted her head as if examining her face from every angle. Apparently deciding there were no bad angles, she nodded to herself. "Not that we're likely to get it with the murderer in jail."

I made a noncommittal sound. If only I could believe that. I'd rest a lot easier at night.

"Speaking of that, I guess you don't really need this information anymore, but I found out about Cecil."

I'd planned to corner Ruth and force her to tell me his whereabouts as soon as we got to Branson. This was much easier. "Might as well tell me," I said casually as I stood to make copies of the to-do list. I'd put one in every room and maybe Lisa would actually read one. "Where is he?"

Amelia smiled at me coyly in the mirror. "Well, the good Lord's the only one who knows that." She turned around to face me. "Cecil's dead. And has been for years."

I sank onto my chair. "Are you sure?"

"Absolutely. I knew it myself, really, but I'd forgotten. Why did you want to know?"

"Just curious. Thanks for telling me."

As soon as she was gone, I called Carly. "Mark Cecil off the list. He's dead."

She gasped. "Then who's CeeCee?"

"Who knows?"

"I'm glad you called. Marta wanted to know if Reagan could ride back to Branson with us. Is that okay with you?"

"Sure. Will she get out of the hospital in the morning? When I was there last night, she wasn't sure."

Carly cleared her throat. "Actually, she's getting out this afternoon."

"And you think I should invite her to spend the night at my house?"

She laughed. "That's up to you. But I figured you would."

"It's weird how protective I feel about her considering how hard she was to take when we first met her." Visiting her at the hospital every day had made me realize more and more how young and vulnerable she was behind that pretense of sophistication and toughness.

"Not really. A lot of the time when you get to know someone, they're different on the inside than they seem to be."

"Good point, oh wise one."

She sighed. "Just thinking about Holly, I guess, and wondering if there was more I could have done to help her."

"You did all you could, Carly. But I'll call Reagan right now and ask her to stay at my house tonight and ride to Branson with us tomorrow." As far as Holly, I didn't say it, but I did intend to do one more thing for her—find out who really killed her.

He who trusts in himself is a fool,
but he who walks in wisdom is kept safe.
PROVERBS 28:26

O n the road again," Carly sang from the backseat.

"Mom," all three of her kids protested.

Beside me in the passenger seat, Reagan smiled.

"You may wish you'd taken a cab," I joked.

She shook her head. "I appreciate you inviting me. This is much more fun than a long cab ride alone. And thanks again for letting me stay at your house last night. You didn't have to do that."

"I wanted to. And Marta seemed anxious to get you back to the Paradise."

A smile lit her face again. "She offered me a permanent job there, singing on the nights they don't have big names. And opening for the headliners when they are there."

"Wow," Carly said, leaning forward. "That's great. Is that what you want to do?"

"Definitely." She turned to look at Carly. "I don't know if you know, but I'm trying to get started as a songwriter. So being around stars gives me the perfect opportunity for them to hear my stuff and maybe record some of it."

I kept my eyes on the road. "Did Holly listen to your songs?"

She turned her head toward the window and for a few seconds didn't speak. "Yes. She even sang a few of them in her concerts. But she never went through with recording them."

"That must have left you sort of in limbo," I guessed.

She looked at me, and I glanced at her quickly. Her face was bright red. "You might as well know. That day you caught me in Holly's dressing room, I was looking for the CD I'd given her that had my songs on it."

If she was telling the truth, that was one mystery solved. And my gut instinct said she was. Of course, the same gut had thought a dead man was a main suspect, so I wasn't sure. "Did you find it?"

"Yes. Just before you came in. I jumped in the closet and stuffed the CD

277

in the waistband of my jeans." Her voice was so soft I could barely make out her words, and in the mirror, I could see Carly straining against her seat belt to hear. "I'm sorry."

I shrugged with my hands on the steering wheel. "I wasn't supposed to be in there either."

"What were you looking for?"

"I don't know, really. Clues to who killed Holly maybe."

She nodded and looked out the window again. "I'm just glad they caught the killer."

My eyes met Carly's in the mirror. Wouldn't our lives be simpler if we believed that?

She nodded as if in agreement with my unspoken words.

When we pulled into the Paradise breezeway, Dani and Marta were waiting. Carly jumped out and got the crutches from the back, and she and Marta helped Reagan into the building.

"Looks like it's up to us to get the luggage, kiddos," I said.

Dani helped, and the five of us loaded everything onto a cart. In the lobby, Ruth and Maurice were at the desk.

Ruth hurried over to me. "I need to talk to you."

Déjà vu. "What's wrong?"

She took my elbow and guided me away from everyone else. "You and I both know that stalker didn't kill Holly."

"How do you know?"

She frowned. "Because Buck did. He was embezzling from her, and he killed her." She looked over at Reagan, who was talking to Marta and Carly. "I'm not sure if Little Miss there knew about it or if she's just guilty of keeping bad company."

Wow. She'd toned down her opinion of Reagan considerably.

"Joey thinks she's innocent. As far as murder goes, at least." Oh, that explained a lot. "I'm not so sure. But either way, I know Buck did it." Maurice waved two room keys at her, and she smiled at him. "We'll talk later," she said from the corner of her mouth.

I nodded, but she was already gone.

"Later" turned out to be about a couple hours later. A knock sounded on our suite door, and when I opened it, Ruth stood there. "May I come in?"

I glanced over my shoulder at the deserted suite. Carly and the kids had gone down to John and Marta's, and I'd hoped to get my Dear Pru letters done and e-mailed so I could join them. "Sure."

Had she watched until the others left? As she walked in, I slid my cell phone off the desk into my pocket. My past experiences had left me a little leery of being alone with people who were possible murder suspects. No matter how innocent they seemed. Appearances could be deceptive.

I motioned toward the couch. "Have a seat."

"You have to help me." She sank onto the sofa.

I sat on the chair across from her. "How can I help?"

"You have to talk to the detective and see why he hasn't at least arrested Buck for embezzlement."

"Detective Jamison?"

She nodded. "I can't talk to him since he arrested Joey like he did. He thinks I'm a crazy old woman."

"Maybe if Maurice went down and told him—"

She held up her hand. "Maurice thinks I should mind my own business and let the police handle it."

"Well, maybe—"

"No!" Tears poured onto her cheeks. "Don't even say he's right. You have no idea what I've been through."

"I know it's been hard with Holly...and then with Joey getting arrested."

She covered her mouth with her trembling hand and shook her head. "That poor boy. Having the past all dredged up like that."

"The past?" I snagged a tissue from the box on the table and handed it to her.

She took it and vigorously blew her nose. I handed her a second tissue. "Thank you."

"The police thought Joey killed Holly because of his dad?" I said as gently as I could.

"Well, because of the accident."

"Accident?"

She twisted the tissues in her hands. "Joey came home from school one day and found Cecil—" Her voice broke and she began to sob.

I moved over by her and put my arm around her, mentally filling in the blank. *With Holly? Dead?*

"—beating me. He was about to kill me." She looked up at me as if to be sure I believed her. "Really."

I patted her shoulder. "I'm sorry."

She stared at the blank TV as if seeing the scene playing there. "Joey ran at him and shoved him. Cecil was three sheets to the wind anyway. He toppled forward and hit his head on the fireplace hearth."

"We called 911. But by the time they got there, he was dead."

"Was Joey charged?"

"Our lawyer had him plead guilty to involuntary manslaughter so he wouldn't have to do but a few months in juvie." She shook her head. "I wish I'd never gone along with that. It was just an accident." She pushed to her feet.

I followed suit. "That must have been awful, Ruth."

"I didn't mean to dump all this on you. I just need you to talk to the detective and ask him about the bank statements."

After our last phone conversation, the last thing I wanted to do was talk to Detective Jamison. Especially to try again to convince him he had the wrong man. But I couldn't say no to Ruth. "I'll try."

"Thank you." She hugged me and left.

❖

Carly and I didn't get a chance to talk alone until bedtime. I filled her in on everything Ruth said.

Her brows drew together. "So do you think Joey did it?"

"Based on him accidentally killing his father when he was a teen? No." Not that I was ready to cross him off the list.

"But you only have his mother's word that it was an accident. What's she going to say?"

I grinned. "Spoken like a true mother. But you're right. And I think if the stalker hadn't shot Reagan, Joey would probably be going to trial for killing Holly right now. So he should be our main suspect."

"He 'should,' but I get the feeling you're not convinced."

"Everything doesn't add up."

"Speaking of not adding up, are you going to ask Detective Jamison about Buck embezzling?"

"Since Marta has the pool ready, I probably won't even see him while we're here. So I'd have to call him. But I might. We'll see what tomorrow brings."

❖

The wail of an ambulance siren woke me.

Carly stumbled into my bedroom. "I just talked to Marta. Ruth overdosed."

"Is she. . ."

Carly shook her head. "Her pulse is thready, but she has one."

I grabbed my clothes and hurried to the bathroom. Within five minutes, Carly and I were on our way down the hall.

Marta met us. "They just took her in the ambulance. I woke Maurice up, and he went with her."

"Why would she do this now?" I asked.

Carly gave me a look I couldn't read.

Marta frowned. "I don't know. She's been talking about starting the museum for Holly. And she actually seemed excited about it." She put her hands on her hips. "Do you think the Paradise is doomed to tragedy?"

Carly and I laughed.

"Marta, our God is bigger than any jinx, so no, I don't," Carly said firmly.

Marta gave us a sheepish grin. "I know you're right. I'd better go tell John what's going on. Since you're up anyway, you might as well get some breakfast while it's fresh."

After she left, Carly nodded toward the breakfast area with its continental spread. "I guess she's right. You hungry?"

"Not that much. But this way we can talk without waking the kids."

We each filled a plate and made our way over to the booth in the corner. "It seems like a year ago when they questioned everyone in this room," she said as we sat down.

"Yeah, a lot has happened. What was that look about awhile ago? When I asked why Ruth would do this now." I took a bite of an orange slice.

Carly picked at a strawberry. "I was just thinking if she killed Holly it could be remorse. Or if she knew that Joey did it, it could be. . .that." She shivered. "That would be terrible."

"Oh, I didn't even think of that. You're right." I pushed my plate slightly away. "I'm not hungry."

"I know. Me either. If you want me to, I'll swim with you; then maybe we'll feel more like helping Marta."

"Great."

❖

By late afternoon, Carly turned to me. "I've made a hundred phone calls today, making sure everyone knows the details about the concert. But every time I use the phone, I think I should call and check on Ruth."

I nodded. "Me, too."

She grabbed a phone book and looked up the hospital number. I waited while she asked for Ruth's room. "It's ringing," she mouthed.

"Ruth? It's Carly. I thought Maurice would answer."

She frowned. "You're by yourself? Oh."

She mouthed to me. "A nurse is with her."

I nodded.

Carly didn't speak for a few minutes, and I could hear Ruth's excited voice, even though I couldn't tell what she was saying. "Oh dear. Would you like for me to come over?"

Apparently Ruth said yes, because Carly ended with, "I'll be right over then. 'Bye."

When she closed the phone, she shook her head. "Ruth says she didn't overdose. Someone tried to kill her."

"Do you believe her?"

Carly shrugged, tears glistening in her eyes. "I don't know. But I'm going over there. Will you keep an eye on the twins? Zac and Dani are going to the mall."

"Sure."

◆

The twins ate Happy Meals while I went over Ruth's accusation in my mind. According to Marta, Buck had gotten into town last night. So he had slipped into Ruth's suite and. . .what? Poisoned her sleeping pills? Switched them out for stronger ones?

I tried to wrap my mind around the possibility that Joey had tried to kill his own mother. I wasn't naive enough to think it had never been done. Maybe he was still angry that she let him go to juvie for a crime he didn't commit. Or did commit. Depending on whether Ruth was telling the truth. Of course, if Ruth was lying. . .I swirled a french fry in ketchup.

"Aunt Jenna!"

I looked up.

Rachel pointed at the blob of ketchup I'd squirted onto my sandwich paper. I'd swirled it all over the place. "Oops." I gave the girls a sheepish grin. "I got distracted."

"Distracted enough to get us a hot fudge sundae?" The mischievous glint in Hayley's eyes made me suspicious.

"I'm not sure."

"Mom gets us hot fudge sundaes all the time," she assured me, an impish grin lighting her pixie face.

"Yeah, even when we're full. She makes us eat them." Rachel jerked away as Hayley nudged her. "Well, she does get them for us."

I pulled out my cell phone. "It's too close to your bedtime for me to decide. I'll just call your mom." I wanted to check on Ruth anyway.

Carly answered on the first ring. "Hello," she whispered.

"I take it you're still inside the hospital."

"Yes," she hissed.

"I don't think they'll care that you're on your cell phone. Was there a sign?"

"I didn't see one."

"Then how's Ruth? Tell her I said hi."

I heard her passing on my message. "She says 'hi' to you, too."

More muted talking between them.

"Jenna, she's worried about the embezzlement investigation of Buck. Would you mind calling Detective Jamison?" She lowered her voice, and I could envision her turning away from the bed. "To put her mind at ease. Please."

Why hadn't I just said yes to the hot fudge sundaes? "Okay. I'll call him. And can you find out—"

"Thanks. Oh, someone's calling on the room phone. See you in a little while."

"Wait. The kids want—Carly? Carly?" She'd hung up on me. I'd wanted to know exactly how someone supposedly tried to kill Ruth. I flipped the phone shut. "Hot fudge sundaes all around."

Hayley and Rachel squealed and bounced up and down.

Twenty minutes later, we were happily finishing our sundaes. "Do you think Zac and Dani are on a date?" Hayley asked as she licked ice cream off her spoon.

I froze midbite.

"No!" Rachel looked up at me, her eyes speculative. "Are they?"

"I have no idea," I blurted. When I'd heard the teens were going to the mall, I just figured it was more of the same hanging out they'd been doing the past few weeks. Now that I thought about it, there had been more teasing (Zac) and giggling (Dani) since we got back from Lake View. How could I not have seen what was right in front of my face?

Hayley set her empty sundae cup down. "Didn't Mom tell you to call him? Maybe she's afraid they're kissing."

"She didn't tell me to call him."

"You said 'Okay. I'll call him.'" Rachel did a perfect imitation of me right down to the overburdened sigh.

"Oh, that was someone else. But I'd better call him, too." I hadn't done anything wrong with Detective Jamison, but knowing he'd been interested in me for more than a friend made me feel guilty. Crazy, but my mind doesn't always work logically. "Let's walk while I talk. Your mom will be home before too long."

Out in the parking lot, I fished his card from my cell phone wallet and punched in the number.

"Detective Jamison." His deep voice sounded hurried.

"Hi. It's Jenna Stafford." I guided the kids across the tiny street and over to the Paradise parking area.

"Jenna. It's nice to hear from you."

"Thanks. But I'm calling with a question." The girls were on each side of me, hanging on not only my arms but also my every word. No doubt trying to figure out if this was more than just a business call.

"What can I do for you?"

"Ruth was worried that she'd never heard back from you on those bank statements."

"What bank statements would that be?"

"Holly's."

"I have no idea what you're talking about."

"You know. The ones I found in Buck and Holly's suite right after the murder."

"You *found* them?" The skepticism in his voice made me grit my teeth.

"Yes. Buck asked me to pack up Holly's things."

"Incriminating bank statements and all?"

Call me a liar, why don't you? "I'm sure he didn't—" I looked up just in time to see Maurice pull into the hotel lot and park. "You know what, forget it. I've found someone I can ask who won't act like I'm an idiot."

"That car almost ran over us." Hayley pointed dramatically at Maurice's little red car.

"Honey, it didn't even come close." We came up beside Maurice's car. I waved.

He raised his hand in greeting and unfastened his seat belt.

"Not today." Rachel started talking very fast. "The night Miss Holly died. Only nobody cared because she died and we didn't."

"It must have been a different one. He wasn't in town when Miss Holly died."

Why would the detective lie to me about the bank statements? But he must have, because Maurice had specifically said he gave them to "Jamison."

Hayley shook her head. "Well, his car was in town that night. Because it had that funny looking thing on the hood." She pointed toward the dollar sign hood ornament.

Maurice had gotten out of the car with his briefcase and was making his way toward us when everything clicked into place in my mind. The bank statements. The car. Ruth's overdose.

19

Do not those who plot evil go astray?
But those who plan what is good find love and faithfulness.
PROVERBS 14:22

I stared at him, the color draining from my face. I turned and pushed the kids toward the back entrance of the hotel. Just as I yanked the key card out of my pocket, a hand closed around my arm.

"Going somewhere?"

"We just got back actually. From McDonald's. Wish you'd gotten here sooner. You could have had a hot fudge sundae."

The kids looked at me then at him. He pulled his briefcase away from his body enough for me—and me only—to see the ugly-looking gun aimed at me. "I need to talk to you." His tone was very polite. Innocuous even. I'd been right earlier. Maurice wasn't treating me like I was an idiot.

I nodded and slowly handed the card to Rachel. "You girls go on in. Your mom should be home soon."

"By ourselves?"

I forced a smile. "You can call Marta if you want to. She'll come stay with you until your mom gets home. But I need to go for a ride with Mr. Seaton."

Maurice's eyes flared, and I had a bad feeling I'd pay for that later. But it might save my life if Carly ever realized something was wrong.

"Wear your seat belt, Aunt Jenna." Hayley pointed at Maurice. "He's *not* a very good driver."

He gave her a tight-lipped smile. "You girls run on along. I'll take very good care of your aunt." He guided me toward the car, the gun a very effective prod. "I really shouldn't leave them behind since you told them my name," he muttered close to my ear.

Rachel was just sliding the key into the door slot.

"Please," I murmured, as much a prayer to God as an appeal to Maurice.

"With them along, you might try something heroic. And stupid. It doesn't really matter." He opened the car door for me, and I quickly climbed in.

Within seconds, he was getting in the driver's side. Relief flooded me as the twins made it into the building and the door closed behind them. What

285

did Maurice really know about what I'd figured out?

Maurice drove without speaking. So I figured the proverbial ball was in my court. And if I wanted to stay alive, I needed to keep it bouncing. "I really don't understand why you're taking me. You almost got away with the perfect crime."

He glanced over at me.

"Embezzlement."

He stared straight ahead and pretended I hadn't spoken.

"Since they have Holly's killer in jail, I would have figured you'd just transfer your money to a secure account on a little island somewhere and live out the rest of your days in luxury."

He grunted. Whatever happened to the idea of a talkative killer? The last time I faced a killer, I could barely get a word in edgewise. "Why don't you just tie me up and leave me somewhere?"

He smiled, and it was not a pretty sight. "That's exactly what I have planned, my dear."

Something wasn't right about that, but I pretended to be relieved. "Good."

"You'd do well to remember what happened to Holly when she took me for a fool," he growled.

This couldn't be good. He'd just confessed to murder. Whatever he'd meant by his cryptic answer, I felt certain he didn't intend for me to live through the night.

Back to the ball game. "How did Holly take you for a fool?"

We pulled up to a stop sign. He pressed the gun hard to my side. I stared straight ahead, afraid he'd think I was signaling to the people in the nearby cars. As we slipped out of traffic and turned into a residential section, he relaxed a little. "I made it look like Buck was taking her money. So she asked me to come up Saturday and not tell anyone. Said it was urgent."

I clasped my hand to my mouth, and he jerked the gun. Maurice Seaton. Maurice Seaton. "CeeCee," I breathed. "We thought you were a manicurist."

He looked like he thought I was crazy. "Holly started calling me that when we were first married. I hated it. I told her it sounded like a girl. Which is probably why she did it." He shook his head. "Anyway, she let me in right after the warm-up show started."

That must have been minutes after she pushed Carly and me out of her suite.

"I told her Buck was indeed stealing from her and then mentioned her leaving him."

"So why would you kill her if she believed Buck did it and was leaving him?"

"Shut up." His face turned red, and I thought sure the ball game was over, thanks to my technical foul. I prayed silently, continuing the ongoing plea I'd started when Maurice's hand had first closed over my arm back at the hotel.

He jerked the car into a driveway and leaned over toward me. I flinched, but he just reached overhead to hit an automatic garage door opener.

The little car glided into the garage, and he hit the button again. The door slid closed behind us. My heart, fairly calm before, was slamming against my ribs.

"Get out."

I carefully considered my situation. Expert advice always says don't go with an abductor. But I had to earlier, or he would've hurt the twins. And at this point, what could I gain from bravely proclaiming, "Shoot me now." The longer I dragged this out, the better chance I had of escaping.

He jabbed the gun against my side again. "I said, get out."

I nodded and climbed out of the low car, ever aware of the gun trained on me. He walked around, took my arm, and guided me to a workbench. My gaze followed his hands as he picked up a knife and laid the gun down. Could I grab it? His hard eyes telegraphed the answer—only if I wanted to be filleted like the catch of the day. Just in case, he stayed between me and the gun as he cut a section of heavy-duty string off a roll and tied it tightly around my wrists.

Satisfied I was securely bound, he retrieved the gun and kept it on me while he got his briefcase from the car. Within seconds, we were outside, and he nudged me toward the stairs going down to the lake. The wooden steps creaked loudly in the dusky dark. Down below, water lapped against the dock.

In high school I went through a morbidly romantic Emily Brontë stage. I'd creeped Carly out by telling her I wanted to be in the water when I died. Now that it looked like my wish was about to come true, was it too picky of me to note that I'd meant when I died of old age? I'd envisioned my husband of seventy years carrying me out into the lake and holding me tightly in his arms, the waves sloshing around us as I breathed my last breath.

As we reached the dock, I was tempted to close my eyes and try to pretend I was old and ready to go, but the practical side of me kicked in. Instead, I examined everything in the fading light. Was he going to shoot me here and dump me into the lake? If he raised the gun, I'd dive into the water. With my hands tied, swimming would be difficult but not impossible.

"We're going for a ride," he muttered, shoving me toward a small boat with a big motor. I looked around. Where was everybody? But I couldn't see a soul who would hear me yell for help.

"Don't even think about screaming, unless you'd like to be responsible for innocent lives being lost." He gave me another push.

I fell into the boat, barely catching myself with my tied hands. "But mine is an innocent life."

He snorted. "Your mama should have raised you to mind your own business."

The nerve of him. *My* mama did fine. His mama should have taught him not to kill people.

But he wasn't through. "I never wanted to kill anybody. But even though Holly thought Buck was embezzling from her, she refused to leave him. Then she started making fun of me. Said he might be a crook, but at least he had the guts to go after what he wanted."

"So you killed her?"

He shook his head. "No. I just wanted to show her that she was wrong. So I told her that I was the one who took the money and that I'd made it look like Buck did it." He shoved me to my knees in the bottom of the boat right in front of the driver's chair and pointed the gun at me.

"Then what did she do?" Not that I even cared anymore, but I was desperate to keep the ball moving, anything to avoid that final buzzer.

"She reached for the phone to call the police. If Buck stole from her, she was fine with it. But after all our years together, she was going to turn me in. Send me to prison."

He sat down in the captain's chair facing me. When he didn't immediately start the engine, I realized he was waiting for a response.

"That must have really hurt."

"I'd picked up a guitar string in the hall, just out of habit. I'm kind of a neat freak."

That's not the only kind of freak he was, but I figured I was better off not mentioning that.

"And when she started to call the cops, I just snapped. Before I knew what happened, she was dead." His voice broke. "I loved her."

I couldn't see his face very well in the dark. Was he crying?

"I'm sorry." Believe me, I was so sorry. Sorry that we ever came to the Paradise. Sorry that Holly had reacted as she had. And sorry that I'd let myself get into this situation. I tried to edge closer to him so I could see if his grip on the gun had loosened in his grief.

"Just be still," he barked. All traces of vulnerability were gone from his voice as he started the boat motor. Within seconds, we were zipping through the black water. I couldn't see where we were going. All I could see was where we'd come from. As the lights of his subdivision faded into the distance, my hope grew dimmer, as well.

Tears blurred my vision. The wind whipped my hair forward, and I twisted my body slightly to the side to get it out of my eyes. We were going so fast. If

I could somehow throw myself overboard without getting shot, the impact with the water would surely kill me. Despair settled in heavier than the darkness.

Oh, Lord, please rescue me.

The boat slowed then stopped. On the shore, a set of bright lights on the bank caught my eye. The campground Alex showed me. I could remember the layout. If I jumped in the water and followed the North Star, I should come up on the bank at the right place. Unless Maurice shot me here while I still knelt in front of him.

By the glow of the running lights, I could see him as he walked toward me. The boat swayed gently with his steps. "I'm sorry." He put his hand under the string that bound my wrists and pulled me up. My legs prickled pins and needles as they came out of the cramped position.

"I didn't want to kill anyone."

I glared at him, any sympathy I had earlier gone with the feeling in my legs. "You'll never get away with this."

"I already have. That's why I didn't worry about leaving those nosy little twins behind. My plane is fueled and ready at the airport. The money I took from Holly is in an account in the Cayman Islands. In less than an hour, I'll be winging my way to freedom."

Well, pin a medal on him. He was right. And I'd be dead at the bottom of the lake. Unless I acted now. I threw my body weight toward him, being careful not to completely lose my balance. I heard him crash and fumble for his footing, but I scrambled up onto the live well and did my best no-hands dive over the side. It might not qualify for the Olympics, but— The thought was interrupted by a loud explosion. A searing pain hit my left shoulder just as I hit the water. The icy darkness swallowed me. The cold made it hard to think, but it also numbed the pain. Instinct brought me to the surface quickly. A spotlight reflecting off the water near me cleared some of the fog from my brain. I dove deep, counting the cost, but knowing that if I didn't take the chance, I was lost.

I stayed under until I was about to lose consciousness, then kicked my way upward, praying I hadn't gotten turned around. I could be propelling myself to the bottom of the lake. Just as I thought sure I'd gone the wrong way, I broke the surface again. The light was nowhere to be found, and the sound of the boat motor faded into the distance as I treaded water, using my bound hands as one large fin.

Choppy waves were all I could see, so I braced myself and bounced out of the water, using my feet to shoot me up. "Oww!" The intense pain made my head spin. Spots in front of my eyes replaced the night sky. "If I faint, I die," I said to the water. I bounced up one more time, not as vigorously. The lights of the campground weren't too far. At least not too far if my hands weren't tied and I weren't possibly dying from a gunshot wound. I couldn't keep bouncing, so I looked up and thanked God for the cloudless night. The North Star shone right over the campground. I swam toward it, pushing through the pain like I used to when I was in training. Not that the coach shot me back then.

My mind was seriously starting to jumble. I began to count the strokes silently. *One. Two. Three. Go toward the star. Four. Five. Six. Three. No. Wait. Go toward the star.* Finally, I just switched to *Star. Star. Star. Star. Star. Star.* With each word, I pulled water toward me with my bound hands and kicked, sort of a variation of the frog stroke I used to do when I was tiny. I kept my focus on the star and let it guide me. But finally I knew I was beat. I couldn't swim anymore. I stopped and my feet grazed against something. I tentatively reached down with my toes and then let my weight rest on solid ground.

Thank You, thank You, thank You, God.

The tears started to flow, and by the time I got to the shore, I was on my knees, sobbing great gulping sobs. "Help." I wanted to lay on the rocks and sand until I could quit crying. Until I could think. I barely knew my name. But I did know one thing. Maurice was going to get away if I didn't get help.

That possibility brought me to my feet. "Help." I called louder as I stumbled into the lighted area around the cabins. "Help!"

One porch light clicked on. Then another. A woman came out of the first house, a little girl clutching her leg. Two guys, a few years older than Zac, walked out on the porch of the second.

"You poor thing." The woman rushed over and put her arm around me. "Go get some towels, Lilly."

The guys took a few steps closer and the tallest one peered at me. "You're bleeding."

"Got a pocketknife?" the woman asked him.

He looked at his buddy, who fished in his pocket and pulled out a Swiss army knife. He reached over and cut the twine.

I clutched my left arm against my body.

"Call 911," I croaked out. The tall guy looked a little afraid of me, but he pulled out his cell phone and dialed.

"What should I tell them?" he said.

"Tell them to send an ambulance, you goose," the woman snapped.

"No, wait! I'll talk." I held out my right hand.

"She wants my phone?" he said to his friend, who shrugged.

The woman yanked the phone from his hand and put it in mine.

When the operator answered, I took a deep breath and tried to ignore the spinning. "This is Jenna Stafford. Get in touch with Detective James. . . Jamison."

"Ms. Stafford, where are you?"

"Tell him Maurice Seaton confessed to killing Holly Wood. He's on his way to the Hollister airport. You have to stop him. Hurry."

"But where are you?"

I told her the campground name then remembered there was one more thing. "Oh. And he shot me."

I don't know what happened to the guy's cell phone when I surrendered to the encroaching blackness and tumbled to the ground.

❖

"Holly would have been so happy."

I smiled at Carly's reflection in the mirror. Her dark curls framed her glowing face. "You look pretty happy yourself. And I don't think it's because of all the stars we're going to see tonight."

She sat down beside me on the vanity bench and absently fluffed her hair. "It's not just because Elliott's here. Although I admit, that is really somethin'. It's also the fact that you're here." She motioned toward the sling that held my arm. "Alive and able to go to the concert. When I heard you'd been shot. . ."

I nodded and leaned forward to touch up my lipstick with my good hand. "It was scary."

"You know, Alex never left your bedside. Even when Mama and Daddy got there, he stepped back but stayed in the room. I think he was afraid to take his eyes off you."

"Probably afraid I'd stumble into another murder." I stuck my lipstick in my purse.

"Very funny. He does worry, but it's because he loves you."

"Yes, he does. Isn't it wonderful?" I knew I sounded like a love-struck idiot, but it was so nice to finally feel that Alex was totally committed to our relationship. "Ready to go watch the concert?"

We met Alex and Elliott in the lobby. As we handed our tickets to the usher, he smiled. "Front row seats. Nice."

"That's what happens when you know the owners," Carly whispered to me. "We shouldn't be mixing Brad Paisley up with the post office guy tonight, that's for sure."

I nodded and waved at Zac and Dani, who were seated midway. Zac blushed a little, and I realized they were holding hands. Guess that explained why they didn't want to sit with the rest of us.

Mama and Daddy along with the twins were seated on the front row with us. Before we even got up there, I could see the twins' bobbing heads. They were thrilled to be seeing so many stars up close and personal. But no more thrilled than the rest of us, probably.

As soon as the performance began, though, there was no doubt that it was a tribute. Even though almost every well-known country music artist appeared on the stage, they selflessly made it all about Holly. In the background the huge screen flashed a silent montage of the queen of country music's concerts as the performers sang her greatest hits and told touching stories about her. Before the night was over, I decided Carly might have been right. There could have been more depth to her than I realized.

When it was over, the crowd went wild. As the cheering and clapping showed no signs of stopping, I glanced over at Carly, who had tears streaming down her cheeks.

I leaned over to speak into her ear. "Holly would have been happy. Even though she was far from perfect, she touched a lot of lives for good."

She squeezed my hand and nodded.

Later, after the stage lights were down and the auditorium was empty, we went backstage to say good-bye to everyone.

Ruth hugged us both. "I've decided to buy the land next door for Holly's museum."

"Here in Branson? Next to the Paradise?" Marta would be thrilled.

Ruth nodded. "It's only fitting. I've been on the phone all afternoon trying to get things ready." She wiped away a tear. "I still can't believe Maurice killed her. He loved her so much."

I hugged her. "I think he did, too, but he just went crazy."

"And to think that he tried to kill me, too. At least running the museum will keep me busy." Ruth twisted the tissue in her hand. "Keep my mind occupied."

Just then, Joey came in, loosely supporting Reagan, who was on crutches. Was that compassion on Ruth's face when she looked at Reagan?

Joey hugged his mother. "It turned out really well. Holly would be pleased with what you've done."

I leaned down and hugged Reagan with my good arm. "You take care of yourself. Stay in touch, okay?"

She smiled. "I will."

"Good luck with your new job. We'll be back to hear you sing before too long."

"Thanks." She looked over at Joey. "I'll at least have someone in the house band that I already know."

I smiled at Joey. "Congratulations on your new job, too, then."

To my amazement, he flashed me an almost sunny smile in return. "Thanks."

As they walked away, I felt an arm around my waist, and I looked up into Alex's twinkling eyes. "I think this is the end of the yellow brick road. You sorry it's over?"

I laughed. "It's been an adventure, but I have to say that Dorothy's right. There's no place like home."

DOWN HOME AND DEADLY

IF YOU LAY DOWN WITH THE DOGS, YOU'LL COME UP WITH FLEAS.

Don't forget to call the groomer to see what time you should pick up Fluffy," Lisa yelled over her shoulder as she headed toward the sauna.

I slumped into my chair and reached for the phone book. Nepotism was alive and well in America, and my so-called career was a train wreck.

Actually, train wreck was probably a little too dramatic. More like an economy car, really. With a dead battery. And me trudging along behind, pushing uphill.

I waved my hand in front of my face, trying to disperse the cloying scent of Lisa's expensive perfume. How did I get here? A year ago I was a valued employee, on the fast track to buying my boss's health club for a good price, with the added bonus of owner financing. Until Bob asked me to show his rich daughter a little about running the club to help her get her confidence back after her recent separation from her husband.

If Lisa had a confidence problem, she covered it well with a large mask of egotism. Ever since she showed up, I'd been edging closer and closer to becoming an indentured servant. I still had all my old tasks. (Lisa couldn't figure out how to actually *run* the club, only how to use the equipment.) But in addition, I was her daytime maid.

"How low can I go?" I complained to the empty office and picked up the phone, a prayer for patience running through my mind as I flipped through the business card index for the groomer's number.

Wait until Carly heard this one. At the thought of my sister's reaction, my gaze went automatically to the family picture I kept on my desk. Or rather to the place it used to be. "I don't believe it." My picture had been replaced by one of Lisa cuddling her pampered pooch.

I slammed the phone down. "That *so* does it."

Without stopping to analyze, I grabbed an empty plastic bag from Lisa's expensive takeout lunch and filled it with my personal things. The things I could find.

I yanked open the top drawer of the desk. There was my family picture.

At least it didn't get thrown out with the garbage. Or stuck in the pool supply closet, like all my paintings from the office wall did when I took a Branson trip awhile back. "She can put up all the modern art she wants now," I muttered as I cleaned out the drawer.

Satisfied I had everything I couldn't live without, I snatched up my keys. "I'm outta here."

I stomped down the hall, pushed open the front door, and crashed into Bob.

"Jenna?" He shifted the box he was carrying to effectively block my exit. "What are you doing?"

I took a reluctant step back into the building. "Leaving."

"When will you be back?"

When your daughter figures out she isn't the queen of the universe. "When you're ready to sign on the dotted line and make me the owner." Same thing.

His face reddened. "Ah, Jenna. I was about ready to do that, actually. But something's come up and I'm a little short on cash. So even if I did sell it to you now, I couldn't owner finance. My accountant. . ."

I hadn't been impressed the first time Bob told me what excuse he and his accountant had cooked up for not selling me the place, and I sure didn't plan to stay around and listen to it again. I put my hand on the box to move it out of my way.

"Wait!" Bob quickly opened the box and pulled something from it. He gave me his most suave smile and dropped the box at his feet. He held up a blue T-shirt. White lettering across the front commanded: GET IN THE SWIM WITH JENNA STAFFORD.

I frowned. He hoped to win me over with the very T-shirts I'd protested? Capitalizing on my Olympic glory (or lack thereof, in my opinion, considering I lost) had been the thing I disliked most about this job. A necessary evil. But definitely not a persuasion point for staying.

His smile stretched wider. "I know how you always hated the pink ones, so I got them in blue."

I sighed. "We both know who asked for them in blue." Demanded was more like it. "And speaking of her. . ." I moved the T-shirt out of my way like a bull charging a red cloth and brushed past him. "You'd better call the groomer to see what time you should pick up Fluffy." The door closed behind me.

Thankfully he didn't follow me.

Something about standing in front of the familiar building with my belongings in a plastic bag made my insides quiver. After months of giving notice then giving in to Bob's pleading to stay, I'd finally done it. I'd quit. I took a deep breath of fresh September air and exhaled slowly. Would I be sorry? Eventually, maybe, but not today.

My cell rang before I got to my vehicle. I glanced at the caller ID. Bob.

Probably couldn't find the groomer's number. I ignored the call and stowed my stuff in the front seat of the SUV. Before I could turn the key, Sister Sledge belted out, "We are family!"

I jumped. Since my old phone was at the bottom of Table Rock Lake, I'd been forced to get a new one. And I still hadn't gotten used to the personalized ringtones my nephew Zac had set up for me. What was it with teenagers and technology? And why did my youthful thirty suddenly seem so old?

At least I had sense enough to know that ringtone was my sister, Carly. Just what I needed—a sympathetic ear.

I flipped the phone open.

She started to talk so fast I couldn't understand a single word.

"Carly. Slow down."

"The. Grand. Opening. Of. Down Home. Diner. It's two weeks from Friday. That's sixteen days." She enunciated her words as if English were my second language. Or third.

Even though buying and refurbishing the Lake View Diner had been Carly's dream, the realization of that dream was proving a wee bit stressful. "I know that. Remember, I made sure I wasn't on the schedule at the athletic club that day so that I could help you?" I started the engine. "Not that it matters now."

"What do you mean, it doesn't matter now?" The frantic tone was back. "It matters to me. I need your help!"

"You've got it. As much as you need." I resisted the urge to peel out of the parking lot as I raged about the injustices I'd endured. She sympathized until finally my white-knuckle grip on the steering wheel relaxed. When I was almost home, I half laughed. "Sorry for ranting so long. But that's it. I'm not working there anymore."

"When I called, I was going to ask you to see if Bob could let you have a few days off. But now, with you quitting, well, this is just perfect." I guess she heard herself, because she hastily added, "Heaven knows I've been so irritated at Bob since he brought Lisa in and made you a flunky."

"Thanks for clearing up any remaining delusions I might have had about my job."

"Hey, that's what sisters are for." Carly paused. "You okay with this?"

"Sure. I will be." I slowed at my street and turned on the blinker then glanced in the rearview mirror. Not a car in sight. So at least my boss hadn't followed me home. "And I really don't want to talk to Bob for a few days, anyway." With any other job, I'd have felt bad about not giving notice, but I *had* been giving notice ever since Lisa came. Bob just hadn't been listening.

"Great. How fast can you get over here?"

❖

"Who put that table with a checker set on it out on the porch?" Alice asked, her graying brows drawn together.

Carly looked up from a booth where she'd spent the morning interviewing wait staff and cooks. "I did."

Alice pursed her lips and nodded.

Carly gave me a look that said, "Can you handle this, please?" and turned back to Vini, a young Albanian who'd done a great job working at the health club for several months. Until Lisa fired him a couple of days ago out of the blue. I'd asked Carly to interview him, so I owed her.

I put my hand on Alice's arm. "You've been working hard. I made some tea awhile ago. Want some?"

Alice nodded. "That sounds good."

I picked up my cell phone off the counter and slid it into my pocket as I pushed open the double doors. Something about the new phone made it hard to keep up with. I didn't even remember putting it there.

Alice followed me into the kitchen. "Don't get me wrong. I'm thrilled your sister wanted to buy our diner, but she sure has some strange ideas."

"Change is never easy." I smiled at my reflection in the stainless steel side-by-side refrigerator. I'd been moonlighting incognito for about a year as local advice columnist Dear Pru. Now I was starting to sound like her in my everyday conversations. "You loved the diner just like it was." I handed her a glass of ice.

She gave me a sharp look.

"I mean, everyone did. Love it," I stammered. So much for being wise. "But it's normal for Carly to want to do some things to make it her own."

"Carly might do well to remember what your mama always says."

I poured tea into her glass. "What's that?" Unlike me, our mama is a fount of wisdom. Hard to know which thing Alice was referring to.

"If it ain't broke, don't fix it." She took a big chug of her tea.

I was pretty sure my mama had never said the word *ain't* in her life, but I had heard her echo that general sentiment before. "Oh. Yeah."

Harvey pushed open the doors. "You know why she's got that table out on the porch?"

Alice shook her head, and I didn't breathe. The table on the porch was just a tiny piece of the bigger picture my sister had in mind. But telling Alice and Harvey had been the fly in the ointment from the beginning. And I wasn't about to take on the task.

Harvey grunted. "She's got some fool idea about people playing dominoes and checkers out there."

Alice gasped. "Did you tell her that this is a diner? The whole idea is to get people to eat and then leave so more people can eat."

Harvey grabbed a hammer from the closet and headed back out. "I told her," he called over his shoulder. "But beneath that soft drawl, she's got a mind of her own."

Did I detect a bit of admiration in his voice? Harvey and Alice had been our parents' friends for so long that I could definitely understand why it was hard for them to see Carl and Elizabeth's little girls trying to make over the diner they'd poured their hearts and souls into all these years.

"Checkers and dominoes," Alice scoffed under her breath as she finished off her tea. "Might as well put rocking chairs out there, too."

I don't play poker. And it's a good thing. Because my poker face wouldn't fool anyone.

Alice looked at me, and her eyes widened in disbelief. "You don't mean it?"

I nodded. Why hadn't Carly just come clean with them about her big plans? She'd convinced herself—and me—that they'd take it easier in small bites. I wasn't so sure.

Alice huffed out. I savored the peacefulness of the quiet kitchen and considered calling Alex to invite him to come help us paint tonight. We needed all the hands we could get. And it'd definitely be more fun with him here. That was a no-brainer. I pulled my phone from my pocket and hit the button that redials the last number dialed.

"Hey, babe."

I frowned. That didn't sound like my fiancé, but I thought sure he was the last one I called. "Alex?"

"I'm sorry. I believe you have the wrong number."

I held the phone out and looked at the screen. It read—"Connected to Me." What did that even mean? I groaned inwardly. "Sorry. My bad."

I pushed the END button just as the double doors opened again and Debbie walked in with a roll of wallpaper in her hand. The waitress had been so thrilled to stay on at the diner that she'd offered to help out with the remodeling. Carly had accepted and gladly agreed to pay her. Even though I had two strikes against me with her—one, that she'd always liked Alex, and two, that she was Lisa's best friend—she'd been nothing but friendly to me.

When she saw me, her eyes widened and she stopped. "Is that my phone?"

I smiled. "No, this is my new—" My smile faded as I remembered the wrong number. I held up the phone. "Does your phone look like this?"

"Yes."

I ducked my head. "I'm sorry. So does mine. Exactly. I haven't had mine long enough to tell it from someone else's, I guess." I held it out to her.

She snatched the phone out of my hand. "Did you use it?"

I stared at her. Talk about overreacting. Even if her cell phone minutes were limited, I'd only had the phone for a minute. "I hit the last call dialed, thinking I'd call Alex, but obviously it wasn't him."

She didn't answer, just mashed a couple of buttons on the phone and stared at the screen. "Did you talk to someone?"

I'd been interrogated by police that weren't this stern. "Just a guy who said I had the wrong number. I'm sorry I got confused."

Her smile looked a little forced, but at least it was a smile. She pushed a strand of her bleached-blond hair behind her ear. "No worries. That happens. I just got mine too, yesterday."

"And wouldn't you know I'd steal it today? We need to get one of those label makers. Remember those? When I was about ten, Mama got one to label things at the cabins, and I labeled the whole house. Even the furniture."

Her smile relaxed. "I do remember those. One summer I went to camp with 'Debbie' in raised white letters on bright blue tape stuck on everything I owned."

Raised voices in the dining room interrupted our soft laughter.

"Do they know yet?" Debbie whispered.

I shrugged. "It sounds like maybe they do now."

With trepidation, I walked over to the door and peeked out. Vini was gone, and Carly stood facing Harvey and Alice, who had their backs to me.

Carly saw me and motioned me to her. "Jenna, come tell them that you think the new name is great."

I looked over my shoulder at Debbie, who shooed me out. "I'll just be in here hanging wallpaper and minding my own business."

"Chicken," I muttered. I walked over to the tense trio. "You have to admit that 'Down Home Diner' has a ring to it."

"What does 'down home' mean, anyway?" Alice asked, her nose crinkling as if a skunk had suddenly crawled up under the diner and died.

"You know what 'down home' means," Harvey insisted. "Country and common." He waved his hand to the porch. "That's why that table's out there, obviously. Checkers and dominoes are 'down home.'"

She narrowed her eyes at her husband. "Whose side are you on?"

"You know I'm on your side. I always have been. I was just answering your question."

Alice took a couple of steps backward, and Harvey pulled a chair out for her to sit on.

Seated, she looked up at Carly, her eyes swimming with tears. "We should have put in the contract that you couldn't do that." She grabbed a paper napkin from the table in front of her and wiped her nose. She motioned toward the small, delicately lettered sign Carly had just finished and placed on the pie counter. "It's crazy enough to be giving police officers in uniform a free piece of pie. But I'd never have thought of anyone changing the name of the diner."

Harvey ran his finger around the collar of his checked shirt. "Actually, remember when Mom and Pop first turned the diner over to us? You wanted to rename it Alice's Restaurant. But Mom had a fit."

For a second, Alice's face opened as if she were remembering a younger her—full of plans and hopes. But then she pinched her lips together and shrugged. "And rightly so. I was a silly kid who didn't know what was what."

I glanced at Carly, wondering how she'd handle the inference. But her Southern graciousness won out.

"I'm sorry I hurt your feelings, Alice," she said softly. "But this is a fresh start for me. And the Down Home Diner is what I need."

My sister, the quintessential steel magnolia.

Alice slumped. "Oh, it's okay. You bought it. You should be able to call it whatever you want. I'm just an old fool."

Harvey sat down beside her and patted her hand. "This is a fresh start for us, too, Allie. Heaven knows we need one. And I think it'll be easier for us to let go of the Down Home Diner than the Lake View Diner."

She nodded. "You might be right."

In unspoken agreement, we left them to their own conversation and walked out onto the front porch.

Carly sat down at the small table that had started all of this and motioned me to sit across from her. She mussed her dark curls with her hand in a mannerism I recognized meant she had something on her mind.

"What's up?" I asked.

She picked up a red checker and tapped it against the table absently. "Nothing really. Not yet, anyway."

"What does that mean? Is it about the diner? Or Elliott?" Ever since I'd gotten engaged a few weeks ago, I'd been wondering about Carly and Elliott. Apparently that old adage about those in love wanting everyone to be in love was true.

"You know Elliott and I are getting pretty serious."

I propped my elbows on the table and leaned toward her. "Yes?"

She turned the checker up on its edge and rolled it from one hand to another across the wooden surface.

"Carly! What's going on?" Patience wasn't my strong point. And she knew it.

"I'm thinking about trying to find Travis," she said in a rush.

"Why?" I blurted out. Her ex-husband, Travis, had divorced her when she was pregnant with the twins and Zac was six. He'd run off with an emaciated model and eventually skipped the country to Mexico. We assumed he left the country to keep from paying child support. I'd loved my brother-in-law once, back before he betrayed our whole family and broke my sister's heart. But going searching for him made about as much sense to me as trying to bring back a bad migraine once it was gone.

She carefully placed the checker back in its original place on the board and looked up at me. "For closure for the kids. And for me, too, really. If we get married, Elliott would like to adopt them, and I'd like that, too. Even though I feel sure we could get it approved on grounds of abandonment, I'd rather have Travis's permission."

I shook my head. "My gut is saying that finding Travis is a terrible idea, Carly. In this case, I can't think of any better advice than to let sleeping dogs lie." Or in Travis's case, let lying dogs sleep, but I didn't say that out loud. "What does Elliott think?"

She bit her lower lip and pushed her curls back from her face. "He agrees with you."

I didn't know what to say. Nobody likes to feel ganged up on. "So how's the hiring process going?"

She grimaced to let me know she knew what I was doing, but picked up the new subject. "Pretty good. I kept Arnie to wash dishes but hired a new guy, too. Same with the cook. Of course, most of the new staff isn't starting until after the grand opening, since Harvey and Alice are going to help out with that. Hard to believe those two were doing half the cooking and dishwashing themselves."

I idly moved a black checker. "They don't have kids," I reminded her. "The twins and Zac would be disappointed if you turned into a workaholic."

She laughed and slid a red checker forward one space. "The twins might be. But now that he's a senior, Zac thinks he doesn't need his mama anymore."

"Is he going to work here after school?" I moved another checker.

She nodded as she responded with a move of her own. "I'll have some part-time hours for him. Most of the waitresses stayed on, though. And I hired Vini as a waiter."

I smiled. "Oh, good. He always impressed me with his work ethic at the gym. He's punctual and never goofs off."

"I hired him already. You can stop the streaming reference message."

"Did you call Lisa about him?" I asked as I considered my next move.

"Didn't think I needed to with you here," Carly said, edging her checker close to being able to jump mine. "Especially since he was honest about her firing him."

I frowned and pushed my black playing piece out of harm's way. "Did he say what reason she gave?"

Carly shook her head and countered with another move. "Just said she fired him for no good reason."

"Sounds like her." With Lisa on my mind, I shoved my checker hard without really thinking.

Carly reached across, jumped over two of my checkers, and scooped them up.

"Wait a minute!" I protested. "I wasn't paying attention."

"When you play on my porch, you should always pay attention," she said facetiously. "Welcome to the Down Home Diner."

❖

"Jenna."

I spun around with the dishcloth still in my hand.

Carly, her dark hair curling around her sweaty face, beamed at me from the kitchen window. "Can you snag the garbage when you're done?"

"Sure. Why not?" I wiped the crumbs from the counter into my hand and waggled my fingers over the trash can. Across the room, Harvey patiently showed Vini how to clean the salad bar at the close of the day. I pushed the kitchen door open with my shoulder. "Carly, if success can be measured by garbage, I'd say your grand opening was a resounding triumph."

Carly looked up from stirring a large pot of tomorrow's soup of the day she already had simmering over the burner. "You think so?"

I washed my hands at the stainless steel double sink.

"She's right." Alice reached across Carly and salted the soup. "Harvey took it out not twenty minutes ago."

Carly put her hand on Alice's. "I already salted it."

"I know you did, honey, but just not enough for bean soup. Beans absorb salt like little sponges." Hearty shakes of salt punctuated each word.

Carly tossed me a pleading look over her shoulder. That old saying about too many cooks spoiling the broth was definitely proving true during this transition period of old diner owner to new.

I gathered the handles of the black plastic bag and cleared my throat. "Alice, thanks to that last rush of police officers we had an hour ago, most of the pie is gone. But there are a few pieces left in each pan. What do you do with those?"

Alice glanced out at the pie counter. "Wrap up individual servings and sell them at breakfast. I'll take care of them." She headed toward the door. "I still don't know about this idea of giving away pie," she said over her shoulder.

When the door swung shut behind the older woman, Carly sighed. "Thanks for rescuing me." She opened a drawer and dropped the saltshaker into it. "Why did I think it would be a good idea to accept their offer to help me out for a while?"

"It was a good idea. Besides, in a few weeks this place will be all yours." I lifted the plastic bags, one in each hand, and slipped out the back door. The door slammed loudly behind me. I stepped off the back porch into the orange glow of the quiet alley. Whoever invented guard lights deserves a Nobel Prize. Or at least a free piece of pie.

I duckwalked to the Dumpster, balancing my burdens. "One, two, three, heave." I threw one garbage bag into the green Dumpster, then let go of the other one. It went flying over the trash bin and landed with a thud. A small noise made me jump.

"Shifting trash," I whispered and tiptoed around to retrieve the bag.

I squinted at the darker area behind the Dumpster then put my hand out to touch the warm hood of a small sports car I hadn't even seen. Why would it be parked here, completely hidden by the huge double Dumpster? The owner took the thing about not wanting to risk having anyone hit his door in the parking lot to a whole new level. I stretched to get the trash bag off the roof and froze.

This car had more than a dent in the door. The driver window was broken out. I snagged the handle of the bag but stopped again. A man I didn't recognize was slumped sideways in the front seat.

"Sir?" My voice was as jagged as the window I was looking through.

He didn't respond. Being careful to avoid the broken glass, I reached in and touched his left shoulder. Still no response. I touched his neck for a pulse.

No pulse. My hand brushed sticky wetness at the same time I saw the dark stain on his shirt, and I knew I was in a deserted alley with a dead body.

Something rustled behind me. I started to turn, but the world exploded. Darkness rushed to meet me.

Dead as a Doornail

"Oww..." I'm not sure if the sound of groaning woke me or if the pain woke me and then I groaned. Either way, I opened my eyes and reached toward the black thing in front of me. At least that's what my brain said for me to do. My arms, apparently trapped under my body too long, weren't getting the signal. I rolled over and ignored the pins and needles as I shifted to sitting. Nausea hit in waves.

My head throbbed. "Oww..." At least now that I was upright, I could identify the black thing as a tire. I rubbed my fat-feeling fingers over my stinging cheek, and pieces of gravel clinked to the ground. Why had I been facedown in the gravel next to a car? As soon as the question flitted through my pounding brain, I knew the answer.

I was in the alley behind the diner.

And there was a dead man in the car beside me.

But the dead man hadn't knocked me out. I turned my head fractionally, wincing with every muscle shift. No captor stood nearby waiting for me to wake. I appeared to be alone, thankfully.

How long had I been out here? I squinted through the dim alley past the Dumpster. The back door of the diner looked miles away. The feeling was coming back in my fingers, and I eased myself up onto wobbly legs and gritted my teeth. "You can do it," I whispered and limped toward the distant porch light.

Finally, my hand closed around the doorknob and turned. I pulled the door open. Debbie, in an apron, didn't look up from where she rapidly loaded the dishwasher. Vini stood at the sink with his back to me.

I stumbled into the room feeling as if I'd stumbled into a *Twilight Zone* episode. Why hadn't someone come looking for me? Alice bustled into the kitchen holding a broom with one hand and a dustpan in the other.

As much out of a need to assure myself that I wasn't invisible to my coworkers as anything else, I opened my mouth to speak. Before I could, the kitchen door swung again, and Carly rushed in, her gaze immediately falling on me. "There you are. Were you cleaning the bathrooms?" She narrowed her eyes. "Why is there dirt on your face? What's wrong? Are you okay?" Her voice rose with each question, and silence filled the room as everyone stopped what they were doing and turned to look at us.

"Dead man."

"What?" Carly peered at me, confusion knitting her brows together.

I tried again. "A man was shot out behind the Dumpster. He's dead."

I heard gasps from every corner. "Are you sure he is dead?" Vini asked weakly.

"Yes," I gasped out. "I think the killer is still out there. Somebody knocked me out." My knees gave way, and they all rushed toward me.

Carly grabbed me around the waist, and Debbie shoved a chair under me. "Call 911," she barked to Vini, whose normally swarthy complexion looked pale and sallow.

"I'll do it." Alice yanked up the cordless phone. "Harvey," she yelled as she punched in the numbers.

"It hasn't been ten minutes since the last police officer left. Too bad they didn't stay a little longer." Debbie grabbed a bag of frozen peas from the huge side-by-side freezer, wrapped a towel around it, and carefully placed it against the back of my head. "Did you see anyone else parked out there? On the edge of the parking lot? Or in the alley?"

Before I could answer, Harvey came running in. "What's wrong?"

Alice shushed him as the 911 operator apparently answered.

He glanced over at me and did a double take. "What happened?" he whispered as Alice rattled off who she was and where she was.

"There's a dead man in the alley," Alice said bluntly into the receiver.

Harvey spun around toward her. "A what?"

"A dead man," she mouthed and waved him away. "He's been shot. And Jenna Stafford found the body. Yes. Jenna Stafford. She's been hurt. Someone knocked her out." She paused to listen. "No, she's conscious now. She seems like she's okay." She listened again then nodded. "Okay." She put her hand over the mouthpiece and glanced at us. "Lock the doors."

Harvey ran out to the front, and Carly stepped over to the back door I'd just come in and turned the dead bolt.

I hugged myself, rubbing the goose bumps on my arms.

Harvey came back in and pulled Alice to him. "Door's locked out there," he said softly.

She nodded, still holding the phone to her ear, occasionally murmuring to the emergency operator to let her know we were all still okay.

Vini, his arms crossed, stood in front of the sink, facing me. The fear in his eyes was like the measles, contagious and uncomfortable. I glanced away to where Debbie stood beside me, holding gentle pressure on the frozen peas at the back of my head and texting on her cell phone with her other hand.

Carly patted my shoulder, and I covered her hand with mine. No one spoke.

She squeezed my hand then stepped over to the stove, lifted the lid off the bean soup, and gave it an absent stir.

"You know if you stir it much after it's been cooking awhile, it'll be bean mush instead of soup," Alice said.

Carly dropped the lid.

"No, ma'am," Alice said into the phone. "I wasn't talking to you."

A siren in the distance cut off whatever Carly might have been going to say. The wailing quickly grew louder.

Red lights flashed through the kitchen window that faced the alley. I had a sinking feeling the ambulance crew was too late for the guy in the car. Almost immediately, blue lights mixed with the red. And still more blue lights.

Alice nudged Harvey. "She says to go let the police in the front door."

Harvey hurried out, and within seconds he was back with two local officers, Seth and Ricky, behind him.

Alice hung up the phone.

"Jenna, you okay?" Seth asked, concern evident in his voice.

I nodded. Debbie took the peas from my head and went to put them back in the freezer.

"You sure?" Seth said.

"I've got a little bump, but other than that, I think I'll live." *Unlike the guy in the alley.* I shivered.

Seth and I had a history. When I first moved back to town and was trying my hand at dating, he'd asked me out—then promptly killed the romance when he assumed that he'd get to work out at the gym for free if we were dating. In light of the dead body out back, that little breach of etiquette didn't stop me from being happy to see him. Or his partner, Ricky, either, in spite of the frown he wore and the notebook he pulled from his back pocket.

"What happened out there?" Ricky asked, the hand holding the pen a little unsteady and a slight quiver in his voice. I had the distinct feeling this was his first murder.

Seth cut him a look and brought his gaze back to me. "Do we need the EMTs in here?"

I shook my head, and at the movement, my hand flew up to cup the lump on the back of my skull. "Ow."

"Get someone in here to look at her," Seth growled over his shoulder to Ricky.

The tall cop put his notebook away then disappeared into the diner.

Seth pulled up a chair next to me and sat down. "You look pretty pale. Is it bleeding?"

"I don't think so." I ducked my head.

He carefully parted my hair and grunted. "No blood, but that's a prize-winning goose egg."

"Thanks," I said dryly. "It's nice to be a winner."

"You're always a winner to me."

Something in his voice brought my gaze around to meet his.

He smiled. "You still dating Alex?"

"Last time I checked she was engaged to him," a deep voice said behind me.

I turned toward the familiar voice. Alex Campbell filled the doorway, his face taut with worry. "You okay?"

I nodded, so glad to see him I couldn't speak.

He covered the distance between us in two strides and bent down to hug me.

Seth jumped to his feet and took a couple steps backward. He even held out his hand as if offering Alex his vacated chair. Alex had been the high school quarterback when Seth was a lowly tenth-grade bench warmer. Old habits die hard.

"Thanks," Alex mumbled, his attention still fixed on me. He released me as he sat down but held on to my hand.

A female EMT came bustling in, her black bag in her hand. She checked my vision and examined the lump on my head. When she finished, she looked at Alex and smiled. "Everything looks okay to me. But you probably want to get her over to the ER to get this checked out. A hit hard enough to knock someone out usually causes a concussion."

Hello? I started to wave my hand to remind her who was the patient here. But I was too tired. I was used to this phenomenon when I was out with the town's most eligible bachelor. Even my new engagement ring hadn't seemed to slow the attention down much. I glanced over at Debbie. Tonight the waitress was more interested in her cell phone, but usually she spoke to Alex instead of me. In Alex's defense, though, he always kept his own gaze fixed on me—which was one of the many things I loved about him.

As soon as the EMT left, Alex turned me to face him. "What happened, honey?"

"Might as well just tell it once, 'honey,' " someone said gruffly.

I looked up to see our chief of police standing in the suddenly popular doorway. "Hi, John." We'd been friends since the sandbox, but my penchant for sniffing out the truth drove him up the wall sometimes.

"You know, Jenna, it'd be funny if it weren't so horrible." He walked in with Ricky right behind him.

Fresh tears sprang to my eyes. "I know." It hadn't been long since I found the queen of country music dead in her Branson dressing room, and less than a year before that, I'd gotten embroiled in the murder of our local newspaper editor. So I knew what he meant.

"You all right?"

"I guess. Physically, anyway."

"What is it with you and dead bodies?"

I shrugged, and an involuntary shiver ran up my spine. Alex put his arm around me and pulled me against him.

"I—"

John held up his hand. "Forget I asked. Let's just concentrate on this one. Tell me about finding the body."

"I was taking out the trash," I stammered. "It was almost closing time." I glanced at Carly.

She nodded. "It was right at eight o'clock. We only had a few stragglers when you went out." Her face flushed, and she spoke to John. "We were busy cleaning, so we didn't notice when she didn't come back right away." She flashed me an apologetic look.

He waved away her implied apology and turned his shrewd gaze back to me. "So what happened when you got out there?"

I told him as coherently as I could. Ricky scribbled in his little notebook while I talked.

"You felt for a pulse?" John said, looking at my apron.

I glanced down and froze at the sight of the rusty fingerprints. Apparently I'd instinctively wiped the blood off before I was clobbered. I clutched Alex's hand tightly and nodded. "Then something hit me in the head from behind."

"Did you lose consciousness immediately?"

"I must have. I don't remember anything after that until I woke up staring at a tire."

"What time did you come back in here?"

I glanced at Debbie, who shook her head. Then Vini, Harvey, Alice, and Carly. They all looked stricken. "It couldn't have been more than fifteen minutes after eight," Carly said.

Vini pointed at Alice. "She called emergency. They will know what time, yes?"

"Yes," John agreed. "So right after you came in, they called 911?"

"Well, once someone noticed me," I said, irritated at the whine in my voice. Still, it had been disconcerting not to be missed. "Debbie got me some frozen peas."

I looked over at Debbie, who was leaning against the wall typing on her cell phone. She didn't even look up at me.

John's brows drew together. "Frozen peas?"

"For my head. But within two minutes, I'd say, Alice called."

John looked at Ricky. "Get me the time of that 911 call."

Ricky nodded and disappeared.

John turned back to us. "Had anyone else been out back before that?"

Everyone shook their heads, then Alice glanced up at Harvey. "Wait. Harv, you took the trash out about twenty minutes before Jenna did, remember?"

John fixed his gaze on Harvey, who nodded.

"Did you see a car behind the Dumpster?"

"I didn't look behind the Dumpster. I knew if I didn't hurry back in"—he glanced at Vini—"the salad bar would be in shambles. I just tossed the trash."

I spoke up. "I wouldn't have noticed the car if one of my bags hadn't gone over and landed on its roof."

Alice took Harvey's arm and put it around her. "Just think, honey. There may have been a murderer right next to you." She frowned. "It's scary to think he was out there with you, Jenna."

"Yeah, scary." I gently touched the goose egg on the back of my head and looked down at my skinned knees. "And painful."

"Do you know the guy's name?" Debbie asked softly, slipping her phone into her apron pocket. From the drawn look on her face, the text conversation hadn't gone well.

John nodded. "J. D. Finley."

Debbie gasped. A couple of other people made noises, but I couldn't be sure who. All of us looked at Debbie. Her face matched her white apron, and tears threatened to ruin her freshly applied makeup.

"I take it you know him?" John said.

She nodded and bit her lower lip. "He's a friend of Lisa's. They've been dating for a while, I guess." She tried to wipe the tears away with one finger, but they tumbled down her cheeks anyway. "I've been out with them a few times."

John gave her a stern look that I knew meant there would be more questions for her later.

She shrugged. "Poor Lisa. This will break her heart." The last word became a quiet sob. Carly handed her a paper towel.

Bob's daughter was lucky to have a friend like Debbie. As far as I knew, few people but her parents would have cared if it were Lisa herself who was out in that car in the alley.

John turned to the rest of us. "What do the rest of you know about him?"

Harvey nodded toward Alice as he answered for both of them. "We knew him."

"Was he in here tonight?" John asked.

"I didn't see him," Debbie said without looking up.

"Me, either," Harvey said. "And I was working the cash register by the front door, so if he'd been in here, I'd have known it."

"Anyone know what he was doing out in the alley?" John asked us all.

No one answered. Finally, Alice spoke up. "Maybe he was supposed to meet Lisa? I mean, if they were dating, maybe they arranged a date here."

I shook my head. "Why would he have parked behind the trash bin to meet Lisa here for a date? That makes no sense."

John apparently agreed with me. He frowned. "Anyone see Lisa here tonight?"

We all shook our heads. Considering I quit my job and gave up my dream of owning the Lake View Athletic Club because of her, I was pretty sure I'd have noticed if my nemesis had been here.

Seth motioned to John from the doorway.

"Be right there."

Seth nodded and disappeared into the dining room. John turned back to us. "If I think of anything else I need to ask, I'll call you."

"Wait. John." I touched his sleeve. "Who is J. D. Finley? Is he from around here?"

"Jenna, I'm sure we'll find out all there is to know about him before this is over, but this is official police business. You need to let us do our job." The "and stay out of it" was implied as he turned toward the door.

"I think finding a dead body puts me right in the middle of it."

He sighed. "Just this once, can't you mind your own business?"

Alex shifted in his chair to look at me. "I'll be right back, hon. I'm gonna ask John a couple of questions. Will you be okay?" When I nodded, he rose, and together he and the chief strode out of the kitchen.

I stood and walked to the staff bathroom to check out my head. No matter how I contorted, I couldn't see the bump, but I could feel it. I blinked my eyes. No double vision. I didn't feel particularly sleepy. And other than feeling a little disoriented from finding a dead body, I wasn't dizzy. I washed my hands and opened the door.

"Surely you know I wouldn't blame you," Alice said as I stepped back into the kitchen.

She and Harvey looked at me and froze.

As Nervous As A Long-Tailed Cat In
A Room Full of Rocking Chairs

Harvey's face lost most of its color, but he laughed. "It wouldn't be the first time you've accused me of turning the burner up under your soup," he said.

Alice's answering chuckle sounded forced. "Of course, you're right. But I'm not accusing you this time. Just saying that I wouldn't blame you if you had turned the burner up in all this excitement."

"I didn't," he said firmly.

"That's fine," she said.

I smiled weakly and walked into the dining room where everyone else had gathered. Whatever that had been about, it wasn't soup.

Carly looked at me as I walked in. "You want me to go to the ER with you?"

"No, I'm fine. I'm going to stay and help you clean up."

"You most certainly are not," Carly said. Alex and John moved closer as if they were her strongmen ready to enforce her decree.

"I will help clean," Vini offered.

Carly smiled at the twentysomething Albanian. "Thanks. And Elliott's supposed to stop by and help, too." She turned back to me. "Go get your head checked out. We've got this covered."

"I'll just go home and rest then. The EMT checked me out, and I don't have any signs of a concussion."

I'd expected an argument from Alex, but before he could say anything, John put his hand on my arm. "I think you should go on down to the ER."

I smiled. "You, of all people, should know how hard my head is."

He frowned. "I can't believe you're joking. You could have been killed."

"Aw, it's nice to know you care."

Alex snorted. John and I had never really outgrown our childhood "one up" type of friendship. Bless her heart, my friend Denise, who married the big lout, always ended up having to mediate.

John shot me a wry grin. "Truth is, Denise would kill *me* if anything happened to you on my watch. If you have any symptoms, you go get it checked out." He sauntered over to where Ricky and Seth were sitting at a booth looking at Ricky's notebook.

As we walked out of the diner, Alex kept his arm around my waist. "You know, in spite of his gruff talk, he thinks of you as a little sister."

"Yeah, an annoying little sister that he wishes he could box up and ship to Siberia."

Alex laughed. "I'm glad to see you getting back to normal. You were pretty pale when I got here."

"Getting conked on the head tends to do that to a person."

His smile disappeared. "You speak from entirely too much experience on that subject."

❖

"Found another body, did you?" The old man from the feed store on Main Street gave me a snaggletoothed grin.

"Yep." I gritted my own full set of teeth into some semblance of a smile and tapped my order pad with my pencil. "What can I get for you today?"

"I'll have the meatloaf special. Gettin' to be a habit of yours, idn't it? Gettin' involved with murder? I'm surprised you're not out back helping the police look for the gun."

His cronies laughed.

"Hush up, Grimmett," Marge Templeton scolded from the booth across the way. "Jenna can't help being in the wrong place at the wrong time."

"Grimmett" ducked his head, his weathered face mottled with embarrassment. Apparently he hadn't realized that Marge was nearby. Her late husband, Hank, had been my first "wrong place at the wrong time." Even though I hadn't actually found the newspaper editor's body, I'd eventually solved his murder. Sort of. And almost gotten myself and Carly killed in the process.

I gave Marge a grateful glance. We shared a bond of having been in a sticky situation together. I knew I could count on her to watch my back. She owned the paper now, and although it wasn't common knowledge, she was also my boss. She and her niece, the new editor, were the only two people besides Carly and me who knew that I moonlighted as advice columnist Dear Pru.

The other old-timers told me what they wanted to eat without incident. As I wove my way through the busy dining area with their orders, I admitted to myself that Grimmett was right about one thing: I'd much rather be out back with the police looking for the gun that killed J.D. But I had sense enough to know John would come unglued if I got anywhere near them.

"Ma'am! Ma'am!" A big-haired lady on the opposite side of the room waved her arm. "This isn't what I ordered."

I glanced around the busy dining area. Where was Debbie?

I made a quick detour to the woman's table, and she gestured toward her plate. "I know you aren't our waitress, but ours seems to have disappeared. I ordered a salad and chopped steak. This is meatloaf."

I took the offending plate. "I'm sorry, ma'am. I'll be right back with your salad."

"Thanks. I heard y'all talking about that guy that was killed here last night. Wasn't he from here originally?"

I shook my head. "Not that I know of."

She nodded to the mousy-looking woman across the table from her. "Didn't your grandma say he grew up here?"

"Yes," the woman said.

"I hadn't heard that." And as much as I wanted to hear more, I knew I needed to find Debbie before Carly lost customers because her wait staff was too slow. "I'll just go get your order."

I leaned over the counter into the kitchen to see if Debbie was in there. All I could see was orders piling up. I glanced over to the salad bar where Vini was dumping fresh lettuce into the huge stainless steel bowl. "Vini, I think Debbie must be on break. Can you help me serve for a few minutes?"

For the next half hour, we worked frantically, sorting out orders and making corrections and apologies.

When the lunch crowd thinned slightly, I thanked Vini. "Can you handle things out here for a few minutes while I find Debbie?"

He nodded.

I looked in the kitchen and even opened the mop closet. But no Debbie. Finally, I went to the ladies' room and peeked in. Empty. I started to let the door shut, but a muffled sobbing drew me back. "Debbie?"

Just a soft hiccup in answer.

"Debbie? Is that you?" I glanced under the stall and saw her scuffed white tennis shoes, still slightly speckled with the butternut paint from the remodel. "I know it's you. You might as well talk to me."

She blew her nose loudly, and in a few seconds the stall door creaked open and she stepped out.

"What's wrong?" I asked.

"This whole murder thing. I just feel bad about J.D. It's so sad." She bent over the sink and splashed cold water on her red, puffy face.

I met her gaze in the mirror. "It is. Do you have any idea who might have killed him?"

"No, of course not. I barely knew him." Her voice quavered, and she fished her brush out of her purse and redid her messy bun. "But poor Lisa."

"Yeah." I thought again how lucky Lisa was to have Debbie for a friend. Most people in Lake View probably wouldn't have too much sympathy for the spoiled princess. "Do you know why he was here?"

She shrugged. "How would I know? Maybe he was coming to the grand opening." Her voice broke. "But he didn't make it." She began sobbing again.

I patted her shoulder. "Debbie, why don't you go ahead and go home? Vini and I can handle the rest of the lunch crowd." It would be easier if we knew she was gone than if she kept disappearing to cry. I hoped Carly wouldn't care that I was sending her most seasoned waitress home during the busiest part of the day. "If you feel like it, you can come back in later."

"I don't want to go home."

"Then maybe you should visit Lisa. I'm sure she's having a hard time with this."

She nodded. "I heard they made her go down to the station this morning and have fingerprints," she whispered.

Her unique way of phrasing that procedure made me fight a smile. "Really? They think she killed him?"

Her eyes widened. "Do you think? They said it's just a formality because she rode in his car a lot. So they can figure out what fingerprints might be there that aren't supposed to be."

I quickly backtracked. The last thing I wanted to do was add to the overworked rumor mill. "No, no, I'm sure she's not a suspect. Eliminating fingerprints that belong there sounds right. And anyway, why would she kill her new boyfriend?"

Debbie's eyes filled with tears again. "Relationships can be hard."

"Yeah, I know. But even though 'breaking up is hard to do,' don't you think it would be harder to kill him?"

She pulled a tissue from the holder on the counter and loudly blew her nose again instead of answering. Should I have mentioned that was a rhetorical question?

I patted her on the shoulder. My mother and Carly were so much better than I was at sympathy and advice. Why did I always end up in these situations? "I'll tell Carly that you're taking the rest of the day off."

"Thanks." She gave a wan smile and left.

I hurried back to the dining room. From the corner of my eye, I saw Harvey directing a couple toward one of my tables. I grabbed two menus and headed over to take their orders. As I neared the table, I recognized Seth's partner, Ricky, and Tiffany Stanton, the mayor's daughter. Tiffany had moved back to Lake View only a few months ago to take a job as editor of her aunt's newspaper, and Ricky hadn't wasted any time in getting to know her. When the tall cop wasn't on duty, you could always count on seeing them together.

Since her parents, Amelia and Byron, sent her to boarding school instead of Lake View High, I hadn't known Tiffany well when we were growing up.

But I'd always thought of her as the Anti-Amelia. She had pretty features, but it almost seemed as if she did everything she could to hide them. Her naturally curly hair frizzed around her bare face, and she usually wore shapeless clothes or men's jeans that did nothing to flatter her figure.

Today, even though she hadn't changed a thing, she looked as radiant as a bride. "What'll you have to drink?" My standard opening line.

"What are you having, Ricky?" She leaned toward him. "Sweet tea with lemon?"

He grinned. "You know me too well."

She beamed at me. "I'll have the same." She waved her hand in the air, and I could tell she was showing off the huge rock on her engagement finger.

When I brought the drinks back, they thanked me.

I pulled out my order pad. "Congratulations on your engagement. Your ring is beautiful. Is the wedding soon?"

"Yes." Tiffany flashed Ricky a coy look. "We don't want a long engagement, do we, honey?"

He ducked his head. "The sooner the better."

She scooted closer and kissed him on the cheek. "We're hoping to get married next month. Although. . ." She pursed her lips as if she had tasted the lemon from her sweet tea. "*Mother* says she doesn't see how we can possibly be ready in a month."

I could understand that. My own wedding was scheduled for Christmas, and even though it was going to be small, I had a checklist that was quickly looming out of control.

"Speaking of your mother," Ricky murmured and stood as Amelia and Byron Stanton walked toward us. I quickly grabbed two more menus while he pulled out Amelia's chair for her to sit down.

I took the mayor and first lady's drink order and hurried away. A few minutes later, as I carefully set the drinks on the table, I glanced at Tiffany. The change was amazing. Her arms were crossed defensively in front of her, and the radiance was gone. "I think you just don't want me to get married." She glared sullenly at her mother. "You've never really wanted me to be happy."

Amelia glanced up at me and gave a nervous laugh. "Honey, of course I want you to be happy. I just think you're rushing this." She looked to Byron as if for support. "We want you to have a wedding to remember, and that takes some time to plan. You don't want off-the-rack dresses for the bridesmaids, do you? And what about your gown?" I'd often thought Amelia was like a Barbie doll with no real feelings or emotions, but her distress was very real.

I took my pad and pen out of my apron. "Have y'all decided what you want to eat?" I asked in my most cheerful voice, then motioned Vanna-like toward the white dry-erase board on the wall. "These are today's specials."

Amelia ignored my motion and glanced down at the menu in her hand. "I'll have the chef salad with blue cheese dressing on the side." She looked at me over her menu. "Carly does make her own salad dressing, doesn't she?"

"Yes, of course. I'm partial to her honey mustard, but the blue cheese is great, too."

Tiffany didn't look at the white board either. Carly was going to fire me if I didn't do a better job of promoting the already-made food.

"I'll have a cheeseburger and fries off the menu." Tiffany smiled at Ricky. "That's what you want, too, isn't it, baby?"

"Sure is." He patted her on the hand. "You always know just what I like."

I saw Amelia's jaw muscle jump as she gritted her teeth. Was her son-in-law-to-be needling her on purpose?

"And you, Mayor Stanton?"

"I'll have the chicken-fried steak and gravy, mashed potatoes, and fried okra."

Thank you, Mr. Mayor. Finally, someone who was ordering one of the specials. Maybe my job was safe for another day.

Later, when I set the serving tray beside their table and began unloading it, they were still discussing the upcoming nuptials.

"We do have an image to uphold, dear." Amelia was again speaking through gritted teeth. She was going to need dental work if she kept this up. "We can't just throw something together, especially if your dad is going to run for the senate." She lowered her voice on the last three words.

Debbie had warned me that as a waitress I would hear lots of personal business and gossip. "We're like the furniture," she'd said. And it looked like she was right.

I set their plates in front of them and headed back to pick up an order for another table. I got busy with my other tables but stopped back by to see if they needed refills.

Ricky pushed to his feet just as I approached. "I'm going to go out and see if I can help the guys," he said as he threw a couple of ones on the table and handed a twenty to Tiffany. "Do you mind handling our bill, honey?"

She shook her head and shoved the money back to him. "Today's my treat."

He glanced at her parents then back at her and frowned. "I'd rather pay for it, okay?" he said quietly.

She glared at her mother then nodded. "Sure, sweetie." She took the twenty-dollar bill. When he was gone, she turned to her mother. "I hope you're happy. You ran him off."

Amelia's elaborately made-up eyes widened. "Why, Tiffany, I did no such thing."

"You know what? I need to go. I'll talk to y'all later." Tiffany dropped a kiss on Byron's forehead and, with barely a glance at her mother, stomped up to the cash register.

Byron stood and retrieved his and Amelia's bill. "I'm going to go on and pay, too." He followed his daughter.

"Well, at least she didn't eat all of that fat-filled burger," Amelia murmured as I refilled her glass.

Indignant on Carly's behalf, I protested. "That's ground chuck—"

Amelia waved her hand. "Never mind, dear. I need a favor."

"A 'to go' box?"

She frowned, but thanks to one-too-many Botox treatments, only her eyes showed it. "No, silly." She glanced at her husband and daughter and lowered her voice. "You're so good at snooping. I need you to find out what you can about Ricky before he and Tiffany get married." She was talking so fast and quietly, I could barely understand her. "We had her last boyfriend investigated. It turned out badly, and she was brokenhearted for a while." She sipped her tea and lifted her hand in a lazy wave to a nearby diner. "We don't want that to happen again," she said to me from the corner of her mouth.

"You know, Amelia, I'm not a PI. Can't you just have a professional check him out, run a background check, that kind of thing?"

She put her hand to her heart as if I'd suggested having him murdered. "No. Tiffany made us promise not to do that ever again."

Maybe she wasn't as managing a mother as I thought.

Her next words dispelled that delusion. "I'd do it anyway, but I'm afraid she would find out." She took a drink. "But you can do it. You ask questions all the time, anyway, so no one would think it was odd."

Thanks a lot.

"Besides, you know John and Seth both. They'll tell you anything." Ha, little did she know. John wouldn't tell me the time of day unless he had to. Well, he wasn't that bad, but he certainly didn't share information with me.

"I guess I can ask them about him. If you really want me to. But he seems like a regular guy to me. Why are you so worried?"

"Tiffany doesn't attract men like some girls do." She glanced at me. "Well, look at her. No wonder she doesn't. I could have helped her, but from the time she was small, if I even made a suggestion about her looks or clothes, she took it as an insult."

Amelia looked toward the door where Byron motioned toward her that he was ready. "Anyway, she hasn't had good luck with men. Ricky seems fine, but we just want to make sure. Will you do it?"

"I don't know. . ."

She tapped her nails impatiently on the table. "I seem to remember I didn't hesitate when you asked me to look into something for you."

I shrugged. What could I say? She was right. In the last murder I'd been investigating, I'd asked her to check something out and she had. "I'll figure out a way to ask John and Seth what they think about him without seeming suspicious. And I'll let you know."

She pulled out a ten-dollar bill and left it on the table. "Thanks."

I scooped the ten into my apron pocket and watched the first lady of Lake View glide across the room.

Poor Ricky. He had no idea what he was getting into.

4

A Watched Pot Never Boils.

Within five minutes, Harvey was ringing up the last few stragglers from the lunch crowd. I was learning the ebb and flow of customers. They all came at once. They all left at once.

I walked over to where Alice carefully filled the saltshakers.

She smiled at me. "I bet you're worn out. Not bein' used to this and all."

I didn't know it showed. Every part of me was longing for a nice, relaxing swim in the club pool. I even would've settled for taking inventory or cleaning the equipment in the exercise room. I sank into a chair and groaned. "My feet may never be the same. I don't see how you've done this for so long. No wonder you wanted to sell this place."

A cloud crossed her face. "It's never easy making a change, though. We've lived in Lake View our whole lives. And Harvey's parents owned the diner before us."

I needed a new subject fast. "I heard today that J. D. Finley was from here when he was young. Is that true?"

"Um-hum," she grunted without looking up.

I waited for her to elaborate, but she concentrated on sifting the tiny white granules into the last shaker.

She finished and picked up the big plastic pitcher full of salt. "With all those police officers out back, I'd better go see about the pies I have in the oven."

I stared at her back. If I wanted to snoop, I was going to have to find someone more loquacious than Alice.

Or—I glanced out at the parking lot where police cars were parked everywhere—I could see for myself what was going on.

I stood and stretched then ambled into the kitchen and poured a cup of coffee. "I'm on break," I called to Carly as I let myself quietly out the back door, clutching my mug casually. No law against an overworked waitress taking a break out back, was there?

Across the small alley the infamous Dumpster loomed. Behind it and to the sides were scraggly woods—land that had probably been cleared less than a decade ago but had been ignored since. Today that little thicket was literally crawling with cops.

I leaned against the wooden post and watched the search.

"Spread out more," John barked, and the officers quickly obeyed.

Thankfully no even looked my way, or our esteemed chief of police certainly would have ordered me back inside.

Just as I drained the last drop of my coffee, an excited yell went up from an area on the very outskirts of the woods.

I stood on my tiptoes and could make out two familiar figures. "Over here!" Seth and Ricky waved their arms. "Found it!"

Lake View's police force descended on them en masse, no doubt trampling significant clues in the process.

I heard John growling at them, so apparently he thought the same thing. Within seconds, they headed back in my direction, John carrying a plastic bag with something small in it. As he drew closer, I squinted at the contents. Undoubtedly a gun, but it looked more like a tiny water pistol. Hard to believe something so small could do so much damage.

Before I could slip back inside, John spotted me. His face grew red, and he twisted his mouth as if trying to think of what to say, but he just sputtered.

I held my hand up in an international gesture of peace. "I'm going, I'm going."

I quickly let myself back into the diner before my childhood friend had a coronary. Sometimes he really overreacted to my tendency to want to know what was going on.

❖

"Wow, Carly. You're a genius." I wiggled my toes in the warm water. "I'm so glad you bought two."

"I can't take credit. I got them because of the advice Alice gave me." Carly sank down in her own chair and immersed her feet in the plastic foot spa in front of her. She groaned and closed her eyes. " 'Take good care of your feet,' she said. 'And they'll take good care of you.' "

"Speaking of Alice. . ." I couldn't believe I'd been so drained that I'd forgotten this. "Yesterday after John let us all go, I overheard Alice say something odd to Harvey."

"She says odd things to him all the time," Carly said without opening her eyes.

"Yeah, but she said, 'I wouldn't blame you.' Or something like that."

She sat up. "For what?"

I shrugged. "She *said* for turning the burner up under the soup."

"Oh. Well, the soup was a little scorched today, I thought. Maybe that's all it was."

"Maybe."

For a few minutes we sat without speaking in the darkened living room of the small cabin on our folks' property that Carly and the kids had moved into a few months ago. With the girls in bed, Zac in his room on the phone, and our heated foot spas bubbling, we'd created a relaxation haven.

"I guess you don't think it was a stranger this time, either, do you?" Carly said tiredly.

I didn't even have to wonder for a second what she meant. "I wish I did, but not really." Each time we'd gotten embroiled in a murder, we'd tried to cling to the false hope that the killer was a stranger. Both of the other two times we'd been sadly disappointed.

"Yeah, me either. One can only hold on to that kind of naïveté for so long."

I squinted toward her. "Aren't you getting cynical?"

She shrugged. "Having a dead man show up at your grand opening tends to do that to you."

"Excuse me for ruining your grand opening by finding a body," I said. "Why do you think he was there?"

Carly kept her head resting against the padded back of her chair. "Well, since I already sound like a narcissist, maybe someone hired him to sabotage my big day."

I snorted. "No doubt. Wonder what the pay is for that?" I asked. "Dying in order to sabotage?"

She snorted back at me without opening her eyes. "Okay then, smarty. I guess it would be too flippant to say that he might have put out a hit on himself to get him out of his relationship with Lisa."

I reached over and shoved her gently. "I think we've officially come down with the eleven o'clock sillies."

"Mama always says the only cure for that is going to bed before eleven," Carly said in a pseudoserious tone.

"Well, Mama should have come over and helped us clean up tonight at the diner," I spouted. "Then we wouldn't be so tired we can't sleep."

"Good point," she murmured.

"I know the difference," I said suddenly.

"Difference in what?" Carly asked, something in my voice alerting her that my silliness had vanished. She sat up and looked over at me.

"This body. This time we don't know the victim. So we have no idea who might have done it."

"Very true," Carly said thoughtfully. "And since he was in fact a *stranger* to us. . ."

"A stranger might very well have killed him," I finished triumphantly, feeling a little rejuvenated at the thought. "And we don't even have to know why."

◈

"Sunday dinner at your mom's," Alex said with a sigh as he helped me clear the table. "One of the many things I missed all those years we were apart."

I waved a fork at him. "You only love me for my mama's cooking?" I teased. "We may have a problem."

He nudged me and motioned to Carly and Elliott, who still sat whispering with their heads together at the other end of the long table. "You think *we* have a problem? At least *we* know the meal is over."

Elliott looked up and grinned. "Hey now, we're not deaf."

"Well, stop the mushiness then, Romeo. You're making me look bad." Alex returned his grin.

Carly laughed. "This from the man who had my sister swept away in a limo to meet him for a private dinner at the marina."

"And then bought her a rock the size of Manhattan a few weeks later," Elliott chimed in.

"And even more romantically, helps me with the dishes," I said, winking at Alex.

"I think that was a hint for us to get busy." Elliott stood and pulled Carly to her feet then put his arm around her and pulled her close. He whispered something in her ear.

The twins came running in, followed by Zac.

"Mom, can we go now?" Hayley's query was more of a command.

"Yeah," Rachel chimed in. "You said as soon as lunch was over we could go get ready for the basketball game."

"Pipe down, kiddos." Zac spoiled his big-brother attitude by adding, "But everyone's goin' down to the courts soon, right, Mom? I want to practice my jump shot before the game starts." He turned to Elliott. "Can't you make her hurry?"

"Hurry a woman? Son, you've got lots to learn"—Elliott winked at Zac—"but I'll do what I can."

"Out!" I made shooing motions at the kids. Then I stopped. "On second thought, why don't you take these dirty dishes in the kitchen and tell your grandma that y'all will load the dishwasher? When you finish, we'll show you who the real athletes are."

"I'll show them how to hold down a lawn chair," Carly muttered.

The kids obediently took all the dishes and exited the dining room, but they were so busy laughing about our supposed athletic ability that Hayley bumped into the door facing. Served her right.

Forty-five minutes later, we were waiting for a few stragglers on the concrete basketball court just past the playground. One of the benefits of being raised at a resort—plenty of room for friendly games. And plenty of extra players. Just as Dad finished going over the rules, the honeymooners in cabin five came running up. "Are we too late?"

Dad shook his head. "The cops are just now getting here." He motioned to where the black-and-white patrol car had pulled into a parking place.

The man stopped in his tracks and put a protective arm around his new wife. "Excuse me?"

Dad laughed and pointed at John, Ricky, and Seth, who were walking across the gravel parking lot toward us. "Don't worry, son. The chief of police has a mean three-pointer, but he isn't worth a dime on defense. And that tall cop gets all the rebounds, but when he shoots, you don't need to worry. He can't hit the broad side of the barn. And Seth? Well, he's just Seth. You'll see."

Everyone laughed, even the newcomers.

A new hybrid vehicle pulled in and bypassed the parking lot, driving across the gravel directly to the basketball court. Before I could guess who the driver might be, Tiffany Stanton emerged. She waved and smiled then walked around the car and opened the passenger door. John's wife, Denise, climbed out, her usually slender frame struggling to hold the extra twenty-five pounds she had gained in the first eight months of her pregnancy. They already had two children, but this was Denise's first pregnancy since turning thirty. John had apparently read that with age came danger. He'd been treating Denise as if she were made of spun gold for the last several months.

The cops had almost reached us when John heard us greet Tiffany and Denise behind him. He spun around to look. "What is she doing here? I told her she needed to rest."

He hurried over to Denise and cupped her elbow with his hand. I would be annoyed by the constant attention, but Denise seemed to be coping very well. Then again, looks could be deceiving. Even though she smiled as she struggled to gain her balance, there was a hint of gritted teeth in the smile. She waved and began walking toward us with John scampering around her like an overgrown puppy.

"I'm okay, John. I needed to get out of the house, and your mom volunteered to babysit." Denise's words floated to us, her exasperation clear in her tone. "I can walk by myself. Why don't you get my chair out of the car?"

Tiffany had opened the trunk, and she stepped back to let John take the red lawn chair. Ricky waved her over to be on his team, and she jogged toward him.

I'd never have thought of her as athletic, but then again she was the opposite of her mother, and I sure couldn't imagine Amelia enjoying a pick-up basketball game or hanging out at the Stafford Cabins play area on a Sunday afternoon, for that matter.

We all stood there gawking at the John and Denise show as they reached us and he got her settled into her chair. By the time he had her situated to suit him, she almost needed binoculars to keep up with the action. He handed her his phone and his portable radio and turned toward us.

As soon as he finished, Dad said, "Denise, you can be on my team. We need a good guard." He winked at me.

Sure enough, John rose to the bait. "She can't play!" As we burst out laughing, he grinned weakly. "Oh, I guess you knew that."

"Go on, honey, you play and uphold the family honor," Denise said, edging her chair closer to where Carly, Mama, and the twins were sitting. "I'll just watch safely from the sidelines and cheer you on."

After the kayaker from cabin 7 joined us, we had twelve players, just enough for three teams of four. We flipped a coin to see who would play the first round. Seth, Ricky, Tiffany, and John drew the first game against Alex, Elliot, Zac, and me. That left Dad, the honeymooners, and the kayaker for the third team.

During a water break, Tiffany and I joined Carly, Mama, and Denise on the sidelines.

"Nice shooting there, Tex," I drawled to Tiffany.

She smiled. "Two years of dating a basketball coach. He was obsessed with the game, and if I wanted to see him, it had to be on the court."

When we went back onto the court, the game moved fast and furiously. We were up by six points when Seth went up for a shot. He missed, but as he came down, he yelled, "Foul!" at Alex.

Alex frowned. "I don't think so."

Ricky walked up to stand beside Seth. "Think so or not, you did," he said to Alex.

"We'll replay." Alex offered a compromise.

Seth shrugged. "Fine by me."

Before we could resume play, though, Denise hollered for John. He gasped and sprinted toward her, no doubt expecting to have to deliver the baby right there on the sidelines. But she waggled his cell phone at him.

We all sat down on the concrete for a short break while he took the call. Zac, Elliott, Alex, and I sat together.

"You didn't foul him," Zac murmured.

Alex shrugged. "It's just a game."

Elliott smiled. "Easy to say when we're ahead."

Zac's face brightened. "We are smoking them, aren't we?"

Elliott nodded. "Nice three-pointer, buddy."

"Thanks. I've been practicing."

I had a flash of realization. Carly was incredibly blessed that Zac and Elliott had such an easy relationship. Amelia and Tiffany were proof that even a blood bond didn't guarantee that kind of camaraderie.

John clicked his phone shut and walked back over to the court. "Seth, Ricky, I need you to come with me. Something's come up. Good game, y'all." The last was aimed at us as the men headed purposefully to John's car. I dashed after them and tried to casually stroll along beside John. Kind of hard since he took one step to my two.

"John, are you going to the station?"

He kept walking.

"Did someone have a wreck? Is anyone hurt?"

Still walking.

But my gut wouldn't let me be quiet. "This has something to do with the murder case, hasn't it?"

No answer.

"John Connor, you make me so mad. All you have to do is tell me what's going on."

Finally, he whipped his head around to look at me. "You're wrong there, Jenna. I don't have to tell you anything. This is official police business. Go play ball."

After the third game, which, by the way, we won handily, the guests went back to their own cabins and the rest of us scattered. Carly and Elliott headed out to the glider under the elm tree. Alex had some work to catch up on, so Mama and I walked over to the porch swing.

"Mama, did you know the guy that was murdered was from here?" I sat down in the swing.

She sat down beside me. "Yes."

"Did you and Daddy know him?" I pushed off the swing with my toe.

"We knew who he was. He left here a long time ago."

"Tell me about him. Where did he go?"

"I don't know all that much about him, honey. And I have no idea where he went."

"I just want to know why he was killed. And who murdered him."

"Honey. . ." Mama pushed the swing with her foot. "I know you. The more you learn, the more you want to find out. And before you know it, you're right in the middle of a murder investigation."

There was definitely truth in what she was saying, but it still stung. "C'mon, it happened right there behind the diner. Plus I found the body." I shivered involuntarily. "It's not like I chose this."

"No, but you choose whether or not to get involved. You know I've always said your curiosity would be your downfall." She turned to look at me. "And so far you've managed to survive, but I pray every day that you'll be safe."

"I appreciate it." I pushed the swing gently. "That's probably what's kept me alive this long." I grinned in an effort to lighten things up a little.

She answered my grin with a frown. "Just wait until you have kids of your own. You've never worried until you've worried about your children." She stopped the swing with her foot and turned toward me. "Your daddy and I want you to promise to stay out of it this time."

"I understand." I wasn't making any promises, except one to myself to keep my mama and daddy from worrying about me.

She reached over and patted my hand. "We're just tired of visiting you in the hospital."

Across the yard, a motion caught our attention. Carly jumped up out of the glider and stomped toward the back of the house. Elliott got up and followed her. She turned and said something that we couldn't hear and waved him away. He walked slowly with his head down toward his car.

I looked back at Mama. "Do you think we should go after her?"

"No. What did I tell you about minding your own business? If she wants to tell us she will."

But I couldn't help noticing the worried expression on Mama's face.

5

Wouldn't That Kill Corn Hip High?

I don't know why it's so hard for John to share any information with me," I complained to Alex as I handed him a piece of cake later that night.

He took the plate. "Maybe you should bribe him with cake."

I plopped down on my couch beside him. "I mean it. He's infuriating."

He took a big bite of cake and made an *mmm* sound low in his throat. "Who said you can't cook?"

Very funny. He knew I'd gotten the coconut cake in the freezer section at Wal-Mart. All I'd had to do was thaw it out. My kind of cooking.

"While you're changing the subject with flattery, let's not forget my basketball-playing ability," I said.

He grinned. "Oh, c'mon, Miss-Used-to-Be-a-Coach, you can play circles around me on the court, and you know it."

"Are you fishing for compliments?" I asked, laughing. "You're as good as you were in high school. And if I remember correctly, you lettered in every sport at Lake View High."

Neuro jumped up on the couch beside him, and Alex stroked her fur. Her purring vibrated the whole room.

"She's complimenting you," I said.

"She's just hoping to get a cake crumb." He ruffled her head, which she usually hated, but she pushed against his hand instead of walking away.

I took his empty plate and put it in the sink.

"Want to go sit out on the porch with a letterman?" He waggled his eyebrows.

I laughed at his silliness and pushed open the back door. We had just settled into the lawn chairs to watch Mr. Persi, my golden retriever, bounding around the fenced-in yard when the cell phone in my pocket rang.

"I'll call them back, whoever it is." I slid it out and glanced at the caller ID. "Weird. It's Bob."

Alex raised an eyebrow. "You'd better take it. If you don't, your curiosity will drive us both crazy."

Even when I was working at the club, Bob rarely called me after work hours. And since the day I quit, he hadn't called at all.

"Hey, Bob. What's up?" Mr. Persi came over and plopped down on the porch between us.

"They came and got Lisa for more questioning," Bob said with no preamble. He sounded so rattled, I wouldn't have recognized his voice if not for the caller ID. "In the police car."

"They took Lisa in? Why?" I glanced over toward Alex, who was absently patting Mr. Persi.

"The gun belongs to her." Bob's voice choked up. "It's her gun. The gun that killed J.D. Her prints were on it. On the gun. They really think she did it." His words were so jumbled, I wondered if he even realized he was repeating himself.

I didn't know what to say. Any platitude I offered would be just that. "Bob, you need to stay calm. I'm sure they'll realize she's innocent." Lisa was self-centered and totally self-absorbed, but that didn't make her a murderer. Or was she? My mind began to race. Had something happened to make Lisa want to kill J.D? Lisa always seemed to think that if she wanted something, it was hers. Maybe in this case she realized she didn't want J.D., so she eliminated him. But like I'd told Debbie, surely breaking up would be easier. And less messy.

"First she married Larry, that abusive—" His voice choked. "Now this. Hasn't she been through enough?"

"Her husband abused her?" Okay, I officially felt terrible. I'd have guessed it to be the other way around, if anything. I couldn't imagine Lisa putting up with being mistreated. But I guess that just showed that anything was possible.

"Yes. And she's finally putting it behind her." He took a shuddering breath. "Jenna, would you come over to the gym and talk to her tomorrow? That is, if they let her come home." I could hear the tears in his voice. "I need you to help me clear her name."

"I'll be there first thing in the morning, Bob. I don't go to the diner until noon."

"Thanks, Jenna. I'll make sure she's there. It means a lot to me to know you're supporting her. I know you've had your differences, but she needs all of her friends around her right now." He lowered his voice, and after years of working with him, I could easily visualize the sheepish expression on his face. "And, by the way, you know you're welcome to use the club pool anytime."

If I'd been the type to kick a man while he was down, I'd have made a sarcastic comment about selling more T-shirts that way, but I settled for, "Thanks. I'll do that."

To be honest, swimming in the lake was getting a little uncomfortable.

ALIBIS IN ARKANSAS

The weather could turn nippy without warning. Yes, I'm a wimp. But I wasn't about to admit to Bob how much I was missing the perks of my old job.

"I'm glad we cleared that up." He stopped speaking to me, and I could hear a muted conversation in the background. Then, "Jenna, Wilma said Lisa just called and they're bringing her home now. I have to go."

"Okay. I'll see you tomorrow morning." I hit the END key and dropped the phone in my pocket.

I looked over at Alex. "You heard?"

He nodded.

"You know it'll kill Bob if Lisa is guilty. She's the light of his and Wilma's lives."

"Not to mention the boss of their lives. They shouldn't have spoiled her quite so much. At least that's my opinion." Alex looked up at the moonlit sky. "We won't spoil our kids like that, will we?"

"Not if we have five or six like you want to. Who would have time to spoil them?" I grinned at him. "Who would even have time to take care of them?" He had been teasing me about wanting a big family. A really big family.

He leaned over and kissed me softly then pulled back and caressed my cheek with his thumb. "You know what?"

I shook my head mutely as I stared into his sparkling eyes.

"As long as you're in my family, whatever size it is will be just perfect."

Mr. Persi barked loudly and pushed between us.

Alex laughed. "At least I have his seal of approval. I'm not so sure about Neuro."

My cat had always been a tad neurotic—hence her name. But after Mr. Persi trotted into our lives and stayed, she quit pulling out her fur. And since Alex had been hanging around, she seemed more relaxed than ever. "Neuro loves you."

"And. . . ?" he teased.

"And so do I."

"I never get tired of hearing it."

Wasn't that perfect? Because I never got tired of saying it.

◆

After Alex left, I thought about what he said about our children. We had truly come a long way since earlier in the summer when he was too busy even to think about a future with me.

When Carly called as I was getting ready for bed, I was still smiling. "Hello."

"Hi."

Her gloomy voice reminded me of the apparent fuss Mama and I had witnessed between her and Elliott earlier. "You doing okay?"

"I'm fine. I'm making a tunnel-of-fudge cake."

"For what?"

She hesitated. "Just because."

Uh-oh. Anytime Carly started baking random desserts, I knew we had a problem. "Yeah, right. So you and Elliott had a fight?"

"No." Her tone was vehement. "We just disagreed about something," she said more quietly.

"Oh," I said dryly. "Thanks for clearing that up for me."

"Enough about us. What about you? Are you getting excited about the wedding? Or has the murder sidetracked your thoughts?"

"The wedding is a means to an end. But I'm excited about Alex and me becoming a family." I stroked Neuro's thickening fur and told Carly what Alex had said earlier.

"God's really blessed us, hasn't He, Jen?" Her words were choked with tears. I just hoped they were happy tears.

"Yes, He has."

We talked for a few more minutes, then I told her about Bob calling.

"Don't you know he's brokenhearted?" she said. "I remember how upset I was when Zac was a suspect in Hank's murder."

"Me, too," I admitted. "That's all I can think about. It's hard for me to feel an overabundance of sympathy for Lisa, but no parent should have to go through that."

"And sometimes it's hard to know where to draw the line at protecting our children from pain."

I had a strange feeling my sister wasn't talking about Bob and Lisa anymore. But I knew from experience that whatever was going on, she'd tell me when she was ready. And not a minute before.

❖

Gail was at the desk when I arrived at the gym the next morning.

Her solemn face lit up when she saw me. "Jenna, what are you doing here?"

"I just stopped by for a few minutes." No need to tell her why I was here.

"Guess you heard about Lisa?"

I nodded. "Bob called me."

"Are you going to be here for a while? I get a break in about thirty minutes, and we could talk."

I shook my head. "I wish I could stay. I have some things I need to ask you, but right now I have to talk to Lisa then get on to the diner." I headed toward the office, but she followed me down the hall.

"Did he give you any details?" She looked around to make sure no one could hear us.

"Not yet. I'll be back to swim as soon as I get a free minute, and we can hash everything out."

She took the hint and went back to her post. As I neared the open door to the office, I could hear Lisa talking to someone.

"They had to release me. I have an alibi."

It wasn't because I was trying to eavesdrop that I stood outside the slightly open door. It was merely that I thought it would be bad manners to barge in when she was busy with someone else. Really.

"A genuine alibi or one you conveniently set up?" a man's voice snarled.

"I told you just like I told John. Someone stole that gun. I've kept it here in the desk drawer for protection, just like you told me to."

The man's voice was low, and I couldn't hear his words.

"Larry, I don't know who else knew it was here or who took it," Lisa said. "If I did, I'd tell the police."

"Because we both know you're so trustworthy?" the man roared.

Finally feeling guilty about eavesdropping, especially now that I realized she was talking to her husband, I reached up to tap lightly on the door. It burst open away from my fingers, and I was face-to-face with a furious man I'd never seen before. "Get out!" Lisa screamed, unnecessarily it seemed, because the man nearly bowled me over in his haste to leave. The overpowering scent of Lisa's perfume followed him out like a cloud.

I stared after him. I'd always heard that Lisa's wealthy, older husband, Lawrence Hall, favored Ricardo Montalbán during his *Fantasy Island* years. Today he looked more like the madman Ricardo played in *The Wrath of Khan*.

"Oh, it's you."

I spun around to face Lisa. "Yes, me." She sounded less than thrilled, but maybe that was more an irritated residue of the argument than it was my presence.

"What are you doing here?" she asked flatly.

Ironic. That was the very question I'd been asking myself ever since I started down the hallway to the office. "Your dad asked me to come by...to see if I can help you sort out your problems."

"My boyfriend was murdered, and even though Daddy always acted like you could walk on water, I'm pretty sure you can't do anything about raising the dead."

Ouch. I took a step backward. Mentally I was picturing myself saying, "Sorry, Bob. I tried."

"Other than that I only have one other problem." She glanced toward the door that Larry had just stormed out of then back at me. "Make that two. Your friend *John* thinks I'm a murderer."

"Are you?"

Her mouth dropped open. "No."

"Good. I didn't think you were."

She sat down in the office chair and stared at me.

I'd shocked her, but at least she'd stopped sniping at me for a minute. "So now that we have that out of the way, do you have any idea who might have wanted to kill J.D.?" I sat down in the chair across from the desk.

She pursed her lips and shook her head.

"I know this is hard, Lisa, but you're going to have to help me. I just have a few questions—"

She blew out her breath in disgust. "There's nothing you can ask me that the police haven't already asked. They wanted to know about my eating habits, about J.D.'s eating habits, about our relationship." She raised an eyebrow. "Personal things." She waved her little cell phone at me. "They even confiscated my phone. And questioned me about it. How long have I had it? Who's my carrier? Did I have another phone?" She sighed. "And then the big question. Why was J.D. behind the diner?"

My heartbeat picked up slightly. "What did you tell them about that?"

"I told them the truth—I have no idea. We didn't have a date or anything that night."

"Was that normal?" I sounded like a detective.

She shrugged. "Well, to tell you the truth, once he took your place here, we saw each other constantly. So we didn't go out quite as much."

I tried to keep my irritation from showing. *Once he took my place.* I knew she said that just to needle me. "So had you known him long? Before you started dating, I mean?"

"No. Not really." She leaned toward me. "You know how you're supposed to meet guys at weddings? Well, we met him at a funeral. His grandmother's funeral. We were instantly attracted to each other."

"We who?"

"Me and J.D." She shook her head. "Good grief, Jenna. How can you solve a murder if you can't even keep up with a normal conversation?"

"I meant who was with you at the funeral? Your husband?" Maybe Lisa's ex saw the instant attraction and understandably resented it.

She snorted. "Hardly. I went with Debbie. J.D.'s grandmother and Debbie's grandmother were friends. Or something like that." She waved her hand in the air, dismissing them as unimportant. "I'm not really sure why, but Debbie thought she should go and didn't want to go by herself. So I went."

"Okay. You met him at his grandmother's funeral. And it was love at first sight. So you started dating and then hired him to work here. Right?"

"Pretty much. He decided to look for part-time work so he could stay here and get to know me better. Luckily you quit not too long after that."

I was speechless with outrage, but she didn't notice.

She dabbed at her eyes with a tissue. "Only now he's dead, and in a way it's all my fault. If he hadn't been so crazy about me, he'd have left town after the funeral." Tears rolled down her cheeks. "Because his grandma didn't leave him anything. Not a penny. And I think he was expecting to get a big inheritance. He was really disappointed."

"He wasn't rich, then?" I'd always had Lisa pegged for a girl who went where the money was.

"Well, he definitely didn't seem rich when we first started going out. He even let me buy my own dinner. If he hadn't been so good-looking I probably wouldn't have gone out with him again." She wiped her eyes once more. "But after a couple of weeks, he started paying for everything. He even took me to Tunica. And gave me money to play the slots. But of course, I didn't tell John any of that."

"Any idea where he got the money?"

"Now, how would I know that?" She rolled her eyes.

"Well, you *were* dating him." I may have sounded a little sharp. Probably.

"And that was the only reason I agreed to be fingerprinted. John told me it was to eliminate my prints so that they could find the killer." She tossed the tissue in the garbage, and her tears dried as quickly as they came. "But now he's using my fingerprints to try and prove I killed J.D. He tricked me so he would have someone to arrest," she snarled. "I can't believe I trusted him."

"Lisa, they needed your fingerprints. And he didn't trick you. How could he know your prints would be on the gun? You have to admit it makes you look suspicious."

"It was my gun, so *of course* it had my prints. It's not my fault someone stole it out of my drawer."

"How long had it been missing?"

"How should I know? I hardly ever noticed it." She shrugged. "I didn't even know it *was* missing. *You* could have taken it for all I know."

I ignored that dig, but I wanted to beat my head against the wall. Or maybe Lisa's head. Not enough to hurt her, of course, but maybe just enough to gently knock some sense into her. Yeah, right.

I couldn't believe she was talking to me like this when all I was doing was trying to help. Deep breath. "Maybe you should tell John the truth. That J.D. didn't have any money, and then all of a sudden he did."

"And maybe you should mind your own business."

"Lisa, what was Larry so upset about earlier?"

She narrowed her eyes. "Since when is my relationship with my husband your business?"

"I. . ." It really wasn't often that I was at a loss for words.

"Look. Thanks for stopping by, but I'll get Daddy to hire a professional. Someone who can prove that I'm innocent. Not an amateur sleuth that got lucky a couple of times." She wiggled her fingers. "So, see ya."

"Right. Well, I have to go to work now." I gritted my teeth and counted to ten as I walked out the door, taking care not to slam it.

6

Happier'n A Dead Pig In The Sunshine

Jenna, can you call Susan and see if she can come in today?" Carly stirred a steaming pot of soup and nodded toward the list of waitress phone numbers on the wall by the phone. "Alice called. She and Harvey won't be in, so I had to put Vini as host." She turned toward me. "I hope he can do it. Do you think he can?"

"Sure. Leading people to a table should be easier than taking orders and delivering food." I reached back to tie the apron around my waist. "Are Harvey and Alice sick?"

"Alice said John asked Harvey to come by the station and answer some questions." She dipped some of the soup into a small bowl and blew on it. "Alice sounded really upset. She said she was going with him." Carly sipped a spoonful of the liquid and frowned. "Taste this."

"Wonder what they wanted with Harvey?" I stared at the soup. That conversation I'd overheard between Harvey and Alice the night of the murder had *not* been about soup. The question was, what *had* it been about?

"I've no idea. But I guess you're going to try and find out." Carly added some garlic powder to the pot of soup. "I don't think John will tell you."

I ignored her allusion to my curiosity and called Susan, who agreed to come in and do an earlier shift. When I hung up, I quickly got into my apron and hit the floor running.

"Welcome to Down Home Diner, ma'am." Vini's voice floated to the table where I was writing an elderly couple's order. I glanced up in time to see a flamboyantly dressed woman pat Vini's cheek.

Her voice didn't float. It trumpeted across the packed diner. "Well, sweet thing, you can welcome me anytime, anywhere."

Vini blanched, grabbed a menu, and fairly raced to an empty table in my section.

"Your waitress will be right with you." He wiped his brow and headed back to the front of the diner, making strange grimaces in my direction. I assumed he meant, "We've got a live one here." I finished the order I was taking and excused myself.

As I walked to the table, I studied the new arrival. She was one of those people whose age isn't readily apparent, but I guessed her to be somewhere in her forties. Her jet black hair was teased within an inch of its life and piled high on her head. Her eyes were so heavily mascaraed I was surprised she could blink. More noticeable was her dress, or lack thereof. We had the standard No Shoes, No Shirt, No Service sign on our door. We might need to revise that.

She had on a skirt and a top, of sorts. The white top was the scantiest of halters, and the skirt, black leather, was short enough to qualify as micro-mini. Her white boots were straight out of the sixties. Beside her brilliantly red lips was a beauty mark. A tattooed snake crawled up her right arm and coiled lovingly around her neck. As I approached the table, she gave me a cheerful grin.

"Welcome to Down Home Diner. What can I get you to drink?" I gave her my standard opening as I pulled my order pad and pencil from my pocket.

"I'll have a beer in a bottle. The best you've got. I'm celebrating."

"Sorry, ma'am. This is a dry county. We don't serve alcoholic beverages. But we have really good sweet tea or lemonade."

"What kinda burg have I landed in?" she asked loudly. "A gal can't even get a drink?" She lowered her voice slightly. "C'mon, sweet cakes, I know you got the good stuff stashed somewheres. Just bring it in a tea glass. I won't rat you out. It ain't every day your ship comes in, but mine did, and I aim to celebrate."

"I'm really sorry. We don't have anything alcoholic on the premises. But our tea is worth celebrating. Tell you what. I'll bring you a glass on the house. If you don't like it, you won't be out anything." Carly gave away pies to police officers; surely she wouldn't mind if I gave tea to keep the peace.

"Well, the price is right. Go ahead."

As I returned with her tea, I noticed others in the café were eyeing our unusual customer with interest. She was returning the favor, meeting glances all around the room. I rattled off the specials and she ordered, but as I turned to hand the order in, she wrapped long fingers topped with pointed, blood-red nails around my wrist.

"Hang on a minute, honey. Let's talk."

"Let me turn your order in." I gingerly disengaged my wrist. "Then I'll take a break. That way I can talk without getting jumped by the boss." I was careful not to say this loud enough for anyone to hear and repeat it to Carly. I really didn't want to get jumped by my big sis. I handed the woman's order through the window to the kitchen and returned to her table. As I sat, she pulled a pack of cigarettes from the small purse she had slung around her shoulder. I must've looked as shocked as I felt, since there were No Smoking signs on every wall.

"What? No smoking here, either?" She shook her head as she replaced the pack. "Man. What do you people do for entertainment?"

"Well, we eat a lot," I deadpanned, and was rewarded with a loud crack of laughter.

She slapped the table with her open palm. "Girlfriend, you are a riot."

"What brings you to our little town?"

"Little is the right word. It sure wasn't to be entertained. Nope. I came on a mission. I am a woman on a pilgrimage, you might say. This little one-horse town is where one of my old mistakes came right. Did that ever happen to you?" She nudged me.

"I don't know." I was confused, and it showed.

"Well, I'll tell ya, sister, I've made plenty of mistakes in my life. I ain't ashamed to say it. But one of my first ones was marrying a weasel. Have you ever done that? You married?"

The kitchen window bell rang. "Not yet." I walked over to pick up her order then set the full plate in front of her. She continued to talk as I sat back down

"Well, take my advice and steer shy of it. And if you do get married, make sure he ain't a weasel. My man, Jimmy, he was slick. And sweet-talking? Why, that man could talk the bark off a tree." She paused to take a gulp of tea. "This tea's good. Anyhow, he was crooked as a snake. See this snake on my shoulder? I got that after Jimmy and me split up. That's my reminder not to fall for any more snakes. Yeah, me and Jimmy got married when I was just a girl. Then I found out he wadn't what you might call honest. No sirree." She took a large bite of mashed potatoes and gravy and kept talking as she chewed. "But we did one thing right. We made wills. You got a will?"

"Yes, ma'am."

"Smart girl. Yep. Me and Jimmy made wills and left all our worldly possessions—don't that sound fine?—all our worldly possessions to each other. I never thought much about it until a lawyer called me a couple days ago. He told me Jimmy had done cashed in his chips in a little one-horse town nobody'd ever heard of. And I'm thirty thousand dollars richer. Best thing Jimmy Dean Finley ever done for me was die."

"You mean—? J. D. Finley was your husband?"

"Ex, honey. I divorced him for reasons we needn't go into, over twenty years ago. But he never changed his will. So I came here on this pilgrimage to see where he bit the dust. And to celebrate."

A loud clatter jerked my eyes to the kitchen area. Debbie stood in the midst of breakage, and I noted absently that her customer must've ordered strawberry shortcake. She looked as if she had been in a wreck, splashed with strawberry juice to her knees.

"I'm sure glad that little lady wadn't bringing my food." My companion winked at me. "I b'lieve you guys need to invest in some superglue for her. Stick that tray to her hands."

"Excuse me a second," I murmured and rushed to help Debbie and Vini clean up the mess. Only Debbie didn't stick around. She simply turned and walked to the kitchen. But not before I saw the tears streaming down her face. Carly was either going to have to find out what was bugging Debbie or buy unbreakable dishes. After we cleaned everything up, I went back to the table.

"Ain't you Mr. Clean? With hair, of course," she remarked sardonically. "That little gal needs to find herself another job. She ain't cut out for waitressing. I oughta know. I been one my own self. Along with lots of other things." A loud bark of laughter followed. "What time do you get offa work, missy?"

"Me?" My mind was blank—or numb.

"Yes, you." She snapped her fingers in my face. "Hello? You do work here, don't you?"

"Oh. Yes." I glanced at my watch. "In about twenty minutes."

"Why don't I wait for you outside under one of them big shade trees? I need somebody to show me around town, and I don't know a soul here. Unless you count poor ole Jimmy's, and that ain't much help." Another roar of laughter.

I debated. A little of this woman went a long way. On the other hand, she'd known J.D. in his youth. Perhaps she could shed some light on who would kill him, or at least why.

"I'll meet you in the parking lot in a few minutes," I answered.

"Good girl." She left a five-dollar bill on the table and gave me a wink. "That's to celebrate my good fortune. I believe in spreading it around."

As she exited, followed by many fascinated gazes, I went to the kitchen to see if Carly needed help in view of Debbie's departure. To my surprise, Debbie, scrubbed clean of strawberries, though still somewhat stained, was dishing up food, keeping her eyes fixed on her work. I went back to waiting tables until the noon surge had subsided then hung up my apron.

I stepped into the kitchen and quickly filled Carly in on my new acquaintance.

"You're going for a ride with a stranger?" she asked, obviously puzzled.

I shrugged. "You'd just have to meet her. I need to find out as much as I can about J.D., and I think she can help me."

"Keep your cell phone on."

"I will," I called and headed out to meet my new acquaintance.

"I was about to come hunting you, honey. But I figured you couldn't get past me unless you went out the back door and hid behind the Dumpster." I shivered. The Dumpster was the last place I would ever hide from anyone.

"Hop in this roadster of mine, and let's see what this little burg has to offer." She opened the passenger door of an older Mustang, fire-engine red and well kept. I climbed in, and she ran around and sank into the driver's seat, turned the key, and revved the engine. I glanced around. All I needed was for John or Seth to run up and write a ticket. I'd never live it down. But we got safely away in a spurt of loose gravel and headed down the main drag of Lake View.

"We get lots of tourists, Mrs. Finley," I began.

She began to look around, even craning her neck to look in the backseat. I clung to the seat belt strap with white knuckles as the car careened from one lane to the other.

She brayed another of her loud laughs.

"What are you doing?" I asked.

"I was looking for Mrs. Finley. If you meant me, my name's Jolene. I ain't been 'Mrs.' nothin' since I was a kid. And I took my maiden name after Jimmy Dean left me. Yep, Jolene Highwater, that's me. Now, little lady, what's your name?"

"Jenna Stafford." I waited a beat, although I doubted Jolene would be the type to watch the Olympics, much less remember one has-been from years ago. Apparently I was right.

"Pleased to meetcha, honey." She removed her right hand from the steering wheel and stuck it out. I shook it and released it quickly, hoping she'd return it and her attention to where they belonged. She noticed my nervousness and laughed again. She certainly was a happy woman. "Jimmy always said I was the worst kinda driver, a polite one. When I talk to someone, I look at 'em."

"Well, we have several hills and curves in this part of the country, so that may not be a good idea." I spoke quickly, lest she look too long and miss a curve.

"You know, I hadn't even hardly thought about Jimmy Dean for the last few years. I'd really put him out of my mind. He was just a youthful mistake, you know?" She looked over at me, and I nodded.

After what seemed like an eternity, she looked back at the road. "But ever since that lawyer guy called, I keep remembering when we was together. I thought there wadn't no good memories, but now most of 'em seem good. Ain't it funny how our minds can play tricks on us?"

It was. My mind was tricking me into believing that if we didn't stop while we talked, somebody might be cashing in on *my* will. "There's a scenic overlook up here on your left that's really beautiful." I crossed my fingers that she'd pull in.

She obligingly whipped the little car in and killed the motor. We got out and looked across mountains faintly colored with fall leaves. My legs still trembled a little, but I walked over and sat down, willing myself to relax.

In front of us, mountain after mountain fell away until they faded into blueness. I never tired of looking at the majestic beauty of this scene. Jolene stared at it a long time without speaking. Almost a miracle. Then she slowly lit a cigarette and took a long drag.

She loosed a stream of smoke and looked at me. "I'd like to ask you a favor." She spoke soberly. "I know we just met, and you don't owe me a thing. But I'm kinda in what you might call a pickle. Turns out I'm the executor of Jimmy's will. He hadn't got no close kin left. So I have to decide how to dispose of the body when they get done with it and release it." She stared out at the mountains then back at me. "I thought I'd just have him cremated and get on back to my life, but now that I'm here, I don't think I can do that."

I wondered again about Jimmy Dean Finley. What kind of life must he have lived to have no one who wanted to plan a funeral for him? "You know, his grandma lived here. She died a little while back. He came to the funeral and just stayed on."

"Yeah? Her and him never did get along when I knew him. But I guess, like they say, blood's thicker'n water. You think I oughta have him buried here?"

"There were folks in town who were quite fond of him," I said carefully. "They might get a sense of closure if you have a funeral."

She snorted. "Closure? Reckon that's why someone killed him? So they could get closure?"

"Do you know why someone might have killed him?"

She threw her cigarette down and ground it into the dirt with her heel. Then she carefully picked up the butt and stuck it into her pocket. "I have no idea. Unless Jimmy changed quite a lot, it coulda been just about anything. Wonder how much a funeral would cost? I could spend a thousand or so of what I'm getting, I guess. After all, if it wadn't for him, I wouldn't have any."

"I could show you where the local funeral home is."

"Tell ya what—you do that later on. Right now I'm ready to find the nearest watering hole. I've had about as much of this dry-county stuff as I can handle for one day."

We climbed into the Mustang, and the engine roared to life. She spun gravel as she peeled onto the road and headed back to town.

❖

The next night, Carly walked into the deserted dining room as I was wiping the crumbs from the last dirty table. "Think you and I can handle the cleanup if I let the others go on home?"

"Sure." We hadn't had a chance to talk since the diner opened. I followed her into the kitchen.

Debbie and Susan both looked relieved when Carly told them their shifts were officially over.

Susan picked up her purse. "I'm dog tired. I'd forgotten how hard this was." She must have noticed Carly's funny look, because she quickly clarified, "I'm thrilled to have the job. It's just been several years since I've waitressed. I'll have to get back in the groove."

"You're doing great," Carly assured her. "Thanks for pulling a double yesterday."

"See y'all tomorrow." Debbie followed Susan out the door. "I'm going home to put my feet up."

Carly and I finished putting the dishes away. Together we walked out to do a last-minute check of the dining room before tackling the bathrooms.

Vini was standing near the front door.

"Vini!" Carly said. "I thought you were already gone."

"No. Is there anything else I can do? I will be happy to put the dishes away or sweep." Dark circles under his eyes made him look exhausted.

Carly and I exchanged glances. "Um, Vini, I told you your shift was over. Why don't you go on home now and get some sleep?" Carly smiled at the waiter. "I appreciate your willingness to work, but we're almost finished."

"Okay. If you are sure there isn't anything I can do." In spite of his agreeable words, he didn't move. "I just wanted to help out. I really appreciate you giving me this job."

"You do a great job. Harvey says lots of people ask to be seated in your section."

"I do my best." He smiled modestly. "I make good tips, too. I think a lot of people just like to hear me talk."

His accent did stand out in our little Southern town. Not to mention his European charm and Italian good looks. And according to Harvey, older women, especially, liked to sit in his section. Maybe because he had the courtliness of an old-fashioned gentleman.

"Well, we have to finish cleaning up, hon." Carly made a shooing motion at him. "You probably need to go on home and study."

"Yeah, I get to clean the restrooms." I pulled latex gloves out of my pocket. "I can't wait."

"Would you like me to help? I can do the men's room." He picked up a pair of gloves.

I glanced at Carly. She must have read my mind. There were some gift horses you didn't refuse. An offer to clean the men's room definitely fell in that category. "Sure. You can if you don't mind." She handed him an apron. With the extra help, it didn't take but a few minutes to finish up the cleaning and put the supplies away. As we gathered up our personal things, Carly stepped back and looked at Vini's face. "Are you getting enough sleep?"

"Between studying and working here, I don't sleep a lot. But I rest plenty." He pulled off his latex gloves. "I need to work all the hours you will let me have so I can make enough to pay for school." He tossed his apron into the laundry hamper. "And I have to maintain good grades, so I have to study a great deal, too."

"Wow, you do have a full schedule. Not much time for a social life, I suppose." Carly smiled at him.

"Social life? What is that?" He grimaced. "The only females I see are right here at the diner. Remember the woman with the snake tattoo?"

I smiled as I thought of Jolene.

"Hiding from her. That is my idea of a social life."

"You need to get out more, honey," Carly said as she carefully locked the front door.

We walked out onto the back porch. Carly locked it, too. We all started out to the vehicles together. Vini veered off toward his old van.

Carly looked at me. "I forgot I parked around front."

I motioned toward my car a few feet away. "I'll give you a ride around there. It's safer that way."

She climbed into the passenger seat, and I started the car.

"Poor Vini. He looked so exhausted tonight. Kind of overwhelmed." My tenderhearted sister sounded distressed.

"Well, no wonder with his busy schedule. I don't think I could face going to school and studying plus working here as many hours as he does." I put the car in reverse and slowly drove around the building.

Carly sighed. "Yeah, and he looked worried, too. I guess he really needs the money."

A sudden memory of Vini standing by the cash register when we'd walked into the dining room an hour earlier flashed through my mind. "You don't think he needed it bad enough to kill J.D. and rob him, do you?" I dismissed the idea as soon as the words came out of my mouth.

Carly shook her head. "No way do I think that sweet boy would even think about such a thing."

"Me either. But you know Mama always told us some people would do anything for money."

"True. But I don't think Vini falls into that category. Do you?" She glanced at me as I pulled up beside her car. "Besides, I hadn't heard J.D. was robbed. Was he?"

"No idea. If he was, that bit of gossip hasn't hit the streets yet." I wondered if

I could pry that information out of John with a free piece of pie. Probably not.

Carly turned toward me. "Not to change the subject or anything, but I hope you have a good time tomorrow." She leaned back in her seat. "Are you nervous about spending the day with the 'in-laws to be'?"

I shook my head. Then I nodded. Then I shrugged. Talk about mixed signals. "I don't know. You know I always loved Alex's parents even when we were kids. I guess I'm afraid our engagement will change things some." I turned off the motor. "But having premium seats at a Cardinals game will be worth overcoming my nerves." I grinned at Carly.

"I'm sure they knew that, too." She climbed into her car. "Have a good time. Call me when you get home."

"I will, but it'll be really late. Don't work too hard without me." As I pulled out of the parking lot, I realized that Carly and I hadn't ended up getting to talk alone after all. Pretty soon we'd just have to sit down and visit.

Dear Pru,

    I've been married three months to the man of my dreams. Our marriage couldn't be better. Except for one minor detail. His parents hate me. They tell him they like me, but I know they don't. They're not rude, but if you could see how stilted they act when I'm with them, you'd know they can't stand to be around me. I really don't know what to do.

                    More Outlaw Than In-law

Dear Outlaw,

    Be patient. Chances are that if you find a common interest and work to get to know his parents better, they'll like you. And even though I know you can't see it, some reserve could be normal for them. Sometimes our imaginations wreak havoc in our lives. Be sure paranoia isn't part of your problem.

7

Everything Is Lovely And The Goose Hangs High

When Alex rang the bell, it was morning but still dark outside. I yanked the door open and pulled him inside. "I need your help."

"Whoa, water girl. What's wrong?"

"Is this shirt okay?"

He looked at my red Cardinals shirt then back up at my face. "Is this a trick question?"

"No!"

"Of course it's fine."

"Just fine?"

"Perfect. As usual," he said with a slightly uncertain smile.

I stared in the foyer mirror at my wild curls. "Why did I leave my hair down? Everybody knows you wear a ponytail to a baseball game." I swooped my hair up and secured it.

"Uh-oh," Alex said.

I turned to him. "Uh-oh *what*?"

"Uh-oh, I didn't get the ponytail memo."

I smacked his arm. "Very funny."

He held up a bag. "But I did bring you something that actually goes with that hairstyle."

I opened the bag and pulled out two red caps emblazoned with the team logo. "Thanks." I froze with it halfway to my hair. "You don't think it's too much for us to be matching?"

He placed his own cap on his head. "Too much?"

"Too. . .like we're shoving our engagement in your parents' face?"

He laughed then stopped when he saw my face. "Honey, let's sit down and talk about whatever's got you so frantic."

"We can't sit down. If we're late, we might miss the beginning of the ball game." Or worse, cause his parents to miss it. I'd looked on the Internet after Alex told me about their engagement gift to us. I felt sure they'd had to pay at least a hundred dollars each for four tickets right behind home plate.

Neuro and Mr. Persi paced around me as if they knew my happy ending

345

was about to explode into a million pieces. I gave them each a pat. "We'll be back late tonight, guys. Zac will be by a few times to visit. Be good and take care of each other."

Alex escorted me onto the porch then put one hand on my back as we walked to the truck. He helped me in and shut the door. I think by now he wasn't sure I wouldn't run.

We didn't speak until we were leaving Lake View, and he glanced over at me. "Want to tell me what that was all about back there?"

"What?" I stared out the passenger window at the trees and pastures flying by.

"The meltdown."

"Just because I had a hard time deciding what to wear? That represents a meltdown?" I joked. "Remind me never to take you shopping with me."

"Fine," he said, a slight frown crossing his face. "Obviously, we're going to spend a four-hour drive pretending that nothing's wrong."

I forced my shoulders to relax and blew out the breath I hadn't realized I'd been holding. "I'm a little nervous about seeing your parents."

"You saw them when they came through town a few weeks ago," he pointed out in a reasonable tone.

"Yes, but then I was just your girlfriend, and they were in town about an hour. This is going to be an all-day thing, including going to their house after the game." I cut my gaze over to him. "And now we're engaged."

He shook his head and tapped his hand on the steering wheel. "Which my parents are thrilled about."

I snorted. "Of course that's what they're going to tell you."

He drove for a minute then sighed. "You want to know the truth? If I married anyone else, they'd be disappointed."

I opened my mouth, and he held up his hand.

"And no, that's not why I'm marrying you."

I sighed. He knew me too well. But he'd calmed my nerves. For now, anyway.

◆

"He's out of there," Coach Campbell roared.

The Cincinnati batter didn't move out of the box, and Alex's dad threw out his hands in disgust. "What was that?"

Demaree patted her husband's arm. "Honey, just because we have seats behind home plate doesn't mean you're the ump."

"Maybe I should be," he grumbled, but his grin gave him away. He leaned forward and looked across his wife at me. "What do you think, Jenna? Was I right or wrong?"

Alex cleared his throat. "Now, Dad. Jenna—"

While Alex was trying to protect me, St. Louis's pitcher wound up for another pitch and released it. The umpire called strike three, and the inning was over.

I laughed and interrupted. "Coach, I think you were absolutely right. He's out of there."

"You always were a wise one," he said.

Yeah, like when I was wise enough to know my swimming career was all washed up. I pushed the negative thought away and scolded myself like Carly and I always did when the kids got a little self-centered. *It's not all about you,* I reminded myself.

Demaree slipped her hand in mine and gave it a small squeeze. She leaned over and spoke softly in my ear. "Forgive our enthusiasm, Jenna. We're so happy that you and Alex are going to be married. I'm afraid we're a little giddy."

"Are you sure?" I blurted out.

Puzzlement crossed her face. "Of course I'm sure. Why would you ask that?"

I shrugged. "No reason, I guess. I know I let Coach down when I lost the Olympics."

Her pretty face grew stern. "Let him down?" she said, no longer lowering her voice. She flashed a look at her husband. "Mike, Jenna thinks she let you down by losing in the Olympics."

His eyes widened with surprise, and either he missed his calling as an actor, or his shock was genuine. "How did you let me down? You were the best swimmer I ever coached. You did everything I asked of you, even when you thought you couldn't. You were a joy to coach, Jenna."

I resisted the urge to go into it further. Now was neither the time nor the place as the first Cardinal batter approached the batter's box. "Never mind," I said, smiling. "Thank you."

By the time the Cards won a rowdy victory, I'd almost managed to stop thinking of Alex's parents as my ex-coach and his wife. If they could get over my early failure and the impact it no doubt had on their lives, surely I could, too. I was a grown woman, after all.

But when we got to his parents' house after the game, all my earlier nervousness returned with a vengeance. I climbed down from the truck. "Whoa, it's beautiful," I said to Alex, as we approached the white two-story house with its bright green roof. "I especially love the front porch and the swing." His folks came out just as I finished speaking. They'd left the ball game only a few minutes before us, but when Alex called them ten minutes ago to tell them we were stopped for road construction, they were already home. One of the joys of being a local and knowing all the shortcuts.

They accepted my compliments and ushered us into the house. We bypassed the formal living room and went straight to the family room, a comfortable area with overstuffed chairs and a fireplace.

And walls and shelves covered with pictures. I noticed one of Alex as I remembered him from childhood. He was so cute, even then. I followed his pictorial progress from infancy to adulthood. All those moments I'd missed. There he was at bat in a baseball game; here he was shooting a long shot on the basketball court. There were pictures of him swimming, camping, graduating college. Holding up his shingle. There were several of him in groups, both formal and informal. None with him and a girl alone. I wondered if his parents wished he'd married someone from his college days instead of the girl who choked under pressure.

"Hey, water girl," Alex said from near my shoulder. "Your wall's over here."

I glanced at him in puzzlement as he turned me to face the wall across the room. Photos of Coach Mike and his pupils. I walked across for a closer look. To my surprise, I was in more than half the photos.

"My star student," Coach said from behind us.

I spun around. "Up to a point."

He chuckled. "Up to the point that Super Girl finally showed she was human by getting sick at the worst possible time? But even then you were the best I ever coached."

I ignored the last part of his comment as politeness and focused on the first part. "You didn't think my illness was just nerves? A way to wimp out?" Until I said it aloud, I hadn't realized that deep down that was what I'd feared all these years.

"Nerves?" he boomed. "Nerves don't cause a 102-degree fever. You had no business competing. If you'll remember, I told you to withdraw, and you refused. And I felt it had to be your decision, since you'd trained so long and hard. Your parents reluctantly agreed with me. But your body couldn't fight infection and win a gold medal at the same time."

"Or any medal," I reminded him just in case he'd forgotten.

Demaree slipped her arm around me and gave me a side hug. "Girl, you qualified for the Olympics. Where's the shame in that? Even if you hadn't been sick, which you definitely were, there are only so many medals. But being there was a victory. You're an amazing swimmer." She walked over and took her husband's hand. "And even more important, in our eyes, you're an amazing person. So don't identify yourself by what you can *do*, but by who you are. You're a beautiful, caring Christian woman who has had some disappointments. But from those disappointments has come determination and strength of character. And we're proud to have you for our daughter-in-law."

I reached up to wipe a tear, and Alex grasped my wrist lightly.

"What a sneaky way of showing off your engagement ring," he said and held up my hand. What a sneaky way of changing the subject.

I loved him.

And his parents.

❖

When we pulled into my driveway that night, I wondered for the hundredth time why I'd been so nervous about seeing his parents again.

Alex got out and walked me to the door. "Want me to come in and make sure everything's okay?"

"I'm sure everything's fine." I glanced at my watch. "Zac was here just a couple of hours ago to let Mr. Persi out."

It was a little before ten. Not too late to give Carly a call. When I got inside, I did, and she answered on the first ring. "I was hoping you'd call. How'd it go?"

I hit the speakerphone button and laid the phone on the vanity. "Great. I had a wonderful time." I slid the ponytail holder from my hair and picked up my brush. "They were so nice to me."

"All that worrying for nothing," Carly teased.

"I guess you're right. You know what?" I ran the brush through my tangled hair. "They're really happy we're engaged."

"Of course they are. They know a good thing when they see it." I could hear the smile in her voice.

"And so do I. I'm so glad Alex and I finally worked things out." I looked at myself in the mirror. Even I could see that I looked happy. "Now if I can just get you and Elliott all fixed up." I teased her.

"You know how mom always tells you to mind your own business?" She laughed. "Well, never mind. That dog won't hunt."

"I guess you're implying that I'm nosy?" Nothing new there.

"Well, if the shoe fits." She laughed. "And we know it's exactly your size. And you have the mate in your closet."

"Okay, silly. But you'd tell me if there was anything I could do to help y'all, right?" I laid down the brush.

"Of course." She lowered her voice. "I'm just not going to rush into anything."

I hardly considered a year "rushing," but Carly would do things in her own time. Harvey was right when he said she had a mind of her own.

"By the way," I said. "Larry was at the club when I went to see Lisa. He didn't seem too happy."

"Lisa's husband? I don't imagine knowing Lisa was seeing J.D. made him happy."

"Well, the thing is, he knew exactly where she kept the gun. In fact, he's the one who told her to bring it to the club and put it in the drawer."

"Did she tell you that?"

And even though she couldn't see me, I blushed. "No, I overheard it when I was standing outside her office."

"Who, you? Nosy? What was I thinking? Eavesdropping, huh?" Carly said dryly.

"No, in this instance I was just waiting politely until she was free to see me," I said piously. "The point is, Larry knew about the murder weapon and where it was.

"Hmm. . ." Carly said. "You know what?"

"What?"

"Didn't you tell me before you quit that Lisa was laying it on thick to some of the members about the club being safe because she had a gun and knew how to use it?"

I slapped my forehead with my free hand. "Carly, you're right. I can't believe I forgot that. But she was bragging to a bunch of guys one morning when I came in."

"So a lot of people knew about the gun. It wouldn't take a rocket scientist to find it in her desk drawer."

"That's true. But Bob specifically said Larry was abusive. And if he was jealous. . ."

"Yeah," Carly said. "We know firsthand that jealousy can lead to murder."

"Oh well, I may find out more tomorrow. I'm going to swim at the club in the morning."

"So you and Bob made up?"

"I guess. To an extent."

"If it's not war, it's peace," she said. "Be thankful for it."

"Believe me, I am."

❖

It felt weird but totally natural to be back at the club pool for my morning swim. I had spent so much time here that not coming for the last few weeks had felt strange. I shook off introspections and focused on getting my laps in. No use crying over spilled milk. Or in this case, chlorinated water. Definitely better than the lake. And so nice to have it to myself. Or so I thought.

"Hey! They let just anybody in here?"

I set a new record for going from a breaststroke to a high jump in seven feet of water. Which Seth thought was hilarious.

"What are you doing here so early?" I excused myself for sounding like a petulant child on the basis of extreme surprise.

"I heard the great Jenna Stafford was working out here again, and I had to come check it out." A grin still marked his features, so at least my rudeness hadn't been too obvious. "Just kidding. Passing by on my way to the weight room. I'll be back later in case you need company." With a jaunty salute, he left, but before I could soak in the solitude, Amelia came in. So much for a quiet swim.

Amelia motioned imperiously.

Like a puppet on strings, I obediently swam to the edge of the pool.

She handed me a towel. "Put this around you and sit with me a minute." She proceeded to a corner table and made herself comfortable.

I followed. Like I had a choice. As I draped the towel over me for maximum coverage and warmth, Amelia looked around suspiciously then leaned forward and put a finger to her lips. Apparently she was channeling James Bond. I glanced around nervously. Were enemy agents about to descend? Was the room bugged? Was Amelia slightly batty?

"What's wrong, Amelia?" I apparently hadn't quite banished my inner pouty child.

"Shh. I don't want anyone to see us talking." She got up and looked out the steamy windows of the pool room doors. Satisfied that we weren't being observed, she resumed her seat. "Remember what I asked you to do for me?"

Oops. I was drawing a blank. "What?"

She pursed her lips and shook her head as if she felt sorry for me for having such a low IQ. "You were going to ask around about Ricky."

"Oh yes. That. Well. . ." Pause for throat clearing and brain searching. "So far, not much." I'd been a little busy trying to help Bob keep Lisa out of jail and find out who really killed J.D. But since Amelia knew I wasn't directly involved with this murder investigation, I knew she'd never buy that as an excuse. And considering that this very moment, Ricky's partner was in the weight room next door, I could make up for lost time. "I've got a plan, though."

"Plans are only as efficient as the planner," she said primly.

I pushed a wet strand of hair off my face and stared at her. Was she insulting me?

Her expression lightened a little. I think she realized she'd almost pushed the "favor" envelope too far. "Please hurry. Tiffany's pushing like mad for me to get this wedding planned."

"Okay, I'll get back to you as soon as I find out anything."

She gave me a terse nod and stood, then with a surreptitious wave of dismissal, sauntered out. I wanted to call out a witty "We've got to stop meeting like this," but I felt sure she wouldn't appreciate it. So I stood and sidled toward the shower room. Even though I loved to swim, I hated getting back in the water after I'd been out for a while.

I rushed through my shower and emerged just as Seth left the men's shower room. How convenient.

He shot me a cocky grin as if I'd set up this meeting on purpose. And even if he was close to right, it definitely wasn't for the reason he was obviously hoping it was for. "Hey, babe, we've got to stop meeting like this," he drawled.

I cringed, glad I hadn't said something similar to Amelia. That old line wasn't as witty as I'd thought it might be when it was said aloud. "Hi, Seth. Did you have a good workout?"

He flexed his muscles beneath his white T-shirt. "Always."

Even for Amelia, I draw the line at admiring another man's pecs. I glanced toward the pool. "Do you swim?"

He nodded. "Like a pro." He apparently remembered who he was talking to, because he said, "Well, I may not be the best in the world." He laughed. "But at least I can swim. Ol' Rick can't swim a lick."

Talk about opportunity knocking. "He can't?"

"Nah, he always says if God intended us to swim, he'd have given us fins."

Mission accomplished. Now anyone with a brain could see that Ricky wasn't suitable for Tiffany. Imagine anyone not swimming. I smiled at my silly thoughts. "Speaking of Ricky, is he an all-right guy?"

Seth frowned at me and stumbled a little. "Yeah, he's okay. Why?"

I waved my hand airily. "I just don't know him that well. . .and now that he's playing b-ball with us on Sunday afternoons, I thought I should know a little about him."

"Like what?" Seth's face darkened.

Unsure whether to abort my mission or keep trying, I forged on. "Oh, I don't know. Like did he move here to take the police job, or was he already here when the opening came?"

"I don't know. I think he had been here a little while when the opening came up. Why?" His eyes were filled with suspicion.

"I told you. I just like to know about people. And I figured you're his best friend, since y'all are partners and all."

He shrugged. "I don't know about best friend. That sounds kinda girly. He's a pal. We don't hang out much, since he and Tiffany have a thing going on." He sent a searching look my way. "You do know about that, don't you?"

"Sure. I saw them at the cabins the other day, remember? Have they dated long? Did he date around when he first came?"

Seth's grin slipped slightly. "Why? You want to take him away from her? Did you forget that big rock on your finger?"

My eyebrows rose. "No!"

He put his hand on my arm and gazed into my eyes. "You've made it plain to me you're engaged, and I'm dealing with that. So why are you asking about other men?"

Eek. I hadn't taken into account that he might be jealous. "Seth. . .I—"

He held up his hand. "I know. You only like me as a friend. But Tiffany's a real sweet girl. And she doesn't need you messing things up for her. So just remember, Rick's taken." He stomped off before I could assure him that I wasn't after Tiffany's boyfriend.

I knew one thing for sure. I'd never ask Amelia for another favor.

Her paybacks were too steep.

Between A Rock And A Hard Place

The next night, I walked out of the diner and glanced at the digital numbers on the front of my cell phone. Only 8:30. I still had plenty of time to run by the *Monitor* and pick up some Dear Pru letters. I drove the short distance, pulled into the empty parking lot, and killed the motor.

I dreaded going into an empty office. But picking up the letters after everyone was gone was the only way to preserve my secret identity. Even though Marge had always told me just to tell people I did some part-time work for the newspaper, she also said not to be specific about what the part-time work entailed.

So I'd gotten used to letting myself in the back door with the key Marge had given me and finding my way through the darkened offices to the desk where my letters were kept. Still, every time I unlocked this door, I thought about Hank Templeton, the former editor. And about his murder. Tonight, as I headed down the hall, I noticed a light shining under the door of the editor's office.

I shivered. Had Hank left the light on for me?

Since I didn't believe in ghosts, I hefted my carryall, wondering how much impact it would have on a skull. Not much, since I'd emptied it before I left home. I glanced around the hall. Unless I intended to yank a picture off the wall and beat the intruder over the head, I had few options. I turned to look for a more conventional weapon and tripped over a trash can.

The office door opened.

"Freeze! I've got a gun and I know how to use it," a woman's voice snarled.

"Don't shoot!" I threw my arms over my head.

"Jenna?"

"Tiffany? Thank goodness. You scared me to death."

"Yeah? Well, my heart's beating a little fast, too."

"Do you really have a gun?" I couldn't resist asking.

"Sort of." She sheepishly extended her hand, with the index finger pointed outward and the others curled in.

"I'll have to remember that next time I get in a tight spot." I grinned.

"I just came to pick up some Dear Pru letters."

"I thought you came on Tuesdays."

"I had a late date last night, and you know I can't come during business hours. There wasn't a car in the parking lot."

She motioned to her sweat suit. "Ricky's on duty tonight, and I was just out for a walk. Thought I'd stop by and catch up on some work."

I nodded. "I should've called you. Sorry."

"That's okay. Neither of us had a heart attack, so no harm done. Come on in, and let's get some letters."

As we walked down the hall, she said, "Aunt Marge says the Dear Pru column has soared in popularity since you took it over."

"Thanks. I wasn't sure at first if I could do it, but with Carly's help, and Mama's, too, actually, I—"

Tiffany stopped and frowned. "I didn't know your mom knew about you being Dear Pru."

I laughed as I walked on into the office. "She has no idea. But Mama has given us so much good advice over the years that with almost every Dear Pru letter, I remember a nugget of her wisdom to help me answer." I pulled a manila envelope stuffed full of letters out of the filing cabinet.

"Lucky you." She stepped inside the office. "I guess I was born a rebel. I've never been good at taking my mother's advice." She laughed. "Just ask her." She sat down in the chair near the desk. "Although, you may have gathered that from the other day at the diner."

"Well. . ." I wanted to be diplomatic, not my best talent. "I did get the impression she wanted you to spend more time planning your wedding." I took several letters off the stack and sat down in the chair beside Tiffany.

"She wants it to be the social event of the season." She shrugged. "Not me. If it weren't for Daddy, I'd just elope. What about you? Have you and Alex set a date yet?"

"We're planning on right around Christmas." I glanced down at my engagement ring.

She raised her eyebrows. "Don't tell my mother you're getting married that soon, or she'll be planning your wedding. Or wait. . . Do tell her, and maybe it'll get her off my case."

"I could probably use a wedding planner." Although truthfully, I agreed with Tiffany. I didn't need a big social event to be married. Our wedding would be quiet and simple. But just as legal and romantic as a bigger one.

"Jenna?" Tiffany's normally confident voice was hesitant. "I've noticed how well you deal with my mother."

Shocked, I bit back a protest. Amelia and I dealt as well as a snake and a frog, with me being the frog. I always feared she might swallow me whole.

Tiffany continued, oblivious to my amazement. "You know, I was always a disappointment to her. She's so perfect, and I could never live up to that."

"Well. . ." I cleared my throat. "Everyone's idea of perfection is different. And a child's perception of her mother sometimes differs from the way others see her."

"How did you see your mother?"

I thought of my mom playing kickball with us when we were little, taking me to the pool, sitting patiently and proudly through endless swim meets, serving as room mother throughout my elementary years, teaching me to pray, admonishing me to pay attention to the preacher. My mom was my cheerleader, my spiritual adviser, my support. My hero.

"Well. . ." I hedged. "My mom's not your average mom. She's more like Super Mom."

"You know, when I came home on holidays, I'd see you and your sister at church with your folks, and I fantasized about being you."

"You're kidding. Why?"

She shrugged and looked a little embarrassed. "You got to live at home all the time. You weren't considered a nuisance who had to be sent to boarding school."

I shook my head. "I'm sure that's not why they sent you to boarding school. It's just that they wanted the very best for you because they loved you so much."

"Is that what you think?" She shot me a pitying look, but I thought there was a hint of hope, as well. "They had an odd way of showing it, didn't they? Actually, Daddy would've let me stay home, but Mother talked him out of it."

"Are you sure?"

She nodded. "Positive. When I was little, it was okay. I wasn't your typical cute toddler, but I was reasonably intelligent. But when I was about six, I hit a growth spurt and gained weight. From then on, I was an embarrassment to Mother. By the time I was a teenager, my weight problem had grown worse and was complicated by that common teen horror, acne. I spent several summers abroad with a nanny. Does that sound like my mother loved me?"

"Teenage years are hard for everyone," I answered, remembering the turmoil surrounding my parents and Carly. "Sometimes the best thing we can do about them is forgive and forget."

Tiffany ran her hand through her frizzy hair. "It's not like I haven't tried. A long time ago, I decided the best way to deal with her is to be myself, only more so. Hence, no makeup, no fancy clothes, no beauty salons. It kills her. And I'll let you in on a little secret. I have a whole closet full of other clothes. When I go out of town, I dress and act like everyone else. I'll never be beautiful like my mother, but I'm passable."

"Has Ricky seen you in your other guise?" I had to ask.

She laughed. "Oh yes. On a few special occasions, I've pulled out my wardrobe stash and gotten fixed up before we've gone out. Only when we were going out of town, of course. I've been to Dallas on business several times since we've been dating. A couple of times he let me get him a plane ticket and hotel room, though he wouldn't stay at the fancy hotel I stayed at. He didn't want to waste my money. And of course, we couldn't travel down together. I don't want Mother to have a heart attack, after all."

"That's nice of you," I said dryly.

She smirked. "Anyway, I promised Ricky that when we get married, I'll stop my little prank. But for now, he thinks it's a good joke on Mother, too."

"You and Ricky must have the same sense of humor," I commented. "Being able to laugh together is a good thing."

"Yes." She frowned faintly. "Though sometimes he is a little flippant about things I feel are important." She hurriedly added, "Not that I'm criticizing him."

"Nobody's perfect," I answered. I could almost feel Amelia at my elbow, urging me on. "Where did you and Ricky meet?"

She rolled her eyes. "That's a crazy story. I hadn't been back in town long, and Mother insisted on buying me a new car. Of course, the little hybrid I wanted wasn't good enough for her daughter, so she got me a gas-guzzling Hummer. Can you believe it? Anyhow, I was cruising through town when blue lights came on behind me. I pulled over to let the officer chase down whatever dangerous criminal he was after, but it was me. Ricky had just joined the force and didn't realize who I was."

I noted that she was as arrogant as Amelia, though in a nicer way.

"When I told him my name, he asked if I was any relation to the mayor. We had a good laugh when he discovered he'd pulled the mayor's daughter over for speeding."

"You drive a Hummer?" I asked, remembering the little Toyota Prius she'd been driving the day of the basketball game. As different from a Hummer as. . .Tiffany from Amelia.

"No, of course not. I drove that one a couple of weeks just to humor Mother then traded it for a hybrid. Going green is best for the earth, you know."

"So Ricky asked you out when he stopped you?"

A hint of color flashed across her cheeks. "Actually, I asked him out. The Garden Society had a big do that weekend, and I had planned to go alone. He didn't know many folks in town, so he was glad to go with me. We hit it off so well, we've dated ever since. And I think he may be the one for me. I've dated some real losers, but I have a good feeling about Ricky. And it will really tick Mother off if I marry a police officer." She must have realized how that sounded, because she grimaced. "That's just the icing on the cake."

"Be careful, though. Dressing to aggravate your mother is one thing, but marrying for that reason would be taking things a little too far."

A flash of irritation crossed her face.

Had I overstepped the bounds? After all, this was my boss I was giving advice to.

"That wouldn't be the reason. Like I said, it would just be a plus."

"I don't know. It seems like it would be a good idea to come to terms with your mother before you make permanent plans with anyone else."

"Is that Dear Pru speaking?" Sarcasm dripped from her voice.

"I've just seen too much unhappiness because of unresolved problems," I answered soberly. "Dear Pru sees a lot of sorrow. I've learned plenty from my readers."

"I'll think about it." She stood abruptly, and I followed her down the hall past the restrooms and break room. Tiffany pointed to a room near the door. "Do you realize that every newspaper Uncle Hank put out is in that room? If we were as up-to-date as most cities, it would all be on computer by now." She sighed. "But we're not."

I knew she was just trying to dispel the awkwardness my unwelcome advice had left between us, but I was curious. I pushed the door open and glanced inside at the rows of newspapers. "Wow. That's a lot of information."

"Yeah, probably forty years' worth at least. And all filed by date."

Wouldn't it be easy to solve a murder if I could organize my mind like this room?

While I was still daydreaming about that, Tiffany cleared her throat. "I've got to run."

As we exited the building, I thought about what I'd learned. Amelia's whole theory about her daughter not being able to attract men was skewed by her faulty perception of Tiffany. Sometimes I felt the same way about solving J.D.'s murder. Like there was a piece of the puzzle in plain sight that we just weren't seeing.

Dear Pru,

I am nearing thirty, and not to be cliché or anything, but my biological clock is ticking. I have met a man I really care for and am considering marrying him. He loves me, but I'm not sure if what I feel for him is love or if I am just settling so that I can have a family.

Not Sure

Not Sure,

If you aren't sure, there's a good chance you aren't in love. Only you can decide if marrying a man you "like" in order to have a family is worth giving up on the real thing.

"Is this my favorite attorney?" I grinned as I imagined Alex on the other end of the phone line.

"It depends. Who's this?" he asked playfully.

"Your favorite waitress."

"Debbie?"

"Very funny."

"Oh wait! I recognize that sarcasm. This is Jenna, isn't it? Then, yes, this is your favorite attorney."

"Good, because I'm about to do something I've never done before and ask a man out on a date."

"Anyone I know?"

I snickered. "You're in rare form today, Counselor. Carly called, and she and Elliott want us to ride to Jonesboro with them to get some restaurant supplies." Before he could make a smart remark about how exciting that would be, I rushed on, "And eat at El Acapulco while we're there."

"That sounds good," Alex said.

An hour later, the four of us were on the road in Elliott's SUV and deep in discussion. With Elliott and Carly in the front seat and Alex and me in the middle seat, we covered everything from religion to politics, all those subjects you were supposed to avoid. How cool that we shared similar points of view on most things.

Halfway to Jonesboro, we started dissecting a Will Smith movie we had rented and watched together. Elliott glanced at Carly. "Keeping his identity a secret was what got him in trouble."

Carly jerked her head around to look at him. "He didn't do it on purpose at the beginning. And if she had known, she never would have gone out with him."

Elliott shrugged. "Still, keeping secrets like that keeps relationships from growing."

"Humph." Carly crossed her arms. "Shows how much you know. They ended up together, didn't they?"

Elliott kept his eyes on the road, but his knuckles were white on the steering wheel. Carly turned and looked out the passenger window.

Alex and I stared at each other in bewilderment. I shrugged. Elliott was just the brother-in-law I wanted. And I was pretty sure he was the husband Carly wanted. So what was the problem with these two lately? Sometimes they seemed thrilled to be together; other times they got upset with each other at the drop of a hat.

"So who do you think killed J.D. Finley?" I asked, more to break the silence than any real hope that my three traveling companions would know.

Nobody spoke for at least thirty seconds, then Elliott's death grip on the steering wheel slowly relaxed. "Well, I don't really know any of these folks very well. Lisa took a few lessons at the country club, and she struck me as a lady who knew what she wanted and how to get it." He kept his eyes on the road.

Carly glanced toward him. "That doesn't mean she'd kill someone, though. Lots of folks look out for number one. And they don't kill whoever gets in their way."

Oh boy. To think I'd been trying to smooth things over. "You're both right," I said. "And the suspect list is pretty sparsely populated. The only other person I've thought of so far is Larry."

"Who's Larry?" Elliott asked.

I told them about Larry and the way he had acted when he nearly ran me down at the gym. And how he'd yelled at Lisa.

"Sounds like a rough character," Elliott agreed. "And you think his motive would be jealousy? If he did it, I mean."

"I guess so. If we knew the motive, I think we could figure out who did it." I glanced at Carly. "Unless it was a stranger like Carly hopes."

He nodded. "I agree with Carly. I don't like the thought of someone from Lake View being a cold-blooded killer."

I smiled at Alex. Finally, I'd found something they agreed on. He gave me a discreet thumbs-up.

At Sam's Club, Alex and I left Elliott and Carly to gather restaurant supplies while we wandered among the books and CDs. Before too long, Alex met a fellow lawyer, and they were soon engrossed in the intricacies of trout fishing: fly fishing versus live bait.

I listened for a while, but finally my attention span reached its limit.

"I'm going to go help Carly," I whispered and received an absent nod in response. "I'll call when we're done."

My stomach was growling, and I figured the sooner we got supplies taken care of, the sooner we could eat. A fajita was calling my name. I headed toward the back and had flipped my phone open to call Carly when I heard her voice, strangely agitated. I closed the phone but could still hear her loud and clear. Apparently from the next aisle.

"I can't help it, Elliott. I don't think it's the right thing to do."

"You think keeping secrets is the right thing? Come on, Carly. I think you're avoiding the issue. Your family is so close. How will they feel when you finally tell them? Someone, probably Jenna, will want to know when you found out. Then what?"

9

Barkin' Up The Wrong Tree

I stayed out of sight but waited for my sister to answer. What was going on?

"I think I know my family better than you," Carly answered tartly.

"Fine." Elliott sounded more resigned than angry.

My curiosity meter was on full alert. Secrets? From the family? Did this have to do with the whole Travis situation? Or was there something else? And what was that "probably Jenna" crack about? I retraced my steps to Alex. I'd lost my desire to help gather supplies, as well as my appetite.

I was thankful Alex was alone when I found him. I quietly told him what I'd heard.

He put his arm around me, and I stood for a few seconds listening to his steady heartbeat. "I know it's hard," he said softly. "But maybe this is something personal between the two of them. And that's really a good thing, isn't it? You *are* hoping that they're getting serious, right?"

"You mean like maybe they're about to get engaged and she isn't ready to tell us yet?"

He shrugged. "I don't know if that's it or not. But she'll tell you when she gets ready."

I nodded. "How do you do that?"

He raised an eyebrow. "What?"

"Make me feel better."

His dimple flashed. "It's a gift. Now let's find the secret-keeping couple and go eat."

I kissed him on the cheek. "Thanks."

"Anytime."

We met Elliott and Carly rolling two loaded carts toward the checkout. "Did you buy out the store?" Alex called, and they laughed. Any awkwardness I felt vanished. Alex was right. Carly would tell me when she was ready.

At the Mexican restaurant, my appetite returned with a vengeance. The swarthy young waiter brought chips and white cheese dip then took our order. He repeated each thing we said as he wrote it down and waited for a nod.

361

"He wants to be sure he gets it right, doesn't he?" I said after he left. As a newly minted waitress, I couldn't imagine how hard it must be to have a language barrier in addition to all of the other difficulties of the job.

"That reminds me of Vini," I said.

Carly nodded. "Speaking of Vini," she drawled, "I wonder if he has problems with his roommates or something. He acts like he never wants to go home."

"Yeah, I've noticed that, too. But he does a really good job," I said.

"I think because English isn't his native language, he pays close attention to all his orders. He makes fewer mistakes than. . ." She put her hand over her mouth and looked at me.

"What?" I looked right back. "I *know* you don't mean me."

"Of course I don't," Carly said. "I just realized it might be unprofessional to discuss my employees."

"So, who *do* you want to discuss?" Alex asked, and we all laughed.

I cleared my throat. "We could talk about employers."

"Now wait a minute," Carly drawled.

"I mean ex-employers, silly. I was just going to say that even though I'm sorry that it took Lisa getting in trouble to do it, I'm relieved that I've kind of made peace with Bob."

"Funny you should mention Bob and peace in the same sentence." Elliott dipped a chip in the cheese dip.

I frowned. "Why?"

He shrugged. "Just that I heard something weird out on the links this week." He stuck the chip in his mouth.

"About Bob?" Alex said.

Elliott nodded then chewed the chip for what seemed like forever. Maybe I was wrong about him being the perfect guy for Carly. Didn't he know I was dying of curiosity over here?

He swallowed. Finally. "I heard he and Wilma were full-fledged hippies back in the day. You know, peace, love, flower power. All that stuff."

"Like when they were teenagers?" Carly asked.

Elliott shook his head. "I honestly just heard bits and pieces, but I think it was more recent than that. Maybe when they were our age."

"So they were old hippies," Alex murmured.

"Speak for yourself," Carly and I said at the same time. We grinned.

"Wonder what changed him?" I mused.

Elliott took a drink. "From what I heard, something big."

"What?" Carly pushed a jalapeño over to the side of her plate. "He got arrested for smoking pot?"

"I really don't know. More than one group of older men have alluded to it during golf games this week for some reason. But still, all I know is that apparently something bad happened out at Bob's place back then. And whatever it was, it put him on the straight and narrow." Elliott took the napkin off his lap and laid it beside his plate.

"I wonder why people are talking about that now," Carly said.

"Because Lisa's a suspect in a murder?" I suggested.

"Everything comes back to the murder with you, doesn't it, water girl?" Alex teased.

❖

"I'm so glad you're feeling better, Mrs. Hanley." I hugged the tiny elderly woman gently. "We've missed you the last couple of weeks."

"It's good to be here." She beamed up at me. "When you're ninety-six, it's good to be anywhere." She laughed as much as I did over her joke. As I moved aside so others could welcome our congregation's oldest member back, I scanned the crowd for Alex.

Finally, I spotted him in the corner, in an earnest discussion with Mr. Foshee, the elder who taught Sunday morning Bible class. I sent up a silent but fervent prayer of thanks that the man I loved loved God.

"Jenna?" Mama appeared beside me. "You and Alex are coming to lunch, aren't you?"

My brows drew together, and I nodded. Didn't we always? Sunday afternoon at Stafford Cabins was a tradition since Carly and I'd moved back to town. I usually contributed green beans or corn, and Carly always brought some elaborate recipe she'd whipped up in her spare time.

"I've got a roast in the oven, but I don't have a salad. Since Carly's not going to be there, do you want to bring green beans *and* corn?"

"Sure I will. But what do you mean Carly's not going to be there?" Alex and I had playfully spent the ride to church guessing what culinary delight Carly might have cooked up for lunch today.

"Didn't she tell you?"

"I'm pretty sure she didn't." I'd been overworked and tired lately, but my mind hadn't quite gone on vacation yet.

Mama smiled. "I guess if she had, you'd have known. She and Elliott are eating together today. But the kids are coming to the house. Zac's taking them home to change out of church clothes and then bringing them on."

"She and Elliott? Alone? This sounds serious. Is it? What exactly did she tell you?" Maybe Carly had finally decided to act on the fact that Elliott was the man of her dreams.

"Jenna, please remember what curiosity did to the cat." Honestly, sometimes Mama treated me as if I were the twins' age. "Besides, she didn't say much. Just that she was eating with Elliott today because they had some things to discuss, and that Zac would bring the girls and come for lunch and basketball as usual. Now you know as much as I do."

"How did she look?"

Mama glanced around the auditorium then back at me with a frown. "What do you mean, 'How did she look?' She looked normal."

"Did she seem excited? Nervous? Happy? Or all of the above?"

"Jenna, you're a darling girl, and I love you very much, but you're slightly batty sometimes. Actually, she told me over the phone last night. But when she slipped into church a few minutes late this morning, she looked normal. That's the best I can do."

"I inherited my battiness from someone," I said with a cheeky grin. "Either I got it from you or you married a batty man. Take your choice." I patted her shoulder.

Without cracking a smile, she retorted, "You got it from your dad's great-uncle Jed. He was crazy as a Bessie bug."

I stared at her, and she started laughing. I joined her. The origin of my "battiness" might be in question. But there was no doubt where I got my sense of humor.

❖

"Carly? It's Jenna. Call me when you get a chance." I hated leaving a message, but I was dying of curiosity. Me and the cat. I patted Neuro, who stretched and yawned before returning to licking her paw.

Okay. Just me.

The phone rang, and I snatched it up. "Hello?"

"Jenna? What's wrong?" Carly sounded groggy as if she'd just awakened. I glanced at the clock. Nope. It was ten o'clock on Sunday night. Not too late to call.

"Nothing's wrong. At least, nothing's wrong with me. Is something wrong with you?" I was babbling. "I mean, we missed you at lunch. Mama said you were with Elliott." Suggestive pause.

Silence on the other end of the line.

"Is he still there?"

"No."

"You want to talk?" Sometimes being blunt is the only way to find out what you want to know.

Silence. Then a hesitant, "If you do."

"I can be at your house in"—I decided I was decent in my sweats and a T-shirt—"ten minutes." Who cared how I looked? My sister might have just gotten engaged. I had to know.

"Why?" Carly sounded bewildered.

"So you can tell me whatever it is you can't tell me on the phone."

"Jenna, what in the world is wrong with you? You're acting as crazy as—"

"Daddy's great-uncle Jed, I know. Mama's already told me."

"I must be dreaming." Carly had progressed—or regressed—from bewildered to completely befuddled. However, when she opened the door for me ten minutes later, she looked so normal that I had second thoughts about my engagement theory.

"Let's keep it low. The kids have school tomorrow, you know. They need their sleep. Besides. . ." She glanced around as if expecting a twin to pop up from behind the couch. "I don't want them to know about this right now."

That concerned face was not the face of a newly engaged woman. "Car, what's going on?"

She looked over her shoulder at the kids' rooms. "I can't really talk about it."

Suddenly, I remembered our conversation the day we played checkers on the porch. "Is this about Travis?" I mouthed.

She nodded and turned away. "But I don't know anything for sure. I should know everything in a few days, and I'll tell you then."

I knew she wouldn't lie to me, so no doubt she didn't know anything *for sure*. But the conversation I'd overheard on our trip to Jonesboro told me that she knew something she wasn't telling me. And unless I was mistaken, her eyes were red-rimmed. Short of whining and begging her to tell me, I had no choice but to give her a hug. "Fine. Tell me when you find out. . .for sure."

"I will," she said and guided me smoothly to the door. No doubt before I lost the tenuous hold I had on my curiosity.

◆

"Pass the popcorn." I nudged Alex. We were watching one of my favorite movies, *Princess Bride*.

"As you wish." Alex handed me the nearly empty bowl.

I elbowed him in the ribs. "Oh, that was cute." The movie had just come to the part where Grandpa explained that every time Westley said, "As you wish," to Buttercup, what he really meant was "I love you."

"I really do love you. You know that, don't you?" Alex turned toward me.

"If you really loved me, you would tell your boss that you're allergic to sunshine and beaches," I teased. He was leaving for a conference in Miami, and we were enjoying a last evening together before his departure the next morning.

Just as he leaned in for a kiss, the doorbell rang.

I grinned. "It's probably Zac. He said he'd try and come by and help me download some songs to my new phone."

"He can wait," Alex said softly and dropped a gentle kiss on my lips. Then he pushed to his feet. "I'll get the door, and you can refill the popcorn bowl."

"As you wish." I grinned over my shoulder at him as I headed to the kitchen. I stuck a bag in the microwave and turned it on. Over the popping I could hear a female voice interspersed with Alex's deeper male one. Not Zac, then.

Alex came into the kitchen, followed by Gail. Her eyes were swollen, and her face was red and splotchy.

"Oh no. What's wrong?" I took the bag from the oven. "Was someone else murdered?"

She shook her head.

"I'll take Mr Persi out for a walk while you and Gail visit," Alex offered. Another thing I loved about Alex. He wasn't nosy like me.

"As you wish." I smiled at him. From the corner of my eye, I noticed Gail's puzzled expression. But it vanished immediately as tears came into her eyes.

"Oh, Jenna, I'm sorry to just drop by like this, but I didn't know what else to do." She pulled a paper towel from the holder on the counter and rubbed her face. "Lisa told the police that she was at work on Friday night during the time of the murder." She started crying. "But she wasn't. And she told me I'd get fired if I told the truth."

"Here, Gail." I motioned to a chair at the table. "Sit right here and let me get you some tea." I poured her tea and set the glass in front of her. "Where was she?" I shook the bag of popcorn into the bowl and offered it to her.

"I don't know. She left early without saying where she was going. She does it all the time. Well, you know how she is, Jenna." Gail absently took a piece of the popcorn. "She never stays as long as she's supposed to."

"Right. Nor does she do the work she should do while she's there." I sat down beside Gail. "So she threatened to fire you if you said she wasn't there?"

She nodded. "I just don't know what to do. I need that job, and besides, without you there, the place would really fall apart if I left, too." Tears rolled down her face.

"We have to tell Bob." I reached for my cell phone. "Maybe he can get Lisa to tell the truth. And I know he won't fire you." I hit the arrow button down to the Bs. I raised my eyebrows, and Gail nodded.

When Bob answered, I explained what Lisa had done.

"I just can't believe she did that. Are you sure?" Poor Bob. He just didn't want to face the truth about his princess.

"I'm sure."

"This is going to look really bad for Lisa, isn't it?" He was the master of understatement. "What should we do?"

"Look, the only thing you can do is convince Lisa to go see John. Have her tell him she was scared and so she lied." I glanced over at Gail to see if she agreed. She nodded. "If Gail has to tell them, it will be even worse for Lisa. Also, she needs to tell them where she was."

Bob agreed, and we hung up. Gail stood and pushed her chair back to the table. "I feel so much better now. Thanks, Jenna."

I walked her to the door. "Don't worry, Gail. Bob and Lisa will go tomorrow to talk to John."

I heard the back door shut and knew Alex was back inside with Mr. Persi. Even though he didn't ask, I told him what Gail had said and Bob's response. When I finished, I frowned. "I wonder where she really was, though."

"Of course you do, honey. I'm sure the police will find out." Alex guided me back toward the living room. "Let's finish the movie."

After Alex left, I called and told Carly about Lisa's false alibi. "Where do you think Lisa was?" she wondered aloud.

"I think we need to find out. Don't you?"

"I'd like to tell you that you need to mind your own business, but I don't think that'll happen. And, after all, the murder did happen on my property. Let's just try and stay safe this time, okay?"

"Of course." It's not like I wanted to be face-to-face with a murderer. Again.

10

If It Ain't Your Tail, Don't Wag It.

Just like every day since the murder, I parked in the back of the diner parking lot as far away from the Dumpster as I could. I always had the creepy feeling that if I looked behind the Dumpster, I would see that little sports car. With a dead man in the front seat. I hurried inside, trying not to glance in that direction.

But just like every day, the questions ran through my head. Who killed J.D. Finley and why? Why behind a Dumpster? I could think of plenty of answers for the first question, but I couldn't imagine why J.D. was parked behind the Dumpster at the diner.

As soon as I opened the door, the delicious scent of apples and cinnamon made my mouth water. Alice was expertly cutting the edges off the top crust of an apple pie. She opened the oven door and put the scallop-edged pie in with several others already turning golden brown.

As I headed into the dining room, I snagged an apron off the hook and tied it around my waist. I grabbed an order pad off the shelf, stuck a couple of pens in my pocket, then looked around at the many empty tables scattered throughout the diner. I waved at John, sitting in a booth alone and in uniform. "We don't seem quite as full today as we have been."

"It's Tuesday." Debbie offered no other explanation.

"And that means. . ." That people aren't hungry? Everyone runs home for lunch? What?

She left me waiting while she took a piece of fresh apple pie over to John. When she came back, she said, "Oh, I figured you knew. A couple of the fast-food places have big Tuesday specials. This is usually our slowest day."

Seeing John gave me an idea. I could get Amelia off my back and use some easy questions about Ricky to get a conversation going with John. Then I would segue neatly into how the murder investigation was going. "Hey, I'm going to take a quick break."

Her brows drew together, and I could see she was thinking about the fact that I'd just arrived, but she shrugged. "Whatev."

I slid into the booth across from the police chief. "We need to talk."

He froze with a bite halfway to his mouth. "Look, Jenna, if this is about the murder, legally I can't tell you anything. When are you going to understand that?"

"This is your lucky day, then. Because my question has nothing to do with the murder."

He looked skeptical but put the bite in his mouth. "What?" he said as he chewed.

"It's about Ricky. . ."

"Ricky? My officer Ricky?"

I nodded. "Okay, I might as well just explain it. Amelia asked me to ask around about Ricky and see what people know about him."

John's face grew alarmingly red, and for a minute I was afraid I was going to have to do the Heimlich maneuver.

"Because of Tiffany, you know," I said hurriedly. "I wouldn't have agreed, but I owe her a favor."

He snorted. "The first lady isn't ever going to think anyone is good enough for her daughter."

"I know that." I was a little ashamed that I'd even agreed to ask, but I had. So I needed to find out something. "Maybe you could tell me something that would reassure her."

"I think Ricky's a good officer and a stand-up guy. He knows what he's doing and doesn't mind doing it. We were shorthanded when he applied. Frankly, he was an answer to a prayer."

I nodded. "Anything else?"

He leaned forward. "Yes."

"What?" I leaned forward, too.

"I thought this pie was free. I didn't know I was going to have to answer a question for every bite."

I tossed my hair over my shoulder and gave him a mock glare. "Fine. Enjoy your pie." I slid to my feet. John couldn't even answer my questions without getting smart when they had nothing to do with the murder. No way was I going to get any pertinent information from him about J.D. Might as well not even ask.

I walked back into the kitchen to cool off. Carly turned from where she was dishing up chicken and dumplings. "What's wrong?"

"John. He won't cut me any slack."

She turned back to the stove. "In other words, he won't give you any information."

"Basically. Anyway, I'm officially going to work now. While I was talking to John, I noticed people are starting to come in."

She grinned. "Slowly but surely we're overcoming the slow Tuesday curse."

When I walked back into the dining room, more than half the tables were full. The word about Carly's cooking was spreading. I quickly got into the rhythm of taking orders and delivering plates heaped with today's specials.

I mentally congratulated myself on doing such a good job. So far I hadn't dropped anything or switched any orders. Although I did fumble a plate when I glanced over toward Vini's section where Harvey had seated Bob and Wilma. I wasn't sure what the etiquette was when seeing your ex-boss after you'd just found out he'd had an unusual past. Knowing he'd been a hippie in another life, I could easily envision him with a long braid and headband, à la Willie Nelson. I resisted the urge to flash him and Wilma a peace sign.

Just as I made up my mind to go over and say hello, Bob jumped up and shook his finger in Vini's face. I couldn't hear the words, but even from a distance it was obvious this wasn't a friendly conversation.

I hurried over just as Vini backed up a couple of steps, his dark eyes wide in his ashen face. "I did not kill him. Why would you say that?" By now people at other tables were craning their necks to see what was going on. I stepped between them.

"Hi, Bob." I nodded toward Wilma. "And Wilma." She gave me a weak smile and waggled her fingers toward me. "Something wrong?" I turned toward Vini. "Why don't you go on and put their order in?" I pointed toward his order pad. "Maybe you can discuss this after they finish eating and there aren't quite so many people here."

Bob looked around the crowded room, his face reddening. He sat down quickly. Vini headed toward the kitchen.

"Is Lisa doing any better?"

"At least she isn't in jail." Wilma answered for Bob, who had his head down. "But now the police just won't leave her alone." She looked over toward the table where Seth and Ricky were enjoying their free pie after their lunch. "They act like they think *she* killed J.D."

"But she didn't!" Bob jerked his head up and slapped his hand on the table. "Vini was the one who had a big fight with him. If he lets my little girl take the rap for something he did, I'll. . .I'll. . ."

"Bob. Stop." Wilma put her hand over his. "Jenna knows Lisa didn't kill him. And if Vini did, well, John or those other policemen will find out."

"So why would you think Vini did it?" I couldn't imagine the soft-spoken foreign student killing anyone. Or even getting angry with anyone.

"You know they worked together at the club. J.D. caught him stealing from the cash register, and Lisa fired him."

"Lisa fired Vini for stealing?" Why wouldn't Gail have told me that?

"Yes." Bob worried the napkin wrapped around his silverware. "So maybe Vini hated him." He glanced up at me. "And maybe he hates Lisa, too." He sounded shocked at the thought that anyone could hate his darling daughter.

"Now, Bob." Wilma patted Bob's hand. "Everyone loves Lisa." I guess Mama was right when she said there's no love like a mother's love.

He flashed his wife a look that said a father's love was just as strong, but maybe not quite so blind. "Anyway, just because it was her gun, they think she did it." He shook his head. "She told the police someone stole her gun a few days before the murder, but they act like they don't believe her." He took out each piece of his silverware and laid it on the table as if his hands couldn't keep still.

"Well, she doesn't know exactly when it was stolen, does she?" I asked.

He frowned. "She kept it at work in the desk drawer. It's not like she pulled it out all the time." His eyes brightened. "Maybe Vini stole it when he took the money."

"Do you know anyone who didn't like J.D? Anyone besides Vini who had had an argument with him?" I just couldn't believe Vini would kill anyone, but if I had learned anything, it was that you can't tell a murderer by the way he looks. Or acts.

"Well." Bob and Wilma exchanged a look. "Harvey. . ." He froze.

"Harvey? Harvey what?"

Wilma cleared her throat and looked over my shoulder.

I glanced back. Harvey was walking up behind me. "Hey, Harvey, what's up?" I slid my pad and pen into my pocket and turned to face him.

"Jenna, aren't you supposed to be working? This isn't even one of your tables. People are starting to complain." His glare included me and Bob. "We've always prided ourselves on good service. I'd hate to think that now that we've sold, that's all a thing of the past."

"Oh my goodness." I'd let my curiosity get me in trouble. Again. And after I had just been bragging to myself about how good I was doing. "Excuse me, y'all. I'll go get your food and then get back to my tables."

As I walked away, Harvey muttered, "Hippie troublemaker." I glanced back at him, but he was stomping away. I remembered what I'd told Elliott on our trip to Jonesboro. It really was odd that suddenly everyone was talking about Bob's flower-child past.

I found Vini, who looked relieved when I suggested that he trade Bob and Wilma's table for one of mine.

Later, when I laid the ticket on Bob's table and turned to go, Bob touched my arm. "Jenna, I know you're helping your sister out here, but do you think there is any way you could work some at the club?" His humble tone touched my heart. "Lisa's so upset that she can't really do much work."

What was her excuse before? I bit my tongue to keep the words from coming out. Mama always told me you shouldn't kick a man when he's down.

And Bob was so down, he was practically subterranean.

"To be honest," Wilma said softly, "Lisa's so sad and upset that she's taken to her bed."

Well, then. If Lisa wasn't going to be at the club pretending to work, I'd be glad to help out. "Carly just hired a new waitress, so I was planning to cut back on my hours here anyway, Bob." I stuck my pad in my apron pocket. "I can work if you need me. I'll stop by tomorrow and pick up a key."

Carly was just grabbing her keys to head out the door when I finished the noon shift. As we walked out together, I told her about Bob asking me to work.

"Would you mind if I cut my hours back so I can help Bob out?" I glanced over at her. "Be honest."

"No, of course not. I don't blame you at all." She stopped beside her car. "But are you sure you're not letting your sympathy put you back in a bad position?"

I shrugged. "I'm not sure, but I just feel so sorry for them." I stopped. "You know I've really enjoyed working at the diner. More than I ever thought I would." I opted for total honesty. "But I guess I didn't realize how much I'd miss the club."

"I understand. Of course you miss it."

"By the way. . ." I glanced around to make sure no one could overhear me. "I found something else out today that I need to tell you."

"What?" She looked around the crowded parking lot.

I lowered my voice. "Remember the other day when Vini was talking about how broke he was and how much it cost for his school?"

She nodded.

"Well, today Bob said that Lisa fired Vini for stealing from the cash register at the club."

Carly gasped. "I can't believe that." She shook her head. "He seems so trustworthy. Are you sure this isn't another of Lisa's 'stories'?"

"I'll ask Gail if she knows what happened. If anyone would know, she would."

"Let me know what she says."

❖

Dave, the personal trainer and weight room manager, was working the desk when I walked into the health club. When he said Gail didn't come in until three, I headed back to the pool room. After some relaxing laps, I was about to head for the sauna when the steamed-up glass doors opened and Gail walked in.

"Hey, girl, Dave said you're looking for me."

"Guilty as charged." I grabbed a couple of towels and wrapped one around my hair and another around my body. "Do you have a minute to talk?"

She nodded. "Sure. My shift doesn't start for another ten minutes. What's on your mind?"

I sat down in a white deck chair and waved her to the one beside it. Déjà vu. Just call me Amelia. I hoped I hadn't motioned Gail as imperiously as Amelia had me a few days ago.

When we were seated, I smiled at her. "I need to talk to you about Vini."

Her eyes widened. "Why? What about him?" she asked. She looked so alarmed that I faltered. Had I been wrong about Vini?

"Bob mentioned that he was fired from the club for stealing. Is that right?"

She relaxed in her chair and snorted. "That's the excuse Lisa gave. But it isn't true."

"Can you tell me what happened?"

"Not to speak ill of the dead or anything, but J.D. was a jerk. And Lisa just followed him around like a puppy dog. I know it made Bob sick to watch them."

"What do you mean? I thought Bob liked him."

"Ha. No way. Bob couldn't stand him. Actually, that's what started the whole thing with Vini. I heard Bob tell Lisa that since membership enrollment was down, we'd have to let someone go." She raised an eyebrow at me. "When you left, so did members."

I felt my cheeks grow hot at the implied praise. No doubt the mass exodus of members was more because of Lisa's inept management than because of the absence of my amazing management skills. "Go ahead."

"Anyway, he told her to get rid of one employee. No matter what Bob intended, he should have known she wouldn't fire her man. So she and J.D. cooked up this little story to get Vini fired."

"How do you know it isn't true?"

"I counted the cash in the register that night. Then I checked with the bank to see how much the deposit was. Every penny was deposited."

"Wow. So do you think they wanted to get rid of Vini specifically? Or just any employee so J.D. could stay on?"

"I think they picked on Vini because they knew he wouldn't fight them on it. Plus, he hadn't been here as long as the rest of us. I'm so glad you hired him at the diner."

"Me, too. So you weren't a fan of J.D.'s?"

"Nope. He and Bob had some kind of history, too. Did you know that?"

"No. What kind of history?"

"I'm not sure. I just heard him say something about telling Lisa about 'our shared past.' I was under the impression that he may have been holding something over Bob's head." She shrugged. "You know, threatening Bob. But I can't imagine why."

"Me either." But I was certainly going to find out.

When she left, I retired to the sauna. In the steamy quietness, I sat for a minute and mulled over the life and death of J.D. Finley. When he drove to the Dumpster, did he have death on his mind? Did he have an appointment with a murderer? Or had it been a surprise attack?

I rolled up a towel for a pillow and stretched out on my back on the hot wooden bench. Closing my eyes, I worked my way down my mental suspect list. Even though Lisa owned the murder weapon, why would she have done it? Had J.D. proven hard to shake as a boyfriend? That seemed a flimsy excuse for murder. More in keeping with Lisa's personality would be if J.D. were the one trying to get out of the relationship. I could see her, in a fit of anger, using her toy gun to take care of the problem. But I couldn't see her keeping it to herself and playing the innocent so well. She really didn't act guilty at all. What if someone really had stolen her gun? The more I thought about it, the more likely that seemed.

And who better than her husband, who seemed like a raving maniac when I'd seen him at the club the other day. And he definitely knew where the gun was. Any man who would beat his wife might also kill her lover. How closely were the police looking at Larry?

My eyes fluttered as I suddenly remembered what Gail had just told me about Bob. It sounded like my ex-boss had motives of his own for getting rid of J.D. The only thing that didn't add up there was him letting his precious princess take the fall.

I sat up and punched my rolled-up towel a couple of times to fluff it again and stretched back out. I wasn't having much luck with the relaxing part of this little sauna visit.

So many people were acting weird. Debbie, even Carly—not that I thought hers had anything to do with the murder—and of course, Vini. He seemed flustered so much of the time, and often he acted like he didn't want to leave the diner. I'm not sure what was wrong about that, but it just felt odd.

On the other hand, he'd hardly had the opportunity to commit murder unless he'd excused himself to go to the bathroom and slipped out back, shot J.D., then slipped in to work without anyone noticing. Which was possible, yes. But probable, no.

And what about motive? He obviously resented J.D. getting him fired, but was the soft-spoken, mild-mannered student capable of cold-blooded murder? And framing Lisa for his actions? I didn't think so. And since I'd had a hard time believing he would steal, and from what Gail said, I was right, I tended to go with my gut feeling about Vini.

LETTIN' THE CAT OUT OF THE BAG
IS A LOT EASIER'N PUTTIN' IT BACK IN

losing time. Finally. Carly had sent Debbie and Susan home already, and Vini and I were gathering the last of the garbage. Since the night Vini told Carly how badly he needed hours—and proven how well he could clean the men's bathroom—he'd helped clean up.

"You know my new rule. I do not, under any circumstances, take out the garbage." I twisted the tie and set the full bag by the door. "Just let me close this other bag, and you can carry them both out."

As I pulled the black bag out of the metal can, I noticed a flash of light. It almost looked like a flashlight had come on inside the bag. I donned some heavy cleaning gloves from under the sink and stuck my hand in to fish it out. When I reached for it, I saw it was my cell phone. It must have fallen out of my apron pocket when I was cleaning and landed in one of the garbage cans. I was thankful that when the side buttons get bumped, it lights up. Otherwise I'd have lost it forever. I wiped it off with a paper towel.

"What do you think? Some of these are pretty sturdy." I showed it to Carly. "Even though it looks like it's on, I don't want to mess with it while it's so nasty. Do you think it will still work after I take it apart and clean it off? I was just learning how to use it."

"Not to mention all that music Zac said he put on it for you." Carly hung her dish towel on the towel rack. "It might be worth cleaning it and trying it out."

Vini picked up the bags and headed out the back door while I took the back off the phone and cleaned the outside of it with a damp paper towel. The inside still looked good as new. I put the battery back in, hit the power button, and was rewarded with the little orange man doing cartwheels across the screen. "Yea! It still works."

I hit the envelope for text messages to see if Alex had messaged me while I was at work. The first received message said, "Waiting for you out back."

"How in the world could he be waiting for me out back?" I held up the phone where Carly could read the message. "His plane left this morning."

"No idea." She shrugged. It hit us both at the same time. The last time someone was waiting out back. . . Was a murderer waiting for me out back? But why would he warn me?

We both jumped up. "Vini!" we screamed in unison. I ran toward the back door with Carly on my heels. We screeched to a halt at the door and looked at each other. Would we find his body on the ground behind the diner?

I pulled the door open and peeked out. "Vini? Are you okay?" No answer. Carly gave me a little shove.

I held on to her sleeve and dragged her out on the back porch with me. "Vini!" I yelled louder. "Where are you?"

Vini strolled up from the side of the diner. "What is wrong, Jenna? You sound upset."

"Where were you? I was worried that something may have happened to you." My voice trembled.

"I went to get my phone out of my van. I forgot it there." He held up a cell phone. "I was going to call Gail."

"Oh." While the two of them were with me, I felt brave enough to look all around the back alley that adjoined the diner parking lot—from the safety of the back porch, of course. As far as I could see, there wasn't a car or another human in sight.

Vini walked into the diner ahead of us. I tugged on Carly's sleeve. "I don't think this is my phone."

"Why?"

I told her quickly about the phone mix-up with Debbie when we were remodeling. As soon as we got back into the light, I checked the outbox. There were several sent messages. None looked familiar. I occasionally sent texts, but I hadn't sent these. The most recent ones said, "Did you leave?" and "Why won't you answer?" There were several that sounded about the same. I hit the button to bring up the address book. Only one number. Very strange. It was listed as "Me." The same thing the screen had said when I'd used her phone the last time I'd gotten it by mistake—"Connected to Me."

I waited until we finished up and Vini was in the break room gathering his things, then I showed the phone to Carly. "You think I should take it to her tonight?"

"No. She'll be here tomorrow." She carefully locked the front door. "Aren't you working the noon shift?"

I nodded.

"Well, just give it to her then."

"See you both tomorrow," Vini called as he left.

Out in the parking lot, I stopped. "Car? Who do you think was waiting?"

"What?" She hit the remote and opened her van door. "See you tomorrow."

"Wait." I put out a hand to restrain her. "Who was waiting for Debbie in the back?"

"The only person in the back was—" A look of comprehension flooded her face. "You think J.D. was waiting for Debbie? But why? I mean, he and Lisa were dating."

"That would explain why he was behind the Dumpster. He was cheating on Lisa with Debbie."

Carly frowned. "That's so cliché. Your boyfriend cheating with your best friend."

"Yeah. I hate to think that Debbie was doing that."

She shrugged. "It happens a lot, though. Now that I think about it, things are cliché because they're common. And as far as I know, J.D. and Lisa were just dating, not engaged."

"Yeah, but Lisa doesn't strike me as one who would take it so well if the man she was dating wanted to date someone else. I wonder if she knew. If she did, would she be mad enough to—" I couldn't finish the thought. Murder is such an ugly word.

"Didn't Lisa meet J.D. when she went with Debbie to his grandmother's funeral? Maybe Debbie felt like he belonged to her and Lisa just horned in. You know, maybe she felt justified. Or maybe there was nothing going on. He could've had a perfectly innocent reason to text that to Debbie."

"Yeah? Name one."

"Well. . ." She thought a minute then rose to the challenge. "Maybe he and Debbie were planning a surprise party for Lisa. Or maybe he wanted Debbie's advice about a gift he was buying for Lisa. Or maybe he was going to ask Debbie about Lisa's husband, or. . ."

"Okay, I get it." I slapped her arm lightly. "I think we should take this to Debbie tonight and find out what it's all about."

"Jen, I'm worn out. I have three kids waiting at home. She can get it tomorrow. The messages will still be there. We can ask her then."

"We'll be so busy we won't have time. Besides, I want to know tonight."

"That's you to the bone. I've gotta know, and I've gotta know now." She grinned at me, but it was a tired grin. "I'm sorry. I just can't go tonight." She yawned widely, covering her mouth with her hand. "I'm nearly dead on my feet."

"No prob. You run on home and get some rest. You look beat."

As she drove off, I considered my options—wait until tomorrow or run by Debbie's tonight. Easy choice.

As I pulled into Debbie's driveway, a light in the living room went off. I parked and walked onto the front porch, clutching the phone. The motion light beside the front door came on, and I jumped then snickered at my nervousness.

I pushed the doorbell button. No response. Since I hadn't actually heard a chime, I decided the bell might be broken. I knocked. And waited. If I hadn't seen the light go off as I drove up, I would have thought nobody was home. Instead, I felt sure that Debbie just didn't want to see anyone. I squinted at the bright porch light shining in my face and glanced down at the phone in my hand.

Didn't want to see anyone?

Or me, in particular?

◆

The conversation at every table was the same. Just one time today I would like to take an order or deliver food to someone who was talking about something besides whether or not the police were going to arrest Lisa. Anything else would do. I'd even settle for hearing about a NASCAR race. Anything but the possibility of poor Lisa going to jail. But that didn't keep me from listening and trying to sift the truth from gossip.

When Harvey sat Marge and Tiffany at a table in my section, I hurried over to take their order. On the way back to the kitchen, a teen was entertaining his buddies. "I heard she was a serial killer and killed at least five people."

At another table I heard an older woman talking about "all those drugs they were using." As far as I knew, Lisa was not a drug user. But what about J.D.? And I didn't catch everything the woman with her said, but it was something about "the sins of the fathers." I wondered whose father she was referring to but couldn't figure out a way to ask her without appearing nosy. Okay, nosier than usual.

A few minutes later, I set Marge's salad down on the table. As I handed Tiffany her salad, I thought about the fact that she had ordered a salad when she was with Marge instead of the "fat-filled" burger she had ordered when she was with her mother. "I'm really worried about Lisa. Do you know if they're going to arrest her?"

Marge glanced up at me. "I've heard several rumors, Jenna. Hopefully we'll get a police report in time to put the truth in the paper." She glanced at Tiffany. "But one of our sources said they found a towel with the victim's blood on it in her car."

A bloody towel in Lisa's car? How had I not found out about this? I tried to cover my dismay. "Did either of you know him? J.D.?" I set their salad dressings on the table. "I heard he was from here originally."

"I knew his grandmother pretty well. And of course I remember all the scandal during his trial."

"Trial?" My voice rose, and a few people glanced toward us. Oh well, anyone who overheard probably just thought I was talking about Lisa's future like everyone else. "Why did he have a trial?"

"I guess you were too young to remember." She paused and tapped her chin thoughtfully. "Well, maybe you weren't even born yet. I've lost track of the years, but it happened a long time ago." She settled her napkin in her lap. "I don't think he served any time." Again she paused. "Hmm. Maybe just probation since he was a minor." If this were anyone but Marge, I would think she was drawing this out on purpose to frustrate me.

"So what'd he do?" Mama was right. Too much curiosity could drive you crazy.

She glanced around the diner. "This isn't the best place to discuss it." She lowered her voice. "You can ask your mother or dad later. I'm sure they remember."

They probably did remember, but Mama had distinctly asked me not to get involved in this investigation. So asking them was out of the question.

Just as I opened my mouth to reply, I heard a loud crash behind me. I spun around. Debbie stood with her hand to her mouth. Broken plates and the remains of more than one daily special littered the floor. Except for the part that was spread down the front of Grimmett and one of his friends.

"Excuse me, ladies. I think I'm needed over there." I snatched a stack of napkins on my way over to the mess. Debbie's lips were trembling, and tears welled in her eyes as she tried to wipe chicken and dressing off Grimmett's shirt. He pushed her hands away and took a napkin from me and handed one to his friend. Debbie stepped back.

Alice hurried out of the kitchen with two damp towels. She handed one to Debbie, who took it and started wiping at the food. Alice bent down beside her and helped. Vini rushed over with a tray, and he and I picked up the broken plates.

Grimmett and his equally unlucky friend got most of the food off their shirts. He turned back to his buddies as if we weren't there. "So like I was saying. . .I heard she caught him in that little sports car with another woman and shot him."

Vini and I exchanged a skeptical look as we finished up cleaning. Right. Parked behind the Dumpster with his secret love. How romantic. And even if he were, where was this mysterious other woman when I found the body?

Grimmett must have had the same thought. He glanced down at me. "Is that true? Since you found the body, you oughta know."

I rose to my feet and dusted my hands off over the tray. "I didn't see anyone else."

"I'm going to try and clean some of this off my apron." Debbie's tears had dried some, but she was still ashen. "Can you cover my tables for a few minutes?"

I looked around the crowded dining room. "I'll try. You go ahead."

I was really busy, but once again Vini and I were able to cover Debbie's tables as well as our own. By the time I realized she wasn't coming back, our shift was over. Now I'd have to run her phone by her house again.

I walked into the break room to gather my things and smiled when I saw Harvey and Alice there drinking a cup of coffee. Suddenly, I had a brilliant idea. I poured myself a cup and sank down beside them.

"How's everything going?" I asked conversationally.

Harvey nodded. "Pretty good."

"Still planning to move to Florida after you finish helping Carly?"

Alice tilted her head as if she could see through my casual questions. "Planning on it."

"I need to ask y'all a question."

"Ookay," Harvey said.

I smiled. "Marge told me to ask my parents for the details, but frankly, Mama's already lectured me about staying out of this murder investigation, so I thought I'd ask you two instead. It's about J.D."

Alice jerked, and her hot coffee splashed down her hand and onto the table.

"Oh no." She clutched her hand.

"Are you okay?" I asked quickly.

Harvey jumped up and grabbed her. "Here, hon, let's get some cold water on that." He bustled her out of her chair to the staff bathroom while I wiped up the mess.

I went to get a damp rag from the kitchen, and when I came back, the couple was nowhere in sight. Had Harvey taken Alice to the ER for her burn? Or were they hiding out to avoid any further questioning? Maybe the whole town was in on some sort of cover-up about J.D.'s past. Or maybe I'd been watching too many old movies.

After Alice's strange reaction, if it was a reaction, taking Debbie's phone back shifted to second on my priority list. First, I had to find out what Marge had been talking about. With that in mind, I looked up her number in my address book. After all, Marge hadn't said she wouldn't tell me; she'd just said the diner wasn't the place to discuss it. Maybe her house would be. One phone call later, I'd been invited by for a glass of tea.

Ten minutes later, still smelling like the lunch specials, I walked up to Marge's door. Had it been only a year ago that I'd stood on this same porch holding a green bean casserole after Hank's murder? So much had changed. Some for the better, some for the worse. I reached out to ring the doorbell, and the sun glinted off my engagement ring. One change in particular was a definite improvement.

Marge opened the door and motioned for me to come in. I stepped past her into a house that only remotely resembled the one she and Hank had lived in. Just as she'd done with her personality since she'd become a widow, Marge had opened up the house to sunshine and light. Bright cheery colors replaced the drab beige walls, and as she ushered me into the living room, the plastic-covered couch was nowhere to be found. "I love what you've done with the place," I murmured as I sank onto an overstuffed red chair.

Her face lit up. "Really? Tiffany helped me. She and I had so much fun picking everything out. We even did most of the work ourselves. But the ideas and the planning were all hers. She's a genius with colors."

I shook my head as I thought of Tiffany's drab wardrobe, dull, frizzy hair, and scrubbed face. Behind that costume, she hid a flair for colors and design. That girl had learned a long time ago how to choose her weapons in the perpetual battle with her mother. "It's wonderful, Marge."

She beamed and sank down onto the loveseat. "So what are you curious about this time?" She took a sip of her tea.

"You mentioned J.D.'s 'trial.' And I couldn't ask Mama and Daddy." I told her quickly about Mama's warning to me to stay out of the murder investigation.

She nodded and went to set down her tea glass.

"So I asked Harvey and Alice."

Marge jostled her glass and almost dropped it. Tea splashed onto the coffee table. She jumped up and snatched a tissue from a dispenser on the end table. "Oh, good heavens, Jenna! Why would you ask Harvey and Alice? They were the very reason I didn't tell you in the diner." She wiped up the liquid and gave me a measured look. "How'd they react?"

I nodded toward her tea. "Alice reacted just like you did, actually. Only hers was hot coffee."

"Ouch," Marge mouthed. "Is she okay?"

"I think so. When I came back from getting a cloth to wipe up the spill, they were gone."

"Of course they were."

"Why? What is J.D. to them?"

She leaned her head back against the chair and stared at the trifold screen as if seeing the past unfolding on it. "Harvey and Alice's only daughter was killed in a car accident."

"When?" I'd known they had one child who died young, but I'd never heard details.

Lost in thought, Marge counted on her fingers then brought her gaze back to me. "Next month, it'll be thirty years."

"What does that have to do with J.D.?"

"He was the one responsible for her death."

And obviously he had a trial. "So he did time?"

Marge shrugged. "I don't remember, exactly. I think they put him in some kind of lockup, but he was a minor, so it was probably a place for juvenile delinquents. Believe it or not, we never talked about him again after his trial."

"Never?"

She shrugged. "Hank put a few articles about his case in the paper, even though I begged him not to. Now I can see that he had no choice, but I was younger then and more naive."

"But the rest of the town just acted as if he didn't exist?"

"Everyone thought that the best thing for Harvey and Alice was to just put it behind them and pretend the accident never happened. Even J.D.'s own grandmother—God rest her soul—felt guilty the rest of her life." She stood and grabbed another tissue. "Back then not talking about it was how people dealt with grief." She wiped her eyes. "It was probably the wrong thing, but it was all we knew to do."

"What happened exactly?"

She considered my question then pushed to her feet. "Honey, I'm just not willing to dredge up the past. We're talking about wounds that are as old as you are. And any healing that has been done is tenuous, at best. Far be it from me to stir things up again."

I could tell I was being dismissed, so I reluctantly stood. Sure enough, she walked toward the front door, and I followed. "But now with J.D. murdered. . ."

She held open the front door and shook her head. "I refuse to think that anybody killed that boy because of what happened thirty years ago."

Out on the porch, I considered her parting statement. "I wish I could be so sure," I murmured to myself as I walked slowly to my car. "I just wish I could be so sure."

12

Your Chickens Will Come Home To Roost

So basically, what you're saying is that you want me to drive the getaway car?" Carly asked.

I plopped down in the chair with my mail on my lap and started slitting envelopes. "That makes it sound like I'm doing something wrong. All I want to do is give Debbie's phone back to her."

"And find out why she was meeting J.D. the night he died and why she didn't come forward with that information." Carly's flippant tone came through my little phone loud and clear.

Before I could answer, she continued, "Oh, and ask her why exactly she put the phone at the bottom of the trash."

"Basically," I said in a small voice, looking at an invitation to Tiffany's wedding shower at the country club.

"Sure," Carly said, apparently resigned to life with my avid curiosity. "I'll pick you up in ten minutes."

"Thanks."

When she pulled up in front of my house fifteen minutes later, I was on the porch waiting. I ran out and jumped in the passenger seat. "You're late."

"Beggars can't be choosers."

"Hey!" I protested with a grin. "Just because I'm trying to do the smart thing and take someone with me when I go to confront a person who may or may not be a homicidal maniac. . ."

The word *homicide* reminded me of the disturbing news I'd learned from Marge earlier, and my grin faded. I quickly filled Carly in.

She wiped at tears with one hand and drove with the other. "How awful for Harvey and Alice."

"I know," I said quietly, handing her a tissue. "And I wonder how taking a life, whether accidentally or on purpose, affected J.D. It must have changed the course of his life."

"Yeah," Carly agreed. "Especially if even his grandmother didn't mention his name anymore."

"Ironic that he came back for her funeral and ended up getting killed, isn't it?" I wondered again if trouble had followed him to our sleepy little town of Lake View. Or if it had been here waiting for him all along.

❖

I knocked on the door of Debbie's tiny house and cast a glance over my shoulder to where Carly waited in her car with the engine running.

When Debbie opened the door a crack, I shoved the cell phone toward her. "I accidentally got your phone again."

She recoiled and shook her head, still not opening the door all the way. "That's not my phone."

"It's the phone you had at the diner the other day." I held it up again to show her. "Remember when we got our phones mixed up?"

"That doesn't belong to me." She opened the door a little more. "I'm telling you, it isn't mine." Her voice rose.

"I know why you don't want to claim it. You might as well come out here so we can talk about it." I really didn't want her to invite me in. I was so jumpy these days, I was seeing a killer on every familiar face.

She hesitated, and for a minute I thought she might slam the door shut and dead-bolt herself inside. But slowly she opened the door and stepped outside.

Her hair was matted on one side and her face creased. I could tell she'd been sleeping, or more likely from the looks of her red eyes, lying in bed crying.

Whatever the truth of the situation was, my heart ached for her. "You need to take this phone to John and explain where you got it."

"No, Jenna. I can't do that." Debbie sounded near hysterics. "You just don't understand."

"I think I do. You and J.D. were seeing each other behind Lisa's back, right?" I checked again to make sure Carly was still there.

"Not really."

"He gave you a cell phone to call him on, but you weren't seeing each other?" I'd figured that much out on the way over, when I'd realized that the one number in the phone that was put in as "Me" had to be J.D.'s. He must have added it in himself and given Debbie the phone. The police had questioned Lisa about whether she had another phone. No doubt they'd found the text messages on J.D.'s phone, but since this phone was also in J.D.'s name, the police didn't know who had it.

"We. . ." She choked out the words. "We kept telling ourselves we were just friends and that Lisa just wouldn't understand us hanging out. But the truth was I was falling in love with him. And I think he was with me, too."

"So why didn't you just tell her?"

"Neither of us wanted to hurt Lisa." She blinked rapidly against the tears filling her eyes, but they spilled down her cheeks anyway.

My guess was that J.D. didn't want to lose his job at the health club, but I could have been wrong.

"We were going to tell her Sunday, but he got killed before we got the chance." She swiped at her eyes with the back of her hand.

"So you threw the phone away?"

"Yes," Debbie spat out the word. Then her voice broke. "And it tore my heart out to do it." She cried harder. "It was my last link with J.D." She was sobbing so hard now, I could barely understand her. "If Lisa killed him, it's my fault." She dug a tissue out of her pocket and wiped her nose.

"Debbie, how could it be your fault?"

"Maybe Lisa found out about us and got mad and killed him." Debbie sobbed.

"If she did, John needs this phone. You should take it to him and tell him about you and J.D."

"No," she said flatly. "I won't. If Lisa doesn't already know and she found out, it would ruin our friendship. And I'm the only friend she has left now."

"I'll have to take it to John. How long do you think it will take for them to find out it was yours?"

"That's just it. It wasn't mine. Like you said, it belonged to J.D." She wiped her eyes again. "I was just using it. You can't prove that I ever had it."

"They already know about the phone, Debbie." I tried my most reasonable voice. "It would be better for you if you just took it to them voluntarily."

"Look, Jenna, don't you see? They're getting ready to arrest Lisa. This will just be the last nail in her coffin." She looked at me. "But what if she didn't find out about me and J.D.? What if she didn't kill him?"

"John will find out." I sounded confident, but I couldn't help remembering how I felt when Zac was a murder suspect. Even though I knew John was conscientious and did his best, I also knew he hadn't had all that much experience with murder.

"As long as they don't have this phone, they'll keep looking. If they have it, they'll just say, 'Here's our proof. J.D. and Debbie were cheating behind Lisa's back, so she killed him.' They won't look for anybody else." She sniffed. "If you give them the phone, what are they gonna do? Arrest her immediately. That's what. Put her in jail and throw away the key. Is that what you want?"

"No. Of course not." She might be right. Lisa could end up in jail. And unless they found another suspect, she could go to trial. Especially if there was a bloody towel in her car.

Debbie interrupted that awful thought. "Why don't you go talk to Lisa? Try to find out if she knew about us. If she didn't know, then the phone doesn't matter. If she did know, then take the phone to John." Now Debbie was the one using her most reasonable voice.

Just what I wanted to do. Confront yet another person who might be a murderer. "I guess I could at least go see her. But if I can tell she knows about you and J.D., I'll have to take the phone to John. And even if she doesn't, I think one of us will have to take it anyway."

"Just wait and see what she says," Debbie pleaded.

I turned the phone off and slipped it back into my pocket. It didn't look as if I'd be getting rid of it today. But I knew someone would have to take it to John. And soon.

◆

"Well, from what you told me about Jolene," Carly said, as we lazily paddled around the lake using foot-power, "Debbie's more J.D.'s type than Lisa is." She neatly turned our paddleboat away from a collision course with the twins.

I smiled as I cycled with my feet, too. "Wait until you meet Jolene. She makes Debbie look like Princess Di. But you're right. Of the two, Debbie is more like Jolene than Lisa is."

"So why didn't he just tell Lisa?"

I shrugged. "Maybe he just wanted to have Debbie as insurance in case things didn't work out. Debbie said they 'told themselves they were just friends.' So technically, they weren't dating. Maybe J.D. was just keeping his options open. And I'm sure he didn't want to lose his job."

"Or maybe he had planned to manipulate the situation in some way but died before he could," Carly mused.

Before I could answer, cold water sprayed us.

"Whooo!" Carly rubbed her hand across her face. "You sneaky girls splashed us on purpose!" Our blue and white paddleboat rocked as we turned and pedaled furiously to try and catch the twins.

"Y'all looked like you needed to have a little fun," Hayley called, grinning over her shoulder at us. "Hurry, Rachel, they're gaining!"

"I'm going as fast as I can," Rachel yelled.

"We're getting too old for this." Panting, Carly looked over at me and grinned. "Besides, they're lighter. They can go faster."

"No kidding." My muscles burned as I pedaled harder. "Youth wins again," I declared dramatically as the twins beat us by inches to the dock, our finish line.

"No more splashing us," Carly told the giggling girls. "Let's just relax and paddle around for a while. That way I may be able to catch my breath."

As the girls paddled their boat across the lake, Carly and I leaned back against our seats and tried to slow our pounding heartbeats. Carly kept an eye on the girls' boat as we talked.

"I can't even imagine what it would be like if something happened to one of them." She nodded toward the twins. "Poor Harvey and Alice."

"Yeah. I feel so sorry for them. I wish we knew exactly what happened." I leaned back and stuck my hand into the cool water. "I hate it that Marge didn't tell me not to mention J.D. to them." I trickled water down my sweaty face. "And Marge won't tell me anything else."

"Did you ask Mama?" Carly fanned herself with her hand. "She would know."

"No." I filled her in on Mama's plea for me to stay out of this case. "So I'm trying to keep a low profile." I relaxed against my seat. "Besides, I need an unbiased report."

"I think most of the people involved are pretty biased," Carly said dryly. "Too bad we can't just google it. But I'm pretty sure something that old won't be on the Internet."

"The archive room at the newspaper!" I turned to Carly. "As soon as we can, we need to go to the *Monitor* office. All we have to do is find the paper with the article in it." I didn't mention that there were forty years of papers to go through. No need to scare her off before we even got started.

"Sounds easy enough." Carly guided us up to the dock. We levered ourselves out of the boat and motioned for the girls to come on in.

While we were waiting for them to get out of their boat and join us, Daddy came toward us with fishing poles in one hand and his tackle box in the other.

"Is it okay with you if the girls and I fish for a while?"

Carly nodded. "Jenna and I need to run an errand, anyway."

Daddy offered the poles to the giggling twins. "Let's see if we can catch some supper."

I glanced at the watch on Daddy's wrist. It was a little after five. Most of the *Monitor* employees should be gone. "Can the girls stay with you until we get back?"

"Of course they can. We may be out here an hour or more, anyway." Daddy rigged a pole for each of the girls, and they sat on the dock with their legs hanging off. "We'll take our catch up to the house when we finish."

"Pretty sure we'll catch some, aren't you, Grandpa?" Rachel said sassily.

"He knows *I* will," Hayley spouted off.

Daddy laughed, and Carly and I exchanged a grin. "They're growing up," she murmured. "Before I know it, they'll be grown and gone."

I stared at her as we climbed into my vehicle. "Are you okay?"

She nodded and stared out the window at the lake. "Just realizing how quickly things can change."

I frowned but concentrated on pulling onto the highway. Was Travis about to come barreling back into our lives? I wanted to ask. But I'd promised myself I'd wait until she got ready to tell me. And I would.

◆

The parking area behind the newspaper office was empty when Carly and I pulled in.

"I'm glad no one is here. I'd rather not have to explain what we're looking for to anyone." I unlocked the door. "Even Tiffany."

I flipped the light switch on in the archive room, and Carly gasped. "Just find the paper with the article in it? I think this may be harder than I thought."

I explained that they were in order by date and that Marge had given me the month and year. So after narrowing our search to that one small area, we began to read.

After about fifteen minutes, I slapped the table. "Pay dirt!" I read the headline aloud to Carly. "Local Teen Killed in Drag Racing Accident."

"Drag racing? No one mentioned that, did they?"

I shook my head and continued reading. "'Fifteen-year-old Sara Coleman, daughter of Harvey and Alice Coleman, was the victim of a fatal automobile accident. Coleman was a passenger in the car driven by Jimmy Finley, age seventeen, of Lake View. Witnesses said Finley lost control of the car when it hit a bump in the road while traveling at a high rate of speed. It then went airborne and flipped several times before landing in a ditch. Finley reported only minor injuries. Police have not yet determined whether alcohol or drugs were involved. The accident occurred off County Road forty-four.'"

"Wow," Carly said. "I'd envisioned something like a hit-and-run or maybe he was drunk and hit her car."

I laid the newspaper to the side. "So she chose to be there." I mulled that over for a few minutes.

"That probably makes it worse for her parents," Carly pointed out. "If she were a totally innocent victim, it may have been easier on them."

"I wonder if he was her boyfriend." I set the newspaper in its place. "Or if she did it on a dare."

"Maybe she just loved to go fast," Carly said.

We found another article dated two weeks later. The headline read: Local Teen Pleads Guilty in Fatal Accident. I read the article aloud. "'Jimmy Dean Finley pleaded guilty to vehicular homicide in Lake View District Court on Thursday. According to police, Finley and passenger Sara Coleman were involved in a high-speed drag race when Finley lost control of his car, which went airborne. Miss Coleman was thrown from the car and killed instantly. Alcohol was a factor.'"

"Do you think there are any other articles about this?" I glanced at Carly.

"We're almost finished with the month. Let's go on and look through the rest of these."

A few minutes later, Carly said, "Oh, here's one!" She started reading. "'PARENTS OF DEAD TEEN SUE PROPERTY OWNERS WHERE ACCIDENT OCCURRED. Harvey and Alice Coleman filed a wrongful death lawsuit against Bob and Wilma Pryor after the death of their daughter, Sara Coleman.'"

She stopped. "Bob and Wilma? What in the world?"

"Keep reading," I urged.

"The lawsuit alleges that the Pryors knowingly provided alcohol to minors while on their property."

I gasped. "I don't believe it."

She glanced back at the article. "Believe it. Listen to this: 'According to unnamed sources, there have been numerous complaints from other parents about underage drinking and drag racing on the Pryors' property.'"

We looked at each other. "There has to be more. At least the trials of J.D. and of Bob and Wilma," Carly said.

I nodded. "And I have to see how they came out."

We began looking through the newspapers for the next month. But it wasn't until December that we scored.

"'J.D. Finley has been sentenced to a year in juvenile detention,'" Carly read aloud.

A minute later I found the rest of the story. "'Local residents Harvey and Alice Coleman have dropped their wrongful death suit against Bob and Wilma Pryor.'"

"Hank kept those last two uncharacteristically short, didn't he?" Carly said.

I nodded. "Marge said she begged him not to print anything at all. I suppose he just put what he felt his journalistic ethics required."

"So that's why Bob gave up the hippie life. . . ." Carly carefully put the newspaper back where it belonged. "And why everyone is suddenly remembering the past."

I nodded. "The question is, did someone remember the past vividly enough to kill because of it?"

13

NEVER MISS A GOOD CHANCE TO SHUT UP

"Miss Jenna." Vini gave me a serious look. "If that woman comes in and pinches my jaw again, I will have to look for another job. Miss Carly will fire me, because I will be rude to a customer."

"Tell you what, Vini. I'll be on the lookout. When Jolene comes in, I'll be sure Harvey seats her in my section. Deal?"

"Thank you. Yes, it is a deal."

Consequently, when Jolene made an appearance toward the end of the noon rush, Harvey seated her at a table in the corner, and I took her order.

"I must be getting back to my roots or something," she commented as I set her sweet tea on the table. "I had that all the time when I was at my gramma's when I was a kid."

"If you don't mind my asking, where are you from? Sometimes you sound like you're from Mississippi, and sometimes from New York or somewhere up there."

"Keeps you guessin', don't it?" She winked. "Actually, you ain't far off. I spent the summers in Texas with my gramma, but my folks lived in New Jersey. Then when I was old enough to make my own way, I went wherever the spirit moved me, from Florida to California and points in between. My trusty Mustang takes me wherever the good times are. I usually find me somebody to hang out with for a while, and then I move on. I'm a pretty good waitress, so I can work about anywheres."

I eyed her short, low-cut dress and stiletto heels, trying to picture Carly hiring her to work at the Down Home Diner. Nope. Couldn't see it.

"Now, let's get down to business. We've gotta hit the funeral parlor and figure out how much a buryin' is gonna set me back. Once me and the mortician come to terms, we need to set a date and get this thing done. I ain't one for havin' a long drawn-out grieving. Jimmy's dead. Let's get him in the ground and get on with life."

Once again, I found myself riding shotgun in the red Mustang. We pulled into the drive of the local funeral home and got out. Jolene checked to make sure her dress wasn't hitched up—or maybe to make sure it was. Then she pranced on her tall, thin heels into the building. I almost ran to keep up. I wanted a glimpse of Tom LeMay's face when he saw her. The plump, bald, middle-aged man met us at the door but took Jolene's appearance in stride.

"May I help you ladies?" His voice was calm and courteous.

"You betcha boots," Jolene answered. "We wanta bury a guy. What's the cheapest funeral we can have in this fancy place?"

Tom looked at me, and my face turned red. I fought the urge to turn and walk out as if I'd never seen Jolene before. Instead, I shrugged slightly and introduced her.

"I got a paper right here that says I'm the executor of Jimmy's will, so I got to do my duty and see him in the ground. I want it done decent, but I don't want to be ripped off, neither. You understand?" She wagged a pointed red fingernail under Tom's chin.

"Yes, ma'am. We aren't in the habit of ripping people off. Now, if you will follow me, I will show you our selection of caskets." He turned, and we followed.

An hour later, we emerged. Jolene was torn between exhilaration and gloom, because even though she'd talked Tom down on the price of his cheapest casket, the funeral was still going to "eat a hole" in her inheritance.

"But that's okay," she assured me. "Jimmy had a big wad in his bank account, and it's all mine. Whoo. . ." She shook her head. "It just goes to show. I never dreamed I'd be an heiress. I may just have to help them rube cops find the killer."

"Speaking of killers, have you thought any more about why someone might have shot J.D.?" I hated to question her outside the funeral home, but I needed to know. "I mean, what was he like? Did he leave enemies everywhere he went? We have very few murders here in our small town. And with him not being from here, I wondered if maybe he brought his killer with him, so to speak."

"Well, honey, if you're hintin' I offed him, you can get over it. I didn't even know where he was till that lawyer dude called me. And he said he had a whale of a job locatin' me."

"I didn't mean to imply anything about you, Jolene. Sorry if it sounded that way." She looked menacing when she was angry, though. I could imagine that snake tattoo shooting its fangs out at me. I hurried to soothe her. "I just thought you might give me some insight into J.D.'s character. But you don't have to."

"That's okay. I fly off the handle a little fast sometimes. Jumpin' to conclusions and missin' as my old gramma used to say." She sent me a forgiving grin. She mused for a minute then continued, "Wonder when Jimmy took to callin' hisself 'J.D.' Sounds right fancy, don't it?"

"I guess."

She ignored my answer. "Now that I think about it, he did make a few folks mad. You know, my best girlfriend back then—Melody was her name—she married herself a rich old man. Took her forever to find one, but she did." She shook her head in wonder. "He was an old coot—bald-headed and didn't have his own teeth. But he was loaded. That's the best kind of man, you know." Wink, wink.

"Well, I—"

She cut off any Dear Pru advice I might impart with a wave of her hand. "So, one night Melody and me have a girls' night out, and we meet this guy, a real hunk. I don't know how she does it, but before the night's over, she gets him to give her his number. The rest of the night, she's all braggin', you know, how she could pick up men without even tryin'. I kinda lost my cool and blubbered to Jimmy, wantin' him to tell me I was prettier'n Melody—which I was—but the next thing I know, he's callin' her and threatening to blab to her husband if she don't let him borrow her fancy car."

"So she was mad at him?"

"I'll say she was. Mad at both of us. Even though I was innocent as a newborn baby. She wouldn't speak to me for a long time. In fact, as long as Jimmy and me was together. She come around after I showed him the door, though. Should we put an obituary in the paper? Sort of let folks hereabouts know when the funeral is?" she asked without ever taking an audible breath.

"I'll take care of it. The editor and I are friends," I answered.

"I knew you was the right gal to take up with soon as I laid eyes on you." She slapped me on the back. Not lightly. She dropped me off at the diner, and I left her to her Mustang and musings and went home to get ready for work at the health club. On the way, I called Marge at the *Monitor*, and together we came up with an obituary for Jimmy Dean Finley.

❖

I stuck my head into Bob's office. "If it's okay with you, I'm going to come by tomorrow night for a couple of hours and see what all needs to be done." I thought it might be easier if I had some time by myself to get reacquainted with the running of a health club.

"Sounds good. Let me get you a key." He motioned me to come inside. "Got a minute?" He made a pushing motion toward the door, so I shut it.

Poor Bob. He'd aged so much in the last few days. "Of course." I sat down. And tried not to think of how often I had dreamed of owning this place. And how aggravated I'd been at Bob and Lisa when I quit. Time to put those thoughts behind me.

He pushed the key across the desk toward me. "I guess you heard that they may arrest Lisa any minute now. I know it's the talk of the town." His shoulders slumped as if the weight of the world rested on them.

I nodded.

Bob leaned forward. "I think she's being framed, Jenna." He lowered his voice. "Some stuff happened a long time ago. And ever since, Harvey has hated me. Remember how he and Hank Templeton teamed up on the zoning board to keep my business outside of town? I think he did this just to get back at me."

"Killed an innocent person just to get revenge on you, Bob?" I wondered if self-centeredness was an inherited trait.

"No. . ." Bob suddenly looked very uncomfortable, as if he hadn't thought this far ahead.

I considered telling him I already knew, but I couldn't think of a tactful way.

"The thing is. . . J.D. was involved back then, too. In the stuff that happened. So Harvey hated us both. This way he killed two birds with one stone." He studied the framed picture of Lisa and Fluffy. "Killing J.D. and setting Lisa up for it settles the score with both of us."

I nodded. In some twisted way, I could see his logic. If Lisa was found guilty, it would be worse for Bob than if he himself was sent to prison.

"You know, don't you?"

I looked up into Bob's questioning eyes. I didn't see any reason to deny it. "How could you tell?"

"I'd braced myself for your questions. I knew as soon as I hinted at the past, you'd want to know it all. But you didn't ask me anything."

"I just didn't want to make it any harder for you than it is already," I said quietly.

He spun his chair around, turning his back to me. When I heard his voice, thick with tears, I knew why. "Wilma and I, we'd just moved here from California not long before all that. She wanted to settle down, but I liked the fact that the kids all thought I was cool." His voice broke. "They made me feel young. I didn't see any harm in it."

I stared at his shaking shoulders.

He shook his head and didn't speak for a minute. Even from the back, I could see he was struggling to keep any composure at all.

"We didn't know about the drag racing, but if I could go back and live that part of my life over, I would. We both told Harvey and Alice how sorry we were. And they seemed to forgive us to some extent. Dropped the suit, which you probably know. But when Lisa was born a couple of years later, all the old feelings of hate boiled up again. They both looked at us like we had no right to have a daughter when they'd lost theirs because of my stupidity."

"So now you think Harvey wants to take your daughter away from you?"

He nodded, with his back still toward me.

"Does Lisa know about this?"

"No!"

"J.D. didn't tell her?"

"No. He probably would've. But he died before he got a chance."

My heart thudded in my chest.

He spun around to face me, mindless now of the tears coursing down his cheeks. "I didn't mean it like that. I didn't kill him."

"So he wasn't blackmailing you?"

"Not really. He just kept reminding me that he had one over on me."

The precursor to blackmail. Reason enough to murder someone? Maybe. But I didn't believe for a minute Bob would kill someone and let his precious daughter take the blame. In my eyes, that fact alone exonerated him.

I stood and put the key in my pocket. "I'm sorry."

He nodded. "Me, too."

I left him to his thoughts.

On the way home, I stopped by Carly's to tell her what Bob said about Harvey being the killer.

"You know, as bad as I hate to say this, the same things could be said of Alice," she said.

"Alice? You're just mad because she bosses you around in the kitchen," I teased her. "*And* she makes better pies."

"Ha. She does not make better pies. She just has more years of practice." Carly fluffed her short curls. "Just wait until you taste the pies I make when I get as old as she is."

"You're right, though. She does have the same motive."

"But not the same opportunity," Carly said suddenly. "Because Harvey took the trash out."

I put my hand to my mouth. "You're right. He could have shot J.D. then walked right back into the diner."

"He would have stayed out there long enough to see you and knock you in the head. But as busy as we were. . ."

I remembered how long it took anyone to realize I was hurt. "Nobody even would have noticed."

14

YOU CATCH MORE FLIES WITH HONEY THAN YOU DO WITH VINEGAR.

Jen?" Carly sounded harried on the phone. "I have a huge favor to ask."

"Let's hear it."

"Is there any chance you're going out to the athletic club tonight?"

"I was planning on it. Why?"

"The girls and I need a ride to school."

"No problem." The school was out near Bob's gym anyway. "Is your car torn up?"

Silence.

"Carly, you still there?"

"I'm here," she said, embarrassment evident in her tone. "Technically, my car isn't 'torn up.' It's more like 'out of gas.'"

Any other time, she'd have called Elliott to bring her some gas or give her a ride to school. I certainly wasn't complaining, but it made me sad to see them drifting apart.

"I'll be right over."

When I pulled up in front of their cabin, Carly and the girls came running out and jumped in.

"How long will your school thing last?" I asked when we got on the road.

"It's an open house," Rachel said from the backseat.

"So there's no set ending time," Hayley finished.

I glanced at Carly. "In that case, why don't you just drop me off at the gym, and I'll work until you pick me back up?"

"Really? That would be perfect. You're a lifesaver."

"That's better than a Dum Dum, I guess." I tossed her a silly smile.

The girls giggled and Carly groaned. "That was corny, even for you."

"Yes, well, I'm getting cornier in my old age."

"You only use that term because you know I'll always be older than you," she said.

"You're probably right." I swung the car into the almost-deserted parking lot of the Lake View Athletic Club and jumped out.

Carly jumped out, too, and ran around to the driver's seat. She gave me a quick hug before sliding in. "Bye, Jenna, and thanks again."

She waited to make sure I was inside before leaving the club parking lot. Ordinarily I would think that was overkill, but with a real killer on the loose, I wasn't complaining. The thought of a "real killer" sent a shiver down my spine and made me glad to hear the hum of voices in the exercise room.

I shivered again when I started looking at the mess that Lisa had left. Her housekeeping skills were on par with her management skills—although I had a feeling it was more of an "I don't care" attitude than not being *able* to do it.

After I'd been cleaning for a while, Dave stuck his head in the door. "I'm about to lock up. You want me to wait for you?"

"No, thanks. I've still got a little more to do here."

He nodded. "Rumor has it there's a ghost in here late at night, so if you hear anything, get your cell phone ready to take a pic."

"If I saw a ghost, the last thing I'd be worried about would be taking its picture."

He shrugged. "Your loss. A photo of a real ghost would sell for no telling how much."

"I'd rather just have peace and quiet and get my job done. But thanks." I glanced back at the stack of junk I was sorting through then thought of something. "Oh, and Dave. . ."

He stuck his head back in the door. "Yeah?"

"Thanks for spooking me before I get locked in here by myself."

"Spook the legendary Jenna Stafford? No way."

He laughed all the way down the hall. I threw myself back into cleaning. I should have turned some music on, because as soon as I knew he was gone, I started hearing little noises. Creaking noises, swishing noises, ceiling fan noises.

A scraping sound from the back door might as well have been a cannon shot. That's the kind of noise that puts all other noises to shame. The kind you can't ignore or explain away. That was definitely something. I cautiously peeped over the top of the cabinet I didn't realize I'd ducked behind.

I heard footsteps, and they were coming this way. No way anyone would have any business in the back room of the club after hours. Well, no one but a cleaning freak like me. Unfortunately, the cabinet was too small for me to crawl into. I wished I'd closed the hall door when I came in here, but all I'd had on my mind was getting the place aired out and cleaned up.

Suddenly, it hit me. Mama had been wrong. All those times she'd warned me about curiosity leading to an unhappy ending for me, she should have told me that cleaning would be the death of me. That would have saved me a lot of prune hands and sore knees over the years. And tonight it might have saved my life.

The footsteps stopped at the door. I wondered if my foot was sticking out beyond the edge of the cabinet. If I drew it in, would it make noise?

Speaking of noise, was that whistling? A whistling killer? "Yankee Doodle," no less. Forget my whole death-by-cleaning theory. Mama was right, as usual. Curiosity would kill me. But I had to look. I borrowed a trick from Tiffany and prayed that my "hand" gun would be as unnecessary as hers had been.

I swung out from behind the cabinet in one fluid motion, bringing my fake gun out in front of me. "Who's there?" I said in my most commanding voice to the shadow in the hallway.

"It is Vini! Who is there?" His voice trembled.

My taut muscles went limp. "It's Jenna."

He stuck his head inside the doorway, and his eyes widened. "What are you doing here?"

"I think that's my line. I work here." I frowned. "If I remember correctly, you don't."

"I can explain." He walked into the room, his face suffused with color. "Or I could, but I do not want to get someone into trouble."

I crossed my arms in front of me. "Well, 'someone' *is* in trouble. It's you. So you'd better start explaining." I was still shaky from the fright he'd given me, which made me sound tougher than I felt. "You came in the back door. Did you break the lock?"

"No." Vini sounded shocked at the idea. "I did not break it. That would be wrong."

"Then how did you get in?"

"I used the key." He dangled a key in front of my face. I snatched it from his hand.

"*Where* did you get this key?" I demanded.

"W—well." He backed up as if he still believed I had a gun. "I—I will tell you."

"Yes. You certainly will tell me."

"Promise not to get her into trouble," he said.

"I can't make any promises until I know the whole story."

He gave it serious consideration then sent me a tentative smile. "I trust you."

I was pretty sure I knew by now who had given him the key. "Sorry I was so sharp with you, but you scared me to death."

"I did not know you were here. I would have been quieter."

"Don't worry about it. Just tell me why you're here."

"I live here."

I'd thought the shock of him walking in on me had been the biggest shock of the night, but I was obviously wrong.

"Vini, you can't live here. This isn't a house. It's not even an apartment."

"Believe me, it is only temporary," he insisted. "The people I lived with— they got transferred and had to move. I had no place to sleep. I could not stay at the college because I did not sign up for a dormitory room. Besides, the dormitory costs more than I can afford."

"So Gail gave you a key and said you could stay here for a while?"

"Yes. You guessed it." He nodded. "She has been very kind to me. She would let me stay at her apartment. But it would not look good."

"So you've been living here for a while?"

"I was sleeping in my van and taking showers here when I worked here. But after I got fired, Gail said I could stay if I didn't tell anyone." His forehead wrinkled. "I hope she is not mad at me. She told me to only come in the back door when the club is empty." He gave me a reproachful look. "No car is out there tonight. So I thought it was empty. You scared me."

"Vini, you can't stay here anymore."

His shoulders slumped in defeat. "Are you going to tell on Gail?"

Bob had enough on his mind. And Vini staying here hadn't hurt anything, really. "I'm not sure. Not right now."

"So I will move my things back out to my van." He turned and walked away.

When he was gone, I picked up my cell phone and made a quick call. "Mama, I know it's late, but I need to rent a cabin for the night." I quickly explained the situation to her.

"We have a couple of empty cabins he can choose from, but you won't be paying," she said firmly.

"Just for tonight," I agreed. "Then we'll figure something out."

❖

The next morning, I hurried over to Stafford Cabins as soon as I knew Mama and Daddy would have the office opened.

The front office was deserted when I walked in.

"Good morning," Daddy called. "We're in the back."

I stepped down the tiny hall to the little break area Mama had fixed up. They were sitting at the table drinking coffee. And holding hands.

I blushed. Would Alex and I still be that much in love after that many years? I had a feeling we would. He was due back from the conference on Saturday. I made a mental note to call him later and tell him how much I looked forward to growing old with him. That done, I turned my attention back to my parents. "You really shouldn't just call out for anyone to come on back," I scolded. "I could have been an ax murderer."

"I suppose you could have," Daddy said thoughtfully, looking at Mama. "But I thought we raised her better than that, didn't you, Elizabeth?"

Mama nodded, never missing a beat. "Of course, if you were an ax murderer, dear. . .it really wouldn't matter whether we invited you in or not, would it?"

I sighed. "Never mind."

"Tell us about Vini."

"Yes. He was up at dawn, sweeping the office porch and straightening the deck chairs," Daddy said.

I smiled, because I could see him doing that. "Well, you know, he came here as an exchange student in high school then managed to get his paperwork to stay on for college. With a limited work visa, he's living on very little money. He was living with a sponsor family, but the husband was transferred to Little Rock, which left Vini homeless."

"Oh my. Bless his heart," Mama said.

I nodded. "He's been sleeping at the club and just eating what he gets at the diner. But he needs a place where he can study and relax." I looked at them and chose my words carefully. I wanted to be sure they knew that helping Vini was something I wanted to do. Not something I wanted them to do.

They were staring at each other without speaking. It was one of those looks that made me feel as if there was a conversation going on that I wasn't a part of.

I continued, "I was thinking that maybe I could pay a reduced fee for one of the cabins. I know you sometimes do a weekly rate, and I've even seen you offer a monthly rate to a few—"

"Hush, dear, so we can think," Mama said sweetly.

I hushed.

"Are you thinking what I'm thinking?" she asked Daddy, her eyes sparkling.

He nodded. "It's an answer to a prayer. Cabin 40."

I just stared at them. "We don't have forty cabins."

Mama laughed. "You remember cabin 40. We named it that because it's out in the back forty." She sipped her coffee and grinned at my still puzzled expression. "In other words, it's so far from the office we got more complaints than it was worth. So when a storm blew a tree across the porch a couple of years ago, we just moved the tree and closed the cabin."

Daddy picked up the story. "We were just talking yesterday about what we were going to do with it. There was some damage to the porch, but the cabin is livable. We can have power hooked back up with no trouble. To pay for his keep, Vini can clean it and work on the porch as he has time. After he finishes that, if he still needs a place to live, we've got plenty of other jobs that need doing."

I frowned. "So you really do want the cabin fixed up?"

Mama nodded. "We've tried to figure out what to do with it."

"It was sweet of you to want to help him, honey," Daddy said. "But a man needs to earn his own way when he can. Keeps his character strong."

"A hand up is much better than a handout," Mama agreed.

I smiled at them and gave them each a hug. "I'll go tell Vini the great news."

❖

I didn't have to be at work at the athletic club until three, so after I made Vini's day, I decided I would do what I had promised Debbie and go visit Lisa at Bob and Wilma's.

I pulled into the circular driveway in front of the elegant split-level glass and cedar house. Wilma answered the doorbell. She seemed genuinely happy to see me. When I told her why I was there, she ushered me up the wide oak stairway and to Lisa's barely opened bedroom door. I turned to ask Wilma if she wanted to go in and tell Lisa I was there. But before I could say a word, she'd retreated down the stairs.

I tapped on the door, and it opened under my knuckles. My guess was that the room hadn't changed since Lisa was a little girl. A pink ruffled bedspread covered the bed underneath the white canopy. It made me think of Barbie's bedroom. And there was Barbie, um, Lisa, in bed propped up on some pillows, a romance novel in her hand.

"Hey," I said, giving her my best smile. "How are you?"

"How do you think I am?" she grumbled.

"Upset, I imagine." I nodded toward the closed blinds behind the frilly curtains. "Would you like me to open the blinds and let some sunshine in?" I took a step toward the window, and a tiny white fur ball came alive on the bed. Teeth bared and growling, Fluffy didn't want me close to her mistress.

I froze then took a step back. The dog retreated to its pillow but kept its eyes focused on me.

"No, I don't need sunshine." Lisa ignored Fluffy and glared at me. "I just lost a, well, a very good friend. In a brutal way. And now the police think I killed him. I'll be lucky if I don't get arrested before I can even attend his funeral tomorrow." She pinched her lips together. "And I never looked good in orange." She was probably right; apparently pink was more her color. "So, yes, I'm a bit upset. I think that's understandable."

"It definitely is understandable. But maybe if you got up and went to the gym, you'd feel better. Sometimes getting that adrenaline pumping—"

She pushed herself up in the bed. "I'm sure you came to interrogate me about something, so why don't you just get on with it?"

My eyes widened. "I came to check on you. People are worried about you."

"Like who?"

"Like Debbie."

I watched her face, but she had no visible reaction to Debbie's name. So I forged on. "You and Debbie met J.D. at the same time, right?"

"Yes, so?"

"What did Debbie think about him?"

"She thought what every woman who met him thought—that he was hot.

And she was right."

"Do you think she was put out that he chose you instead of her? I mean, y'all met him at the same time, you both thought he was attractive, but he chose you."

"Well, come on. I mean, I love Debbie and all, but look at her and look at me. Can you see any guy choosing her when I'm available?" She smirked. "No. J.D. was mine for as long as I wanted him. I just had to decide whether I wanted him or if I was going back to Larry."

She really was totally self-centered. "Speaking of Larry," I said. I sort of felt odd calling him Larry. I'd always heard him referred to as Lawrence, but Bob and Lisa both called him Larry, so I decided to follow their example. "How did he feel about you and J.D.?"

"Poor Larry." Lisa lost some of her composure. "That's my biggest fear." She swiped at a tear. It even looked real. Maybe there was a heart in there somewhere. "He was so jealous. What if he decided to have it out with J.D. and just lost control? I don't think I could bear to be the wife of a murderer." She shivered and continued. "Besides, if Larry killed J.D., it was partly my fault. He was always possessive. That's one reason I left him. I just had to have some breathing room."

"Oh. I thought—" I came to a stop.

"You thought what?" Comprehension washed over her face. "Ooh. Dad told you that story I told him. About how Larry was abusive. Well, I had to say something. Dad adores me. But he expects me to stay married unless I have a good reason not to. So I gave him a good reason." She shrugged.

I just shook my head. This girl was the queen of situation ethics.

"I'm curious about something." I hadn't planned to ask this question, but now that I was here, I had to know.

"What about?"

"Rumor has it that there was a towel under your car seat with J.D.'s blood on it. Do you know how it got there?"

She frowned. "I heard that, too, but I had no idea it was there."

"Wonder how it got there?"

"Well, Sherlock, I suppose it had to be either one of two things. Either J.D. cut himself shaving or something and stuffed the towel under there himself. Or someone planted it."

I ignored her "Sherlock" dig in favor of getting information. "Which do you think happened?"

She shrugged. "Since someone stole my gun, my guess is the same person planted the towel in my car. I just can't figure out who would want to hurt me like that." She reached over and rubbed Fluffy's head. "Or hurt my precious baby, either."

"They hurt your dog?" I asked, eyeing the tiny ball of fluff. Other than occasionally baring its teeth, it looked fine to me.

She put her hands over the dog's ears. "Fluffy's not just a dog. She's my baby." I was wrong. Lisa wasn't totally self-centered. After all, she had spared a thought for her "baby." "And if I'm upset, she gets upset."

"I understand." I had a neurotic cat, didn't I? "Some animals are sensitive to their master's moods." And I'm sure if any animal was sensitive, it would be Fluffy. And Lisa probably had more moods than most.

"I think I'll call Dad and have him take Fluffy out to Larry. He's the only person who loves her as much as I do."

Just one more errand for poor Bob to do for his princess. On the other hand, this would be a perfect opportunity for me to check out Larry in person. "Or I can run Fluffy out to Larry's."

"Oh." She gave me a measured look. "I suppose that would work."

Talk about gratitude. Not that I expected any.

She called Larry and told him I was coming then gave me directions and stressed that Fluffy only traveled in a cage. At least she got out of bed long enough to get all of the dog's things together. She actually packed a suitcase for the canine.

I lugged the suitcase to my car first then came back for the dog.

"Remind Larry this is only temporary," she told me. "As soon as this mess is behind me, I get her back."

"I'll tell him," I promised.

I was almost to the top of the stairs when Lisa called me back. And to think I'd thought my days of being summoned by her were over when I quit the club. "Yes?" I said. I lugged the small dog carrier back up to her room.

She looked up from her novel as if I were bothering her. "Oh. I wanted to ask you something. I don't usually listen to rumors, but I heard J.D.'s ex-wife was in town. They say she's really trashy. Is that true?"

I stared at her. I was taking her dog to her husband until she could get over her boyfriend's murder. And she was asking me if someone else was "trashy." "You'd have to be your own judge of that, Lisa," I said softly and let myself out the door.

"I'll see for myself at the funeral tomorrow anyway," she called haughtily as I walked down the stairs.

Fluffy, in the carrier by my side, barked in reply. But I just kept walking.

15

Better Than A Poke In The Eye With A Sharp Stick

"How do you talk me into these things?" Carly settled into her seat and buckled in.

"You mean you don't enjoy going with me to confront possible murderers?"

"Don't act so surprised," she drawled. "I told you the first time you dragged me into trying to solve a murder that I'm a big chicken."

"Well, now that we know he didn't abuse Lisa, what do you think the chances are that Larry did it?" I asked.

"You said he's really jealous, so I'm not sure." She glanced at Fluffy in her carrier in the backseat. "I guess it all depends on how he treats the dog."

I grinned as I guided the car into the fringes of Lake View's ritziest neighborhood. "So murderers are mean to animals as a general rule?"

"Probably. You're the expert on murder, not me."

I turned into a private drive and drove through the imposing gates and up a long driveway to an even more impressive house.

We sat for a second rubbernecking at the mansion on the hill. "Doesn't that just make you want to call the butler to bring high tea, dahling?" My English accent was atrocious, flavored as it was by an Arkansas drawl.

"Ignore her," Carly muttered to Fluffy as she got the carrier out of the backseat. "She gets goofier when she's nervous."

"She's the one you need to watch out for," I said to the dog. "She gets clumsy when she's nervous."

Carly snickered. "True."

In spite of our warnings to Fluffy, we made it to the front door without incident. When I pushed the doorbell, loud, rich chimes sounded inside.

A middle-aged woman wearing a white blouse tucked neatly in a knee-length black skirt opened the door. We told her our names, and she showed us to a spacious room with floor-to-ceiling bookshelves and a bay window complete with window seat. Fluffy jumped wildly in her carrier, making sharp yelping noises and scrabbling around. Carly handed me the plastic box, and I set it on the floor but left the door latched.

"Mr. Hall will be with you in a moment." She backed out and closed the double doors behind us. It occurred to me that was what they always meant in old books when they said someone withdrew.

"This must be the withdrawing room," I whispered to Carly. She looked at me as if I'd lost it. "Never mind," I muttered. Jokes that have to be explained are never funny.

Before we had time to get nosy, the double doors opened again. "Good afternoon." Lawrence Hall was a good twenty-five years Lisa's senior, but his white hair and sharp blue eyes gave him a distinguished man-about-town look. All smiles and gracious host, today he did remind me of Mr. Rourke from *Fantasy Island*.

"Ah, I see you've brought my baby home." He bent down toward the carrier where Fluffy was making happy squeaky noises. "Thank you." He opened the carrier and lifted Fluffy out. He was rewarded with a long pink tongue licking him all over the face.

While he was talking baby talk to Fluffy, Carly looked at me and shrugged. I knew she was remembering our conversation in the car about whether murderers were nice to animals.

Larry gave us a sheepish grin. "I've missed her."

I smiled. No kidding. We'd never have guessed.

He sat down in a leather recliner with Fluffy on his lap.

"Would you ladies care for some refreshment?" Without waiting for a reply, he rang a bell on the table beside his chair. The woman who had shown us in entered with a tray holding three glasses of iced tea and a plate of home-baked chocolate chip cookies.

Larry handed us each a glass of tea and held out the plate for us to get a napkin and a cookie.

"Thanks," we chorused.

"Nice weather for September, isn't it?" he said just as Carly and I bit into our cookies. I've always wondered why people offer someone food then immediately start a conversation.

We nodded.

He cleared his throat and tried again. "The Cardinals look like they might go all the way this year."

I took a sip of my tea. "If they can keep their offense hitting like they have the last few games, they definitely have a chance."

Larry's aristocratic eyebrows rose. "Ah, a fellow baseball fan."

"She went to St. Louis to a game the other night and sat eight rows behind home plate," Carly said.

Larry looked at me and nodded. "Nice seats. . . Sometimes I think we miss the feel of being a part of the crowd in our private box."

"Daddy always says if you can't smell the popcorn, you might as well be watching it on TV," I said without thinking.

And that was the end of the baseball conversation.

Carly and I exchanged a glance. I'd wanted to talk to Larry, but the atmosphere was so stilted that it was hard to ask questions like I usually did. I cleared my throat. "We'd better be going."

"Wait." Larry leaned forward and set his glass down. "How's Lisa?"

"She's having a pretty hard time."

"We all reap what we sow, don't we?" His voice was hard.

I winced. "Yes, I guess we do. But then again, we all make mistakes." I wasn't sure Lisa had hit rock bottom yet. And it obviously wouldn't hurt her to do some serious soul searching, but I still pitied her.

Larry rang the bell, and the maid appeared. "Please take Fluffy outside for a walk," he commanded.

The maid quickly took the little white dog and left the room.

Larry turned back to us and crossed his arms in front of his chest. "I offered to hire a lawyer for her, but she said Bob was taking care of it." A strange expression crossed his face. "Looks like she's going to need a good one."

"Do you think she killed him?" Carly asked, and he and I both looked at her in surprise. She shrugged. "You know her a lot better than we do."

He considered her question then shook his head slowly. "She's been tired of me for at least three years, and she didn't try to kill me. Why would she decide to murder to get rid of a boyfriend?" When he said the word "boyfriend," the veins in his neck stood out and his face grew red.

Thoughts of Debbie and her cell phone secret flitted through my mind. But after visiting Lisa, I was convinced that she didn't know about J.D. and Debbie. No one was that good an actress.

"But if she did have a strong motive, do you think she's capable of murder?" Carly persisted. I gave her a mental thumbs-up sign. Sometimes when I least expected it, her inner Nancy Drew kicked in. It always made me proud.

"Aren't we all capable of murder in the right circumstances?" Larry gave Carly an enigmatic smile.

She stiffened, and I waited for righteous indignation to spew forth. She surprised me.

"In what circumstance would you, for instance, be capable of murder?" She smiled sweetly at him, tilted her head to one side, and waited for an answer.

"Oh, I don't know. It would take more than my wife running off with a guy for me to kill him, if that's what you're getting at." And he smiled right back at her. "I might be tempted to kill *her* in that instance. But not him."

"And yet. . ."

"And yet, Lisa's not dead." He smiled. "It's all wrong, isn't it? Is that why you came out here? To ask me if I killed this guy?"

"Well." Following Carly's lead, I spoke more boldly than I normally would. "Do you have an alibi?"

"I don't need one. Unless you have a badge stashed somewhere on your person, and I don't think you do, I don't have to answer to you."

"So you refuse to say where you were the night of the murder?"

"I refuse to answer impertinent questions from meddling women who should be minding their own business. There. Is that blunt enough for you?"

His chilly smile never faltered as he stood and gestured to the door.

"Ladies? Let me show you out. Thank you for bringing Fluffy. Give Lisa my regards." His voice hardened. "And tell her I won't wait forever for her to come to her senses. Good-bye, ladies." And with a mocking bow, he ushered us out the front door. It closed with a definite click.

"That went well," Carly commented wryly as we exited the gates and headed home.

❖

"I hate funerals," I complained to Carly as I pulled on one black shoe and looked around for the other one. "If Jolene hadn't pressured me, I wouldn't go."

"Oh, who are you kidding?" Carly pitched me my other shoe from the closet. "I'm the one who should be complaining about being dragged along. You know what you always say about the murderer returning to the scene of the crime. You wouldn't miss this, and you know it."

I ducked my head. "You know me too well. But I do feel sorry for Jolene. She's kind of obnoxious, but she doesn't know anyone in town, and she was once married to J.D."

"I feel sorry for her, too, I guess. But I could do it from a distance. Especially since most of my employees seem to be taking off to go."

"Most of your employees? Who besides Debbie?" I gave her a sheepish grin. "And me?"

"Vini."

"Vini?" That was a surprise.

"Apparently Gail asked him to go with her. I think they kind of like each other, but they're both too busy or too shy to do much about it."

"Wonder why Gail is going?" I'd understood she hadn't been fond of J.D. when they worked together.

"Gail's a younger version of us, Jenna. Raised by a Southern mama to do the right thing whether you want to or not. He was a coworker, and it's the right thing to go to coworkers' funerals."

"I wonder if any of his grandmother's friends will be there."

"They might. But with all the trouble he apparently gave her, they might not."

"But he did come to her funeral," I reminded her.

"Yeah, probably just to see what he could get." Once again my sister sounded cynical. "Are you almost ready?"

"Yeah, Jolene wanted to pick us up here, but I convinced her to meet us at the funeral home. Wonder how Tom will do with the funeral?"

"Oh, I think he can handle it. Assuming no one gets shot." Carly referred to the last funeral we'd attended.

"Don't even think that!" I shuddered. "I just meant since he didn't know J.D. And since at least one current girlfriend, and possibly two, along with the ex-wife will probably all attend. It could be awkward."

"Or it could be illuminating. Maybe someone will confess to his murder."

I shook my head. "Somehow I doubt that."

As soon as Carly and I entered the funeral home chapel, Jolene strutted toward us. In deference to the solemn occasion, she had on her black halter today with a black leather skirt and black boots that came up over her knees. Her snake tattoo matched her eye liner perfectly.

"You've got to be kidding," Carly hissed in my ear from behind.

"Serious as a heart attack," I murmured. "Just wait." I'd tried to paint her a word picture of J.D.'s ex-wife, but obviously my description had fallen short of the reality.

I introduced the two women, and Carly expressed polite condolences.

Jolene slapped my arm with the back of her hand. "Girlfriend, didn't you tell your sister that dying was the best thing Jimmy Dean ever did for me?"

Carly's eyes widened, but she didn't say a word. She and Mama were both so blessed with knowing the right thing to say that I kind of felt better that Jolene left her speechless.

Tom LeMay, the funeral director, motioned Jolene toward the back. She waved at him and turned back to us. "When this is done, we need to go out and celebrate."

Again Carly didn't utter a word. Not even an "It was nice meeting you."

When Jolene was gone, we found a seat halfway down the aisle, and Carly suddenly rediscovered her voice. "I can't believe I let you talk me into this. That woman is crazy."

I shrugged. "She's odd. But she's honest. Sometimes that's refreshing."

Carly's face paled. "What do you mean by that?"

I frowned. "I don't mean anything by that. Why?"

Before she could answer, a stir at the back of the small crowd drew our attention. Lisa, dressed in an elegant black dress and flanked by her parents, walked past Jolene as if she weren't there. Lisa held a dainty handkerchief to her eyes, but Bob and Wilma looked grimly forward. Each held one of Lisa's elbows, but she didn't look heartbroken enough to faint. In fact, either her mascara was very waterproof or the handkerchief was a show. I saw no tears. They took a seat across the aisle from us, but they didn't look our way.

A murmured conversation behind us caused me to look back just as Tiffany and Ricky slid into the pew behind us.

She leaned forward. "Hi." She spoke in the low tones people often adopt in funeral situations. "I don't usually cover funerals, but since this guy was murdered, I figured I might get a column out of it for the paper."

"I doubt there will be many people here," I responded.

"That's why I dragged Ricky along." She patted his hand tucked around her elbow. "I thought it'd look more respectful if there were a few people attending."

"I brought Carly for the same reason," I said.

Like Carly, Rick looked as if he'd rather be anywhere but here, but he mustered a smile.

"Yep, that's me. The pew-filler," he muttered.

"It's so nice to have someone who doesn't mind giving up his free time when I need him." Tiffany gave Rick a dazzling smile.

Over Tiffany's shoulder, I saw Gail and Vini come in. Vini looked extremely uncomfortable and kept tugging at the tie wedged around his throat. Gail had the appearance of someone performing an unpleasant duty. She and Vini sat toward the back and spoke to each other in whispers without looking around at all.

An elderly couple entered next. They spoke briefly to Jolene and settled themselves directly in front of me. After a few moments of getting settled, the gray-haired woman turned around to me.

"Excuse me. Were you married to Jimmy? Someone said his wife was here."

"That woman at the back is his wife." Her husband nudged her and spoke loudly enough to be heard all over the building. "She told you that. You should've worn your hearing aid. Now turn around here and quit meddling."

I bit back a smile. Would that be Alex and me in forty years? I glanced at them again. They looked vaguely familiar, and I was pretty sure they were the couple who talked loudly during the last funeral I attended.

"I was Mindy Finley's closest neighbor and best friend for thirty years. If I want to ask questions about her grandson, I will." She twisted back to face me. "I hadn't seen Jimmy since he was a kid. He used to stay with his grandma sometimes. He worried her to death with his constant shenanigans. She bailed him out time and time again until she had nothing left to give." She shook her head. "But he had the nerve to show up at her funeral looking for an inheritance. Now he's got himself killed."

Her husband tugged at her, and she turned around without waiting for any comments from me. Just as Tom started to escort Jolene to the front of the funeral parlor, the door opened and closed quickly and someone sat toward the back. I glanced around as discreetly as possible to see if I could spot the newcomers. Harvey and Alice. Came to make sure their nemesis was really gone, I guessed.

Across the way, and also on the back row, was a woman with a black dress, black hat, and glasses. I peered at her and nudged Carly. "You're right. Down Home's staff is almost all here. Debbie's even back there."

Carly nodded dully, and I turned my attention back to her. "Are you sick?"

She shook her head.

Before I could question her further, a loud *"Psst!"* brought my attention to the aisle.

Jolene had stopped right beside me with Tom LeMay still on her arm. She looked at me and motioned around the sparsely populated room. "So which one was J.D.'s girlfriend?"

Heat crept up my face. I glanced at the spectators, who were all watching me. Debbie had taken the sunglasses off and was staring at me, wide-eyed. Lisa glanced toward me then looked away. "The one in black," I whispered.

Before she could press me, Tom tugged gently on her arm. "Miss Highwater, we really must begin."

She waggled her fingers at me and walked to the front and sat down.

Without warning, "Born to Be Wild" blared from the speakers. Everyone jumped. Jolene had apparently done a little tweaking of the funeral plans that she and I had made together. When the song finished, a man in a black suit got up and read the obituary. Then he cleared his throat. For the next few minutes, he spoke in fairly generic terms about how quickly life passes by and how awful it is to waste it.

Even though I knew what he said was true, my mind started to inventory all the people who might have killed Jimmy Dean Finley, their motives, and their alibis. Beside me, I suddenly felt Carly shaking. I looked over and drew in a sharp breath. Tears were coursing down her face, and she was quietly sobbing. "Carly?" I whispered. "Are you hurting?"

She shook her head.

"Are you sick?" Sympathetic tears were pricking my own eyes, even though I couldn't imagine that we were crying about J.D.

Another shake of her head.

I handed her a couple of tissues from the box in the pew beside me and put my arm around her. "It's okay," I murmured, all thoughts of suspects and alibis vanquished from my mind. "What's wrong?" I tried one more time, but she shook her head yet again.

"I can't talk about it here," she whispered, each word punctuated by a quiet gulp.

"Then let's go somewhere where we can." I stood, helped her to her feet, and guided her to the back and out the double doors. No doubt we'd be the talk of the town, but I didn't care what people thought. The important thing was figuring out what was wrong with Carly.

Out in the courtyard, she quit trying to hold it in and started sobbing harder. My legs trembled as we sank onto a wrought-iron bench. "Car?" I wiped her curls back from her face. "Did you know J.D.?"

As she shook her head, relief coursed through me. Followed quickly by extreme confusion. "Why are we crying?"

"It's Travis," she choked out.

My heart jumped. Her ex-husband had been found. "He's here?"

She looked up at me, dark mascara tracks trailing down her cheeks. "Jenna. Travis is dead."

16

The Hard Thing About Business Is Mindin' Your Own

O h no." I reached over and took Carly's hand in mine. "I'm sorry."

We sat there for a few minutes without speaking, letting the cool breeze dry our tears as they fell. My natural curiosity was strangely dormant. A man I'd considered a brother had lost his life. He'd lost any hope of a second chance. Of reconciliation with his children. Had it seemed worth it to him after the initial infatuation was over? I guess we'd never know. Nor did it really matter now. Any lingering bitterness I had toward the man who'd broken my sister's heart and almost broken her spirit faded away to a deep sadness.

"He's been dead four years," Carly said softly.

"Four years?" It seemed incredible that we hadn't known. I'd googled his name more than once on the Internet, just to see if I could figure out what happened to him once he walked out of our lives so completely. Why hadn't I at least found an obituary?

"He died in Mexico," she said, as if answering the question I didn't ask. "That's why there was no record of it here."

I nodded. "I guess that makes sense. Was he ill?"

She looked over at me, her dark curls falling across her face. "He was shot to death. It was apparently a drug deal gone bad in a small border town. The local authorities kept it as quiet as possible."

"So this is what you and Elliott have been fussing about? Travis being dead?" I really couldn't see how that had turned into a source of such conflict.

She nodded her head and stared at the water bubbling in the small fountain in front of us. "It took awhile to find out for sure if the Travis that died was"—she cut her gaze to me and grimaced—"our Travis."

"And you didn't want to tell me until you knew for sure. I understand that."

She squeezed my hand. "Thanks. I knew you'd understand. I didn't see any sense in you or Mama and Daddy having to grieve if it wasn't true. Especially after you found J.D.'s body. It just brought it all so much closer and made it more real." She nodded toward the funeral home. "Just like in there. The preacher could have been preaching Travis's funeral."

I thought of his words about how quickly life passes and how awful it is to waste it. "You're right."

"The main thing Elliott and I disagree about is telling the kids."

Suddenly, the cryptic things Carly said over the last few weeks made sense. How far do you go to protect your children from pain? "You don't want to tell them."

She jerked her hand away and pushed to her feet. "I don't want to *hurt* them. I'd rather just marry Elliott and never tell them anything about their dad. At least not until they're adults."

"But Elliott feels like they should know." I stated the obvious.

"Yes! He says he doesn't want to start our lives together as a family with a deception hanging over us. Even though I understand what he means, every time I picture telling them, I just can't do it."

"So what are you going to do?"

She shrugged and stuck her hand in the cool fountain water. "I guess we're not going to do anything. We're kind of at an impasse."

My heart ached so much for her, but even Dear Pru had no wise answer for her. I stood and pulled her into a hug. "I'll be praying for you."

She nodded. "Thanks."

Dear Pru,

My husband has found someone else, and we're in the process of getting a divorce. We have a four-year-old daughter, and he wants joint custody where she will stay with me through the week and spend weekends with him. His values are very different from mine, which is one reason for the divorce. Should I agree to these conditions? If so, how can I be sure my little girl will continue to believe what I believe to be right from wrong?

Concerned Mother

Dear Mom,

You may not have a choice in the custody arrangements. Teach your child your values by living them as well as stating them. Refrain from bad-mouthing your ex, especially in front of your daughter. And pray a lot.

After the funeral, I headed home and changed into my oldest T-shirt and capris. I had the rest of the day off, and I knew just what I needed. Two hours with a good book and my deck chair. Some sun, some shade, and maybe even a little nap.

I reached for my book from the shelf and recoiled as I saw the tiny flip phone. I'd stopped short of putting a blue label with DEBBIE on it, but I had put it out of the way so I'd quit getting it confused with mine. But how long was I going to keep it? I picked it up instead of the book and ran my finger over the shiny surface.

I hadn't counted on how conflicted I'd feel about Debbie's phone once I decided that Lisa definitely hadn't known about Debbie and J.D.'s "friendship." If I turned it in, they'd surely arrest Lisa, because if they had the weapon and the towel with J.D.'s blood on it, all they needed was motive. If I didn't turn it in, the guilt was going to eat me alive.

I groaned inwardly. Why hadn't I left this silver burden with Debbie that day on her porch? Sometimes I reminded myself of that obnoxious eight-year-old at every pool across America. You know, the one who feels she's responsible for everybody's well-being and can't even enjoy swimming for the weight of the responsibility. "Mama! Timmy's getting close to the deep end. Katie's not wearing her floaties. . . . Debbie threw evidence in the trash."

I started to put the phone back on the shelf then stopped. Getting rid of this once and for all would relax me more than lazing around in the backyard.

"Sorry, big guy," I murmured to Mr. Persi, who had started scampering through the house as soon as he saw me change into my yard clothes. "I'll be back in a few minutes, and we'll do it then." I glanced down at the faded jean capris and my 2004 National League Champs Cardinals shirt. I looked bad enough that I wouldn't purposely go to the store but not so bad that I'd hide in the floorboard if I had car trouble and needed help. "I won't even change clothes," I told the golden retriever. "We'll play as soon as I get back."

Neuro gave the dog a pitying look. I could imagine her saying, "Are you really buying this?"

I rubbed my hand across the cat's head. "I mean it. You could go outside, too, if you wanted to."

She jumped down, her tail high, and ran to the living room. She preferred the coolness of her window perch where she could watch us romp but still be completely pampered and comfortable.

I smiled. Who was I to question how Lisa and Larry fawned over Fluffy? I talked to my pets and filled in the blanks in their parts of the conversation.

At the thought of Lisa and her Fluffy being separated forever by jail bars, I snatched my car keys from the hook and ran out to the car.

Debbie answered the door, still wearing her black dress.

Since she had less motive than Lisa for murdering J.D., I'd decided to take my chances. "May I come in?"

She stepped back, and I walked into the tiny living room. It was neat and clean. Incredibly clean. From the way Debbie had been acting at work, I'd imagined empty wrappers and bottles lying around.

She saw my glance and apparently realized what I was thinking. "I clean when I'm upset."

I nodded. That would explain the vacuum marks still on the couch.

I shoved the phone into her hand. "I can't keep this."

She looked down at it and dropped it.

It hit the hardwood floor and flew into pieces.

Debbie gasped. "I didn't mean to do that."

We both scrambled for the pieces. "It's just the battery cover," I said. But my hands trembled as I put it back on.

"Do you think it still works?" she whispered.

"If it could survive the diner's scraps, it can surely survive this." I hit the power button, and we watched the light come on.

"Now what?" she asked.

I shrugged and set the phone on her end table. "Now it's all yours."

Panic flitted across her face. "Jenna! You can't do this. You're the one who fished it out of the trash."

"I won't make that mistake again."

Suddenly, the phone made a little beep, and we both jumped. "What was that?" I asked.

She bent down and gingerly picked it up. "I've got a missed call."

"You do?"

Her eyes widened, and she put her hand to her chest. "You don't think?" She mouthed the words, "J.D.?"

"No!" I shook my head. "Definitely not."

"What if it is? What if he's in a witness protection program or something and he's not really dead? And I don't call him back?"

"Fine. Call him back."

She shoved the phone at me. "You do it."

"No, ma'am." I crossed my arms in front of me and conjured up a mental picture of the little eight-year-old girl at the pool. It wasn't my fault if Debbie was going off the deep end. "If you want to call, you do it."

She fumbled around and pulled up the missed-call number. "It's not his number."

Why was I not surprised?

"But it wouldn't be if he was in hiding somehow." She took a deep breath and pushed the SEND button. "It's ringing," she whispered.

I nodded, leaning toward her in spite of myself.

She obligingly stepped closer to me and held the phone where we could both hear.

"This is Chief Conner. Who is this?" an angry-sounding male voice barked.

John. Of course. Why hadn't I thought of that?

Debbie's face paled, and she raised her eyebrows at me.

"Tell him," I mouthed.

She shook her head.

"Hello?" he growled.

We just stared at each other again. "Not my responsibility," I kept repeating to myself.

"Listen! The phone you have is evidence in a murder case. Bring it to the Lake View police station immediately. We have ways of tracing the geographical position of this phone call. It will go easier for you if you bring it here."

Debbie gasped loudly and flipped the phone shut.

She sank down on her freshly vacuumed couch and burst into tears. "This is just too much," she sobbed.

My new resolve wavered. It had been a hard day. Debbie had already been to the funeral of someone she cared about.

I sat beside her. "I'll go with you."

She reached for my hand. I took hers. She palmed the phone to me and slipped her hand away. "I can't do it, Jenna. If you do it, maybe you can calm John down."

"Ha!" Had she ever seen me with John?

She pushed her blond hair out of her face and looked at me. Tears still flowed freely down her cheeks. "I mean it. You have to at least try. I'll stay here and change clothes. . ." She ducked her head again. "And get ready to be arrested."

"Why would they arrest you?"

"Withholding evidence? Or maybe he'll think I killed J.D. so that Lisa can't have him." She picked up a needlepoint pillow and buried her face in it.

Why had I thought I could let other people handle their own problems? I sighed. "I'll take the phone to John and talk to him."

She pulled the pillow down from her face and hugged me. "I have a confession."

"What?" I braced myself, not sure I could keep any more of her secrets.

She grabbed a tissue from the coffee table and wiped her nose. "I used to think you weren't good enough for Alex."

I blew out the breath I'd been holding. "I'm sure you were right." Debbie had never made it a secret that she would like to go out with Alex.

She sighed. "Nah, I was wrong. And if you can keep John from making a mess of this, I'll sing at your wedding."

I laughed softly. "Thanks."

◈

"I'm Jenna Stafford. I need to see Chief Conner, please," I informed the uniformed officer at the front desk. He chewed his gum furiously for a minute while studying my face as if memorizing it for future reference. Probably thought he'd be seeing it on a wanted poster. "Please? It's important."

"Hold your horses," he said and picked up a phone. He punched a button and spoke in a low tone. "Jenna Stafford to see you, Chief." He looked disappointed at the response but waved me toward the inner sanctum. "Go on in."

John, writing at his desk, looked up when I walked into his office. "Hey, Jenna. What can I do for you?"

I cleared my throat. I needed to get a grip on this situation quickly if I wanted it to go as I planned. I slipped into the seat across from him. "I want to make a deal with you," I began.

He held up his hand in the tradition of traffic cops everywhere and half smiled. "If you're going to tell me who you think the murderer is, I'd rather you didn't."

"No. I don't know who did it," I said quickly. "But I do have a problem connected with the murder. In a way. Only it's not, really. But you think it is."

"Instead of telling me what I think, why don't you tell me what you're talking about." John leaned back in his high-backed leather chair and crossed his arms across his chest.

I took a deep breath. "Here's the thing. The cell phone you're looking for is in my purse."

17

If You Can't Hunt With The Big Dogs, Stay On The Porch

John slapped his forehead, and red crept up his neck. "Why am I not surprised?" He held out his hand. "Where did you get it?"

I nudged my purse under my chair with one foot. "That's actually a funny story."

He wasn't laughing. "Save the story and just tell me where you got it."

"It was in the garbage, of all places."

"You know what, Jenna? Let me have the phone; then you can tell me, in little bits and pieces or however you want to, all about finding it." He snapped his fingers lightly.

"Wait. I need you to promise me something first."

This time he was the one who drew a deep breath. In fact, I thought I heard him counting under his breath. Patience is a virtue. Maybe he was developing his. "I don't make promises, and I don't make deals. This is not television. Hand. Over. The. Phone. Now."

"Well, I did make a promise. I promised the person who had this phone that I'd talk to you about it before you made any rash decisions."

He pushed himself out of his chair and put his palms on the desk. "What I do with information received and pertinent to an ongoing investigation is not your affair. Give me the phone."

I leaned back instinctively. "The person who had this has a really good alibi for the time of the murder. I don't think she could possibly have killed J.D., but there is some information on the phone that could do her harm."

He took pity on me. Or else he was just sick of having me in his office.

"Jenna, give me a little credit. If this isn't helpful, we won't use it. And I have yet to make information public in a current investigation." His hand was still stretched toward me. "Who had the phone? Whose garbage was it in? And how did you end up with it?"

"I was gathering garbage at the diner when I spotted something. I fished around and found the phone. At first, I thought it was mine. It's exactly like mine, so that was a natural assumption." I looked at him to try and gauge his reaction.

Stone-faced.

"Anyway, when I went to check a message from Alex, there were several messages I didn't recognize. Then I found my phone in my purse."

"So who does the phone belong to?" He held out his hand. "Never mind. Just let me have the phone, and I'll find out."

"I'd like to." I glanced at his unyielding face. "The thing is, the person who had this phone doesn't want Lisa to know that she had it."

"This phone is evidence in a murder investigation. So far I've purposely avoided asking you how long ago you found it. But you don't even want to know what it would be like if you're charged with withholding evidence or being an accessory to murder." John glared at me. "Tell me what you know and quit playing games."

"Okay." I caved. "J.D. and Debbie were just starting to see each other behind Lisa's back. Debbie doesn't want Lisa to find out." I reached down and picked up my purse. "They were planning to tell Lisa, but then he got killed."

"Or J.D. went ahead and told Lisa, and she got mad and shot him," John murmured. He looked quickly at me. "Ignore that. I was just thinking aloud."

I didn't like the direction his thoughts were going. "I thought Lisa had an alibi." I pulled the phone out of my purse and laid it on the desk.

"Not an airtight one." He looked me in the eye. "But you're sure Debbie does?" He picked up the phone and flipped it open as if the murderer's name were written in the keys.

"Well, she was washing dishes in the kitchen at the diner." But did she have an airtight alibi? I couldn't say positively that she hadn't left the diner for a few minutes. How long would it take to run out back, shoot an unsuspecting victim, and dash back inside? And even follow me out and knock me in the head? Anyone at the diner easily could have done it. But there was the fact that she was possibly the only one who knew he was supposed to be out there. Unless he had a whole bevy of secret girlfriends.

"So you can say for sure that she never went outside?" John searched my face as if he could see the questions running through my mind.

I reluctantly shook my head. "Not positively."

"Well, then, don't expect me to make you any promises. I will do what is necessary to bring a killer to justice. But I will not harm any innocent bystanders if I can help it."

It wasn't the promise I wanted, but I had to be content with that.

❖

"Reporting for duty," I said as I breezed into the kitchen. Getting rid of Debbie's phone yesterday had done a lot to lighten my burden of responsibility. If I could keep Lisa out of jail and figure out how to solve Carly's problems, I'd be batting a thousand.

Carly smiled at me. "Just in time." She wiped her hands on her apron as she went to the large refrigerator for more ingredients. Whatever she was cooking, the aroma was delicious. Alice nodded to me from the stove. Funny how well they were working together now when Alice and Harvey had only about a week left on their agreement to help out.

"You should bottle that smell," I told them as I got my own apron and checked the pocket. Yes, my order pad and pencil were there. I was ready for business.

Carly grinned. "If only we could figure out how."

I was glad to see her smiling. She'd told me last night on the phone that the funeral had been therapeutic for her in a way. And that with God's help she was closer to figuring things out. I'd been praying ever since that God would work it out. He was so much better at handling things than I was.

"Anything I need to know before I go out there?" I asked.

She shrugged. "Harvey's seating folks, and Susan and Vini have their hands full. Debbie called and said she's under the weather." She sent me a questioning look, and I shrugged. I'd told Carly the whole thing on the phone last night. And I didn't know anything new.

I pushed the swinging door and was immersed in the hubbub made by happy diners. I waved to Harvey to let him know my section of tables could be put into use and headed to the menu stand. The next couple of hours passed in a blur. I had the fleeting reflection that this job wasn't so bad. Hard, but interesting. Mostly hard, though. My thoughts were scattered when a familiar voice trumpeted my name.

I looked up.

"Hey, Miss Lady, how much longer are you chained to that apron?" Jolene wended her way through a maze of tables to me, conversing the entire way. Presumably with me, but loudly enough for it to be a community conversation. "I came to tell you bye-bye."

"Have a seat, Jolene," I murmured, in the hopes she would follow my example and talk more quietly. "Let me bring you a glass of tea."

I left a menu on the table and went to the counter. I returned with her tea. "Can I get you anything to eat?"

"Nah, sweetie. Thanks, but I ate a late breakfast at the hotel. I just thought you and me might have a little heart-to-heart before I head out."

"I can't leave, but I can take a break for a few minutes. Let me clear it with Harvey." I went to his station and explained that I would be on break for the next ten minutes, grabbed myself a glass of tea, and went back to sit with Jolene.

"So, you're heading out, huh? Where to?"

"You know, girl, I been thinking about that a lot. I ain't had what you might call roots since I was a little kid in pigtails. Now I got this money, compliments of Jimmy-boy, God rest his soul, and I think I might just make a down payment on a little house somewheres. My granny's place in Texas comes to mind. I 'magine her old house is tore down, but I b'lieve I could find me something reasonable around there. I might just go back to waitressing my own self. I'd make enough to pay the bills, and I'd have a life like most folks have." She beamed at me like a first grader showing her mother a good report card.

"Jolene, I think that's a great idea."

"Seems kinda funny, don't it? Jimmy and me never did have what most folks would think of as a good marriage. He never was one to make a honest living. More times than not, I was the one who took care of him." She shook her head in wonder. "But here I am, fixin' to buy a house, and it's thanks to him. The Lord surely does work in mysterious ways, don't He?"

"He sure does," I agreed. I took a sip of tea. "Jolene, I hope things work out well for you."

"Why, I'm sure they will, chickie. You can't keep a good woman down. Speaking of women, you never did introduce me to Jimmy's latest flame."

I sent a brief prayer of thanksgiving that neither Debbie nor Lisa was at the diner.

"No, I didn't. And she's not here right now."

"Ah, well, I guess I'll live without meeting her. I'm ready to blow this burg and hit that little watering hole in the next county. Then I'm off to Texas." She stood and leaned down to envelop me in a scented, smothering hug. "Don't take life too serious, girlfriend. It'll be over before you know it." She gave me a cheery grin and headed to the door. She detoured through Vini's section and pinched his cheek before he could dodge. "Been a pleasure seeing you, sweet cakes. Every single time." And Jolene Highwater was gone. The effect was of a gentle breeze after a howling windstorm.

The ringing of my cell phone jerked me to attention.

"Hello?"

"Jenna?" Debbie's voice could've scorched my ear. "Forget about me singing at your wedding." She spat the words at me.

"Why?" I replied guardedly. But she talked right over me.

"I've spent the last hour at the police station. Doesn't that sound like fun? Well, it's not. Being accused of murder is not a joke at all. I knew this would happen. But nooo. You had to take it into your own hands. Well, from now on, just butt out of my life."

I bit back the reminder that she'd asked me to take the phone to John and talk to him on her behalf. And that I'd done exactly that. "Debbie, calm down. Did John actually accuse you of murder? That doesn't sound right."

"John didn't come right out and accuse me of murder." She was a little less agitated but still touchy. "But I could tell he was suspicious. He really gave me the third degree."

"Well, he would have to question you. After all," I pointed out in a reasonable tone, "you withheld a valuable piece of evidence." She began sputtering, but I continued, "He isn't still suspicious of you, is he? I mean, he didn't threaten to lock you up or warn you not to leave town, did he?"

"No," she said quietly, as if my words were finally soaking in. "And he did say he wouldn't tell Lisa unless he has to. So that's a plus."

"See? Doing the right thing is good." I reminded myself of Pollyanna.

A muted growl from the other end of the phone warned me to tread lightly. "And think of it this way: You won't have to worry about it anymore."

"That's true." She was almost back to normal. "Tell Carly I'll be in for the evening shift." She hung up without saying good-bye, but I was thankful to get through that conversation with a whole ear. I went to the kitchen to give Carly an update. We had the break room to ourselves, so I told her all about Debbie's irate phone call.

"Well, it's best for Debbie to get it out in the open. I'm sorry if she hurt your feelings"—she smiled at me—"but you were right. And getting your ears blistered is a small price to see that the right thing is done."

❖

I turned off the water. Was that my phone ringing? I hoped it wasn't an emergency, because whoever it was would have to wait until I dried, dressed, and towel-dried my hair.

Finally, wrapped in my robe, I checked my voice messages. "Miss Stafford, this is Lawrence Hall." It took me a second to realize it was Larry. That cleared up the mystery of which name he went by. "Bob Pryor asked me to call you and tell you that Lisa's been taken into custody." He left his number in case I needed more information then ended the message.

I glanced at the clock hanging by the front door. It was only 8:30. I considered my options. Dry my hair and go on to bed. Toss and turn all night wondering what happened to Lisa. Or go down to the police station and offer moral support and comfort to Bob and Wilma. Not to mention have a little talk with John.

An easy decision.

I quickly dressed, combed out my hair, and stuck it up in a messy bun. At a quarter till nine, I pulled in front of the station and headed in.

"I'd like to see the chief, please," I said to the desk sergeant.

"I'm sorry, ma'am; he's in a meeting at the moment."

"Will you tell him that Jenna Stafford is waiting out here to see him?" I smiled at him. "I just need to talk to him for a minute."

"I'm sorry, ma'am." He leaned toward me. "He told me not to interrupt him."

"Well, I'll just sit out here and wait if you don't mind." I turned to sit in one of the chairs near the desk.

"If you'd like, there's a waiting area just down the hall on your left." He pointed. "There are some people in there already, but the chairs are a little more comfortable."

"Thanks. I'll go down there. Will you be sure Chief Conner gets my message?"

"Yes, ma'am. I'll tell him as soon as he comes out."

Bob and Wilma were huddled together in the corner when I walked in. They wore identical shell-shocked expressions.

Bob stood and came toward me. "Jenna, thanks so much for coming. We've hired an attorney, but he has to drive in from Little Rock."

I gave him a one-armed hug. "I'm so sorry."

He returned my hug, but as soon as he released me, he began pacing. "He said for Lisa not to answer any questions, but I don't know what she's saying in there. They wouldn't let us go in with her."

"I'm sure her lawyer will be in soon." I bent down and gave Wilma a hug. "He'll get this straightened out." I sat down next to her.

"Bob, stop pacing." Wilma leaned her head back and closed her eyes.

"Jenna, you've been around this kind of thing. Can you think of anything else we can do?" Bob sat back down in the chair on the other side of Wilma.

"You just need to stay strong." I wished I had a better answer for them.

"You know, you spend your life protecting your child, and then something out of the blue like this happens." Tears rolled from Wilma's closed eyes and made tracks down her cheeks. "It makes you wonder. . . ." Her voice trailed off. I held my breath while I waited for her to say something more. Or for Bob to answer her.

When no one said anything, I patted Wilma on the back. "Why don't I go and get us something to drink from the vending machine?" I left them to their painful memories and headed out the door. "I'll be right back."

I walked down the hall to the outer office where I had seen the vending machines. A uniformed sleeve brushed my arm, and I looked up into Seth's smiling eyes.

"Hey, Nancy Drew. What are you doing here?"

"Larry called me." I stuck some bills into the machine and hit the button for water.

"Lisa is in there with John right now. I feel sorry for her folks, but we've got enough on that girl to put her away for life now that we have the motive."

18

What Goes Around, Comes Around

I stared at Seth. Now they had a motive. Which I had handed to them on a silver platter. Lisa was frighteningly self-centered, and if she had known her boyfriend and her best friend were cheating on her, well, murder wasn't so far-fetched. But I was convinced she had no idea. I just had to convince John.

"I don't think she did it, Seth." I hit the button again and watched another bottle fall out.

His eyebrows drew together. "She had motive, the weapon belonged to her and had her fingerprints on it, his blood was on a towel found in her car, and her alibi won't hold water." He ticked each item off on his fingers. "And now she's lawyering up. You just don't want to believe it because of her parents."

"I don't want to believe it because she didn't do it, Seth. Is there any way I can talk to John?" I clutched the three bottles of water to my chest.

"As soon as her lawyer gets here, he'll probably want to talk to her alone. When he does, John will come out." He'd no sooner said that than the front door burst open and a distinguished-looking, black-haired man in a three-piece suit pushed open the double glass doors and rushed up to the desk. "And I think he just arrived." Seth said the last words in a whisper.

After the desk sergeant showed the attorney to the room where Lisa waited, I dropped off the water to Bob and Wilma then hurried back into the hallway so I could catch John as he came out of the interrogation room.

I touched his arm when he stepped out the door. "John, could I have a minute?"

"You again? You're just like a bad penny." It didn't sound like a joke when he said it. "You have exactly"—he looked at his watch—"five minutes. That's it." He motioned me into his office. "And I'm only giving you that because you came through with the motive."

"This is all wrong. Lisa didn't kill J.D." I pushed the door shut. "She had no idea he was cheating on her. So she had no motive."

"Jenna, just go on home and let me do my job." Déjà vu all over again. Hadn't he said those exact words when he brought my nephew, Zac, in for questioning in an earlier murder case? And look how wrong he'd been then.

"I'm not trying to keep you from doing your job. I'm just trying to keep you from looking like a fool." I resisted the urge to stomp my foot for emphasis. "I'm telling you, she had no reason to kill him. I've talked to her about it."

"Riiight." He drew out the word and shook his head. "And you think she'd just confess to you if she did it?" He looked at his watch. "I guess Bob has convinced you that she's being framed?"

"I believe she is being framed. If she'd used her gun, she'd have taken it back home with her and gotten rid of it. And why would she put a bloody towel under her seat?"

He flinched.

"Everybody knows about that. I heard it at the diner."

He nodded. "Small towns."

"And like I said, she didn't know about Debbie and J.D., so you don't have motive."

He tapped his watch as if maybe it had stopped. "Look, I feel sorry for her parents just like you do, but I can't let a murderer go free because I feel sorry for her family."

"You're making a mistake if you charge her with murder."

"And you're making a mistake if you continue to try to tell me how to do my job." His voice rose. "But, for your information, I haven't officially charged her. Yet." Another glance at his watch. "Your time is up."

Bob and Wilma were still sitting exactly as they had been when I first walked in. The only difference was the unopened bottle of water each held.

I sank into the empty chair beside Wilma and put my arm around her but could find no comforting words. The two of them were silent as the grave. I cleared my throat. "Did Lisa give them her alibi?" I hated to pry, but both John and Seth had mentioned that it wouldn't hold up.

"Yes." Bob closed his mouth on that one word. Okay, this was weird. He had been so forthcoming before. Now suddenly he clammed up?

"And the police didn't believe her?" I was fishing for information.

"They believed her. They just said she had time to drive by and shoot J.D. first." He looked down at the floor. "Thanks so much for coming by, Jenna. Lisa's lawyer is here now, and I guess there's nothing you can do." He looked at Wilma. "Except take Wilma home for me."

She shook her head. "I'm staying with you."

"No, honey, go on home. You'll need to get some rest so you can help us tomorrow." He gently took her hand and helped her to her feet. "Please go home. I don't want to have to worry about both my girls."

Still clutching her water, Wilma kissed him on the cheek. "Okay. But call me if you know anything. No matter what time it is."

◈

After I walked Wilma in and was pulling out of her driveway, my phone rang. I flipped it open. "Hello?"

"Jen?" Carly's voice trembled.

"What's wrong?"

She laughed. "Nothing."

"Nothing? You sound like you've been crying."

"Happy tears this time."

"Oh?" I slapped the steering wheel with one hand. "Spill it, Sister."

"Elliott asked me to marry him. And I said yes!"

"Carly, that's fantastic." I forced myself not to ask any questions about the Travis situation. If they'd worked it out, that's what mattered.

"Jenna, he took me out to eat, and after dessert he got down on one knee." She laughed again. "You should see the ring. It's perfect!"

Tears pricked at my eyes. "I can't wait to see it."

"Then he told me that if I chose not to tell the kids about Travis, he would respect that, because he wasn't going to throw away our happiness by being stubborn."

"I knew my future brother-in-law was a great guy."

"He's a wise man, too," she said softly. "I've been praying hard about it, and I've decided to tell them. And Mama and Daddy."

"Oh, Carly. . ." Relief coursed through me. "I'm proud of you."

"Thanks, but I want more than your admiration. I want your support."

I turned my signal on and negotiated the turn into my driveway. "Name the time and place. I don't have to go into the gym until three tomorrow. And if I need to, I can get someone to cover for me."

"Tomorrow morning for breakfast."

I killed the motor. "At the diner?" Strange place for a family meeting.

She laughed. "Since Alice and Harvey only have a couple more days, I'm letting them handle the Saturday morning crowd alone. I'm cooking at my place."

"You sure you don't want me to pick up some bacon biscuits?"

"Cooking will help me stay calm. Just come hungry."

◈

The next morning when I got to Carly's cabin, she met me at the kitchen door.

"Calm yet?" I murmured as I wiped flour from her face.

She wrinkled her nose at me. "I'm glad you're here. I can't decide whether to tell them about the engagement after I tell them the other or not."

"Why don't you just play it by ear? Is Elliott coming?"

She shook her head. "He thought the kids—especially Zac—would be able to show their true feelings better if he wasn't here."

"He's probably right." Zac had been ten when his dad left, and even though he seemed to be crazy about Elliott, he'd need time to grieve.

"The twins will be—"

A knock on the door sounded in the middle of Carly's sentence.

"—fine," she said as she went to let Mama and Daddy in.

Mama held out a glass bottle of orange juice. "Fresh squeezed," she said and hugged Carly.

"She squeezed it herself," Daddy assured us.

I stared from Mama to Carly. "Why didn't I get any of those genes?"

"No one wants a carbon copy of themselves, dear," Mama said. "You're unique." She started pulling glasses from the cabinet for the orange juice. "Speaking of which, are y'all going to Tiffany's shower this afternoon?"

"Yes," I said. "We both are." Carly had protested, but I'd insisted.

"Want me to pick you up?" Carly asked her.

"Sure."

"Jenna?"

"I need to go on to the club to work after the shower, so I'll take my own car."

The twins came bounding in. "Is breakfast ready?"

Carly nodded. "Go get your brother and go to the table."

Forty-five minutes later, we'd all finished our bacon, sausage, eggs, and homemade biscuits. Zac pushed back from the table. "I've got to go, Mom. I'm supposed to meet the guys at the basketball court."

Carly held up her hand and laid down her napkin. "Not yet. Let's all go in the living room." She stood.

Zac frowned. "Why?"

"Just because," she said softly.

"Don't you want us to clean off the table first?" Rachel asked.

"No," Carly said. "We'll do it later."

"Uh-oh," I heard Hayley whisper as we made our way into the other room. "It must be something bad."

In the living room, the twins sank to the floor with their backs against the paneled wall. Zac slumped spinelessly in an overstuffed chair. I sat beside Mama and Daddy on the sofa.

Carly stood in front of the blank TV and faced us. She gave a nervous half laugh. "I know now why people start off by saying, 'There's no easy way to say this.' Because there's really not."

Daddy put his arm around Mama and gave Carly a gentle smile. "Honey, bad news usually goes better quickly. If it's good, then you can drag it out."

She stared at him as if absorbing his words. "Okay then." She looked at the kids. "It's about your dad, Travis."

The twins looked mildly curious, but Zac snapped to attention. I heard an indrawn breath from Mama. Daddy tightened his arm around her shoulders.

"What about him?" Zac's voice was as brittle as ice, his face expressionless.

Carly looked one more time at Daddy as if weighing his advice then looked back at Zac. "He's dead, honey."

Zac's stern demeanor melted. His eyes widened, and he looked like he was going to be sick. "When did he die?"

"Four years ago."

Zac recoiled, and I could see him doing the math, calculating where he was and how old he'd been when his dad died. "How?"

Carly hesitated, and I could tell by the rapid blinking that she was fighting tears.

"We have a right to know," Zac said harshly.

I glanced at the twins. They were quiet, but their expressions were more curious than upset.

Carly's brows drew together. "You don't have to demand information, Zac. I'll tell you everything I know."

"That'll be a switch," he muttered.

"Zac. I just found this out."

"They didn't notify you when he died?" he said in a disbelieving tone.

Carly shook her head. "I hired a private investigator a few weeks ago to try to find him. And this is what he found out." Her voice quivered.

Zac pulled a pillow off the floor and clutched it to his chest. "So how did he die?"

"He was shot in a little border town in Mexico," Carly said.

I could see Zac's brain working. He really is an intelligent young man. A variety of emotions flitted across his face.

"Shot? Was he into drugs? Or something else illegal?" His voice was thin.

"Honey, we don't know what happened. Just that he was found in a seedy part of town and had been seen with a known dealer. I'm sorry."

Zac shrugged. "Does Elliott know?"

Carly shot me a look of panic.

"Why?" I asked.

Zac's mouth was a straight, tight line. Finally, he spoke. "I just figured if he found out that was the kind of dad we had, he might not want anything to do with us."

Carly put her hand to her mouth. The tears she'd been fighting filled her eyes. "Zac, Elliott loves you."

"And us," Rachel said firmly.

"And you girls, too," Carly agreed. "And he knows that no one is all good or all bad."

"Remember that story I used to tell y'all?" Daddy spoke up. "How there are two wolves inside of you all the time fighting to win?"

The twins nodded quickly. Zac hesitated, but he nodded, too.

"A good wolf and a bad wolf," Hayley said.

"And which one is going to win?" Daddy asked softly.

"The one you feed," Zac muttered.

"Your daddy fed the wrong one, honey," Mama said. "But that has nothing to do with who you are."

Carly gave me a questioning look, and I nodded. We could all use some good news.

"I have one more thing to tell you all," Carly said.

"More about Da—him?" Zac asked.

She shook her head. "This is about us. All of us." She smiled at her kids. "Elliott and I are getting married."

"Married?" Rachel said, her voice high. "Whoo-hoo!" She jumped up and tackled her mama. Her sister was right behind her. They danced around Carly. Mama and Daddy stood, and each reached over the top of the twins to hug her. When they stepped back, Carly looked at Zac. "It's a lot to take in all at once," she said. I knew she was giving him a chance to retreat quietly.

He stood and nodded. "It is. But it'll be cool not to be the only guy around this house." A hint of a smile touched his solemn expression. "Maybe I won't be so outnumbered anymore."

And just like that, he was gone to play basketball, the twins hot on his heels. Carly smiled at Mama and me. "Who wants to see my ring?"

"Now I'm the one who's outnumbered," Daddy said, but he did stay to admire his daughter's engagement ring.

❖

The only comfort I had was that Mama looked as disconcerted as I felt. She gave me a weak smile and placed the paper plate on her head. I did the same.

Carly giggled. "I wish I had a camera."

"Hush and put your own plate on," I growled.

"Now use these markers, and without taking the plate off your head, draw your idea of Tiffany's dream house. When we're done, she'll choose her favorite drawing, and the winner will get a prize." The tanned blond beamed at us as if she were giving us all a wonderful opportunity.

"The prize had better be a house in Florida," I muttered to Carly.

"Right on the beach," she agreed.

Tiffany, sitting next to me, snickered. "Y'all do look ridiculous."

"I think the bride should have to play, too," Denise said loudly from the other side of Tiffany. "And I don't think John would want me reaching up.

Didn't they used to say that wasn't good for the baby?"

"That's an old wives' tale," one of the Anderson sisters said from across the circle, clutching her paper plate on her head.

"Look it up on the Internet," said the other sister, who was eighty if she was a day. "You'll see." She turned to the hostess. "Are you going to tell us when to draw?"

"Be patient. Everyone has to have her plate on her head before I can start," the blond said with a pointed look at Amelia.

The mother of the bride lifted her tanned arm and placed the paper plate on her head.

While Tiffany was selecting the winner, I wandered over to the table to refill my empty punch cup. I picked out some almonds and cashews and put them on my small crystal plate. One of the Anderson sisters—I could never tell them apart—strolled up beside me. "Don't you work over at that health club for Bob Pryor?"

"Yes, ma'am." I added a few mints to my plate.

"That poor man. I heard that he may lose everything, even his house." She ladled some punch into her own cup and gave me a sideways look. "Is that true?"

"I haven't heard that." I set my cup down on the table and nibbled on an almond. "Why would he?"

"That hoity-toity daughter of his." She sipped her red punch. "She's in all kinds of trouble."

"Oh." *Now* I knew what she meant. "You mean because the police think she might have had something to do with murdering J.D. Finley?"

"That good for nothing Finley boy? His grandma spent her life's savings bailing him out of one thing after another." She wiped her lips daintily with her napkin. "But that's not what I meant," she said impatiently. "I was talking about the gambling."

"Gambling?" I parroted. "I don't know what you mean." I glanced around the room to see if anyone was listening to our conversation. Everyone was enthralled with the dream house pictures. "Bob hasn't mentioned anything about gambling."

"That girl of his. She's lost a lot of money over there at that gambling place in Mississippi." She tipped up her punch cup and downed the remains. "Tunica. That's where she said she was when that boy was shot." She wiped her lips. "And from what I hear, she goes there all the time. Musta cost her daddy a pretty penny."

"Come on everyone, sit back down," the blond hostess called. "We're going to play another game."

"Tiffany, you leave the room," she said. "Just go out in the hall and wait awhile." She made shooing motions with her hands. "We'll call you back in a few minutes."

Miss Anderson and I walked back to find seats. Amelia scooted over to sit beside me.

As soon as Tiffany left, we were given a piece of paper and a pencil with instructions to write as many facts as we could about her. What she was wearing, her birth date, her fiancé's name, her wedding date—the list was long. I held my blank paper in my hand and tried to remember exactly what color Tiffany was wearing.

"Psst." Amelia jogged my arm. "Just forget it."

"Forget what she was wearing? I thought we were trying to remember." I tapped my pencil against my teeth then threw a guilty look at Mama. She always hated when I did that.

"Forget about finding out about Ricky," she whispered as she wrote a couple of things on her paper. "I've decided we don't need to know." I sneaked a peek over her shoulder. Oh yeah. Yellow sweater. I remembered now. Blue skirt. Surprising that Amelia had paid so much attention.

"She's going to marry him anyway," she said out of the side of her mouth. "So I'm butting out." She wrote several more items down. I resisted the urge to copy them onto my sheet.

"Okay. If you're sure." I'd exhausted all my resources anyway. Seth and John.

I quickly wrote Ricky Richards down on my paper. At least I had one answer.

After Tiffany was called back into the room and we went over the answers, I realized that all the guests, even Carly, had listed more information than I had. And Amelia, who got every answer correct, was the lucky winner of the bow-covered paper plate hat.

As I helped carry things to the car with Marge, Tiffany, and Amelia, Marge congratulated Amelia on having the most correct answers. "Well, she is my daughter," Amelia said dryly. "I probably know her better than most people." She glanced at Tiffany as she put a pile of gifts in the back of the Prius. "I'm aware of those little tricks she thinks she is pulling on me."

Tiffany turned to stare at her. "What tricks?"

Amelia continued to address Marge and me. "Dressing frumpy and wearing no makeup. But I've seen pictures of her dressed to the nines and beautiful."

Tiffany reddened. "I don't know what you're talking about, Mother."

"Of course you do, darling," Amelia drawled. "I even understand why you do it."

"Really?" Tiffany widened her eyes. "Why don't you explain it then?"

"You resent the fact that I sent you away to boarding school." Amelia glanced at Marge. "And that I nag you all the time about your clothes, your weight, everything." She smiled. "That about sum it up?"

I could see the emotions flit across Tiffany's face. Surprise, anger, sadness, and finally resignation. "Yeah, I guess it does."

"Someday after you have children, I'll explain it all to you. Although by that time you may understand." She looked at Tiffany. "No, you're stronger than I ever was. You won't ever get it."

Marge looked at her sister and niece then at my face, which I could tell was red. "It's nice to see you two finally clearing the air, but maybe we should continue this at home?"

That idea definitely had my vote.

◆

Midafternoon, I'd just gotten to the athletic club when Bob walked in, still in his rumpled clothes from the night before. "Jenna? I need to see you in the office."

I dropped the stack of towels I was putting away and hurried to the office on his heels.

"I have something I want to ask you." He shut the door.

"Is it Lisa?" I blurted out.

"Is what Lisa? Where?" Bob cast a confused look around the office as if he expected his jailed daughter to pop up from behind the file cabinet or crawl from under the ratty rug.

"What did you want to ask me?"

"Oh. Have a seat." Uh-oh. This wasn't sounding too good.

I sank into a chair in front of the desk.

He cleared his throat. "I've decided to sell you the club."

Could've Talked All Day And Not Said That

If you want it, I'll start the paperwork immediately. We agreed on a price three years ago, and I'll honor that. I know I promised to finance, but I'm in a bind, so you'll have to find your own financing."

My heart pounded. Now that I knew about Lisa's gambling problem, everything made sense. Even though I'd been waiting forever for Bob to actually come through with the sale, it bothered me that he was doing it under duress.

He continued, "Any bank in town knows the Lake View Athletic Club is a solid business, so you shouldn't have any trouble getting backing. The books are in order, and I'll send them to whatever bank or S & L you want me to."

I just sat there. I didn't know what to say. My turn for throat clearing. "I appreciate the offer," I finally choked out. "But I need to think it over. Can I get back to you on it?"

"I need a decision by tonight. This is a one-time chance, Jenna. I've got other potential buyers, but I promised you first shot, so I'm giving it to you."

My eyes widened. He was going to sell the business. And quickly. To me or to someone else. "Can't I have until Monday?"

He shook his head. "I have to know by tonight."

"In that case, I'll need the rest of the afternoon off."

He nodded. "I understand."

I stood, grabbed my purse from the filing cabinet drawer, and walked out to my car. My mind whirled as I drove away.

When I got to the edge of town, I pulled my cell phone out and punched in Alex's number. He had gotten home during the shower this afternoon. Straight to voice mail. I left a message and pulled into the Stafford Cabins' drive like a homing pigeon.

For a while, I walked the banks of the lake, mindlessly skipping stones until my phone rang.

"Hi, honey, I got your message."

My heart warmed just hearing his voice. I still hadn't fully realized the fact that I didn't have to make big decisions alone anymore. "Welcome home. I'm sorry, I know you're tired from your trip, but are you free for a few minutes?"

"I'm always free for you. What do you need?"

"An ear. You got one?"

"Hey, you're in luck! I've got two. Where are you?"

I told him, and ten minutes later he was there, pulling me into his arms and kissing me soundly. "Oh, wait," he said as he released me. "It was my ears you wanted. I got confused."

I laughed, amazed by how much lighter my heart was already. Whatever we decided together, God would work it out.

He took my hand, and we walked along the lakeshore. He glanced over at me. "So what's on your mind?"

I frowned. "Bob wants to sell me the club."

"So how come you're acting like he sold it out from under you?"

I tugged him to a stop. "Well, for one thing, he's not financing it, which was part of the promise. For another, I have to let him know tonight. And he threatened me. Sort of. He mentioned that he has other people interested in buying."

"So what do you think is going on?"

"I think Lisa's been arrested and has a gambling problem, and he needs money."

He turned me to face him. "And why does that make this decision difficult?"

"I don't know. I feel guilty, I guess, like a vulture circling its prey." Even though no one was in sight, I instinctively lowered my voice. "I *am* the one who turned in the cell phone that gave John the motive to arrest her."

He brushed my hair back with his free hand. "Did you do that to hurt Lisa? Or because it was the right thing to do?"

"Because it was the right thing to do."

"So that has nothing to do with this. From the way I understand what you're telling me, Bob is going to sell the club. With or without you. Right?"

I nodded.

"Let me ask you something. If Bob had made this offer before you knew about Lisa's problem and before she got arrested, what would you have done?"

"Jumped on it with both feet."

"Well, then, get on your jumping shoes, water girl. If it was a good deal then, it's a good deal now."

"What about all the paperwork?"

He dropped a kiss on my forehead. "Lucky for you, you're looking at the king of paperwork. Let's go find a banker who wants to get rid of some money."

"At this hour on a Saturday?"

He grinned. "I'm also the king of connections."

"Who knew I was marrying royalty?" I held up one finger. "Just a sec." I palmed my phone, flipped it open, and punched in a phone number. "Hello, Bob? It's Jenna. I've made my decision. Start the paperwork, and I'll start the financing process."

When I hung up, I looked at Alex. "I can't believe it's really happening." I grinned.

He put his arms around me. "You're not going to get so busy with your new business that you'll want to postpone our wedding, are you?"

I smirked. "And give up my chance to be your queen? Never."

◈

Monday morning Bob and I signed the initial paperwork.

"We'll keep this under our hats until it's all finished," he said.

I nodded. "As far as everyone is concerned, I'll just start back to work for you full-time today."

"Doesn't your sister need some notice?"

I laughed. "She practically pushed me out the door. She knows where my heart is."

"That's one reason I'm so glad you're the one buying it," Bob said softly.

"Thanks. The bank says they'll have the financing by Friday. I'll take that day off to take care of everything. We'll sign the paperwork in Alex's office that afternoon."

"And you can celebrate Friday night as the new owner," Bob finished.

I laughed. "Yeah, probably by just coming here and soaking in the fact that it's mine."

Later that afternoon, Bob paged me to the office.

He looked up from his desk when I came in, his eyes wild. "Jenna," he said, his voice hoarse. "Gail can run the club awhile. I need you to drive me somewhere."

I took in the fine sheen of sweat on his brow and his pale complexion.

"Bob?" The words "heart attack" flashed across my mind like a neon sign. "Are you okay? Should I call an ambulance?"

"Ambulance? What are you talking about? Can't you drive me downtown without making a federal case of it?" He gave me an irritated glance. Okay. Something was seriously wrong. Bob could be exasperating at times, but I'd never seen him like this. I grabbed my keys and followed him out to the parking lot. As I slid behind the wheel, I glanced at him. He looked more normal, but his hand shook as he fastened his seat belt.

I put the car in gear and headed out of the parking lot. "Look, Bob, if something's wrong, it might help if you tell me about it."

"If something's wrong? My only child is in jail and likely to go through a nasty murder trial. She's taking the rap for someone else." He cleared his throat. "I'm going to fix that. Take me to the police department." And he clamped his lips shut.

I glanced at him, wondering if he had a weapon hidden somewhere. Was he going to bust Lisa out of jail? When we arrived at the station, I pulled up to let him out, but he motioned sharply to the small parking lot next to the department, and I obediently pulled in.

"Come on. Let's go in," he said gruffly.

I frowned. What did he think I was going to do? Play Bonnie to his Clyde?

He glanced back at me. "I may need you to back me up. I'm not sure how this is going to go," he muttered.

I trailed him into the building.

"I need to see Chief Conner immediately," he barked to the young guy behind the desk. We were ushered into John's office where John courteously offered us chairs.

I sank into the ugly plastic chair, but Bob remained standing. He leaned over John's desk, placing both hands flat on the surface.

"John. I'm here to confess."

"What did you do, Bob? Let your business license expire?"

"I'm serious. I killed that guy."

I was glad I was sitting down. John glanced my way with raised eyebrows. I held my arms out, palms up. I was just the driver.

"Bob," John said sternly, "what you're doing is a serious offense. You can't present false information to a police officer. Why don't you go on home and think this over some more?"

"What you're doing is illegal, too. I confessed to a serious crime. You have to question me."

"Fine. What were you doing the night of the crime?" John spoke in an official tone.

"Drat it, John. I'm serious." Bob glared at him. "I killed a man. I'm confessing to it. You have no choice but to lock me up."

"Bob, go on home. Your daughter is fine." John patted him on the shoulder. "Things will look better in the morning."

Bob's sudden lunge was so unexpected that John had no time to react. I leaped to my feet. Two officers rushed into the room in response to the shouts, or maybe to the noise the chair and desk made when Bob turned them over. They cuffed Bob a little roughly, but their chief was nursing a bruised eye, so I couldn't blame them.

"Jenna..." Bob turned his head as they shoved him out of the room. "Go by and tell Wilma what happened."

Thanks a lot, boss.

Wilma didn't take it any better than I thought she would.

"This is so crazy. First my child; now my husband. What is John thinking? Bob could no more kill someone on purpose than I could."

"Um, Wilma, to be fair, Bob didn't give him much choice. He sort of slugged John."

"Oh my goodness. This is making Bob so crazy. He's never hit anyone in his life. He was all about the 'peace and love' thing. What was he thinking?" She twisted the towel in her hands. "I have to do something. Let me see. What do I need to do?"

"Why don't you lie down?" I suggested. "I'll get you a cold glass of water."

"Lie down?" She stared at me as if I'd suggested she leap off a cliff. "Why would I lie down? And I'm not thirsty, thanks. I need a plan." She twisted the towel harder then stretched it out. She looked up at me as if she'd forgotten I was there. "Jenna, run along, honey. I've got things to do."

This family was in serious need of therapy. I left before I needed it, too, and headed back to the gym, where I spent the rest of my shift fielding questions about Bob from Gail and Dave.

❖

"This better be good," I muttered. I hated being awakened by a ringing phone. My heart was in high gear and my brain wasn't engaged. Never a good scenario.

"Hello?"

"Jenna?" A voice I didn't recognize. I struggled to see caller ID, but my eyes were blurry from sleep. "I need your help."

"Who is this?"

"Oh, sorry. This is John. Could you come to the station, please? I can send a car for you if you wish."

"I have a car, thanks." This was a strange conversation, but I tried to be polite.

"Did I wake you up?" John's voice was tinged with amusement.

"What time is it?"

"Um, about six o'clock." He sounded a little sheepish.

"Then you woke me up."

"Sorry. I didn't look at the clock until just now." But Wilma's down here, and she's asking for you."

"I'll be there in thirty minutes." I rolled out of bed and headed to the bathroom.

I was only a couple of minutes late, and I knew I looked like a contestant for the police lineup. I was ushered straight to John's office where Wilma occupied the chair I'd sat in yesterday. Compared to how she looked, I was ready for a beauty contest. Her hair stood out every which way, and her eyes were swollen and bloodshot. Almost as bad as John's eye, I noticed.

And she was crying. Not loud wails, just a soft, hopeless weeping. I took the chair next to her and put an arm around her shoulder.

"Wilma?" My mind went blank. What do you say to a woman whose husband and daughter are both in jail?

"She came to confess," John spoke wryly. "Tell us one more time what happened, Mrs. Pryor."

"I was mad at J.D. for breaking up Lisa's marriage. I followed him to the diner and shot him with Lisa's gun." She spoke in a monotone, and her voice was so low I had to strain to hear it.

"Will you sit with her just a minute, Jenna?" John left the room but returned shortly leading Bob. When Bob realized Wilma was in the office, he stepped forward and took her hands.

"Honey, what are you doing down here? Didn't you read the note I left?"

"Note? No. I didn't find a note." She glanced at me and back to him again. "Jenna stopped by and told me where you were. I came to turn myself in."

"Turn yourself in for what? What are you talking about?" Bob looked at Wilma as if she had morphed into an alien. Or at least grown an extra head.

"For murder. I killed J.D."

"Wilma," Bob fairly roared. "You wouldn't hurt a fly, and we all know it. Don't we, John?"

"Do we?" John retorted. "The way I remember it, if someone confesses, I have to take them into custody and question them. Isn't that the way you heard it, Jenna?"

How unfair. Leave me out of this. I tried to send telepathic messages to John, but he wasn't picking up my signal.

"Isn't that what Bob said yesterday?"

He didn't get to be chief of police by not being persistent, obviously.

"Wilma couldn't have done it." Bob cut John off. "We left the diner and went straight home to watch that 'bad boys' cop show." He turned to look at his wife. "We watch it every Friday night. She was with me the whole night, and I'll swear to that in any court of law you want to take us."

"Is that right, Wilma?" John asked gently.

"Yes. He's right, of course."

"Well, Bob, congratulations. You've given Wilma a good alibi."

"Now, honey, go on home and let me handle things." Bob gave Wilma a peck on the cheek and guided her to the door.

"Just a minute, Bob." John's voice hardened. "You do realize that when you alibied Wilma, you also alibied yourself?"

Bob looked stunned. I guess a night in the slammer had diminished his thought processes.

"Now, why don't you both go on home and leave the police work to me?" He shook his head as he walked out of the office.

Dear Pru,

My boyfriend and I have been dating for three months. I have always known that he smokes dope now and then, but the other day he offered me a joint. I said no, thanks, and he laughed at me. He said I need to learn to live. I said it was more like learn to die. He hasn't called me since. Should I call and apologize?

Who's the Dope?

Dear Who's,

It's not you. Unless you call and apologize. Then there will be two dopes in this equation. What you should do is thank your lucky stars that he quit calling you. Go out and make friends who have fun without depending on substance abuse.

It'll All Come Out In The Wash

Funny how I'd thought it would be perfect if Bob would sell me the athletic club. I'd just never imagined that Lisa would have to be arrested for murder in order to make it happen.

Bob had spent all week trying to get her out of jail, and I'd spent all week trying to get the paperwork through. I felt guilty that I'd succeeded and he hadn't. But however it had happened, the bank called at four and said my money was ready. I had an in with the lawyer, so after I picked up the check, Alex stayed open late for Bob and me to meet at his office. Together we'd transferred ownership.

Five minutes before closing time, I pushed the double doors open and stepped into the Lake View Athletic Club—finally mine.

"Hey, boss, is this a sign of things to come? Showing up right before we close?" Gail asked jokingly as I walked by where she was gathering her things. "Bob told me. Congratulations."

I nodded. "Thanks." No matter how overbearing and annoying Lisa had acted, it was hard to enjoy the victory knowing she was sitting in a jail cell.

"There are a couple of stragglers. Want me to stay around? Or are you going to lock up?"

"I'll lock up. I'm not staying too long."

Seth and Ricky came by from the showers, gym bags in their hands. "Hey, Jenna. How's it feel to finally own the place?" Seth asked, his cocky grin firmly in place. I hoped he'd gotten over his misplaced affection for me.

"Good. Thanks."

Ricky nodded. "Congrats on your new venture."

"Does this mean you're going to be too busy for all those questions?" Seth asked.

Ricky cleared his throat and looked uncomfortable. "We need to go, man."

"Aw, don't be shy around Jenna. In between her amateur investigating, she's been real curious about you, too."

My face grew hot. Seth and his jealousy. He thought I'd been asking about Ricky because I was interested in him romantically. Amelia was going to kill me.

So much for being subtle.

"I—"

Ricky flashed me an easy smile and slapped Seth on his shoulder. "Your jealousy is showing, man. But I'm pretty sure she's taken, and so am I. So let's get going."

Seth followed him out, and I turned to Gail with a grimace. "What is it about men? Once you're attached, they suddenly find you irresistible."

"I wouldn't know," she muttered.

I frowned.

Her face reddened. "Sorry."

"Vini?"

She nodded. "Not that he knows I'm alive. As anything other than a good friend."

"He doesn't know what he's missing." But he would pretty soon if I had anything to say about it.

She gave me a wry grin. "Who needs men? I think I'm going to go get some New York Super Fudge Chunk and drown my miseries in ice cream."

"Good idea. I'm going to go see if the office looks any different now that it's really mine."

In the office, I glared up at the wall. Lisa had once again replaced my beach scenes with modern art pictures. I sighed. At least I knew where to find them this time. She'd done the same thing when I was away in Branson, and I'd had to search the whole place before I finally found them in the janitor's closet next to the pool.

As I jogged down the well-lit but deserted hallway, I slipped my cell phone from my pocket and into my hand. The emptiness of the huge building creeped me out. It was the same way when I was at the newspaper office late at night. So many tiny unexplained noises punctuated the quietness.

When I opened the door to the pool area, shadows from the underwater lights rippled across the surface of the Olympic-size swimming pool. The familiar sound of the pumping system soothed my nerves. Maybe some people would consider that creepy, but my mood lightened, and I slowed to a walk, smiling at the blue octagon of water. This was one place that I didn't need other people around—this was my safe place. Suddenly, the realization that I actually owned the pool surged through me. I fought the urge to run to the locker room, get into my swimsuit, and dive into the deep end. There'd be time for that after I retrieved my pictures.

I unlocked the janitor's closet and pulled the string to turn on the lone lightbulb. Without wasting any time, I squatted down to look behind the shelves. Sure enough, there were my pictures. Same as before. But never again. Unless I decided to retire them and redecorate. And even then, I wouldn't put them in the chlorine-saturated air of the pool closet, something Lisa had no doubt done on purpose.

Still squatting, I put my cell phone on the floor behind me and gently slid the wooden frames from their hiding place. A manila envelope tumbled out with them. I propped the pictures against the wall and sank down cross-legged in the open doorway. With Lisa's penchant for hiding things here, there was no telling what the envelope contained. And with my penchant for being curious, there was no chance I wouldn't open it.

When I turned the envelope up, two newspaper clippings fluttered into my lap. I caught the first one and held it up to the light. It was from a Memphis newspaper, *The Commercial Appeal*.

FOUL PLAY SUSPECTED IN DEATH OF COP'S WIFE, blared the headline. I scanned the article. Judy Richardson had been found dead at the bottom of a stairwell in the apartment building where she and her husband, detective Eric Richardson, resided. Bruises on her shoulders and back indicated that she had possibly been pushed. Although not officially a suspect, Mr. Richardson was listed as a person of interest. Investigation was ongoing.

I squinted at the photo of the young cop. He looked so familiar. My eyes went to the date of the article. Five years ago. I glanced at the photo again. Suddenly, my heart jumped. Even though I'd never heard that name, I knew Eric Richardson.

I didn't know why these clippings were here, but I did know one thing. I'd promised Amelia I'd let her know if I found out anything about her future son-in-law. And that lopsided grin definitely belonged to Ricky Richards.

I reached behind me for my phone; then my hand froze as the second headline caught my eye: LOCAL DETECTIVE EXONERATED IN WIFE'S MURDER. Police detective Eric Richardson had an airtight alibi for the time of his wife's murder. He and a local businessman were fishing at Tunica Lake during the time of the murder. "I will cooperate with the police in every way to find the murderer of my beloved wife, Judy."

I pulled my hand back. What purpose would be served by calling Amelia? He'd been through so much. No wonder he'd changed his name. And if the presence of these clippings was any indication, exonerated or not, his past had followed him to Lake View. Had someone been blackmailing him? Even though he'd been cleared, Amelia probably wouldn't take it very well that he'd been suspected of killing his wife.

I skimmed the rest of the article. Police had been about to arrest Richardson when local businessman J.D. Finley came forward with his alibi. I sucked in my breath. Someone had been blackmailing him all right.

But he'd apparently gotten tired of it.

I reached for my phone again. "How could I have been so stupid?"

A searing pain shot through my hand. I jerked around and tried to get to my feet but stumbled onto my knees. A tall shadow loomed over me, a big black boot firmly planted on my hand.

"Too smart for your own good if you ask me," Ricky snarled. I stared up into the barrel of a gun, complete with silencer. "Asking questions about me was a big mistake."

"My hand," I breathed. He ground his boot like he was stomping a bug. I bit my lip to keep from giving him the satisfaction of hearing me cry out, but I couldn't hold back a whimper. Hot tears spilled onto my cheeks.

"Stand up nice and slow," he ordered, all trace of "good ol' boy" gone from his voice.

I cradled my hand against my stomach and pushed to my feet.

"If you'd have kept your nose out of things, this would have all been over."

"Is that what your wife did?" I asked, blinking the tears away. "Asked too many questions?"

He jerked my arm, and I winced. "Judy's death was an accident! I lost my temper and pushed her. I didn't mean for her to die."

"Was J.D.'s death an accident, too?" I croaked out.

He laughed, and my blood ran cold. "I planned J.D.'s killing down to the last detail."

"So he was blackmailing you?"

"J.D. did a job and got paid. But he made the mistake of thinking he held all the cards when he found me again. At first I went along with him. I paid him what I had left of Judy's insurance money, but he got greedy."

He shoved the gun barrel into my ribs. "Too bad Bob's no-good daughter is in jail. I could set her up for killing you, too. Guess you'll have to have an unfortunate accident instead. I'm sure she hid some of your stuff up in the attic, and that staircase is so narrow. . . ." He nudged me forward.

I dragged my feet, my brain racing. If I struggled, he'd shoot me, but as we neared the pool, a memory flashed into my mind. Seth had said Ricky told him, "If God intended us to swim, he'd have given us fins."

We walked by the ten-foot marker, and I stumbled. He instinctively reached toward me. I slammed my body hard into his, grateful to see the gun go spiraling through the air just before we hit the water. A second later, my bright idea didn't seem so bright. He couldn't swim, but he had a death grip on me. Literally.

In every lifesaving class I'd ever taken, we'd learned how to keep someone from drowning you while you were trying to save them. But we'd learned nothing about how to let them drown and save yourself. Not that I wanted him to drown. I just needed him unconscious. Right now our futures were joined and looking pretty dismal. He pulled my head under again.

Suddenly, I felt and heard another splash. As my lungs burned for air, I groaned inside. Had he brought an ally with him? A lookout who'd come to rescue him and finish me off? I struggled to the surface and saw that the third person in the water was Seth, who did indeed seem to be trying to rescue Ricky. Panicked, Ricky continued to claw and fight. Seth drew back his fist and clipped Ricky on the jaw.

Ricky's grip on me immediately relaxed, and I scrambled away from the men and over to the ladder. I climbed out of the water and was debating running when I spotted the gun at my feet. Just as Seth came out of the water dragging Ricky, I snatched it up and pointed it toward the two men.

Seth's eyes grew wide. "Jenna Stafford, have you lost your mind? I had no choice but to knock him out. He was drowning me. And you, too, for that matter."

My slippery grip wavered, but I forced myself to hold steady. "Put him down."

He obeyed me and backed up a step with his hands up. "What did I do?"

"What are you doing here?"

He dropped his gaze to the floor. "Uh. I saw Ricky's car in the parking lot and yours. And I. . .I. . . Doggone it, Jenna. I wanted to see if my partner had gone after the girl he knew I—" He dropped his hands. "I wasn't breaking in or anything. And what about you? Why did you two decide to go for a swim with your clothes on?"

Ricky groaned, and I trained the gun on him. I could see the truth all over Seth's face. All Seth was guilty of was jealousy. Ricky was definitely in it alone. "It's a long story." I motioned with the gun toward the newspaper clippings still lying on the floor in the closet doorway.

With a wary look at me, Seth walked over and picked them up. I kept one eye on the still unconscious Ricky as I watched Seth read the articles. A gamut of emotions flitted across his face. When he finished, his cheeks were red with anger. "He's the killer?"

I nodded. He picked up his cell phone from the side of the pool and called for backup. Within minutes, sirens wailed through the quiet night.

❖

"Jenna!" Carly waved a paper at me as she and Elliott walked up to the basketball court. "I meant to tell you, this came to the diner yesterday." She handed me a postcard.

I looked down at the picture, a cartoon of a red mustang and a leggy blond.

"I don't believe it." I grinned. "Listen to this. 'Hey, chickie, I finally planted my roots practically in my granny's backyard. And the next-door neighbor is a really nice fellow. A preacher, no less. Did I mention he's single? Wink, wink.

Thanks for hanging with me when I was in need of a pal. Jolene.'"

"A preacher?" Carly shook her head. "That man won't know what hit him."

Zac dribbled his basketball up to us. "Y'all ready to choose teams? I got Elliott."

Elliott held out his hands, and Zac threw him the ball. He passed it to Alex, who made a jump shot.

When they were gone, Carly turned back to me. "Alice called yesterday. She and Harvey are settling down in Florida. She told me they'd found a little diner for sale, so she keeps having to remind Harvey what the word *retired* means."

I smiled. "Sounds like they're happy. Bob came to the club yesterday. First time he's been there since we signed the papers three weeks ago. He didn't come right out and say it, but he hinted that Lisa's in a twelve-step program for her gambling problem. He said something like, 'It'll take a lot of work, but Lisa's got a good man behind her,' so I assume she and Larry are working things out. Oh, I almost forgot. He also said that Lisa had asked J.D. to take my pictures to the pool closet. Apparently he decided to stash his blackmail stuff there, as well."

"Well, look who's here." Alex walked over from the court to stand beside me as Seth sauntered toward us. He relaxed slightly as Tiffany emerged from the other side of the truck and jogged in Seth's wake. "Hey, y'all, ready to play?"

Tiffany appeared to have lost weight since Ricky's arrest, but she wore a smile along with her fitted jeans and cute T-shirt. Her hair was pulled into a casual ponytail, but she looked good. And happy.

Seth stepped back to let her go first, and I suddenly remembered him being so defensive with me when he thought I was trying to steal Tiffany's man. What had he said? That she was a "real sweet girl"? Tiffany might get her happy ending after all.

"Hey, Seth. John too scared of gettin' whupped to show up?" Alex asked.

"Oh, didn't you hear? Denise went into labor right after Sunday school."

Carly glanced at me. "Do you think we should go over to the hospital and check on her?"

Seth shrugged. "You can if you want to, but she had the baby about an hour ago, and everything's fine."

"Wow. That was fast," I said.

"Yeah. It's a girl." Tiffany winked at me. "John said that since she was so curious and impatient, he and Denise were thinking of changing their mind about what to name her."

Alex grinned and put his arm around my shoulders. "Let me guess. . ."

Seth nodded. "Yep, but then they decided Lake View only had room for one Jenna."

We all laughed, and Seth and Tiffany walked on over to the basketball court.

Alex pulled me close and brushed a stray curl back from my face. "I sure am glad Lake View has you. I can't imagine our lives if we hadn't found each other again."

I stared into his blue eyes, and in that moment my whole life seemed to click into place, as if I were seeing the big picture for the very first time. Alex's mother's words echoed in my head. All the disappointments and trials in my life—not winning the Olympics, losing a student, and even not buying the health club right away—had just been part of my path. But God had taken that path and used it to bring me to where I stood today. In Alex's arms.

I couldn't have asked for anything more.

Sisters **Christine Pearle Lynxwiler, Jan Pearle Reynolds,** and **Sandy Pearle Gaskin** are usually on the same page. And it's most often a page from their favorite mystery. So when the idea for a Christian cozy mystery series came up during Sunday dinner at Mama's, they became determined to take their dream further than just table talk. Thus, the Sleuthing Sisters mystery series was born.

Christine writes full-time. She and her husband, Kevin, live with their two children in the beautiful Ozark Mountains and enjoy kayaking on the nearby Spring River. **Jan,** part-time writer and full-time office manager, and her husband, Steve, love to spend time with their two adult children and their granddogs on the lake or just relaxing at home. **Sandy,** part-time writer and retired teacher, works with her husband, Bart, managing their manufacturing business. With their daughter off to college, she hopes to devote more time to writing. The three sisters love to hear from readers by e-mail at sleuthingsisters@yahoo.com.

You may correspond with these authors by writing:
Christine Lynxwiler, Sandy Gaskin, Jan Reynolds
Author Relations
PO Box 721
Uhrichsville, OH 44683